MW01489870

Getting There

Gerry Boylan

Synergy Books

Getting There
Published by Synergy Books
P.O. Box 30071
Austin, Texas 78755

For more information about our books, please write us, e-mail us at info@synergybooks.net, or visit our web site at www.synergybooks.net.

Publisher's Cataloging-in-Publication available upon request.

LCCN: 2010923527

ISBN-13: 978-0-9843879-2-2
ISBN-10: 0-9843879-2-7

Cover Image: Dennis Hallinan / Hulton Archive / Getty Images

"The Christmas Song." Music and Lyric by Mel Torme and Robert Wells. © 1946 Sony/ATV Tunes LLC, Mel Torme Trust. © 1946 (Renewed) EDWIN H. MORRIS & COMPANY, A Division of MPL Music Publishing, Inc. and SONY/ATV MUSIC PUBLISHING LLC. All rights on behalf of SONY /ATV Tunes LLC. Administered by SONY/ATV Music Publishing, 8 Music Square West, Nashville, TN 37203. All rights reserved. Reprinted by permission of Hal Leonard Corporation.

"NURSE!" By MARTIN E. MULL © 1975 CHAPPELL & CO., INC. (ASCAP) All rights reserved. Used by Permission of ALFRED PUBLISHING CO., INC.

"I Remember" From Patsy Moore's lyrics to "I Remember," performed by Dianne Reeves.

"HAPPY TOGETHER" Written by Garry Bonner and Alan Gordon. Copyright © 1966, 1967 by Alley Music Corp. and Bug Music-Trio Music Company. International Copyright Secured. All Rights Reserved. Used by permission of Alley Music Corporation. Reprinted by permission of Hal Leonard Corporation.

"Always" by Irving Berlin. © Copyright 1925 by Irving Berlin © Copyright Renewed. International Copyright Secured. All Rights Reserved. Reprinted by permission.

"Try to Remember" from THE FANTASTICKS. Words by Harvey Schmidt. Copyright © 1960 by Tom Jones and Harvey Schmidt. Copyright renewed by Chappell & Co. owner of publication and allied rights throughout the world. International Copyright Secured. All Rights Reserved. Reprinted by permission of Hal Leonard Corporation.

"Ain't No Sunshine" Words and Music by Bill Withers. Copyright © 1971 INTERIOR MUSIC CORP. Copyright Renewed. All Rights Controlled and Administered by SONGS OF UNIVERSAL, Inc. All Rights Reserved. Used by Permission. Reprinted by permission of Hal Leonard Corporation.

Young author photo: Austin Andres
Current author photo: Robert Bruce Photography

Thanks to Mike Campbell for assorted quotes.

10 9 8 7 6 5 4 3 2 1

This book is dedicated to Kathy—Kathleen McGrane Boylan. She did rescue me when I was lost and continues to do so to this day. She has been my best reader, my best friend, and my true love. Together we made a life and a family, which is how this lost soul was found.

"I remember thinking we were worlds apart,
and then I heard your words and they spoke my heart.
I remember thinking I was too far gone,
and you reminded me that there is no such thing."

—Dianne Reeves, "I Remember"
Words and music by Patsy Moore

Notes on Long-Distance Hitchhiking

The hitchhiking proposition is straightforward. I'll stand on the side of the road, stick my thumb out, and expect that while you're driving by in a car, you'll stop and pick me up and take me as far down the road as you're going. Hitchhikers believe that the general nature of people is charitable and that a ride will appear. The typical driver behind the wheel sees the hitchhiker and thinks, *That guy has got to be out of his freaking mind if he thinks I'm going to even look at him, let alone pick him up!* Both views turn out to be correct, although the hitchhiker spends a helluva lot more time waving his thumb around to prove his point.

Hitchhikers and the people who pick them up share a few things in common. Both have an appetite for risk, more so than the regular Joe, and overall are a just a tad odd. Not surprisingly, a number of hitchhikers become salesmen and entrepreneurs. Often, they are quite successful, although more than a few end up in jail for selling drugs.

There's a special biology to road life that's different from that of our daily lives, creating both turmoil and fodder for stories, which are finely polished and embellished by hitchhikers for consumption by the uninitiated. Some tales are stretched too far and become outright lies. Yet other stories, while seemingly out of *Ripley's Believe It or Not!* are achingly, stunningly, absurdly true.

Most of the time, road life can be uncomfortable, numbingly boring, and generally unhealthy. The hitchhiker waits and waits for someone interesting to pick him up, and for something, anything, to happen. Like a bolt of lightning, change comes—too exciting and often addictive.

The starring road in this story is I-75, almost 1,700 miles of concrete and asphalt running through mostly uninspiring landscapes with a few notable exceptions, like the Great Smoky Mountains and Michigan's Straits of Mackinac. I suppose my story would have been an easier tale to tell starting in Sault Sainte Marie, Michigan, and finishing in southern Florida, following the same path as I-75. But, like life, the story gets convoluted, confusing, and messy; it doesn't follow a straight line.

It's strange to even talk about hitchhiking today. It's rare to see a hitchhiker anywhere, especially a cross-country ride-seeker. From the mid-1960s through the early 1970s, though, it was a frequent sight, nothing out of the ordinary. In Canada, where they encouraged hitchhiking by offering a chain of nearly intolerable youth hostels, it was like an ecosystem out of control; hitchhikers seemingly bred and birthed like gerbils until the Canadian highways were clogged with zombie-like creatures standing on the side of the road, eyes vacant, thumbs dangling by their sides.

Perhaps the present is just an evolutionary nadir of hitchhikers, and before long, they'll appear again, like the crows that seemed wiped out by the West Nile virus. Just when you couldn't remember their familiar cackle anymore, one smart-ass crow after another started cawing in the trees again.

Meanwhile, the story you're about to read vaults back and forth between 1973 and 2003, and sometimes it's jarring. Please forgive me the youthful pathos in the 1973 chapters and the wizened, chin-stroking observations of thirty years later. It was a wild ride, and I have a twisted pride that I'm still here to report it.

Here's the truth of the matter: until I was fifteen, I lived in the pleasant suburban bubble of the late 1950s and '60s—like a regular Beaver Cleaver. There was nothing in my life to suggest I would grow up to be an axe murderer or an astronaut. If my life had continued down that neat and tidy path, I'm guessing I would have become an insurance salesman with a bulging belly and a weekend drinking problem. But when I was fifteen, my life blew up. The next five years were anything but ordinary. Not only did life seem to have dealt me a bad hand, but I played my cards poorly.

Toward the end of this period, my life became unhinged from conventional mores, and the result was frightening and exhilarating. What would have seemed bizarre or extraordinary became almost expected. I say "almost" because it was clear to me even as a teenage hellion that a life teetering on the edge of control should be neither anticipated nor welcomed. Through most of this part, I was a mess. But toward the end, the astonishing and absurd meshed into a chaotic miracle. That's the story I want to tell you.

I didn't turn out to be an insurance salesman. But I did have a weekend drinking problem until the summer my daughter was born, and that was the end of that. And while there was always the temptation to ride the fantastic plume of the road again, the thought of sleeping under a highway bridge was a good wake-up call. I am satisfied, truly satisfied, with a wife, a daughter, friends, a job with a decent health plan, and a 401(k).

I'm a middle-aged, retired thrill seeker who likes to think he can remember the skills needed to avoid the bull's horns, and if gored, how to survive a wound. I remember the thrill and fear of living a preposterous life, but I left the port of youth and immortality decades ago. At the heart of the story is how my soul lost its way and how good people shepherded it back home.

Chapter 1

September 2003

The silhouette of a man, arm outstretched, thumb skyward, appeared on the shoulder of the road. I took my foot off the gas, ever so slightly, but my two passengers immediately noticed, looked up, and saw the hitchhiker.

"Dad, no. There's no room!" I glanced in the rearview mirror of the van and caught my college-bound daughter rolling her eyes in futile protest.

My wife of twenty-nine years put her book down on her lap, removed her reading glasses, and smiled, revealing her diastema. Turning to our daughter, Roberta, she said, "Dear, you know your dad, and—"

"I know, Mom, believe me, I know," Roberta interrupted. "Dad's Rules of the Road. Rule number one: always pick up a highway hitchhiker unless you think he's a bad guy. But, Daddy, with all my stuff, where are we going to put him?"

"We'll find room, sweetheart. And remember, those road rules are for me, not you. Don't you be picking up any hitchhikers, no matter how good or good-looking they are," I reminded her. Opportunities to offer words of advice to my daughter were disappearing as we closed the distance to dropping her off for the start of her college career. I gulped hard. Christ, this was going to be long ride if I started blubbering this early. I was going to have to pace my emotions.

I reached up and tapped the rearview mirror, positioning it to give me a better view of my daughter in the backseat. I didn't want to miss seeing any remaining vestiges of the little girl who had dominated my life for eighteen years. I knew that college would complete the inevitable transition that had begun during her teenage years, turning me into a dad without a clue. She caught me looking in the mirror, smiled, and shook her head before looking back at her college folder. She was prepared. She was a well-organized, focused student who wasn't naive about boys, drinking, or drugs, because her mother had been having frank discussions with her since she was twelve—conversations that made me blush.

The day of my daughter's birth was a pole vault over my wrecked childhood. I was a dad! Every day that I was a father—a good dad—was a step further away from the unfinished slumgullion stew of my youth. After we dropped her off at college, those steps would be hers, headed away from us. Christ, I wasn't remotely ready for this.

My name is Luke Moore. I'm fifty years old, and I'm surprised as my friends and family that I made it this far. I survived a lot of shit that was thrown at me, and even more I stepped into all by myself. But here I am today, a psychologist with a good practice focused on troubled teens, which still amuses my lifelong friends. In spite of my profession, I am the father of an unusually well-adjusted, nearly grown-up daughter, and I'm married to the woman who figured out how to pluck me out of the maelstrom. I'm stable and don't take many risks. Really. You may think picking up a hitchhiker, especially with your wife and daughter along, is risky. Not for me. I can spot a bad apple on the side of the road a half-mile away. There are not many hitchhikers on the road today. Not like in my time. But if I see one on the side of the road, long-distance hitchhiking, and if he sells me, I can't turn him down. It's one of the Rules of the Road.

As we passed the young man, I looked in the rearview mirror. He had turned and put his hands together as if praying, and he mouthed, "Please." *Nice touch,* I thought. I eased my wife's silver Chrysler Grand Caravan onto the shoulder of the road, about a hundred feet past the shaggy-haired hitchhiker, who sprinted as best he could with a full backpack. My daughter was already clearing space in the van, pushing loose items further into the back, obscuring the view out of the van's rear window. I pushed the button for the automatic side door opener and the door obeyed just as the winded hitchhiker appeared.

"Man, thanks a lot for stopping. I've been out here for hours." The young man had a baseball hat on backward and five earrings rimming his left ear. I could never remember which pierced ear signaled you were gay, and if multiple earrings meant you were more earnest about being gay than if you wore just one. He eased into our van's bench backseat, next to Roberta. Her face betrayed mild mortification at having to spend time with a complete stranger. The hitchhiker found room for his pack at his feet, leaned forward from the van's backseat, and extended his hand to me, saying, "I'm Tom Lutac, headed to Houghton to get back to school at Michigan Tech. Thanks for the ride."

I took his hand and grasped it firmly, not letting go until I told young Tom, "Pleased to meet you, young man. I'm Father Danny O'Roarke, and I'm out of uniform today. And this is my sister Molly Malone and her sweet daughter Moira Malone, my niece, who is also off to college in the Upper Peninsula, at Lake Superior State. Which means we'll be able to get you north of the bridge." I spoke in an almost convincing Irish brogue. Tom Lutac's eyes widened a bit as he sat back into the seat.

Looking at the young hitchhiker in my rearview mirror made me grin and cringe, remembering the thrill of the road and the roar of its danger. It would be fun drawing his story out. It would make for a good yarn at the reunion I was driving to after settling our daughter in at college. The symmetry would not be lost on my childhood friends, those old Lost Souls who knew me when I looked like a 1970s version of young Tom Lutac.

Traffic was clear just outside of Pinconning, as I accelerated quickly onto northbound I-75. It was an autumn Michigan day, dry and clear, the unfiltered sun warming us through the windshield. In the side-view mirror I could see my reflection, the sunlight highlighting the creases of age and the fading scars on my face. I wore the old wounds like a retired bullfighter. I felt, more than heard, the cosmic hum, an incantation from the past. It was faint, but I would pay attention if it grew louder. At fifty years old, I was on the downside of immortal.

Chapter 2

March 1973

I stood on the interstate highway like a matador. One foot touched the solid white line that separated the highway from the road's shoulder, and my arm and thumb stretched outward with a purpose, challenging the cars as they flew past. I was standing forty miles outside of Knoxville on the southbound shoulder of I-75. It was past midnight; the traffic was thinning and the night air coming off of the Great Smokies was cooling quickly. I had covered this ground twice before, hitchhiking from my home base in Royal Oak, Michigan, a northern suburb of Detroit, to Florida. My cross-country treks began two days after I barely managed to graduate from St. Mary's High School in 1971. Two years later, I was a veteran long-distance hitchhiker, with over 100,000 miles logged from my home base in Michigan, reaching Santa Fe, Los Angeles, Seattle, Calgary, and other scattered points in North America.

My parents had been dead for five years. My mother was truly dead, gone and buried. My dad's heart was still beating, but to me he was a ghost, put far away in what I imagined—what I hoped— was a Count of Monte Cristo-like dungeon. He didn't exist to me, except in my nightmarish version of purgatory. But don't we all endure a dose of this kind of melodrama in our lives? And isn't it a perfectly logical response to hit the road with twenty bucks and see how far it will take you? I thought I was a very well-adjusted whack job, thank you very much—maybe just half a bubble off center. At least that's what I tried to convince myself when I stood on the side of the road, hundreds, if not thousands, of miles away from a home that didn't exist anymore, as the rain increased and the odds of getting picked up dwindled.

I always stood close to the road. Drivers had to see my face or they wouldn't pick me up. (Road deviants and predators were the exceptions to this rule.) The regular folks who pulled over for me and my fellow road warriors needed to make a connection. Although the cars were sometimes only inches from my thumb, it rarely occurred to me to be afraid. I knew it increased the danger, but as I saw it, the improved odds of snagging a ride overrode the risk. I had thought the process of hitchhiking through, and after thousands of brain-numbing hours on the road, I generally knew what worked and why.

Cross-country hitchhiking was about traveling from one place to another, not about taking the scenic route; it was primarily free transportation. That's why the interstate highway system was effective for hitchhikers. It was four lanes of direct routes with cars wheeling from one destination to another with a purpose. Interstates were the CliffsNotes of travel.

The best place to stand was just past where the merging entrance lane met the main freeway. That allowed the drivers entering the freeway to see me early on, and if they were going to pick me up, to stop in front of or just after me, before they reached full speed. Traffic volume was paramount to hitchhiking success, and a major highway like I-75 carried thousands of cars, not the trickle found on most two-lane highways.

I had learned to never take a ride that dropped me off in the middle of a city; there was no place for cars to pull over. City police were suspicious, unaccommodating, and numerous, and they weren't there to protect a hitchhiker from the kooks, weirdos, and rednecks hurling poorly reasoned epithets or beer cans. Turning down a ride was always a last resort, but usually a smart decision. This was a lesson learned after walking seven miles to get out of downtown Atlanta after being threatened by Fulton County's finest. After that debacle, I would either wait for a ride that took me past the city or hitchhike on the interstate ring roads that circle around medium-to-large cities, bypassing the cities' centers.

I figured I had ten seconds or less to make the driver of a car racing on the interstate look at me and then acknowledge that I was a fellow human being. Nearly all drivers tried their best to look away. They changed the radio station, glanced into the rearview mirror, or simply stared straight ahead—anything to avoid eye contact and acknowledge I was a person standing on the highway, begging them to stop and be a Good Samaritan. The basic human appeal of aiding someone was easily overridden by the images of a hitchhiker robbing and maiming a driver, or worse.

The percentage of people who ignored their mothers' advice not to talk to strangers or to pick up hitchhikers was miniscule. Those people were nearly always men—usually single, divorced, or in a troubled relationship; salesmen; or old men in hats. Their need to pour out their stories over a long stretch of road to a total stranger, a captive for hours, overcame fear or their mothers' admonishments.

My analytical view of hitchhiking odds grew out of the boredom and loneliness of hundreds of hours standing on asphalt or cement in conditions usually too cold, hot, or wet. Here's how it added it up: only one car in thousands would stop for a hitchhiker. About 30 percent of interstate drivers were women, and women very rarely picked up hitchhikers. This limited the natural selection to the 70 percent of drivers that were men. Of these men, only about half would even look at a hitchhiker. A healthy percentage of the remaining candidates detested anyone outside their normal day-to-day experience. They looked directly at me and my hitchhiking contemporaries with self-righteous head shaking, or with eyes shooting darts of death and smoke coming out of their ears. They were appalled by our assumed countercultural, amoral lifestyle.

Mainstream society was largely left out of the hitchhiking equation. The eligible driver who would consider picking me up was the proverbial needle in the haystack, only moving at seventy miles per hour. In spite of the poor odds, cross-country hitchhiking worked because of the risk-taking slice of the driving population and other at-the-margin folks. These included hippies in VW vans, drunks, and anyone who had hitchhiked in their lives, including grizzled Dust Bowlers who talked of hobo camps and encounters with less-than-healthy women, and of how they had lost the teeth that left large gaps in their smiles.

While hitchhiking was a waiting game, a little planning increased the odds of getting a ride. No matter how long I had been on the road, I made an effort to keep my appearance presentable.

I pushed my not-quite-hippy-length blond hair behind my ears. I didn't wear hats because they implied I was hiding something. Many people felt the same way about beards, but since I felt mine had finally grown in nicely I was too vain to give that up; I did keep my whiskers trimmed and neat. In summer, my T-shirt was always tucked into my jeans, and I stood up straight and smiled. I completed the pose by keeping my arm out, bent slightly at the elbow. I was a paragon of uprightness. All right, that's a stretch, but I knew that it was crucial not to appear threatening. At twenty years old, I was a wiry guy, just under five feet eleven inches tall and weighing in at 150 pounds—when my pockets were loaded with change. I didn't look menacing. It was more the opposite reaction. When I smiled, I was told by more than one driver that pulled over that I looked like a grandson, or the boy next door; maybe a little mixed up, but still polite to his family and neighbors. This was an important edge in trying to sell the reluctant chauffeur. It's embarrassing to admit, but I used to practice a shy, unassuming, and appealing smile using the small pocket mirror I kept in my knapsack. Yep, when traffic disappeared, I would pull out my little mirror and try on a jaunty smile or two for mass consumption, and then add bedroom eyes in case a couple of chicks would drive by and find me irresistible. None ever did, but that didn't stop my inane practice sessions.

My only defense for the variety of offbeat activities I engaged in while on the side of the road was boredom. The truth was that I was jaded and, in some ways, a weird dude. I wasn't sure if all that time on the road by myself gave me way too much time to think, allowing eccentricities to slip into my psyche, or if I was just wired differently. Don't get me wrong: I don't think I was loopy-eyed strange. Around my friends I could be a guy's guy and swear, spit, grunt, and vulgarize with the best of them. Alone, it was a different story.

As a hitchhiker, I was implacable in my technique, although I did silently curse every thousandth or so car that passed by. But I was always selling.

"Hey, lady, look this way. That's it. I'm harmless—just need to get on down the road. Okay, not you, but what about you, buddy, in the nice Corvette? Probably not. Never been picked up by a Corvette, but this old Bonneville, with you, old-timer, you're a likely suspect. C'mon, make it happen," I sang out.

Over time, I developed good instincts, singling out the older model car in the slow lane, spotting the profile of a man with a hat, or the Camaro with the elbows of two young pot smokers sticking out the windows, or the slightly weaving, slow-moving car at night with a driver trying to avoid a DUI.

I worked them all, willing the strangers to pull over. My final hook, when traffic was light, was to keep eye contact and smile at every car. Even if the driver didn't look over, I would turn and catch them looking in the rearview mirror. Drivers couldn't help themselves. They wanted to catch a glimpse of the hitchhiker, much the same as people who didn't want to gape at a crippled person couldn't stop themselves from taking a sidelong glance. My technique was to turn, drop my arms to my sides, open my hands, and let my face say to the driver, "I'm really okay. You'll really be glad you helped me."

It didn't often result in a ride, but it bolstered my belief that I had some control over the generally powerless proposition of hitchhiking. I was certain my years on the road had fine-tuned my skills of persuasion. I believed that I could will direction in my life and, if not necessarily control my fate, at least smooth the rough edges. I gave my theorem credence because, after two years on and off the road, I had managed to avoid any serious harm, in spite of many close calls. This was my proof that a combination of willpower and proper planning would result in me finding a good place in the world.

This, of course, was delusional, considering I was poor, alone, and without any apparent prospects. In spite of the obvious, I was indefatigable in my belief that I would find money when needed. And success. And, in time, love. Why wouldn't things work out? Delusion and indefatigability were a potent combination.

And that's how I found myself in Tennessee, hitchhiking way too late at night and feeling the chill of the springtime mountain air. A spark of "road doubt" had just begun to slip into my mind. Road doubt, a.k.a. "the road willies," occurred when common sense started to overcome youthful immortality and half-baked "I can control the universe" theories. It had to be pushed deep into the recesses of a hitchhiker's mind, especially this hitchhiker. Once a little road doubt wormed its way into my head, it started to bore deeper, and before I knew it, I would be back in the suburbs wearing a funny little hat, flipping burgers at Bertha's Hamburger Depot. When road doubt visited, I concentrated harder on willing my short-term destiny to include getting picked up by a nympho blonde schoolteacher, who was cruising the highway looking for an unassuming, bedroom-eyed stud-meister like myself to satisfy her unrelenting need for sex. Though fantasies were fairly effective in warding off road doubt, the nympho blonde schoolteacher never did pick me up. I guess that's why they're called fantasies.

After all the reflection and strategy, hitchhiking was a gamble. You stood out there on the edge of the road and took a chance. That's what I was doing on that damp night in the Middle South.

I had been dropped off about forty-five minutes prior by Lonesome Lefty Pawlicki, "the most lonesome Polack you'll ever meet," he had said when he picked me up near Conway, Kentucky. Lonesome Lefty was a typical driver in the sense that he didn't have a lot to lose and had a few stories to tell. I had trained myself to listen to drivers, even while dozing off. My head would bob up and down, moving with the motion of the car, and I would have just enough concentration to hear if the driver's inflection signaled a question. Then I would then murmur an assent or uh-uh and reengage in the conversation for a while.

Many of the drivers were indeed lonely, and their stories were often wholly fabricated, or a retelling of an incident that would have turned out better if fate had been kinder. Eventually, their true, sad stories came out, along with the reasons they were alone and facing life with a smile that needed dental work. They were hungry for companionship, conversation, and attention from any quarter, including hitchhikers.

Lonesome Lefty was a child left behind. Born to a fifteen-year-old mother in a rural shack above the Great Saltpetre Cave near Conway, he grew up fatherless. His mother sold cigarettes, candy, and gas at Stuckey's without the prospect of upward mobility. School didn't take for Lonesome Lefty. He dropped out after the sixth grade, and after a series of low-paying jobs, he eventually worked his way up to a well-drilling crew. His right hand was crushed on the job in 1959. Lonesome Lefty told me his dismal tale, which I listened to with a respectful but jaundiced ear. I heard a lot of stories on the blacktop that defied even my jaded view of the world.

"On that fateful day in May at the Atwaters' farm, we were puttin' in a well at the son's house in the back eighty. Goddamned Leo Murphy was always forgettin' to tie down the well rods on truck number two. Everyone knew Leo was an accident waitin' to happen, and that day, the accident happened to me. A stack of those rods rolled off the truck, clatterin' all over me. One sorta speared me, is what I understand, on this hand here." He held out his mangled, frozen hand for me to view. "I got some pretty good knocks on the head, and when I woke up I was in the county hospital. That was it for me in the well-drillin' field. There ain't no one-handed well drillers. That job was the best money I ever made."

This part of the story was likely close to the truth, but the tales he told me of righteous drinking, beautiful women aching for him, and chauffeuring Jerry Lee Lewis were open to serious questioning. I had introduced myself as Bill Brown when I settled into the front seat of Lonesome Lefty's '66 Bel Air. Bill Brown was one of my many pseudonyms. I grew tired of telling my own story and found solace and challenge in making up new personas as I traveled. Lonesome Lefty finished his ramble and turned to me. "So what did you say your name was, friend?"

"Bill, Bill Brown, but my friends call me One Ball Bill," I said, straight-faced.

"Say again, friend, did you say One Ball? What's that for?"

"Well, Mr. Pawlicki—"

"No, call me Lonesome, friend," Lonesome Lefty interrupted.

"Well, Lonesome, it's a long story. But if you're interested, I'll tell you my tale of woe that left me with just one nut."

"Yes sir, One Ball, I would like to hear that story, if'n you don't mind telling it."

I had already told a rendition of the saga of One Ball Bill to another unsuspecting driver on this trip, but Lonesome Lefty was the perfect audience, gasping and making eyes as I told the wholly fabricated tale. I smugly concluded the story with the line, "My best friend called out to the rest of the team, 'Make room for One Ball Billy,' and the name just stuck."

This was my talent. I prided myself on my command of language and my ability to stretch and bend any story into a tale that barely resembled the truth. My vocabulary came from doing crossword puzzles with Mom from the age of eight. I never worked on them by myself, only with Mom; it was our thing. The storytelling talent came from Dad. I was proud of the skill, but not the source.

Lonesome Lefty Pawlicki was astonished at my story. "Friend, that's the damnedest thing I ever heard," he said. He looked at his crushed hand, resting on the steering wheel, in a different light.

The remainder of the ride was in that easy zone in which two individuals with nearly nothing in common had spilled their guts about their lives; there was nothing much sacred left to be embarrassed about. We rode on and swapped anecdotes about ourselves and our hopes. Lonesome Lefty was looking forward to Kentucky; he had a caretaker job in a small apartment complex. One Ball Bill was rolling to Atlanta to meet with an admissions counselor at the prestigious Emory University. Both of us were lying.

At the end of the four-hour ride, it was past midnight, and Lonesome Lefty left me off at the top of the exit ramp. We exchanged a left-handed handshake with a pair of direct looks and sincere "good luck's."

I stepped out of the car, shouldered my bag, and walked down the entrance ramp. Traffic was thin, and a misty rain watered the road and my denim jacket. I pulled my collar up and moved my arms and hands to attract attention. Rain is not a friend to hitchhikers.

Subtle techniques didn't work when a hitchhiker was getting soaked. While rain might evoke some initial pity, very few drivers wanted a sopping wet beggar in their car. Adding a hat or the hood of my poncho made me look wet and ominous. Rain was also the friend of road predators. They knew a drenched hitchhiker with diminishing prospects for a ride was more likely to ignore his instincts and make a poor decision about whether or not to accept a ride. A seasoned hitchhiker develops a sixth sense about the "bad ride" and can read a driver whose intentions might include more than just moving down the road.

The rain turned from a spatter into a steady light rain. I sighed and pulled out my bright yellow, ninety-nine-cent K-Mart parka to wear over my denim jacket. As I slipped the parka on, I saw a large car, a Ford Galaxie, approaching me fast. I noticed the inside dome light was on, illuminating a young woman who was touching a cigarette to the bright orange coil of the car's lighter. As the car shot by, the driver looked up and over toward me as she puffed life into the cigarette, a smile in her eyes suggesting she might consider stopping. I had an instant of hope. I thought I could reel her in. But her eyes riveted back to the road. I turned to watch, hoping to catch her glancing in the rearview mirror, but instead saw a pair of headlights bouncing crazily across the median that separated the two-way traffic. The Galaxie's brake lights brightened, telling me the woman saw the danger. The oncoming lights were attached to a battered pickup truck lurching at high speed and fixed like a torpedo on the woman's car. The Galaxie swerved right. Too late.

The crash happened less than a hundred feet from me. Images flickered rapidly at me as if backlit by a strobe light. The pickup's front bumper hit the Galaxie almost straight on. The vehicles exploded into each other, accompanied by an excruciating scream of metal and glass. The pickup pushed the hood and engine of the Galaxie up, up, until the car flipped on its side, slid across the gravel shoulder, and came to rest on the grass just off the highway's shoulder. I was close enough that shards of glass bounced off me like rock candy.

I stood frozen, oddly curious about the noise caused by the accident. A television show I saw as kid, featuring natural and man-made disasters, flashed through my mind. No one who survived the various scenarios could accurately describe the sounds.

"It sounded like a train."

"I don't know, it was like a needle scratching across a record."

They had no point of reference. Neither had I, until my family's home burned to the ground. The screeching, hissing noises of that fire and this accident were my version of Dante's *Inferno*—the sounds of the gates to the anteroom of hell opening in welcome.

My shoulders shook involuntarily and jarred me from memory to the present. The events leading up to the accident had played out in stunning fast-forward. I couldn't think in a straight line. The sounds and sights of the crash scene didn't synchronize. I picked a few pieces of glass out of the creases of my parka, heard the engine of the dying car hiss with steam, and watched pieces of airborne metal settle on the highway. I blinked my eyes hard, trying hard to snap out of my shock and ran toward the vehicles as the traffic came up fast on the carnage, stopping sharply behind me. The cars' headlamps illuminated the twisted truck lying in the middle of the road. The lights shone into a cab filled with steam and smoke. The driver's body had pushed through the windshield and lay in an impossible position on the crinkled metal that used to be the hood. Drivers left their cars and moved toward both destroyed vehicles, catching up to me as I looked inside the truck for other bodies. A lean, mustached man with a filterless Camel clinging to his lips reached the body on the hood The cigarette dropped from his mouth and he wailed, "Oh my God! Oh my God! Oh my God!" He reached out and held the broken body's wrist, looking for a pulse that wasn't there. I sprinted over to the overturned Galaxie, but the woman wasn't in the car. Stumbling away from the car and down into the tall grass off the highway shoulder, I looked for something I didn't want to find. Hearing a groan—not a good sign—I waded through the grass toward the fence that separated the highway right-of-way from a cornfield.

I almost stepped on her. She was lying on her back, her face untouched, only a sheen of rainwater covering her skin and short dark hair. I dropped to my knees and saw that her arms and legs were bloody. She moaned lowly, and I put one hand on her forehead and supported the back of her head with the other. Her eyes fluttered open and looked at me quizzically.

"What... where am I?" she stammered quietly.

This was more than I had bargained for when I hit the road looking for a chance to get away from both the humdrum of the suburbs and my own sad-sack past. I choked back the bile and vomit that were moving up my throat. Here I was with an accident victim in my arms, looking to me for help. I wanted to run as fast as I could in the other direction. I had to find a way out of this shit, but there wasn't one.

"You've been in a car accident. You've been thrown out of the car. I'm Luke. I'm going to help you." I was shivering as I looked down, and in spite of the blood and rain and circumstances, I thought, *Wait a minute, this girl looks familiar. No way. Who is she?*

She tried a smile, lips trembling, and said, "Thanks, you're an angel."

I positioned myself cross-legged and cradled her head and shoulders in my lap. I waved my arms, shouting, "Hey, over here! Fast! I need help, medical help, fast!"

The group of travelers who had stopped at the accident scene had increased. Two young men heard me and ran toward us. I tried to wipe the rain-blood mixture off her arms with a fast-food napkin I kept in my coat jacket. She began shaking, so I pulled my jacket off and covered her. The two men, about my age, reached us out of breath.

The first stopped abruptly and said, "Is she dead? The other guy up there on the pickup is dead as old dirt."

I replied, "No, she's alive, but she's gonna need help fast. Can you help?"

"You bet, kid," the second man said. "A semi driver up there on the road called the accident in to the state police with his CB. We'll run back up there and get an ambulance on the way, pronto."

"Okay. See if you can find blankets and if anyone here is a doctor or a nurse. She's hurt badly."

The two men sprinted back up the rise, and I stroked her forehead. Looking closer, I saw her legs were shredded from being tossed through the windshield. I felt liquid where her head met the palm of my hand, and it was thickening. *There must be something I can do.* But I hadn't gotten past the Tenderfoot level in Boy Scout first aid, and I didn't want to move her or touch her further until the ambulance arrived.

My head buzzed as it hit me: *I do know this girl. She's Annette Brady! I used to razz her family about being the Brady Bunch since they had four or five kids. She was in the class ahead of me and moved out of St. Mary's Parish and out of state about five years ago. Christ, her sister Kate was in my class. How can this be? God, she's cold. Hurry up, someone! How badly is she hurt? What should I do? Help me, someone, help me!*

Annette moaned slightly and opened her eyes again. "I can't feel anything. I think I'm going to die here."

"Oh, no, you are going to be fine. Help is on the way, hold on."

She smiled weakly. "Hey, you look worried. It's all right. I know I'm going to die. But listen to me. I need to tell you something before I go."

"Please, please, Annette, hold on here . . ." I pleaded, calling her by name, but her eyes were tired, afraid, yet full of anticipation; I don't think she recognized me. I leaned in close and she whispered to me, stopping to catch her breath between jumbled pieces of a story, a request—no, more like a demand. She talked fast, trying to give me a backstory. I could only hear fragments. She asked me to finish something she had started.

She choked and gasped, "Promise me you'll try to put them back together. Promise me."

"I promise."

Her eyes looked past me into the night sky, which had begun to clear.

"Look," she whispered, and I followed her gaze to where rays of moonlight pushed through the clouds, creating a nighttime rainbow of silver, gray, and blue. "That's where God lives."

A pulsating sound filled the air and surrounded us. The tone grew and undulated and changed direction. Through my deep anxiety, I heard and felt the sound and thought, *Celestial hum.* As the sound melted away, I felt oddly peaceful, serene.

The group rushed back from the road with a nurse in tow, who knelt beside me and Annette in the grass and mud, and took Annette's pulse.

"She's gone, son," she said. I looked up at her, my tears mixing with the fresh rain streaming down my contorted face.

"I know," I cried, "I know." Annette's body hung lifelessly in my lap and arms. My chin slumped as I clung to her.

I wasn't a matador. I wasn't an immortal hitchhiker. I was a mildewed dishrag at the bottom of a goddamned laundry basket. I was nothing, and in a horrible coincidence, a beautiful girl I knew had just died in my arms in the middle of a field in Tennessee. This was a shitty deal all around. I wanted out of this fucking field and out of this life. I wanted to go back to a home that didn't exist.

The rain turned to mist and the accident scene was professionalized by the police and firemen. Eventually, a cop led me by my elbow back to an ambulance for a once-over and a report. As I sat answering questions, I thought this surely must be a sledgehammer sign to get my life back together. I would go back to Royal Oak and get a job, get a girlfriend, help out my family, maybe even shave off my beard. Alas, I have a short memory for ugliness and lots of practice pushing the crap under rocks. Then I remembered I had a promise to keep that I barely understood. I wasn't off the road quite yet.

Chapter 3

September 2003

While my ignoble past still plays out in my current life, I'm usually too preoccupied with everyday messiness to notice it. A trigger, like finding the infrequent hitchhiker to pick up, can snap me back hard. A familiar shiver crept up the back of my neck as I recalled Annette and the aftermath that cajoled and then shook me back into a life worth living. I let a few minutes pass to see if the young hitchhiker would break the ice first. He did—weakly, in my snobbish opinion.

"So, Father O'Roarke, I see you enjoy classic rock," the young man said, his earrings sparkling in the sunlight. Our minivan's CD player was on low volume playing Eric Clapton's "Layla."

"Clapton is the real deal, if you know what I mean. A guitar genius. I mean, that guy can really play. He's a—"

"Yes, I enjoy Eric Clapton's musical ability. He has stood the test of time. Of course, I also enjoy a rousing rendition of the 'Hallelujah Chorus.' I say, young fellow,"—I inserted a slight Queen's English accent here to throw him off—"are you a follower of our Lord Jesus Christ, and if so, are you also a member of the One True Church?"

I didn't have to look at my wife and daughter to know one was smiling with chagrined amusement and the other was cringing with anticipated embarrassment.

"Ya know, Father O'Roarke, I was just having this conversation with my mother the other day. Now, I don't want to lie to you, especially since you're a priest and all, but I have done a fair amount of sinning in my life. However, I have found the straight and narrow, and yes, I am a follower of Jesus, but I have not yet committed to any one church. But I am most interested in getting your advice, since we will be spending some time together."

This was much more promising than I could have anticipated—a bullshit artist. The boy's answer included his mother, a commitment to Jesus (a lie?), and a plea for my counsel—meaning he expected lunch. Even my wife looked away from her book and gave me a sideways, sardonic smile. This lad had potential!

"That's a very thoughtful response, Mr. Tom Lutac. But I think you overestimate my counsel. I am most interested in learning how you came to Jesus. I'd love to hear your step-by-step journey. Then maybe we can trip the light fantastic on why the Holy Roman Catholic Church possesses the real road to heaven."

Yes, I laid it on a bit thick, but what the heck? It's serve, volley, serve, volley, if you're really good at handling yourself out here on the road. I also knew I could only keep this tête-à-tête going until we reached Roscommon, about fifty miles north of us, before both my daughter and my wife would make me stop and 'fess up to young Tom.

This was a major concession to family life. A good story spun on the road should stay there, taking on a life of its own. But my wife and daughter bound me to a promise years ago: I would identify when a story was real and when it was imagined. After Roberta started repeating some bedtime yarns in elementary school as true stories, I had to face the unpleasant truth that there was some disparity between my strict family policy about telling the truth and my own stories, which were mostly outright lies. For example, Roberta had insisted, quite correctly, that there was no way I could had intercepted a pass in a high school football game with my faceguard and run back fifty yards with the ball still lodged in my helmet for a touchdown—but I convinced her it was true, anyway.

Our agreement was that I could still tell tall tales, but that at some point soon afterward, I would let the listening, aggrieved parties know the score. When it came to stories that were largely true but embellished beyond belief, we had an uneasy family truce. I knew this repartee with our hitchhiker was far more amusing to me than to them. But I was easily entertained. Fortunately, my wife was asleep at this point, book in hand, with her blonde hair pushed against the headrest. Unlike me, she could peacefully sleep anywhere, at any time. She was fifty-one years old, ten months older than I was. Our years together had worn well on her. Her skin was still supple and smooth, with only a few wisdom lines branching out from her eyes. Her tranquil beauty is what did it for me. Thirty years after we met, I still knew I had married very, very well—way out of my league. Isn't that the definition of love?

"Where should I start, Father O'Roarke? With my sinning days or my redemption?" Tom asked.

"At the beginning, Tom. Always at the beginning," I replied.

A red-and-blue I-75 road sign in the familiar medallion shape came into view, disappearing as quickly as it arrived. The sign was embossed into my road memories and could start a flood of regret and exhilaration. I leaned back into my leather captain's chair, adjusted the sixteen-position power seat, half-listened to Tom, and half-remembered how uncomfortable it could get on the road. What I didn't know was how unpredictable and bumpy this road trip was going to get.

Chapter 4

March 1973

Unfamiliar middle-Tennessee road signs flew by as I sat trembling in the front seat of Rita McDermott's greenish 1970 Pinto. The rain-washed light from the car's high beams reflected off the crested I-75 sign. I closed my eyes and wished away the past dismal years, pretending my mom was driving. I wished the I-75 sign was in Detroit and I were on my way home from a Sunday afternoon visit to the historical museum, where I'd walked hand-in-hand with my little brother over the cobblestone streets. My eyes opened, and I was still cold, wrapped in a police blanket, and traveling with a stranger.

I felt like I was in a vacuum as the wreck became an anesthetized memory. I couldn't remember how long it had taken for the police and ambulance to arrive. The paramedics lifted Annette's limp body and awkwardly carried it up to the road before putting her on a gurney. I could see the woman in the nurse's uniform talking to the paramedics and cops in the rain. The ambulances and tow trucks started to leave and the road flares subsided. Officer Miller, who had walked me through the accident, excused himself and talked with his partner and Rita, the nurse, on the side of the road. The cops determined the statement they had was adequate for tonight, but wrote down the address from my driver's license, which was my sister Ann's house in Royal Oak.

That's how I found myself with Rita. She was on her way home from work when the crash had stopped traffic in front of her. When police told her I was a hitchhiker with no place to go, her maternal instincts were stirred. She couldn't leave a bloodstained, sopping boy, who had held a girl in his arms until she died, as a courtesy guest of the Tennessee State Police. The police were grateful when she volunteered to take me, because they didn't really know what to do with a shell-shocked, Yankee hitchhiker who seemed to have done the right thing. Rita knew her husband, the owner of a small construction firm, would not be happy that she was bringing home a "straggler," as he liked to call anyone without a brush cut and job. She didn't care what he thought, though, and knew he would be asleep, as always, following her afternoon shift at the local hospital.

Rita McDermott gently chatted me up on the ride to her house. She told me about her only son, Ricky, who had enlisted in the U.S. Marines at age eighteen and was halfway through his one-year tour of duty in Vietnam. She didn't ask me a lot of questions, and I was grateful. I could feel my pulse pounding in my temples and through my eardrums. I tried to be polite and give her reassuring information about my Catholic school background to make her feel safe with me in the car. There was no need. Rita McDermott was not a nervous person.

The car ride and arrival at the McDermotts' ranch-style home was mostly a blur. I found myself standing in their upstairs bathroom staring down at familiar black-and-white checkerboard tiles on the floor, peeling off my wet, blood-stained clothes. I took a deep breath as I showered, and fought a rush of shivers. It took a while to compose myself. I put on the robe that had hung on the bathroom door and turned down Rita's offer of a meal when she knocked on the bedroom door. She said good night, and I found myself in Richard Jr.'s bedroom, which was plastered with orange University of Tennessee football posters. On a shelf sat a Johnny Bench autographed ball on a pedestal next to family pictures.

I hope Ricky makes it home. And I hope I make it home. I lay exhausted on Ricky's bed, my eyes frozen open. I couldn't sleep. I stared at the plastic light fixture attached above to two light bulbs, and tried to think of something other than blood and skin and the smell of gasoline mixed with rain and death. It worked, but a far worse image emerged. It was the face of my dad. The face of a hapless murderer who shamed all he touched and ruined my life—but not for forever. I vowed to my mother I would not let him drag me down his lifeless trail. But I had to admit, the battle was nearly tied since the fire. The apparition of his face on Ricky's ceiling roiled my gut as I forced back the urge to puke. *Goddamn it, he is not going to make me sick again!* I sat up and wiped my mouth with the back of my hand. *Focus on the positive.*

I closed my eyes and could see my mom on the side porch calling me back to pick up the brown-bag lunch I had forgotten. I ran back to her, grabbed the bag, and was off again without stopping. I made it to the street and heard her call. When I turned, she blew me a two-handed kiss with a smile that shone straight through to my nine-year-old heart. I opened my eyes. *Her spirit will win, not Dad's. I'm going to make it.* My shoulders shook and I sobbed. I wept for Mom, my sisters, and my brother. I wept for Annette and for myself. When there were no tears left, I caught my breath. I let myself fall back onto the bed, and the welcome darkness of sleep took me.

I woke up early, hearing the first birds, and was jarred by the unfamiliarity of the bedroom. I never did get comfortable with waking up in a different place every night. I repacked my bag, dressed, used the bathroom, and walked gingerly downstairs toward the smell of the coffee in the kitchen. Richard McDermott Sr. sat at the small kitchenette table, cradling a cup. He looked at me coolly.

"Your wife let me stay here. I'm on my way. Please thank her for the kindness." I was accustomed to the discomfort of meeting strangers and pushed the necessary information out quickly.

"I don't know what Rita is thinking sometimes. I don't cater to vagabond hitchhikers, but I understand you had a rough go of it last night. Sit down and have some coffee and a biscuit, or I'll never hear the end of it." Richard harrumphed and shook his head as I set my backpack on the floor and sat down across the table from him.

I slathered the warm biscuit with soft butter and homemade raspberry preserves, and steered the conversation to Tennessee football, avoiding the obvious conversation-killer subjects like Vietnam, Nixon, and the debate over whether recreational drug use was no worse than kicking back three scotches a night. Richard begrudgingly warmed to me when I mentioned something about the Southeastern Conference and UT's football prospects next fall (thank God for *Sports Illustrated*), and he offered me a ride to the highway—"Only because it's on the way to work." The offer ensured I would soon be on my way out of town and just a hippie blip on his radar screen, one that he could yuck about to the guys at the construction site. I thanked Richard, but told him I was going in the other direction, to UT's main campus.

He surprised me. "Okay, fella, that's not too far out of my way. And my wife wants you to take this with you." He passed a paper grocery bag to me. "Your clothes from last night had to go, but you're close enough to my Ricky's size, so Rita put together some of his old stuff for you." Even though it was clear that Richard was under strict orders from Rita to help me out, his gruffness was more personality than meanness.

"Thank you. You're good people," I said as Richard opened the kitchen door with another harrumph. He drove me to the middle of campus and pulled over in front of the John C. Hodges Library.

"This should be as good a spot as any," he said.

I reached for the door handle and heard Richard clear his throat nervously. I looked over and he asked, "So, I'm wonderin.' How did you keep out of Vietnam? You ain't got a college deferment." I could easily see the chip on his shoulder.

"My lottery number was 359," I replied.

"Ricky's number was 71. One or two numbers higher and he'd be working on my crew with me this morning." Richard McDermott's eyes brimmed. He brushed his tears with both sleeves of his flannel shirt. "I guess that's the luck of the draw, young man. You remember how lucky you are, you hear?"

"Yes, sir," I replied.

"Well, good luck to you, son."

I stuck my hand out, looked Richard straight in the eye and said, "And good luck to you, Mr. McDermott. I appreciate all you and your wife have done for me. Don't worry about me showing up for a handout. I can take care of myself. And, Mr. McDermott, while I'm not much of a praying man, I will say a prayer for your son and his safe return. Godspeed to your family, Mr. McDermott."

His head pulled back as he withdrew from my firm handshake. For an instant, he thought I was making some kind of statement about the war. I meant what I said and didn't let my eyes waver from his when I said it.

His eyes welled up again and he said, "I appreciate your prayers. Godspeed to you and yours."

I hopped out of the car and asked the first heart-stoppingly ripe coed I met where I could find the student union. I found an empty table in the union overlooking the sprawling, redbrick University of Tennessee campus. I moved the clothes from Rita's bag to my knapsack and found an envelope with a ten-dollar bill and a note. "Luke, be careful with your future," Rita had written. I was grateful for the note from a gracious southern lady.

These were tumultuous times, and thousands of mothers worried about their absent sons. With Vietnam ending badly and with disco starting to gain an indulgent toehold, it was as challenging a time for parents as it was for their children. It made sense Mrs. McDermott found solace in a stranger's son. I had filled the role before.

The University of Tennessee churned with action on this sticky spring day. Whenever my travels took me to a college, the visit would affirm my conviction that I would eventually have to attend. There was just too much great energy. UT's student union hummed with surging hormones, hangovers, ambition, energy, self-centeredness, and naïveté. Many of the women who buzzed past me were achingly beautiful and matched by ruggedly handsome young men. Everyone seemed a little taller to me.

I had hoped—and as it turned out, guessed correctly—that Annette's sister, Kate, attended UT. A rationale for honoring my promise to Annette and a simple game plan had come to me in the McDermotts' bathroom. Standing in front of the sink, brushing my teeth, I had noticed some dried blood on my arm, which I had missed in the shower. I had scraped at it with my fingernail. It had popped free like a scab, hit the sink basin, and swirled down the drain. The sight reminded me that the accident and the promise were real; I couldn't leave last night behind like another unimaginable bad dream. Over the past years, I had a nearly perfect track record of running away from every commitment I made or should have made. I wanted to cut and run from this situation, too, but Annette's dying request was watering my dehydrated conscience.

If I was going to half-believe in my I-can-control-fate philosophy, at least I was going to admit that fate existed. And it was pretty obvious that destiny had just whacked me upside the head. I somehow suspected that more than coincidence led Annette Brady to sail past me in her car. That twist of fate, combined with the rest of the night, was earthshaking. The promise she extracted from me was complicated and not completely clear. Standing in the bathroom, I was spooked. I shivered. Whatever it was, whatever it meant, I took this promise seriously.

One of the last conversations I had with Mom before she died was about trust and promises. She sat me down at the kitchen table, which was the center of my family's universe, and gave me yet another "Guideposts for Life" sermonette.

My brother and sisters were eating a summertime lunch of peanut butter and jelly on white bread, (no crusts for my younger brother, Donnie), apple slices, and cold, white milk with Oreos to dip for dessert. The Oreos disappeared, and we all dashed pell-mell toward the side door and an afternoon of kickball, tag, and hole-digging. I was halfway out the door when Mom clasped my shoulders like a C-clamp.

"Luke, before you go out to play, let's have a little talk."

My sisters Ann, Angela, and April laughed as they raced out the door. "Time for Luke to learn the Rules of Life," April yelled.

"Life according to Momma Moore," Angela chipped in.

"Pay attention, Luke, Mom's going to give you a test," Ann finished as the door slammed behind them.

Mom frowned. "Don't say a word, Luke. You're old enough to begin being responsible for your life and my job is to get you ready. Get that look off your face. This will not be as bad as your sisters say. The only test is how you use what I'm going to tell you. So sit right down and let's talk."

I did as Mom said, focusing more on her oval face framing the blue eyes I had inherited. She was the loveliest of women to me. Her blond hair was tied back during the day as she managed her brood. In the evening, when Dad came home (if he came home) she would let her hair down, brushing it out in the hallway mirror.

She would turn to us kids at the dining room table and ask, "How do I look today, my little chickadees?"

We would shout out on cue, "Good enough to eat, Momma!"

Mom would smile broadly, showing a slightly chipped front tooth she wore with pride and a dimple on each of her cheeks.

There was a story behind that tooth. She had won the elementary school one-hundred-yard dash, leaning forward in front of the fastest boy in the school to break the ribbon, before falling forward and breaking a tiny piece of her front tooth.

Dad suggested she get it capped, and she laughed and said, "Trygvi, dear, this is my badge of honor. And I get to tell the story of how I won the race every time someone asks me about it." Mom was the storyteller.

I was thirteen years old that summer, and about every three months she would pick a topic, and I would listen. Kindness and Charity, Truth and Courage, Justice and Liberty—she provided a combination of the Ten Commandments and the Golden Rule. I listened because Mom was the most important person in my life and ignoring her would have been unthinkable, even if I didn't have a lick of interest in the topics. I did love to hear Mom talk, a strand of hair falling over her forehead, which she would push back over her ear, not missing a beat in her quest to teach her child how to live. This last talk was shortly before she died, and I replayed it in my mind over and over again.

"Luke, when you make a promise, it's important to keep it. It's not something you take lightly. It is far better not to make a promise than to break one."

She announced she was finished with the lesson by saying, "I know you're going to grow up to be a fine young man, Luke Moore. Now go on and live your life."

I scurried out of the kitchen chair and headed for the screen door.

"Luke," she called.

I stopped at the door and she blew me kiss. "I love you, Luke, darling."

I blushed red and smiled. I didn't tell her I loved her, but I did.

That's what I thought about that morning while standing in the McDermotts' bathroom in Knoxville, Tennessee. I hadn't a glimmer of a thought about how I would fulfill the commitment. Given the circumstances, I normally wouldn't have had a problem letting myself off the hook. But the combination of Mom's advice ringing in my head and the wild confluence of events that had crashed into my life made it certain I couldn't walk or run away.

Step one: find the Brady family. It was a one-step plan, but I figured I'd play it out and see what happened. I remembered the family had moved to Knoxville from Royal Oak. The Bradys were unusual in our Catholic school because Mr. and Mrs. Brady were divorced and Mr. Brady was never around or mentioned. I remembered that Kate Brady was smart and most likely in college. I had a vague memory that one of my Royal Oak classmates had stayed in touch with the Brady girls, and that they still lived in Knoxville. Someone had mentioned Kate attended the University of Tennessee. I concluded that it made sense to try to locate Kate Brady, who might remember me from St. Mary's, even if it was a half a lifetime ago. Which is what I had in mind as I approached the information desk at the student union. It was hosted by a curvy brunette with a name tag that read, "Mary Ellen, Pigeon Forge, Tennessee."

"How can I help you, darlin'?" asked sweet Mary Ellen. After telling her a story about how I was Kate Brady's cousin making a surprise visit, I left with Kate's address on a UT hospitality napkin, directions to her apartment, and a weekend activities sheet, including an invitation to a keg party on Saturday night. I was more than a trifle embarrassed that I left the union with an erection working its way down one pant leg. Apparently, even in the most stressful of times, hormones keep pumping testosterone.

I walked out into a bright, mid-South morning, looking for Kate. Having a task was a novel feeling; the trade-off of being on the road was swapping purpose for adventure. I was always searching for, and generally empty of, satisfaction. I didn't feel empty today, even if I wasn't certain how to categorize the search for the Brady family. I needed to find Kate, talk to her, and, more than likely, hold her and be held. As I walked, I attempted to prepare myself, to envision the grieving scene: a distraught Kate comforted by friends, or perhaps by her parents and family.

I strolled across the older part of the campus, hiked up a hill, stood in front of the impressive Ayres Hall, and watched a group of students listen to a long-haired but well-groomed student exhort, "We're old enough for war, but not old enough to choose our classes, according to this administration. We've had enough!" The small crowd urged the speaker on with all the contemporary exhortations: "Right on! Power to the people! Y'all keep telling it like it is!" The southern accents were exotic to me, and the rabble-rousers were more rousing than rabble.

UT wasn't Ann Arbor, but it had plenty of life. While sports and Greek life were priorities, the sixties and early seventies had pushed collegiate life into a wild, rebellious party that included liberal drug use, sex as sport, and mass streaking, a scene that was soon imitated on campuses throughout the nation.

It struck me that springtime smelled and looked different in Knoxville. Sweeter than in Michigan. The dogwood trees, cherry blossoms, and azaleas were just past their peak bloom, and a breeze covered the ground with petals. I strolled off campus and into the Fort Sanders area, so declared by a historical plaque. I stopped and bought a five-cent lemonade from an enterprising seven-year-old girl who was chaperoned by her grandmother. When Grandma Rainey learned I was from "up north," she thought it was her civic duty to offer me a quick history tour of the neighborhood and city of Knoxville. The "fort" was in transition from what used to be the finest neighborhood in Knoxville to burgeoning student ghetto housing. Close in to Knoxville's downtown and the university, enterprising real estate sharpies were subdividing the grand Queen Anne and Victorian homes, cramming as many as five or six apartments and up to twenty students into the houses. By providing little maintenance, they made a tidy profit. The homes were still beautiful, with unique architectural details including Palladian dormers, bell turrets, and richly detailed gables.

I followed the map on the napkin to a large brick home with a distinctive, almost church-like facade and an elegant ribbed turret dome off to one side. A young woman was looking off a balcony at 1633 Clinch Avenue, my destination.

As I stepped over a tree-root-buckled sidewalk toward the house, a car door slammed behind me on Clinch, accompanied by laughter loud enough to turn me around. Walking away from the car and toward me was a stunning young woman. It took a moment to recognize Kate Brady. She had been fifteen, quiet, studious, and just a bit pudgy when her family moved to Tennessee. She was now a mature woman in very short cutoff blue jeans, a yellow tank top, and an early tan. I forgot my mission and admired her. She hitched her overnight bag up on her shoulder and stared back, pushing her shoulder-length brown hair over the straps of the bag. I could see faint recognition narrowing her eyes as she questioned how she knew me, but she couldn't find my name or a place with which to connect me.

My first words, "Hi, Kate," were overwhelmed by a loud voice from the girl on the balcony, screaming, "Kate! Oh my God, Kate!"

Kate and I turned and looked up at the distraught young woman shouting from the balcony. She disappeared for a moment and then pushed through the front door of the house, running toward Kate with an anguished face. She reached and hugged her, holding her tight.

"Oh, God, girl, where have you been? We've all been looking everywhere . . ."

Kate stopped her, pulled back from the embrace, and said, "What's going on, Adell, what's happened?"

"Oh, Kate, it's Annette, she was in a terrible accident . . ."

Kate's expression fell from confusion to understanding. "How bad? Is she in the hospital? Oh, my God, is she . . ."

"Kate, I'm so sorry, we didn't know how to reach you." Adell embraced her again. Kate sobbed. Watching the scene, my chest tightened and my eyes teared up. I turned to walk away. *This is not the time,* I thought.

I tried to pass the sobbing women and whispered, "I'm sorry for your loss, Kate."

Kate turned and faced me.

"Who the hell are you? I know you from somewhere, but what are you doing here? Why are you crying?" she demanded.

I was stunned, but cleared my throat and told her, "There's no simple way to say this. I was with Annette last night . . . when she died. I, I grew up in Royal Oak and went to St. Mary's with you . . . and your family. It's just the worst, worst thing I can imagine . . ."

I couldn't go on. I had seen that look on her face before, on my brother's and sisters' faces when we knew Mom was gone. Kate and I stood facing each other, confused and raw. At this instant, our lives were braided together.

Kate's roommate Adell broke the silence loudly, taking charge.

"Jesus Christ, did I just hear you right? You know Kate and you were with Annette last night? That's right out of *The Twilight Zone.* My God, let's get you inside and find out what in the hell is going on here." Adell put her arm around Kate and pushed me on the back toward their apartment. She sat Kate and me down at a dinette table, where I told them my story.

"Beyond belief, beyond belief," Adell repeated.

Kate was in shock. "I believe you, but beyond that, I can't think at all. My head hurts so bad." She held her head in her in hands and massaged her temples. Standing up, she pursed her lips and said, "I need to get home. Adell, I need you to drive. Luke, Luke Moore, right? You need to come with us, but I'm guessing you already know that."

"No problem, Kate. I'll do whatever you need," I said.

"I can't even begin to know what I need or what I'm doing. Let's just get home." She pushed the tears from her face and readied herself to join her family in the rituals of grief and mourning.

The Bradys' family home reflected the "old money" of Knoxville's Sequoyah Hills neighborhood. The large, white-columned home surprised me. There were no houses in Royal Oak that matched the grandeur of the Brady manor. I could remember the Bradys' old home—melting into the standard fifty-by-eighty-foot lots in Detroit's suburbia. In Sequoyah Hills, the lots were measured in acres, and the wide streets rolled, curved, and were lined with dogwoods, catalpas, and shagbark hickories.

The Brady house and grounds were magnificent, grander in scale than the impressive neighboring homes. The driveway to the Bradys' front door was at least a hundred yards long and split into a circular drive in front of the antebellum entrance to the mansion. A driveway led to a large garage behind the house, with a mother-in-law apartment above it. There were several cars parked on the drive, including a vintage Cadillac, a late-model Lincoln, and other luxury automobiles, distinguished in comparison with Adell's beat-up Chevy II.

Adell parked while Kate and I entered the house through the back door, leading into what looked like a restaurant kitchen, far larger than the postage-stamp-sized kitchens in Royal Oak. Kate led me through an archway with intricate carved woodwork, which opened into a spacious, enclosed sunroom that ran along the back of the house. A series of large picture windows opened onto a view of the Tennessee River, which ran along the back of the property. The Bradys were assembled there, surrounding Mrs. Helen Brady, whose auburn hair was brushed high into a bun. She was seated in a wingback chair upholstered with an elegant Sunbury jacquard fabric, absorbing the early afternoon sunlight.

Helen Brady was a striking middle-aged woman, but her face was darkened with loss, her eyes dull from lack of sleep. As I recognized her pain, my temples began to throb in the dizzying presence of relatives and friends. The handsome children—two boys, Matthew and Michael, and Kate—looked lost.

Kate rushed over to her mother and covered her with an embrace. "What do we do, Momma?" Helen Brady held her only surviving daughter tightly. Kate curled in the chair, half in her mother's lap, as Helen stroked her hair.

"Momma, she's gone. Annette's gone."

"I know, Kate. Our light is gone."

The stricken family huddled around Mrs. Brady.

I stood watching with Adell. Mike Brady stood and hugged Adell.

"Who's your friend, Del?" he asked.

I stepped forward and extended my hand. "I'm Luke Moore." Heads turned in the room as the brothers registered faint to familiar recognition.

Adell blurted, "He was the last to see Annette, honest truth." The room froze, almost changing colors, and then became frenetic. The boys crowded me.

"What's Adell talking about?"

"You know Annette?"

"Hey, I remember you now—you went to St. Mary's. What are you doing here?"

The awkwardness of their sorrow left for a moment as they focused on me. They were polite but dogged. I was transfixed by a look across the room from Mrs. Brady. She wasn't talking, but I could hear her. *You've been touched by my Annette, haven't you? Yes, I can tell now. Come here, young man, and let's get to the truth of it.*

"Let him be, boys. Young man, come over and sit with me," Mrs. Brady ordered.

I found my way to a seat on the ottoman, sharing it with Kate's legs, and within inches of Mrs. Brady.

"I don't recognize you, but I do remember the Moore family from Royal Oak. I worked in the St. Mary's cafeteria with your mother, Roberta. She and I helped organize a Christmas show. I remember her well. She had glow about her when she was with her children."

Helen Brady paused for a minute, the memory coming into focus. "Oh, Luke, now I remember. We heard the terrible news here in Knoxville. Oh, son." Her own pain transferred to the memory of my past. I wasn't ready for this, any of this. I was confused as she pulled me close to her.

I'd never liked getting emotional, especially around people I didn't know. Worse yet, I did not like being the center of attention while both these wishes were being violated. It was painfully clear that here, it was going to be unavoidable. I was going to have to tell my story and how it led to Annette.

A thought flashed through my mind. On my first hitchhike to Florida I had been picked up by an old man who used to barnstorm as a wing-walker for those old biplanes. I had told him that I could never do his job.

He replied, "Oh, it's not so bad. After you take that first step, there's really no turning back."

I took the first step. The roomful of friends and family watched me compose myself. I took a handkerchief Mike Brady offered, sat up straight, and took a full breath.

"Mrs. Brady, I need to tell you about how Annette died in my arms last night." The room shuddered; Mrs. Brady's eyes narrowed on me.

"Tell us son, about you, about our Annette. You can see we need to know," she gestured to the crowded room gathering close to me.

Surrounded by childhood faces in a foreign setting, I pulled myself together. I told my story. A true and horrible account. I wasn't acting or conning now to get down the road or to finagle a free lunch. I had never before said aloud how my young life had been ruined. It finally poured out. I told the truth, but even at this most vulnerable point, I did not tell all. I breathed deep, ignoring the pounding at my temples.

"Let me start from the beginning. I have three older sisters, Ann and the twins, Angela and April, and a younger brother, Donnie. We all went to St. Mary's, but I think Kate and I were the only kids in the same class. But Matt and Mike, we played B-ball on the outdoor courts at St. Mary's."

They nodded their heads in agreement. They remembered. But not this next part—they didn't have a clue what came next in my family's sordid story. The Bradys were already in Knoxville when our own personal Twilight Zone visited the Moore family. I had to be out of my frigging mind to tell this story. Little did I know at the time that if any family would understand, it would be the Bradys.

I took a deep breath. *Christ, they lost their sister and daughter last night, suck it up and let them hear a story so shocking that it might distract them from their grief.*

"As my mom used to say, 'The shortest distance between two places is a straight line,' so here it goes. In 1968, when I was fifteen years old, my dad murdered my mom. Yes, my dad murdered my mom."

I could feel the familiar bile of hate rising quickly up my throat. I choked it back.

"The short story is, my dad had run up some big-time debts with mob bookies, and I guess if he didn't come up with the cash, it was strike three. That, along with a big-time drinking problem, convinced my big, bad dad that killing my mom for life and homeowner's insurance was the solution. He suffocated my mom in bed and then set the bedroom on fire. He woke all of us up and pushed us outside and then cried when he said the fire was too far gone to try and rescue Mom. My brother Donnie was only nine years old, and he didn't listen and ran back to the house after my mom. By the time he was pulled out of the house, Donnie had burns covering almost half his body. That was five years ago and he's still going in for skin grafts. The autopsy on Mom, along with a talkative barmaid who over-served my dad at Sid and Wally's tavern, caught up with him. He was convicted of first-degree murder, and he's in Jackson Prison for the rest of his godforsaken life.

"My oldest sister, Ann, was twenty at the time, and she managed to keep us together in a rented house in Royal Oak. Me, I turned into a total asshole—excuse me, Mrs. Brady, a total idiot—and barely graduated from St. Mary's. Two days after high school graduation, I packed up my backpack and hit the road. I've hitchhiked over fifty thousand miles in the last two years, and I guess you could say I'm growing up fast. I go home every three or four months and work odd jobs. My family and best friends are still in Royal Oak, but I need to be away, a lot. I was on the road, hitchhiking from Kalamazoo to Florida to visit Vincent Delgado, who also used to go to St. Mary's before moving to Miami, when Annette's car passed me last night. That's my story so far. Telling it out loud, it's all so unreal.

"It's funny growing up and going to a parish school like St. Mary's. We all come from big families, and you know one or two kids because you're in the same class or take swimming lessons together, and you become friends, and somehow that connects you to the rest of the family. It really becomes a pretty big extended family.

"What I'm trying to say is that it wasn't just a freaked-out coincidence that I happened to be standing on the side of the road last night. And, hard as it is to believe that I held your sister, your friend. . . . your daughter in my arms last night, what seems important is that I saw her in the car before the accident.

"I recognized her, she saw me, and she was alive. In that instant, I felt something. I don't have a clue what it was, but that connection, of Annette fully alive, is what I think I'm here to tell you about. She was vibrant and beautiful. She was caring and kind, and I saw all that in an instant before the crash, hard as that may be to believe. I guess you know about the accident. She was thrown from her car when the truck hit it head-on. I found her by the side of the road and she was hurt badly, but peaceful. I held her, and as broken as she was, her eyes were still shining. I don't know how spiritual Annette was, but she looked up at an opening in the night sky just before she died, and pointed.

"'That's where God lives,' she said. Those were her last words. You know, I don't think she was seeing God like they say just before you die. I think she wanted me to know where God was. I'll never forget that."

All of this shot out; it was the first time I had spoken my sadsack story out loud, and the emotion of my losses and the Bradys' grief caught me. My lips quivered and my face contorted.

"I haven't known much happiness for a long time, and here I am with Annette dead in my arms, and as horrible and as awful as the whole thing has been, I felt at peace, almost joyful. But this can't be how to find joy."

I buried my face in my hands and shook until my shoulders heaved. My speech released the Bradys' thin veneer of serene mourning into a genuine Irish wake. Annette's friends and family began weeping as they reached out to touch and console each other. I joined in, mourning for more than Annette. Mrs. Brady sat up and held Kate and me together. Her face shone through her tears. It was as if I could read her thoughts. *One was lost, one was found, but something is still not complete. That's all right. All in due time. All in due time.*

Chapter 5

September 2003

I watched the red-and-blue I-75 road sign shimmy in traffic wind. I thought back to how this highway had carried me to the Bradys. It made me wince and yield a wry smile. I did a lot of growing up in Knoxville in 1973. It's an understatement to say my life on the road helped develop character, even though I wasn't receptive to the lessons at the time.

After my life on the road ended, with just a hint of encouragement, or induced by three or more beers, I could unwind a poignant, funny, or sad road story with ease. As the years spun out, the stories became better with practice and embroidery. It dawned on me that a fair share of the stories worth retelling were actually about the experiences off the road. I had thumbed with a guy on I-90 in South Dakota one summer with a good take on it. He was from upstate New York, Cohoes, taking a year off school to travel and raise some hell.

He told me, "You know, dude, hitchhiking brings life right to your front door. What I mean is that we're kinda like magnets out here. Much of the time we're up here on this strip of cement or asphalt trying to get to the next place. But I've been picked up all over the country and taken off the highway into people's lives. Some are pretty scary, some are sad, and some are very weird. Most times, it's just dudes or dudettes our age saying, 'Hey, let's hang out and have some fun.' As a result, I know a whole lot about south-erners, backpackers, hunters, demolition derby drivers. You name it, and I'll bet I've met 'em. They've taken me to their favorite fishing holes, bowling alleys—hell, even their churches. Add that to the stories we hear about while we're in the car, man, and we have a bird's-eye view of Americana. That's what the road is all about, man. It's about the people and their stories, not ours."

* * *

As it turned out, our hitchhiker, Tom Lutac, had a pretty good story to tell. He told us he was a student at Michigan Tech, in the Upper Peninsula. He was recovering from a bad freshman year in which he majored more in pot-smoking and beer-drinking than in business administration. Tom reported that at the end of the year, he had succumbed to a lovely coed's imploration to take a hit of windowpane acid. He visited God many times that night, and when he came down from the trip thirty-six hours later, he could finally talk. A week-long, LSD-psychosis-tinged hangover led Tom to the college chaplain, who escorted him back to God, this time without the hallucinogenic, and he was born again. He told the story well enough that I wasn't quite sure whether he was a true believer or a very good bullshitter.

I half-bought that the transmission on his car had blown and it was going to take two weeks for repairs. He needed to be back at school the next day, and he couldn't afford a bus. He had hitch-hiked once before when his car broke down, and now, with his strengthened Christian faith, he felt safe under the Lord's care.

The weak point in his story was his backpack, which looked well used and scuffed heavily on the bottom, a sign of a lot of time on cement, not the ground of the great outdoors. His face wore a weariness that belied his story of a plain-vanilla upbringing in the working class Detroit suburb of Hazel Park. No, it was more than that. As I looked back at him, I saw that I've-been-to hell-and-back-look that assorted lowlifes carry guardedly.

My daughter had fallen asleep, completely uninterested in Tom's road to redemption, and my wife was wrapped up in finishing her book. He started to pepper me with questions about the priesthood, another sign of a resourceful traveler or con man: be prepared with your own story, but keep the focus on the listener. It prevented making mistakes in your own story, and you might learn something useful.

We were past Roscommon and approaching Grayling. I was running out of steam on my priesthood ruse. I had explained my vocation decision: God spoke to me during a high school debating meet. I had answered Tom's questions. Did masturbation violate the celibacy vow? No. What does it feel like to actually turn wine and bread into God's blood and body? It is the moment of truth for every priest. If you aren't transfigured by this ritual every time, the priesthood is not for you.

Tom asked, "Father O'Roarke, what do priests do for a good time?"

I sang loudly, "Celibate! Celibate! Dance to the music!"

My singing woke Roberta. My wife closed her book smartly, glared over her reading glasses sharply and said, "Bathroom stop, among other things, dear," with a downbeat emphasis on "dear" that told me I had gone too far again.

Roberta woke up and chimed in, "Yeah, Father, we need a break and a confession," with dripping sarcasm on the "Father."

"If you insist, ladies. Grayling is thirty miles up the road. We can get some lunch and maybe some fishing supplies. That work for you, Tom?"

"Yes, sir, Father O'Roarke. I love to fish. Maybe we can swap a few fish stories."

"I thought that's what we were doing," I answered as I accelerated to pass a slow-moving truck and get us up the road a little faster toward the liberation of a good old-fashioned confession.

Chapter 6

April 1973

I remained in Knoxville for a week, attending the wake, funeral, and an assortment of other grief-related rituals. While I was a stranger, my witnessing of Annette's final moments and the wildly strange Royal Oak coincidence meant I was treated with care, but from a distance. No one quite knew what to make of me.

Every morning I woke up in Knoxville, I felt numb. Granted, part of the anesthetic was due to official imbibing at the wake, combined with unofficial post-wake nightcaps, with an emphasis on the plural. I wasn't alone. Kate was numb. All of the Bradys were numb. We went through the motions and emotions of sorrow together, the same pit in our guts, the same stomach tightness, dry throat, and fog that had lasted the week following my mom's funeral.

For several days, I hung out with Matt and Mike Brady in their rented house near UT, a hangout for southern hippies and frat and sorority types, all interested in smoking the currently popular blond, mind-piercing Moroccan hashish that was sold in rock-hard, aromatic chunks the size of dice for ten bucks a gram. Pot, hash, and drinking had helped blur the lines between rednecks, college kids, and long-hairs in the seventies South. I couldn't keep up with the heartier drinking and general party constitution of the Brady boys. I sweated out my hangovers playing pickup basketball in the hardscrabble Cal Johnson Rec Center.

I spent more time with Kate and her roommate Adell. It was healthier, and I had the distinct impression that I might get laid. I was in mourning and shock, but my twenty-year-old libido was still in perpetual hormonal overdrive.

In any case, I didn't have illusions that I would land up in cozy coitus with Kate. It would have been too twisted, not to mention the fact that I didn't think I was in her league. Adell was another matter. She welcomed me into her bed like a favorite cat. Although any purring on my part turned quickly into primal growls.

I didn't get invited into many beds, even in that bridge era between free love and disco drug mania. I didn't have the single-minded confidence my sex-successful best friends in Detroit possessed, that ability to woo and sway a woman into a wild night. They managed to engage in sex as sport. Sex, for me, was looking to sink that desperation shot as the buzzer sounded, only to watch the ball clank off the rim. All this was aggravated by a physical condition I tried to force out of my thoughts on a daily basis.

On the first night at Adell's apartment, we drank a bottle of Boone's Farm apple wine, but Kate went to bed after her first glass. As Adell and I finished the first bottle of wine, she told me, "Luke, you're a cute thing that's been through a lot. While don't you curl up with me tonight? We can chill and have some fun!"

"That—that would be great, Adell." I lamely looked for some interesting line to follow up on what sounded like an offer for a carnal romp. Nothing clever came to mind, mostly because my brain was paralyzed by a combination of dread and horniness. I gulped back the cheap wine, knowing that the chance to get laid by Adell was going to overcome the discomfort I would feel over her discovery of my ugly secret.

After a few more gulps of wine, Adell stood up. She first leered and then switched gears; smiling demurely, she reached out for my hands, pulled me up off the sofa, and led me into her bedroom. Halfway between the door and her unmade bed, she spun me around and began to undress me. As she unbuttoned my shirt, my heartbeats reached drum solo rapidity. My thoughts raced to catch my heart. I was losing control. It was my typical reaction to intimacy. I was frightened.

She felt it and said, "Calm down. Luke, I'll be gentle with you."

Hell, I didn't want her to be gentle. I just wanted what she was about to see to go away. There was no way to avoid this moment,

I knew. And since I was hornier than a two-peckered billy goat, I tried to ease her into it. As she reached my third button on my shirt, I held her hand away.

"Adell, before you go any further, you should know something about me. I have some nasty scars, burns on my chest and back. A few on my thighs. It's not pretty, Adell, and some girls get grossed out. I thought I'd spare you the surprise."

She listened and continued to unbutton my shirt. She saw the scarring; the mottled color of skin grafts that had successfully re-encased my organs. Furthering the mess were hairy patches on my chest and back, the burns having destroyed some hair follicles and encouraged others. I was resigned to the ugliness, but grateful it hid under my shirt, only raising embarrassment at intimate times. I knew that compared to my brother, Donnie, I was lucky. Adell drew in her breath as she saw my chest.

"There's another part to my story I don't tell many people."

She listened quietly as I laid out the night my life turned to ashes and smoke.

"On the night my dad set the fire, it wasn't a fireman who went into the burning house to drag out my brother, Donnie. It was me. My big sister April was holding him as we watched the fire burn. He pulled away from April and ran toward the burning box of fire our house had become. I watched him head for the front door, and I knew he was going after Mom, even though the firemen were already in the house. I ran after him. It wasn't courage that made me chase him. I was pissed off at him. I caught Donnie halfway up the burning stairway that led to the second floor and our parents' bedroom. As I grabbed him we slid down the stairs, and the second floor began to collapse on us. I managed to pull Donnie out the door, but we were both on fire by the time we fell out of the house. Our sisters put the fire out with their robes, but the polyester pajamas on Donnie melted into his skin as the flames disappeared. We rolled and screamed, our sisters crying and screaming. The firemen started spraying something on us and through my shock and the chaos, I saw my dad's blank face. That's when I knew he had set the fire. We were rushed by ambulance to the University of Michigan Burn Center. They stabilized us, but my little brother was in rough shape. He had burns all over his little body. My burns were limited, compared to him. It was a goddamn nightmare. I would rather forget everything about that night, but these burns are a reminder every morning and every night."

Adell's eyes were wide as she listened with her hand on her chin. She shook her head and then did something unusual. She didn't tell me how my body was appalling or make an excuse to leave or look at me pitifully, which were reactions I had previously encountered. I'd say the expression on her face was curious.

"Can I touch your scars?"

"Sure. They feel like leather," I said.

"Well, sweetie, let's just hope the rest of you is as tough, 'cause I have plans for a long night of fun," Adell laughed and pulled me close, her arms around my neck.

"Your heart is pounding like a tom-tom. You just calm down a little bit. We're going to make love long and slow tonight."

"I'm just a bit nervous. It's been awhile, and to be honest, I'm just not that comfortable with my shirt off in front of a beautiful woman like you," I told her.

"Well, sugar, you keep sweet-talking me, and we're going to get along fine. We do need to go over a few ground rules."

Adell's voice was suddenly all business. "I may like my sex, but I don't have any intention of getting pregnant or some nasty disease. I take birth control pills, so I'm taking responsibility for that. And you will take the responsibility for wearing this."

She reached over to her dresser for a box of conveniently placed Trojans, which she handed to me.

"Hopefully, those will be enough for tonight, honey. Just tell me honestly that you don't have crabs, scabies, or any VD or some wicked thing I can catch. Then we can move on to the fun."

"I'm clean, Adell. Unfortunately and fortunately, it appears, I haven't slept around as much as I would have liked to. And I have to admit that I haven't ever had a conversation like this."

"Luke, I saw too many girls who showed up at college the sweetest, nicest girls you could know and after getting drunk, they land up in bed with some senior who gives them a gift like herpes that lasts a lifetime. You ever see a herpes blister, Luke? I have. One of those young girls showed me her sores with tears in her eyes, asking me, 'What am I going to tell my boyfriend back home?' What a way to grow up too fast, too much, and too soon, huh?"

I must have looked a little pale and not too sexy after listening to this rather disquieting version of the most sought-after thing in my life.

"Oh, look at you Luke, I do believe the moment has been spoiled. I can fix that. Now listen up, I have an idea that will be fun for both us," Adell said.

She took me by the hand and led me to her dresser. Reaching into the top drawer she pulled out two orange bandanas and handed one to me.

"Roll that up, just like this," she explained as she folded her bandana into a headband shape.

"They're blindfolds. We'll both put them on and see where our blind selves take us. You game?"

I laughed, "I'm game." I put the bandana over my eyes and tied it on the back of my head.

Adell pulled me close again and whispered into my ear, "I'm going to undress you now, real slow. Then I want you to undress me, real slow. I don't like the get drunk, get naked, and get screwed college sex, Luke. It's a lot more fun if we take our time. Now, after you get my clothes off, maybe we can find our way back to the bed. Or maybe not," Adell laughed and I laughed with her, my heart still hammering out a frenetic beat.

With both of us in darkness, I relaxed while she taught me how to enjoy making love. Standing naked and blind, I was confident for the first time with a woman. Adell guided my hands from her toes to her forehead and I learned to improvise and linger as I explored the curvatures and cambers that compose what men yearn for most in life. Adell taught me that taking the time to learn the artistry of woman's body was what turned sex into giving instead of just taking. My hands grew stronger and more assured as I found what made Adell purr with alacrity. My God, it was exhilarating!

After that night, no matter what I did during the day or evening, I found my way to Adell's bedroom during my first week in Knoxville. Without bandanas, I continued to discover her creative lovemaking streak that didn't include the bed. I had my first out-of-body sexual experience as she demonstrated the art of deep tissue sexual massage. I mean really deep tissue, in places I wasn't sure tissue existed. I thought she might have to scrape me off the ceiling after that somewhat unsettling rendezvous.

Abruptly, Adell called it off after a week.

"Luke, you're great fun, but you're going to be gone sometime soon, and I have a social life beyond some sex-crazy boy from Michigan. I love ya, dear. But, I'm not in love with you and you're not in love with me. Let's end this on a high note, okay? Our couch is quite comfortable to sleep on."

I protested, but she was right. A direct hit on the situation. I really liked Adell, and the truth be told, I was tender in the, well, tissue.

How does a person become like Adell Malloy? How did this particular young woman, who was more interested in whether her shoes and purse matched than her grade point average, have a naturally blind eye to my striking disfigurement? I viewed her use of bandanas on our first night as brilliant, worthy of a first-rate therapist. She matched virtuosity in the bedroom with guileless perception. I learned a lot from Adell. You didn't have to be a genius to be wise.

Kate Brady was the counterweight to their college room-mate arrangement. The two had been friends since the first week Kate had moved to Knoxville and began the tortuous junior high school ordeal. Kate was an outsider, a Yankee, and her family had inherited wealth, but also a scandalous past from both sides of her family. Adell was a gangly adolescent with working-class parents. Their alliance began then and had endured.

After I was cast from Adell's bed, Kate and I shared our days and evenings. This coincided with a breakup of Kate's serious, long-standing relationship with her boyfriend. Within a week, we spent so much time together, just talking, we had become friends. I was her shoulder to cry on.

The end of Kate's relationship with a scion of the wealthy Tay-lor clan surprised her mother, who had thought Kate was the most predictable and stable Brady child. Her boyfriend was bright, well groomed, polite, jut-jawed, and rich. Kate considered him conventional and could easily envisage the programmed life that lay before her if she committed to the long haul. At nineteen, Kate wanted something different, without knowing what. Annette's death and my bizarre arrival had brought transformation to her doorstep. She was ready for adventure.

* ✱ *

The headaches retreated as I returned each night to the comfort of the Salvation Army overstuffed leather couch in Kate and Adell's apartment. There was a ready supply of Rolling Rock as I sat in my road jeans and T-shirt and listened to Kate's story about her life and family. The natives of Knoxville were keen to tell their family stories, so I obliged southern folklore intertwined with history of the city. Kate's family took this penchant to a new height. Like my family, the Bradys had been on a Wild Mouse roller-coaster ride that began before Kate was born.

"I knew the basic story of my mom and dad's family saga when we lived in Royal Oak. But Mom always gave us the *Reader's Digest* version. Once Annette started asking questions, Mom gave a lot of one- or two-word answers. It's not like she tried to hide anything from us. It was just too painful for her to talk about. Over time, we put most of the pieces together. And when my grandfather died and we moved to Knoxville, the whole sordid truth came out like a cold bucket of water splashed on us kids. It's quite a story, Luke, rivaling yours. Interested?"

"You bet. Let me be the judge of the family with the most lurid past," I said.

"Go grab a couple of cold ones from the fridge. This is not a short story."

Kate told the story like a historian, keeping her distance from her lineage.

Mrs. Helen Brady was a Prescott, of the Knoxville banking Prescotts, an ancestry that carried prominence, power, and distinctive idiosyncrasies. Helen Prescott was the only living heir of the family's significant wealth. Her father was Walter William Prescott II, who invested in Knoxville real estate and politicians while fiercely reigning over the First National Bank of Tennessee. He built a fortune rivaling any in the South, while controlling politicians, newspapers, and businessmen with ruthless tentacles.

The Prescotts were a part of Knoxville's heritage of stubborn, late eighteenth-century Scots-Irish settlers. While the town had developed into a conservative, religious bastion of the South, its early history of independence was far different. Originally known as Scuffletown, it was a frontier territory built on commerce, including all the timeless vices. Growing up, Helen Prescott was shielded from the family business interests, enjoying the perquisites of wealth while her considerably older brother, Walter William III, was groomed to inherit his father's power. Together, father and son ruled Knoxville while Helen, like a puzzle piece of background scenery, was genteelly bred for a marriage to a suitable and acceptable groom.

Helen found her own way, excelling in music with a marvelous talent for piano and a voice that quieted rooms when she sang. Her performances were usually reserved for church, and by the age of six, she soloed with the adult choir. By age sixteen, her voice covered six octaves, with a quality, clarity, and strength that moved the Presbyterian congregation closer to God than the pejorative words of the cranky minister.

As she grew through adolescence, Helen's voice gave her opportunities to sing in public concerts, her parents' pride outweighing their smothering nature. Her talent led her to New York City in 1949, at the age of eighteen, to attend Juilliard. There, she met Curtis Brady, a journeyman pianist who had barely made it into Juilliard and was hanging on in his junior year. He was a short, muscular young man; handsome in a ruddy, Irish sort of way. His father had made a fortune in Detroit, manufacturing the curtains that covered windows in touring cars in the twenties, before the advent of glass windows. He was a serial entrepreneur, always on the edge of making and losing a fortune.

Curtis was oblivious to his father's business interests, sharing his mother's affinity for society-building activities in the arts. Curtis knew in the first month at Juilliard that he did not have skill to become "the talent," as the obviously gifted were called. But he did embrace the art and music scene of New York City.

Meeting Helen Prescott gave him the chance to brush up against greatness, and when she began to fall in love with the *bon vivant* with a carpenter's tan, he did not discourage her. Curtis was ambivalent about love and marriage, but as he approached graduation at Juilliard, it became apparent to both that there was suitability to their relationship. Their parents were surprised when letters indicated the romance.

The Prescotts knew this was not a perfect match, preferring a Knoxville-bred mannequin with manners, but the Bradys' ability to buy their way into the Detroit society scene was just enough to ensure an acceptable social level where Helen could settle. A career in music was rife with potential misadventures. This was safer. Of course, they believed Helen and Curtis would settle in Knoxville. Helen Brady would be a blooming rose, not a garden out of control.

The wedding in Knoxville in April of 1951 turned out to be the social apex for both families. Newlyweds Curtis and Helen Brady didn't tell their parents until after their honeymoon in Havana that they weren't leaving New York City, and in fact had already rented an apartment in the city and accepted jobs: Curtis as the manager of an art gallery, and Helen as a music teacher and occasional performer in the city. Their families reacted angrily. Both sets of parents arrived in New York after phone calls and threatening letters did not provoke the expected reaction.

The harangue lasted for hours in the young couple's Upper West Side apartment. Helen and Curtis were obdurate, and eventually their parents left angry. Walter Prescott seethed with Scottish stubbornness and a thirst for revenge. He pulled his support immediately and cut off Helen's access to her trust account. She would have nothing until she and the wastrel husband succumbed. The Bradys angered quickly, but forgave faster.

The loss of current income was not entirely unexpected to the newlyweds, but the freezing of Helen's substantial trust account was a surprise. They downscaled to a basement apartment and life began anew for them. Within eighteen months, the first child arrived, though even that could not thaw the relations with Helen's family.

But the Prescotts' mean grip on Knoxville begun to unravel like a ball of kite string when a scandal they couldn't hush up overtook the family. Helen's brother, Walter William Prescott III, had been shot dead by his young mistress. The murderess was not only his mistress, but also the family's sixteen-year-old black maid. As it turned out, she was pregnant with Walter William III's child. Walter's concubine had told him about the pregnancy, standing in his mahogany-paneled study. He fired her summarily, putting a ten-dollar bill in her hand as he escorted her out the kitchen door while uttering not a word. Three hours later, she entered Walter William's house through the kitchen and marched to her lover's study, where she knew she would find him finishing his day. She rushed to the front of his massive desk, aimed, and fired an ancient pistol. One shot, an eyelash below the left eyebrow, was all it took. His head pitched back just a bit, and then he lurched forward, meeting the desk with a thud.

William Prescott III was declared dead on arrival at the hospital. A picture appearing in the newspaper the next day showed his father, an ashen Walter William II, leaving the hospital. A mistress was acceptable to Knoxville society, but the pregnancy of the teenage black maid and the shooting was rich scandal fodder. The Prescott men were hardly loved, liked, or admired. They had been feared. The squalid affair created a fissure in the Prescotts' power. It proved to be an unraveling thread.

The scandal went beyond Walter's death. The maid was tried as an adult and sent to prison for second-degree murder. The maid's child, the blood heir of the Prescotts, became a ward of the state after the baby boy was legally excluded and exiled by Helen's father. The Prescotts would never recognize an illegitimate mulatto borne by a maid, and the child would never see a nickel of their money.

A murmur of public discontent bubbled up, beginning with letters to the editor in the competing papers calling on the Prescotts to accept some responsibility for the child and arguing the girl should be in juvenile custody. After a lifetime of controlling his world, Helen's father, Walter II, watched the levers of power rust shut. With the death of the heir to his fortune and power, he bitterly withdrew, rarely leaving the Sequoyah Hills mansion. The businesses, including the paper and bank, were sold. The fortune remained large and protected, but as his influence dissipated, Walter Senior's mood blackened and his frustration fed his anger over Helen's rebellion. Even his own daughter had betrayed him. He would not listen to his wife's pleas to reconcile with Helen, refusing to even mention her name.

I interrupted Kate's story. "Man, Arthur Hailey could write a novel from this story, Kate. My God, there's money, murder, sex, prison, family secrets—there's even a bastard! And your grandfather is right out of central casting for bad guys. He is lower than a gnat's navel. This story is completely freaked out. Things get better from here, right? Your family does land up rich, living in a mansion, after all."

"Get a hold of yourself, Luke. Remember this is my family, and I'm not exactly thrilled or proud I'm related to Walter Prescott II, you know. Listen up. It doesn't get better until it gets worse."

"Sorry, Kate. Keep going. I'll be a good listener for a change."

* * *

Curtis and Helen both knew they couldn't afford to live in New York with a growing family. When Doris Brady called in 1960, asking Curtis to consider to a job offer from his father, Helen told her husband to listen. She was mildly surprised that she was considering moving to Detroit. Curtis was adamant about staying in New York, almost panicked at the thought of moving to Detroit. But they couldn't make the budget work. Eventually the decision was made with the agreement that Curtis would remain behind in New York for three months to settle the part-ownership of the art gallery.

One month later, Helen found herself in a small, but comfortable, three-bedroom bungalow in the Detroit suburb of Royal Oak, Michigan, with a real yard and neighborhood. She was soon organizing bake sales and assembling a choir at nearby St. Mary's Catholic School, where she had enrolled her oldest children Three months turned into six, and finally, Curtis found his way to the bungalow just weeks before Helen was due with Matthew. His return to Detroit was difficult, then tragic.

Curtis's father, Morgan Brady, had invested heavily in a real estate venture and brought his son in as a partner. Less than a year after Helen and Curtis arrived in Royal Oak, Morgan Brady died of a heart attack, leaving Curtis in charge of a business that needed cash to service the real estate debts. The whole operation was ready to tip over, and Morgan Brady's death brought out the worst in the bankers who foreclosed. A life insurance policy was all that was left to pay off the debts and keep Doris Brady in her home with a small annuity to keep her financially afloat. Curtis found work playing in a piano bar. He explored the potential of opening an art gallery, but Detroit's entire 1960s art culture would fit into a few square blocks of New York City's Soho.

While the children were thriving in suburbia, Curtis's and Helen's relationship was numbed by the routine of it all. Money had always been tight in New York, but there were endless diversions.

Here there was no escape for Curtis. He was suffocating because his well-kept lifestyle secret could not be hidden in Detroit.

While Curtis Brady loved Helen and loved his partnership with her, he cheated on his wife regularly in New York, almost exclusively with men. He had been extremely discreet in New York, and the liaisons were planned, intense, and then terminated. He was adamant about secrecy, and as a result, he qualified his lovers' suitability based on their stability. He and Helen had enjoyed their love life, but it was never the fulcrum of their relationship, rather existing on the same level as their love of music or the children. Being discreet with the cosmopolitan homosexual denizens of New York was far more plausible than in Detroit, where, for the most part, the homosexuals successfully hid their sexual predilections. Finding and assessing lovers was extremely difficult, and finally, a badly concluded relationship with a young Methodist deacon was his undoing. The deacon called the house one night and walked Helen through the litany of the relationship. While Helen was stunned, she composed herself—a Prescott trait—and walked her husband to a local park, out of earshot of their kids, where they sat on swings, talking it out. For Curtis, it was the end of a long slide. He couldn't reconcile his innate, now uncovered homosexuality with the rest of life in Royal Oak. In spite of Helen's pleadings, he left their home the next day, returning to New York. He sent a check every month in varying amounts, but other than the money, he left family life behind.

Helen was crushed and despondent, her prospects for a full family life shattered. With limited funds, she had no choice but to contact her parents, but in spite of her mother's protestations, her father, Walter William, would not be moved. She was on her own. With a near-penniless Doris Brady as her only ally, she found work in a secretarial pool and as a music teacher at St. Mary's. Doris babysat and Helen worked. After the workday, she would put the children to bed and then go out and sing in Detroit jazz clubs, find four or five hours of sleep a night, and start over again.

She had also earned her real estate license and was soon her agency's top selling agent. Bit by bit, she worked her way out of a financial and emotional hole. The children thrived in Catholic schools. She had carved out a place for herself. Doris Brady had become her best friend, and the irony was not lost on Helen. Doris provided Helen with stability, a loyal friend who gave with no expectations other than her role of grandma. Doris Brady's unselfishness touched and changed Helen, and with Doris's encouragement, she began singing in church again. She also found that Annette had inherited her talent. Together, they filled St. Mary's Church with harmonies that talked to God. While Helen gained faith, she also watched with motherly pride as Annette's skill grew. But beyond the skill, Helen felt a light surround Annette when her daughter raised her eyes to the top of the church in song. She ascribed it to motherly pride until other church members told her they saw the light changing in St. Mary's choir loft whenever they sang. Helen never dated, never considered another man in her life. It just wouldn't work. But she was happy with friendship, security, family, and a newly found view of God.

A phone call from her mother in December of 1967 changed everything again. Walter William II had died the night before of a stroke, and Helen's mother was extremely ill. She flew to Knoxville to find her mother in the advanced stages of pancreatic cancer. Martha Prescott was in agony, but for the first time since she married Walter Prescott, she was free. Helen learned her mother had set a meeting with the family lawyer to change the Prescott will that had excluded Helen and had instead designated most of the money to the City of Knoxville for a Walter Prescott Park. Martha Prescott had loathed her husband and his hate-filled, vengeful life. Now, at the end of her life, she cried to her daughter for forgiveness and made things right. Within a week, Helen buried her mother and was heiress to a fortune and the family home on the Tennessee River.

The decision to move to Knoxville was difficult, but aided by Doris Brady, who simply said, "Let's go." Together with the mother of her homosexual, estranged husband, she packed up the family's meager possessions and moved. As a family, they made an odd combination, and it was easier not to mention Wayne Brady, the missing husband, father and son. Doris was a naturally nurturing grandmother, and her grandchildren and daughter-in-law adored her. The children finished the school year, and in June 1968, moved to a life filled with the privileges of wealth.

Helen Brady made one thing clear; the gift of wealth came with responsibility. The Prescott fortune was an interlocking set of assets and had to be actively managed. Helen was astute and conservative about managing the money, very quietly putting it to good use in the community. Annette worked in a youth center that Helen had anonymously funded. The staff talked of the "miracles" she worked with the desperately poor youth. She had a reputation for fearlessness and kindness. She simply didn't worry about the poverty and crime in the area surrounding the center. She fiercely protected her protégés, once shouting down a craving junkie with a knife who tried to hold up the center for its petty cash box. The gangs gave her respect and leeway because she taught their younger brothers and sisters, and even their kids, how to sing.

Kate grew up in Annette's loving shadow and didn't mind at all. She knew Annette was special, and it allowed her to be the bookish, introspective person she wanted to be in adolescence, avoiding the glare of any light at all. She read voraciously: literature, romance novels, William James, *Reader's Digest.* She quietly excelled in school and tested very well at St. Bartholomew's Academy in Knoxville, where all the Brady children attended. She started to bloom just as high school ended: not ready to move souls and take on the world like Annette, but easily making and keeping friends. The Brady boys were handsome and athletic, and took to partying at a young age, worrying their mother. The family wealth eased the transition to Knoxville, and the family took to their southern, Knoxville roots quickly.

In 1971, Doris Brady died suddenly, passing away in her bed on a crisp fall night. It was a great loss for the family and caused the re-emergence of Curtis Brady, who attended the funeral in Royal Oak. The children were by then all aware of their father's predilection for men. The funeral reunion was discomfiting. Everyone involved was filled with a bitter mixture of remorse and confusion over the loss of a treasured mother, mother-in-law, and grandmother, and the emergence of a shamed father and husband. Annette played ambassador, choosing measured forgiveness of her father. As a result, an uneasy connection was made by the rest of the family and Curtis Brady at the wake. He only stayed a short time, but Kate remembered hugging her father for the first time in years as he left.

Kate's history lesson ended with the family's return to Knoxville after the funeral and how the cycle of the Prescotts' wealth touched her family. The Bradys had thrived in Knoxville. Helen Brady felt she had achieved a sense of stability and predictability for her family. Annette's death shattered the tranquility.

"Now you know the real story of the Knoxville Brady Bunch. At least the facts. What the heck happens now for Mom and my brothers is anybody's guess."

"And for you, Kate," I said.

"Yeah, that's for sure. Mom tells us not to be ashamed of our family tree, but her eyelids start twitching whenever the subject of Dad comes up. She says, 'We are who we are, and every family has a few secrets stuffed in the closet. In the case of our family, I prefer to think of our family story as being rich, colorful, out of the closet, and front and center.'"

"Well, I gotta hand it to you, Kate, the only family story as weird as yours, is mine. It's probably why we get along so well."

I raised my bottle of Rolling Rock. "Here's to rich and colorful families!"

"To rich and colorful!" Kate agreed. We clanked our bottles together.

"And our past is not our future," Kate added.

"Agreed," I said.

The story meant more to me than Kate could know. Puzzle pieces that had hovered above my promise to Annette now fell into place. The picture wasn't complete, but I had an unfamiliar faith that the rest of the image would emerge.

My time in Knoxville was bittersweet. I made true friendships forged under trying and poignant circumstances. But the truth be told, after two weeks, I was restless again. Both Kate and Adell made it clear I was welcome to stay as long as I liked. The Brady brothers also offered to let me stay in their unused apartment bedroom rent-free until I found work. There was the rub: I needed to get a job and start carrying my weight, or my role as mystical, welcome guest would turn quickly into that of a raffish leech. It was time to move on.

Finally, one evening, while eating pizza with Kate and Adell, I again brought up that my original plan before the accident was to hitchhike to Miami to visit my friends, the Delgado brothers, who had moved from Royal Oak during high school. The shock of the detour to Knoxville had made me think of home and my family. Returning to Michigan seemed to be the right direction. Kate's reaction surprised me.

"Luke, I'd like to come with you. I can still drop my spring classes, and I need to see life from a different place for a while."

I replied, "You're kidding, right? Leave college, your apartment, everything paid for, and leave your well-dressed and rich boyfriend, Biff, to come with me? Yeah, your mom would be loving that decision."

"His name is Cliff, smart-ass, and he is an ex-boyfriend. I need a change, Luke. I've thought a lot about leaving Knoxville. Annette told me moving to Atlanta for a year was the best decision she ever made. I know my mother will think I'm overreacting to Annette's death. The truth is, I miss Annette every day. I'm not sure how I'm ever going to get over knowing she'll never be there to answer the phone when I call. And that might be part of the reason I need to leave. I don't want to get smothered by my mom. On top of it all, I'm just plain tired of my life. I'm twenty years old and all I've ever done is moved from one square to the next. I'm ready to try something different. You have to admit Luke, leaving with you would be something different," Kate argued.

"Different ain't necessarily smart, Kate, and I oughta know," I replied.

"Don't go getting religion on me, Mr. Throw-Caution-to-the-Wind."

"Hey, Kate, I just know that you don't want my life."

"That's true, Luke. I want my own life and maybe just a little taste of yours."

We finished our pizza and played three-handed euchre with Adell, who was unusually quiet. Kate was animated, talking about how she needed some real change in her life, and a return to her Michigan roots seemed like a good fit. I didn't agree, but Kate's company on the trip back was a plus to me. I wasn't going to encourage her, but if she made up her mind to leave, I wouldn't say no. But there was no way I was going to get between Helen Brady and her daughter. Kate was on her own with her mom.

That night, Adell curled up next to me on the sofa and told me, "I really want to leave, too, you know, but I can't just pack up and go, like a rich kid can."

"I'm not rich, Adell," I said.

"I know, you're dirt poor and Kate's rich. You have nothing to lose and she can lose plenty and still be rich. Either way, both of you can pick up and leave without much to lose. It's the only thing that's the same about the filthy rich and the rotten poor. But us folks in the middle have to stick around and live our lives out." Adell replied.

"You could join us great unwashed, rotten poor," I said.

"What, and leave my wardrobe and shoes behind? You're out of your mind, Luke Moore!" We laughed, knowing our current places in the world. As the night ended, I asked Adell if she would go out on a proper date with me before I left. Maybe a dollar movie and a hamburger and malt afterwards. I wanted to thank her for what she had done for me. She was a generous gal.

As my restlessness to leave Knoxville grew into the seeds of plan, Kate was making her own decision. When I told her I was leaving in the next day or two and definitely returning to Royal Oak, she grabbed me by both hands and told me emphatically, "I'm going with you, Luke, no two ways about it."

We talked it through. I had no objection to traveling with this beautiful friend; a hint, a hope that something more than friendship might develop was not very far back in my mind. Kate had not been back to Royal Oak since moving to Knoxville, and while seeking an adventure, we would not be charting the jungles of Borneo. As expected, her decision to leave Knoxville and her studies at UT became a grand battle with her mother.

"Kate, there's no way on God's green earth that your mother is going to let you leave, let alone hitchhike."

"Remember this, Luke: I'm a Brady, too. I'll make it work, you wait and see."

That afternoon, I listened to the struggle between mother and daughter from the safety of the Bradys' spacious kitchen, sipping sweet tea.

"Kate, don't throw away your life because of this tragedy. I need you, Kate. You're my only daughter now!"

"Mom, please don't lay that responsibility on me. I'm not happy. I wasn't that happy before Annette died, and now I'm just sick and tired of being here. I don't want to be your only daughter. That's way too much attention and pressure for me. You and I both know Annette would play that role better than me."

Helen Brady's face was lined from lack of sleep over the past weeks and the creases deepened as she listened to her daughter. Kate's comment hurt because Helen was closer to Annette than any of her children. She knew Kate was making a rash and immature decision, but she was exhausted and emotionally spent. She just couldn't fight with her youngest daughter. And she remembered the battles with her parents. If she managed to keep her in Knoxville now, she would eventually lose Kate anyway. In a move wholly inconsistent with her life since moving to Knoxville, Helen Brady capitulated and gave a vexed blessing, with conditions.

"Kate, I give up. I can see I'm not going to change your mind, but you're still my daughter. Let's come to an agreement on this."

She laid out her stipulations: Kate must take a bus with me, absolutely no hitchhiking. Kate must check in with a designated friend of Helen's from St. Mary's upon arrival and stay with her until suitable living arrangements could be found. And finally, Kate had to promise to come back to UT and finish her education the following fall term. Kate agreed readily, knowing that once released from her mother's cloak, she would make her own decisions. Her first lie was in failing to purchase a bus ticket. She would hitchhike with me, Kate had decided, and she told, rather than asked, me. She was her mother's daughter. We didn't imagine that an innocent hitchhike down the road would imperceptibly nudge the course of our young lives in a direction we would have never predicted. Sometimes it is the little decisions that make all the difference.

Chapter 7

September 2003

The miles clipped by as we approached Grayling. I looked ahead and squinted, but I already knew the two figures posed next to a rapidly upcoming road sign were hitchhikers. It surprised me because we were miles between exits. As I took my foot off the accelerator, my passengers looked up in unison and saw the young man and woman. As we passed them, I saw the only baggage they had was a gas can, and I remembered recently having spotted a yellow Pinto on the side of the road.

"Dad!" and "Luke, dear," were simultaneously spoken by my wife and daughter.

"I know we don't have room, but they ran out of gas. The next exit is a mile and half north. We can fit them in for that short haul, can't we?"

Our new passengers hustled up to our door, out of breath, as Roberta grumbled her assent after a look from her mom. They scrunched into the van as we quickly gave our introductions and summarized histories, knowing we were only going to have a three-minute relationship. We dropped the pair off at the Shell gas station at the next exit, and our excursion resumed as if our fleeting, good-neighbor encounter had never happened.

However, the girl stirred a memory for me. It was her hair, close to the same color and length of Kate Brady's when we set out on our trip from Knoxville twenty-odd years ago. Funny, I could remember that detail after all these years. I pictured her in the corny hat and cringed. We had to be out our minds to simply hitchhike to Royal Oak so soon after Annette's death. Surely if Mrs. Brady hadn't been disabled with grief, it never would have happened. What a nimrod I'd been for not even giving a casual thought that fleeing Knoxville with Kate was not in the charted waters of acceptable social behavior. I was way out there. Yet that outing began decades of friendship with Kate Brady.

I glanced in the rearview mirror for another glimpse of my daughter. My God, she's all grown up now and within spitting distance of the age when Kate and I were when we left Knoxville. What adventures lay in front of her? Had I done my job as dad well? Had I overdone it and left her unprepared to deal with the mean-spirited pricks out there in the world? Was she ready to deal with the darker face of life, the evil that slithered out of human beings when you least expected it? Did she inherit my scary view of the world? There was more than enough to agonize about with a child. The truth was that I was more worried about letting her down than I was about her upsetting my life. She was a marvel of my life, growing up in a relatively straight line of typical behavior and superlative accomplishments. She was so normal it was extraordinary; it brought tears to my eyes.

Parenthood was the continuation of a grand adventure. I hadn't observed the shared qualities of parenting and hitchhiking before. Were there similarities? With the highway, you can look back to where you've come from, but it doesn't reveal much about what lies further down the road. Same with parenting. Both are exhilarating, frightening and humbling. And with both, I wondered if I knew what the hell was I doing.

That's where it ended. I didn't face the adventure of parenthood alone. I watched as my wife enjoyed her perfect sleep, her relaxed face tilted easily toward me, her body vibrating almost imperceptibly with the motion of the van. My easy sleep disappeared the day Roberta was born. Not my wife, who could log into a deep REM slumber within seconds of offering the final kiss of the night. Her last words every night were, "Never waste a kiss. I love you, Luke," reminding me not to proffer a half-hearted kiss at the end our day, but to buss with the stirring emotion of our youth.

Without her as my counselor, I would have zigged when I should have zagged with Roberta. I would have flinched when a backbone was necessary and barked when a purr was appropriate. In spite of my education and training, I would have been hopeless as a parent without her. Parenting was akin to operating on a precipice, yet with a partner, it was not nearly as frightening as the emptiness of a night on the Dakota plains, solitary except for the companionship of my discomfort. The upshot was that in spite of my genetic quirks, I became a good dad and husband because of my daughter and wife. Maybe not a straight line of logic to get there, but this met the best of my expectations for a well-lived life. My soul still carried pockets of black sadness and rage, but on the whole, I was a content man. Considering the path, and reflecting on how it played out, it was a miracle of sorts.

Chapter 8

April 1973

K ate and I stood at the bottom of exit 134, just outside Caryville, Tennessee, thumbs out. Adell had given us a good head start north, driving us the fifty or so miles up I-75. I said my good-byes to my new friends in Knoxville in one evening, short and sweet. After two years of hitchhiking, I'd been to a lot of places and met a lot of people I knew I would never see again. I had a different feeling about Knoxville, but I didn't want to get all syrupy about leaving. I steered clear of Kate's good-byes to other people , knowing that her leaving was going to be one emotional gusher after another. I was also a convenient person to blame for Kate's departure. The last person I wanted to see was Mrs. Brady, whose sharp eyes would have shot a hole right through my subterfuge. Nope, I steered wide and clear and insisted that we leave early in the morning.

The roadside good-bye with Adell was brief, but not sweet. She knew, as I did, that I was leaving neither as a fledgling boyfriend, nor as a short-term fling. I respected her and told her so. She was angry that Kate was leaving, and mixed up about my role. Standing on the side of the road next to her car, Adell hugged me tightly. Normally, the slightest scent of this kind of poignant intimacy would have given me the screaming meemies. With Adell, I took it in stride and gave myself a little credit for not breaking off until she let go of me and grabbed hold of Kate. Now the emotional thunderstorm began: two dear friends at the ripe old age of twenty were saying good-bye to each other. They both knew it was the end of being young together and were miserable about it. They didn't say much, just held each other as only women can. When they pulled apart, they grasped each other by the forearms and looked at each other, still crying, memorizing each other's faces.

"We'll always be friends, right, Kate?"

"Always, Adell."

Adell started for her car door, brushing her tears and running nose with her sleeve. "You take care of this girl, Luke, or you'll have all of the Brady family and half of Knoxville after your rear end."

"I'll do my best."

She turned the ignition key in the old Chevy II, which wheezed before starting. Through the open passenger window, she called out. "I'll miss you, both of you. God bless you." She put the car in reverse and illegally backed off the on-ramp, pausing at the top to wave before driving out of sight.

Kate stood behind me on the highway wearing a dopey rain hat on top of her ponytail. I had explained to her that not looking too good was important and had picked out the hat for her. This get-up was clearly not in her style wheelhouse. She was both elated and nervous at the outset of this trip, and I tried to keep her expectations low. Even though we weren't leaving for an exotic vacation and Michigan had been home before, she was taking a risk, and it was exhilarating.

I was careful to tell her the rules of the road without scaring her. This was my territory, the one place where I was the big dog. My direction was simple: take my lead. I would size up the drivers and the car situation before getting in, and if I didn't like the feel of it, she should be prepared to get away from the car, fast. I told Kate to be patient; it might take a while to get from one place to another. I did not tell her that hitchhiking with a woman was a blessing and a curse. The rides definitely came faster, but the intentions of the drivers were often not pure. The driver could be a harmless dreamer who, after dropping off the female hitchhiker, would daydream what could have happened in his fantasy scenario. Or there was the danger of a more aggressive voyeur who was coarse and direct in his desires, not about to force his will, but ready to get verbally nasty. The worst scenario was encountering a straight-up twitchy pervert, in which case, the situation would end badly—it was only a matter of how bad.

We stuck our thumbs out and watched as the cars glided by. After a minute, I began my road patter, first under my breath and then louder: "Hey, whaddya say, need a ride here, what's your plan, Stan? Pull-over-right-here-right-now. Not a chance, Lance? Whaddya say, Ray? Just-a-little-ride-here-for-me-and-my-partner-she's-a-rookie-a-virgin-of-sorts-at-this-road-thing-and-we-don't-wanna-get-a-bad-at-ti-tude. Do we? Don't be a pain, Wayne, we're cool, O'Toole, just taking a hitchhike, Mike. Be a pal, Al. Don't be a killjoy, Roy. We just need a little ride action, how-about-now."

Kate watched me in my element.

"Hey, Luke, you sound like my mom when she sings scat, but you're not even close to a key known to the human ear."

I didn't let the mild insult interrupt my concentration. I prattled on for a few minutes until there was a lull in the traffic.

I turned to Kate, arms outstretched. "No luck yet, but it's a beautiful day in Tennessee."

"I'm fine, Luke, but don't ask me to sing your road song. You're going way too fast for me."

"Just passing the time, trying to reel them in," I noted.

We talked on and off while I kept my eye on the road, continuing our conversation while focusing on prospective rides. The road loosened people up, and with a little bit of gentle encouragement, the door could open on a rash of family and personal secrets probably best left for their priests, therapists, or bartenders to hear. Early on I found a concerned look, nodding of the head, and the use of words like, *hmmm, really, I hear ya brother,* and *whew,* could open a torrent of twisted stories. Or, you could make friends very fast by hearing unvarnished truth from a road-relaxed companion. Kate and I had already had a history of loose lips. Out here on the road, she revved up and gave me an earful.

"I didn't mind you sleeping with Adell," Kate told me. "She's a friend for life, but she can land up in bed with the wrong guy. I'm no saint, but Adell worries me. I think guys your age are always in heat, and it's not my job to satisfy your mindless need to jump the bones of every chick you meet."

"Gee, Kate, maybe you could be a little bit more direct about your opinion of men. Sex is not the only thing on our minds."

"Luke, look me in the eye and tell me that in the last five minutes you didn't think about having sex now, in the past, or hopefully sometime in the near future."

I paused for a second, remembering that, just a minute before, I had recollected a stolen stare at Kate leaving her apartment's bathroom wearing just a towel and, as she turned, the flawless lines of her derriere appeared and bounced in perfect biological rhythm down the hall to her bedroom. Now, that was a libido-raising experience. Damn, I wasn't going there.

"No, I don't think I have. Nope, not in the last five minutes. But, I think I get your point."

"You're lying, Luke, and you know it. And I'm sure you get my point. I don't fault you. You can't help yourself. Just don't be so stupid as to think women don't know what's going on, unless we're drinking shots of tequila, and then all bets are off and we act just like men."

This was a good time in the conversation to nod seriously and say, "Hmmm."

Kate segued into a description of Cliff Taylor, her ex-boyfriend.

"The man was just so damn unsurprising and dull. I swear he was born to be married to a Vanderbilt coed who is blond, perky, and full of gushing praise for her handsome husband. That's not me, Luke. Now, you—you're the exact opposite of Cliff. Who could have a clue what you were born to do with yourself? This much I do know, Luke Moore: you were not born to be a penniless wanderer living by your wits."

"Hey, according to the gospel of Kate Brady, I'm a sex-crazed vagrant hobo. Let's hear more about that dull ex-boyfriend of yours and what a cad he was, and leave me out of this."

"Luke, I like you a lot. It's clear that you're smart, funny, and different from any man I know. You're also screwed up, and yet I don't think you've given up trying to get on with your life. I trust you and I think you're strong from all that you've survived. I know I will be safe with you. I'm guessing we will be friends for a long time, even though we've only really just met." I heard the words *friend* and *I like you a lot,* when I was still more than half-hoping there might be more between us.

It took about half an hour before a yellow Z-28 Camaro pulled over fast, kicking stones and dirt up on the gravel shoulder.

"C'mon, Kate." I picked up my bag and handed Kate hers. We trotted up to the car. Looking inside, I saw a young, maybe eighteen-year-old, blue-collar worker, who had probably taken out a big loan to buy his brand-new muscle car. The longneck beer bottle between his legs and small cooler on the passenger seat didn't trouble me, and neither did his first words.

"Hey, I gotta a day off and girlfriend in Lexington, need a ride?"

"Thanks, thanks for stopping." We exchanged nods. He opened the door and held the seat back for Kate and our bags. Kate hopped in, I followed, and as the door slammed shut, I leaned over to shake the driver's hand, "Hey, I'm Mickey Martin and this is my fiancée, Rhonda."

"Pleased to meet you both," said the driver. We were off.

Our driver jabbered on about his girlfriend and his car, which had a name. He was talking so fast I was confused whether the car's name was Roxanne and his girlfriend's name was Rhoda, or "vicky-verky," as my old geometry teacher Sister Jean Romunda used to say. I put on my best I'm-really-interested-in-what-you-have-to-say-look and then daydreamed. I could see Kate peripherally in the backseat. The motion of the car and the wind lightly buffeting her hair seemed to mesmerize her. Her eyelids fluttered before settling peacefully, and her chin bobbed against her chest as she slipped into car sleep. She was lovely. I felt the slightest flicker of worry tickle my instincts, which worried me, because in spite of all my poor choices, my gut check for danger was uncanny. I was a lucky man to be traveling with her, but I sure as hell needed to keep her safe. I grinned as I realized I was worrying about someone other than myself.

Chapter 9

September, 2003

I glanced in the rearview mirror again, and saw my Roberta rocking into road sleep. Her chin was bouncing much the same as Kate Brady's had when she slept through our ride north to Royal Oak in 1973. Times were different then. The thought of hitchhiking as a means of transportation, or for the simple adventure of it all, would never cross my daughter's mind. Heck, I think I knew where Roberta was every moment of her life until she was sixteen. I was almost maniacal in making sure she wasn't going to put herself in harm's way. I was the parental equivalent of a reformed, self-righteous drinker, smoker, or—even worse—a newly puritanical ex-sinner. Yep, have all the fun, find religion, and then swear it all off, not only for yourself, but for the rest of the world.

That would be me with my daughter. No way would I let Roberta get into a situation where she could make a very bad decision that could hurt her forever. I had to balance this with my professional training that acknowledged children needed opportunities to make good and bad decisions and learn from them. More times than not, Luke Moore as an over-the-top dad won out over Dr. Luke Moore, child psychologist. And hell, I was working with kids that seemed to be born pushing the limits of authority, like myself. Structure was a good thing, right?

When I taught at Wayne State University, I had written a paper theorizing that every generation was more rebellious, creative, and risk-taking than the generation preceding them. When the defiant, risk-taking generation grew up, only a fraction kept their promise to give their kids the freedom their parents had resisted. Using my generation as an example, we crazies from the sixties and early seventies were scared silly that our kids would follow our example. We were now the watchful, controlling majority, and we knew from personal experience that it didn't make as much sense for our daughters and sons to take some unknown pink pill and wash it down with cheap wine just to see what happened. And we knew that quaaludes were not an appropriate aperitif for vodka and hashish. Our parents hadn't had a clue that peyote or Michoacán gold bud existed, and didn't have a context for understanding why we would want to ingest them in the first place. But we did.

I may not have known from personal experience what Ecstasy or the drug of choice in 2003 was like, but I had a frame of reference to understand why kids would take it. Even with my personal history and training, I still knew that I wasn't a match for controlling what my daughter would do. Innovative teenagers trump parental intervention every time. I am a savvy parent and took every possible step, observed all signs, and tracked down every lead to keep Roberta from harm at an early age, knowing it could be to no avail.

I also knew full well that all that teeth-gnashing oversight was officially over when I dropped my daughter off at Lake Superior State University. My troubled youth practice has taught me that kids get to bad places from all different directions. I found no consistent socioeconomic background that predicted how a kid transformed from recreational bad actor to a big-trouble addict, whether the trouble come in the form of booze, drugs ,or any of the high-risk behaviors. Where environment did make a difference, a big difference, was in increasing the odds that a miscreant could recover. Kids without a support system were far more likely to relapse into bad behavior. And even with all the support and good intentions in the world, there are some of us who can't win the battle against bad decisions. It's like a buried, genetic time bomb.

My paper was not well received by my colleagues, who saw in it more experiential opinion than scholarly research. They were right. I had a lot more fun with a short article I wrote for *Psychology*

Today, the only highlight of my intended career as a pop psychologist. The title of the article was "Rock-and-Roll Pharmacy," which proposed that today's drug company executives were the same guys selling lids of pot in college dorms: enterprising entrepreneurs still making a buck making people feel better. I asserted that the big pharmaceutical companies' introduction of New Age products to make people my age feel and perform better were the direct results of our rock-and-roll heritage.

Viagra and Prozac are the best examples. I'd give odds that the same guy who peddling "Spanish fly" powder in the 1960s as a sure-fire way to turn a churchgoing Catholic girl into a nymphomaniac, became a middle-aged drug company marketing executive. I can see him daydreaming in a business meeting when, bingo, it hits him! As a kid, his problem was excessive and embarrassing erections. Now the problem has reversed. As with most marketing, self-serving guys, the light bulb went off, and voila!

Nobody seemed to care this was an opinion piece, and everybody but the drug company execs seemed to love it. I had offers to write more articles, but this one article was the depth of my clever ideas. Fortunately for my career, the world never runs out of kids in trouble, and at least I'm pretty good at my job.

I was more than glad Roberta hadn't shared my delinquent clients' fate; she'd escaped any serious harm so far. And Kate Brady managed to survive our trip twenty years ago. She was a strong-minded woman who could size people up quickly. Kate figured me out and let me know it in a direct, yet nonthreatening manner. She was a natural psychologist, and when I find myself stumped with a troubled youngster, I remember her.

"The truth works pretty darn well. And there's no sense being mean about telling it. But there's little sense not telling it like it is, either," Kate Brady told me. She was right.

"Luke, the Grayling exit is in one mile." My wife jostled me out of my daydream.

I slowed the van. Roberta and Tom, who had also nodded off, woke to the changing speed of the van. I slipped the minivan off I-75 and into a Shell gas station with a Subway attached. As I pulled up next to the gas pump, my daughter reminded me it was my turn to come clean and face the music with Tom.

"Dear, dear, Father, and I mean that in only a kind and deferential way. Surely now is the time to tell our passenger here the full story of Father O'Roarke? As the good Lord tells us, the truth will set us free. Isn't that right, dear old Father?" Roberta was laying it on thick. Of course, I appreciated the effort.

"Yes, dear, you are correct and wise. You would have a great future in the nunnery in Adrian, my dear. I dare say you could reach the top-gun level at the nun big house. You could be Mother Superior if you set your mind to it," I told my daughter.

"That's a fine compliment, Father, although my goal is some-day to be a superior mother, like my blessed mother sitting next to you," she shot back.

"Oh, brother, cut the crap, you two," my wife piped up, giving us both a feigned withering look. She turned and addressed our hitchhiker in the backseat.

"Tom, these two just can't help themselves, but I can. This man next to me is my husband, who is going to buy us submarine sandwiches and over lunch give you a truthful accounting of our unusually boring life. Right, dear?"

"Absolutely, my dear," I replied.

Tom look perplexed. "Pardon me for asking, ma'am, but does this mean you're married to a priest?"

My wife shook her head and Roberta and I exploded in laugh-ter. Could a day be better than this?

Chapter 10

April 1973

It's 526 miles from Knoxville to Detroit. The AAA TripTiks advise it's a ten-and-a-half-hour drive, figuring an average speed of fifty miles per hour, which includes one meal, two gas and three rest area stops, but not including a Mystery Spot visit. That's the sane approach to interstate travel.

Flub Fitzgibbons, who had picked up Kate and me just south of Williamston, Kentucky, could make the Knoxville-to-Detroit run in just under six hours, with a six-minute stop for gas. At least, that's what Flub figured at the rate of ninety-five miles per hour. Flub liked to figure, so he told us. For example, Flub calculated the gas mileage in his 1961 Cadillac would be down to nine and a half miles per gallon traveling at this high rate of a speed. The Caddy's oversized twenty-eight-gallon tank would need to be filled up twice and would have less than one gallon left in the tank, providing for a small margin of error, when we arrived in Detroit. No matter that Flub wasn't going from Knoxville to Detroit; this was simply his observation. He was only headed up the road thirty miles. No doubt this was going to be the fastest thirty-mile segment of the trip for us. Just under nineteen minutes, Flub figured.

The trip *was* fast, and Flub was too busy rattling off mathematical oddities we didn't understand for us to learn much about him before he let us off in Florence, Kentucky, not far south of

Cincinnati. I didn't try to engage Flub in conversation. Everything we told him was fed back in dissected, mathematical terms. "How's the weather?" was answered with, "Central Kentucky is three degrees above the norm for March, with precipitation falling below the average by two-tenths of an inch. Year-to-date temperatures and precipitation are above average by point-six degrees and four-tenths of rain, respectively."

Flub was odd, but harmless and helpful, digging into his cooler and giving us two sixteen-ounce Pepsis and a large Baby Ruth to split just before we said thank you and hopped out of the car.

So far, four rides had taken us close to 250 miles in a little over seven hours. Kate looked at her watch and told me it was almost 5:00 p.m. Traffic was moderately heavy, moving slowly south away from downtown Cincinnati, the road flooded with commuters driving home from work.

"What's next, Corn Chex?" Kate asked.

"Ooh, another corny attack," I winced.

"Nothing's worse than those stories you've been telling those poor people who have been kind enough to pick us up, you lunatic. But if you ever tell another driver that I'm your deaf-mute sister just graduated from Saint Rita's Special School, I'm blowing your cover!"

"Hey, Kate, you did a wonderful imitation. I especially liked the fake sign language routine, but I think it was wasted on Flub," I said.

"What was up with Flub, Luke? There are some strange people in the world aren't there?"

"Yeah, and the people we meet out here are a bit on the fringe. But we're making good progress, Kate. It would be great to be pushing past Cincinnati and Dayton by dark. But this is a tough little stretch of road here. Traffic is too heavy and we need to get a ride that gets us past Cincinnati by ten miles or so. There's just no place to stand from the Ohio River until we're past the northern suburbs."

"Okay, boss, I just want to know when I can take this stupid hat off."

"Hey, the Gilligan look favors you, Kate."

We talked easily on and off as time passed and dusk approached. My road chatter slowed as the day wore on, and stretches of silence were comfortable. Kate leaned, then sat on her backpack and sighed as another group of cars passed us by.

"Not our day, is it, Luke?"

"Not yet," I said.

"It's okay, Luke. I still can't believe I'm out here with you. This isn't so bad. A girl could get used to this kind of life, don't you think?" She wore a wicked, sardonic smile.

I laughed and shook my head. "Kate, when your mother finds out we didn't take the bus, your ass is grass and so is mine. And she will find out, and I do mean both of us will be scorched. How could I let you talk me into this? A nice, air-conditioned bus would have already pulled into the Detroit bus station by now."

"Luke, it took me all of two seconds to convince you to take me hitchhiking. You are the easiest boy I know. I think, charitably, that anyone who's wearing a bra could get you to hitchhike to China. And if a girl wasn't wearing a bra, you'd be thumbing to the moon with her!"

"Hey, I am not that easy! I'm very selective who I take out on the road," I retorted.

"Yeah, right, Mr. Moore. All I know is that I'm glad we're doing this, rotten luck or not. And you're right, Mom is going to come unglued when she finds out. It will be a first for this quiet, unassuming second daughter of Roberta Brady. She'll live, and I'll make sure to take the blame. This is a wild time for me, Luke. Three weeks ago, I was a coed going to frat parties at UT, with an ex-boyfriend who had just about convinced me to get back together, and a big sister who was my hero. My idea of a big time was drinking one or two beers too many and dancing up a storm.

"Look at me now. I'm sitting on the side of the road in Kentucky with a man who was a boy I barely knew in Royal Oak, who miraculously held my beautiful sister in his arms when she died. And the incredible thing is that I am comfortable and happy. I'm having myself an adventure! What in the world has happened to me?"

Kate was smiling, but with tears in her eyes.

"I'm not sure what to tell you, Kate. It seems to me that what happened to you, happened to me when my dad set fire to our house. My little cocoon caught on fire, and the normal little boy disappeared in a heartbeat. Death happened. Life happened. Everything is new, messy, and uncomfortable, and we try to figure out a way to keep going on. Me, I just keep moving as fast as I can, trying to keep a step ahead of the day my life changed. I don't want to think about how great things were when my mom and brother and sisters were together just living our simple little suburban happy lives. That was a sweet and sappy time. Even my dad, who is one screwed-up guy, was part of those good times. It makes me so, so angry that he fucked it up for the rest of us."

I was red-faced and furious just thinking about my dad. I was so goddamned angry, I could not remember when or why I ever loved him. I hated my dad and tried my best to keep him out of my thoughts at all times. When he did creep into my head, like in a dream when we were all together at the dinner table, laughing and being a family, I would wake up nauseous.

"Oh, Luke, I'm sorry. Our tragedies do seem to be a bond, sad as that may be. I am glad that I'm here with you. You are a good man, Luke."

"Let's not start down the victim's road, Kate. I'm glad you came with me, and I'll face the wrath of your mom with you. It's worth it. Let's get back to the business at hand of getting us the hell out of here and to Royal Oak, Michigan, where friends and family don't know where I am and wonder if they'll ever see me again."

"All right, Luke, I'm going to focus all my good karma on you, and we'll get us a ride."

"That's exactly what we need, Swami Kate. Watch and observe as I inveigle a luxury car with power reclining seats, a cooler of beer, and sandwiches, to pull over and give us a single ride to Detroit."

I took my position close to the road and talked to every car that passed for the next ten minutes, working them, willing them to end our drought and build on Kate's positive energy. Ten minutes turned into thirty, and the drivers ignored my SOS.

I exploded, stringing together a hostile, seamless litany of unsavory epithets at the un-hearing drivers who sped by.

"You-goddamn -shit-for-brains-fat-assed-fungus-eating-noo-dledick-butt-ugly-boot-sniffing-head-so-far-up-your-ass-you're -eating-your-own-breakfast-son-of-a-bitch-canoodler! Stop your cars and pick us up!"

"Well that seems to be working, doesn't it, oh, wise Road Master," Kate responded.

I turned and said, "Oh, yeah?" and tackled her, wrestling her off the shoulder of the road and down the grassy embankment. We lay on our backs, laughing, watching the first stars emerge as I cursed our poor luck. A car door slammed above us. I jumped up, pulled Kate up, and we scurried back up to the roadbed. We reached the top of the slope and were suddenly looking straight up at two towering Kentucky State Troopers.

My experience on the road taught me that state troopers across the country were usually the most professional, best-trained, straight-as-an-arrow cops that travelers, including hitchhikers, met on the road. Other than the rare rogue state cop, their treatment could be expected to be the same: fair, accompanied by an all-business countenance. For some reason, varying from state to state, they also had ridiculous uniforms that were supposed to render respect, but often caused me to think, "Why do these guys wear those funny hats?"

Both of these Kentucky troopers were unusually large. They had to be at least six foot seven or taller, with wide shoulders and barrel chests. I would have thought they were twins, except their chrome name tags spelled out Officer Purtell and Officer Verla. They were wearing Smokey-the-Bear-style hats, tan uniforms with shoulder epaulets, mirrored sunglasses with oversized frames, and tight-fitting nylon pants with one black stripe on the outside of each pant leg, which was tucked into each knee-length black leather boot. One officer was standing directly in front of our bags, and one stood at the car with his hand close to the large pistol strapped on his belt.

"You two, stand still! Provide me with picture identity," Officer Purtell directed.

I had plenty of experience in dealing with various police. This sparseness of words and the absence of friendly banter meant that we should do exactly as told. The giant trooper's approach was a signal that this was a serious situation. There was something odd about these guys. Part of it was the bright, bluish light reflecting off the police car and framing the officers in rays that forced Kate and me to squint.

Then, I heard a deep, rumbling sound in the distance. It immediately reminded me of the sound I had heard, almost felt, when Annette died. A chill crawled up my spine. The sound rolled over and past me like a fast-moving cloud. I looked at Kate, who seemed oblivious to the reverberation. Her hands shook as she pulled her driver's license out of her wallet and handed it to the trooper. He examined our licenses and removed his sunglasses with great drama. His coal-colored eyes focused on me.

"Young man, this is not a good place for you to be, especially with this young woman. Do you understand me?"

"Yes, sir, I do," I replied.

"Good, you won't want to meet me again on this highway, or any other street, road, or highway."

"Yes, sir." I picked up my bag and motioned to Kate to follow me. As the trooper reached his car and began to open the door, he looked at me and gave me the nod. Reflexively, I nodded back.

That's unusual, I thought, *a cop giving me the nod.*

When I reached the bottom of the entrance ramp, I paused for Kate to catch up with me. "You okay?"

"Oh, sweet Jesus, Luke, I thought we were in some kind of trouble! They were so big, and they didn't say anything, and I really don't know what kind of law we're breaking hitchhiking. Lord, I was scared!"

"Well, those guys were all right. Technically, they can ticket us, and if they really want to cause us trouble, bring us to the station on a vagrancy charge. The state cops usually don't want to do any more than keep us off the highway. They're pros. If you're not an idiot, they tend to just do their job and move on down the road. But there was something eerie about those guys. I mean, I've seen big cops before, but those guys seemed close to seven feet tall. And, they looked like identical twins. And, I can never remember a state cop giving me the nod. What was that all about?"

"The nod?" Kate asked.

I smiled. "The nod is a universal acknowledgement between men."

Kate asked, "Of what?"

I replied, "That we're guys and we're cool with each other. It's an important sign of respect. It tends be an equalizer between car jockeys, greasers, jocks, country-and-western types. You name the group of men, and a nod can start an interaction off on the right foot."

Kate looked at me like I was from Mars. "What is it that makes men think the sun and the moon revolves around them? It's just a nod, for Christ's sake, not a deep Socratic insight. But whatever you say, Nod Man. Maybe a more important question is: what do we do now?"

I was learning quickly that Kate had a handy rapier to readily skewer me, and sometimes it was best to simply smile and shake my head. This marked some progress on my part in understanding women and how to survive with them. We walked down the exit ramp toward the group of fast food restaurants and gas stations.

"We don't have a lot of choices. We can get something to eat, wait a couple of hours, and try again here and hope the cops don't come back. That's not a very attractive option. We can stand on the entrance to the ramp and hope the police don't come by. We can walk a couple of miles and try further ahead. My vote is let's eat and decide later—how about you?"

"Okay, how about Karen's Kafe over there? It looks safe."

Kate pointed to a white clapboard restaurant with pink trim on the windows and doors.

"Karen's it is," I agreed.

As we trudged down the off-ramp, I asked Kate, "Did you hear that sound, kinda like thunder, while the two cops were talking to us?"

"No, Luke. What did you hear?"

"I don't know. I think my eardrums are screwed up or something." I shrugged it off.

Karen's Kafe had three booths and a counter with eight seats. The place was nearly empty as closing time approached. Karen's served basic staples, open at 6 a.m. for breakfast specials at $1.09; lunch with hamburger baskets and a milkshake priced at $1.99, and pot pie dinners, including salad and drink, for $3.49. It was open after dinner until 8 p.m. to accommodate the sporadic trucker clientele who appreciated clean bathrooms and the pie of the day.

The waitress's name was Lucy Zoeller. She told us that truck traffic had slackened at the Florence exit since a new truck stop with showers and cut-rate diesel had opened last summer at the Barber Road exit, five miles up the road. I ordered the hamburger basket and Kate the pot pie dinner. We talked with Lucy while we ate, and found her to be like a bartender, sans the booze.

Kate sat at the counter, waiting for her coffee to cool and working on a slice of blueberry pie while I used the tiny restaurant's restroom. Lucy successfully prodded Kate to tell her our story, while I was taking advantage of a clean restroom. While the restroom was clean, the walls were paper-thin, with the rather unappetizing result that voices and sounds could be heard between the seating area and the can. I could faintly hear Kate and our waitress chatting, first about college life and then about me.

"So, how do you know this guy isn't a complete wacko in disguise? I mean, you've only known him for such a short time," Lucy inquired.

"It's been short, but eventful. I know more about Luke than many of my college friends, Lucy, and while I'm not so sure what will happen next with him, he's a friend I trust."

"I suppose, but you be careful. How you doing for money?" Lucy asked.

"I'm fine. I have a credit card, but you know, it's funny, I haven't talked about money with Luke once since we met on this trip. I don't have a clue how much money he has."

"Eighteen dollars and sixty-two cents," I answered as I walked back to my stool, overhearing Kate's last comment.

"Luke, I don't care . . ."

"Hey, it's okay, Kate. It's a pretty good question. I can make eighteen dollars go a long way. But it doesn't include a hotel room. If we get stuck here, you may have to spring for a cheap room. I'm not sure you're ready for a night under a highway bridge yet. But, Kate, I will pay you for half the room, some day in the future, either in cash, or I'll work it off. I keep track of all my debts, every one, and someday when I make some real money—and I don't have a clue how long that will be—I'll pay everyone I owe back."

Kate nodded as Lucy said, "Okay, hotshot, you talk a good game. How about you give me a hand cleaning up this place? You do that and dinner will be on the house."

"You've got a deal, ma'am, except I insist the tip is cash," I said, and handed Lucy a dollar.

"Deal," Lucy said.

The three of us cleaned the entire restaurant in half an hour.

"Okay, look, you two, I've made a lifetime of mistakes bringing losers home—and I'm only twenty-three—but what the hell, I'll give you a place to sleep tonight, and if you can wake me up, I'll try to get you a ride past Cincinnati in the morning," Lucy said.

We jumped in her 1968 Rambler and drove across the bridge from Kentucky into Cincinnati, Ohio. Lucy lit her Newport 100 and proceeded to unload a litany of bad luck, swearing liberally about her con-artist, drug-dealing ex-boyfriend, who wheedled her out of six hundred dollars, her life savings to date.

We walked up three flights of stairs to her tiny, two-bedroom apartment with a view of the freeway. Lucy opened the door to the smell of stale beer and cigarettes, tinged with a light scent of a garbage bin that needed emptying. The living room was strewn with clothes, empty beer cans, and half-filled Chinese take-out containers. Lucy's roommate, Cindy, sat on one of five lawn chairs, the only furniture visible, smoking pot from a bong while watching television and barely acknowledging Lucy's arrival with two strangers. The apartment displayed the lack of order in Lucy and Cindy's life. The accommodations were not surprising to me. Residents of the low life and border-low life were far more likely to lend a floor for a night's sleep than people that had something to lose. Although Kate was familiar with minimal student budgets and low-rent housing, she didn't have much experience with this kind of life. I knew it wasn't an easy life to escape.

Lucy showed us the kitchen and the bathroom, and pushed her dirty laundry out of the way to make a spot on her bedroom floor where we could sleep. She offered Kate and me the first of many Old Milwaukees. We sat in the lawn chairs watching the local nightly news when a newscaster began to talk over the picture of an overturned tanker spewing smoke.

Cindy said, "Hey, Lucy isn't that your exit?" Lucy stared at the screen and said, "I'll be damned, that's gotta be right where you two were thumbing tonight."

Kate and I looked on in disbelief. The announcer described the accident time as approximately 7:00 p.m. The tanker had blown two tires, skidded, and then tipped before sliding off the road. The news footage showed exactly where we had been standing.

"Jesus, you're right! Look, Kate, that's where we were! Christ, if those cops hadn't chased us off . . . ," I said.

"Oh, my God! Those cops saved our lives, Luke!"

"It appears that way." The entire episode was very eerie. I remembered the horn, almost like a warning, and the strange look of the cops. What was going on?

We drank more Old Mil's than were good for us and smoked joints with Cindy and Lucy, chattering about the two giant troopers and trying not to think about "what-ifs." My beer-induced sleep was heavy, without dreams or much rest.

I woke up groggy, hearing a pounding on the apartment door and a muffled, but loud, female voice calling, "C'mon, Lucy. Get your skinny butt up and answer this door." I saw Kate look up from her space on the floor and heard Lucy on her bed snoring heavily. I was close to Kate on the floor, curled up in a fetal position inside my sleeping bag, half awake. Kate pulled herself up, slightly unbalanced, walked to the door, and opened it with the security chain attached.

"Can I help you?" she politely asked.

"Yes, you can, hon, I'm here for Lucy's wake-up call. Let me in, will you?"

Kate complied. A tall, leggy blonde in a short pink waitress uniform, with her hair tied back, brushed by her and went straight to Lucy's bedroom. Kate followed, catching up to watch the stranger grab Lucy's shoulders, put her face inches from Lucy's, and scream, "Wake-up call at the Hotel Lucy! Gotta get movin'! Time's a wastin'! We have a restaurant to open. Let's go, Lucy, now!"

Lucy woke up with a start and a look of bewilderment. She recognized the blonde and then tried to turn and cover her face with the pillow. The blonde wasn't having any of it, and gently, but firmly, held Lucy by the shoulders. In a more civil tone, she said, "Come on, girl, it's almost six. We need to be moving. Get yourself up and into the shower. Now!"

Lucy apparently knew better than to argue, and slowly sat up in bed with the blonde holding on to her elbow. Shuffling, Lucy allowed herself to be steered into the bathroom.

The blonde emerged when the sound of water started, and introduced herself to Kate. "Hey, I'm Marta Czechowski. Sorry to be a loud bitch, but this happens every Tuesday morning. She closes the restaurant Monday night and opens Tuesday mornings, and she either parties late or gets hammered and can't answer the bell without a little help. Where did you and your Sleeping-Beauty boyfriend meet Lucy?" Marta nodded toward me.

I feigned sleep.

"Oh, that's Luke Moore. I'm Kate Brady. He's not my boyfriend."

Kate explained our experience of the previous night and our destination while following Marta into the kitchen. Marta reached for coffee fixings and moved beer cans and other detritus out of the way on the kitchen counter. She muttered, "How can she live like this? That girl has a heart of gold, but she lives in this pit, picks up strays . . . nothing personal, but she can get herself hooked up with some bad actors. Oh, well."

Marta cleared off the small kitchen table, sat down, and read the morning newspaper she had brought with her, waiting for the coffee to finish. She offered Kate a section. Lucy shuffled into the kitchen just as the coffee stopped dripping, almost dressed in her waitress uniform.

"Right on time, Lucy. Grab a cup and let's go. I made it strong. Listen, Kate, we have to go. You said Lucy was going to give you a ride to the highway, but she works through lunch today. I have a 2:00 p.m. class at the community college, which is on the way out of town. When I finish my breakfast shift, I'll swing by at noon and get you and Sleeping Beauty. You'll be ready, right?"

"Absolutely, and thank you so much, Marta. And thank you, Lucy, for letting us stay here last night," Kate answered.

"No problem, girl," Lucy said.

Marta nudged Lucy out the door. I heard the conversation as my hangover emerged. I was content to let the events of the morning unfold and try to catch as much sleep as I could, even though the floor was hard and I had cottonmouth.

After finishing her cup of coffee, Kate spent the morning cleaning Lucy's disheveled apartment, except the roommate's bedroom, as I rested. The roommate's door was shut tight, though unintelligible sleep-talking interrupted by snorts and horse-like snoring sounds came through the door. Kate and I had watched Cindy drink at least eight Old Milwaukees while chain-smoking cigarettes and joints. Lucy had whispered to Kate that Cindy was "going through a rough patch. I just hope she has next month's rent money."

Kate finished cleaning Lucy's bedroom as the sun slanted through the bedroom window and splashed me fully awake. I pulled myself upright and ran my hands through my matted hair. My T-shirt was pulled up to reveal my scars. I saw Kate look away.

I stretched and grunted my way to the tiny kitchen, rinsed out a mug, and poured myself a full cup of coffee. The caffeine was waking me up, which wasn't all good. Kate followed me into the kitchen, depositing two handfuls of grunge in the nearly overflowing garbage canister. She was rushing around, acting too busy to talk.

"Kate, let's talk a minute."

"I'm working here, Moore."

"Take a break, Mrs. Clean."

She pushed her hair out of her eyes. "What's so important?"

"I'm wondering if you know about these bad boys?" I lifted my T-shirt above my stomach.

She looked me in the eyes, looking away from the burns. "Keeping a secret is not Adell's strong suit."

"You know, day by day, it's not that big of a deal. But I can't go to the beach and go swimming without every little kid pointing and parents looking away embarrassed. I can't take off my shirt to work outdoors or play basketball or run. It's definitely weird to be ugly."

"Luke, you're not ugly," Kate interrupted.

"Maybe not with my shirt on, but with my shirt off, people see a disfigured guy, a mutant. Their first reaction is to look away, but they try very hard to get a sneak peek. I know they wonder how or what happened to me, but in the end, it's the same whether you have a birth defect or an accident or a disease. If you're marred, ugly as a result, the first reaction is 'ugh,' the second might be distaste, the third might be pity—none of which are gratifying from my wounded perspective. Worse are the ugly-minded bastards who get a kick out of going after the guy with the birthmark or the girl with a harelip. That's ugly on ugly. Those morons—I swear they're usually white, heavy beer-drinking guys in their early twenties with their paunches just beginning to show—draw attention to the birthmark ugliness, make a spectacle, and make it so goddamn worse. When you're ugly, you either fight or run, and pain or shame is the sad result either way. The ironic thing is that before I was burned, I was a real smart-ass. I could cut up just about anybody. Although I can't remember going after an ugly, I definitely went for the weak spot. You didn't want to be too short, tall, fat, dumb, or uncool and try to take me on, or I'd be back at you like a crazed boomerang. I lost friends and made enemies.

"After the fire and burns, I realized what an idiot I was. My real friends closed ranks to help me. I don't think one of them consciously thought, *Hey, he's vulnerable now, he won't attack anymore.* It was more like, *He's hurt, and we can help.* And after the first time someone made fun of me, they lashed back for me. So, I'm ugly, but it's all right, because it's part-time. I see a kid with bad acne and think in some ways I have it better than him.

"Now, Lord help anyone that goes after an ugly person with me around. They'll get an ugly's revenge and a new asshole from me."

Kate sighed, "Luke, you're an honest dude, all right. But one minute you sound like a cuddly cocker spaniel and the next like a pissed-off porcupine."

"Maybe not so honest, just can't quite keep my mouth shut, so this blather just shoots out. Enough early-morning philosophy, I've got a cheap-beer headache, and you look fresh and ready to go. I overheard your conversation with the bossy chick that picked up Lucy. Sounds like good luck to start off the day with a prearranged ride. Good work, Kate."

"Not that I had much to do with it. The girl's name is Marta, and she certainly isn't shy. She'll be here around 11:00 a.m."

"Well, I'm up now. I'm going to see if I can run this apartment complex out of hot water and sober up," I said.

After showering, I came out of the bathroom with a towel wrapped around my waist and walked into the apartment's main room to see Kate in the kitchen, putting some muscle behind her goal of making the tarnished faucet shine.

"Kate, you did all of this? Damn, you are one good maid, not to mention a karma builder."

Kate smiled and noted my bare chest, and somehow this simple gesture drew us closer. I was normal, not ugly in her eyes, if only for a few moments in a stranger's apartment.

I dressed and left the apartment, finding a 7-Eleven nearby. I bought half-a-dozen assorted day-old doughnuts, a bunch of bananas, a package of oatmeal cookies, and a quart of orange juice. Back at the apartment, I spread out our poor man's buffet on paper towels. We sat at the kitchen table reading our books. I was in the last chapter of Camus's *The Plague,* a step up from my last book, *Hotel.* I hadn't kicked my habit of trying to impress friends or even complete strangers that I was a budding intellectual by reading highbrow books. I struggled through them and then devoured Arthur Hailey's stuff. Kate had begun Salinger's *Franny and Zooey* (I thought she really was a promising intellectual*)* when loud, weird noises from Cindy's bedroom reached a crescendo.

"For Christ's sake, it sounds like a goddamn garbage disposal in there," I laughed.

"No, I think it sounds like a porcupine and hyena having sex," Kate exhaled.

"How unladylike, but accurate. I'd go look, but I'm afraid of what I'd see."

The noise continued unabated for about fifteen minutes, but neither Kate nor I had the gumption to open the door and find out what was going on behind that closed door.

At noon, Lucy's fellow waitress, Marta, knocked on the apartment door. Kate watched, bemused, as we introduced ourselves and each surreptitiously sized up the other. Marta was taller than me by about an inch. Her pink waitress skirt contrasted with her tan, lissome legs, which I found extraordinarily attractive. She wasn't uncomfortable with her height, and stood with her shoulders back, apparently proud to acknowledge her fulsome figure. I didn't want to be caught admiring this striking woman. When she turned to lead us out of the apartment, her sashay was too much to ignore. Kate, seeing my open mouth and bug-eyes, slapped me on the back of the head and whispered, "Stop gawking, you horndog!"

Kate soon found herself in the backseat of Marta's 1966 VW Bug, bound for the highway, listening to Marta and me talk like we'd known each other for years. We talked about our families, Vietnam, our dreams, the future, Kundalini yoga, Zen. Marta mentioned she was married, but unhappily. I took a breath and thought, *Shit, a husband.*

An intense conversation continued. I was like a first grader telling his mom about his first day at school. I told her about my burns and my insecurities, a deviation from any previous road conversation strategy. She told of her worries about marrying so young, her family's poverty, and plans for the future. By the time she deposited us just past Dayton an hour later, it was if we had ended a satisfying first date. But Marta was turning back south to a community college class and her husband, and I was returning to the road. I stepped out of the car and held the front seat door for Kate. I reached back into the VW and took Marta's hand, engaging her eyes to say good-bye. She smiled and leaned forward, giving me an open-eyed kiss. The wind created by passing trucks shook the car, muffled our words.

Marta merged her car onto the highway with the turtle-like acceleration of the Bug. I smiled and raised both of my eyebrows at Kate, who obviously wasn't pleased. I had opened up to this stranger immediately and in a different way than I had with Kate.

"Well, and here I thought you weren't the lady's man. That was pretty fast action there, Luke. A beer cooler in the backseat would have got more conversation than I did."

I couldn't stop smiling. "Marta is unusual, isn't she? She was straight with me without reservation. That kind of honesty, that openness . . . I could spend a lot of time with her."

"Luke, you just met her, and she's married, and she's gone," Kate noted.

"Yeah, that's true, but she is camping in northern Michigan this summer, and I know when and where." I held up a folded piece of paper and put it in my top pocket.

"I'd be careful there, Luke. She comes with a lot of baggage."

"Christ, Kate, I'm the King of Baggage. All I know is I'd like to continue that conversation with Marta. And, you know, it could be a very long conversation. She's beautiful, she's honest, she thinks, she cares. I like her laugh . . ."

"Luke, you just met her. You can't fall in love with a married woman, who you just spent an hour with in the front seat of an old VW in the middle of Ohio, just because she has good legs, paid some attention to you, and gave you a little good-bye kiss! Wake up, boy!"

"Calm down, Kate. Hey, stranger things have happened. Let's get going here. We're four hours from Detroit. Put that cute hat on and let's get a ride."

It didn't take long before Kate found herself in another back-seat, a 1971 Buick LeSabre, listening to me introduce ourselves to our driver.

"I'm Little Pierre Ouellette, and this is my friend Babette Ouellete. I know we have the same last name, but we're actually not related. Her Ouellete has one *t* and my Ouellette has two *t*'s. We're trying to make our way back home to Quebec City. We just finished a Mormon mission, praise God, in Guatemala, Belize, and Mexico, and we are so anxious to see our families. You'll probably want to know why I'm called Little Pierre—well, of course, there's a Big Pierre . . ."

Kate listened to me earnestly play the Mormon missionary role with a ridiculous story that seemed to amuse Louis Palmer, a pencil-thin office furniture salesman with a pinched mustache. She settled back into her seat, hopefully ready to use her high-school French when called upon. But the scowl on her face meant she was still dwelling on Marta. Maybe she was a tad bit jealous of Marta worming into her territory with me so quickly. *That would be nice,* I thought. Of course, I was wrong.

Years later, we laughed as she told me what she was thinking in the backseat of Louis Palmer's car. *I like this guy, but not as boyfriend material. No question that, like any twenty-year-old guy, he'd hop into bed with me in a heartbeat. Yes, that University of Tennessee Human Sexuality Psych course was right. Men between the ages of sixteen and twenty-one think of sex over one hundred times per day. Over six times per hour, once every ten minutes, confirming that men are indeed pigs and ruled by their uncontrollable lust. Luke is no different, but at least he turned away from me when he made his crotch adjustments, indicating he is a polite pig. I'm interested in the other nine out of ten minutes when a man's attention could be diverted from lust and focused on the rest of life, including paying attention to me. It's true I'm interested in the lusty one minute, but not as the sole reason for living, the opposite of a young man's view. Luke is a man, therefore a pig—a polite oinker who is very interesting in his un-horny moments.*

The drab Ohio farmland flew by as I discussed with Louis Palmer Mormon values and how polygamy was a good thing.

"What do you think about that, Babette?" Louis asked Kate.

She joined the farce. "*Oui,* Lou-ie, *oui,*" she said in a passable French accent, "I do think women should have more than one husband."

Now we're having fun, I thought. With Kate on board, I relaxed a bit, pushed my road anxieties back, and began to look forward to what the road would bring us next.

Chapter 11

September 2003

We walked through the line at Subway and selected the bread, ingredients, and condiments for our submarine sandwiches. My wife, Marta Czechowski Moore, instructed Tom to order the largest two subs he could invent, one for now and one for the road. We sat down at an empty Formica-top booth in the faux restaurant in the corner of the gas station's too-bright interior. I looked around this contemporary combination restaurant, convenience mart, souvenir shop, and ice-cream stand, where you could buy anything from fast food to fishing supplies to a socket-wrench set. It was a far cry from the Sinclair gas station of my day that only offered cigarettes, one pop machine, and six selections of candy. Sitting in the unpadded seats, we unwrapped our sandwiches in awkward silence. It was time for confession.

"Tom, the truth of the matter is, I'm not Father O'Roarke. This is not my niece and sister, and I am not a Catholic priest. I'm actually an escaped mass murderer who has kidnapped—"

"Dad, stop it and get to the point," Roberta demanded.

"The point is that I'm an incurable story teller, and that I used to hitchhike quite a bit when I was your age. I would entertain myself by making up stories about myself and telling them to the drivers who picked me up. It became a bit of a habit, and when I picked you up today, I reverted back to my former self. Please excuse me.

I'm really Luke Moore, and this is my vivacious and insightful wife, Marta, and my lovely and charming daughter, Roberta. While I'm not a priest, I am a child psychologist. No wisecracks, please."

"And a member of Fibber's Anonymous," Roberta said.

"That's enough, young lady," Marta said. "Show some respect for your father. In this case, as in the past, we have been your dad's enablers. Even though we may stop him from going too far, we do like the stories. Tom, we're sorry for misleading you. I hope you're not too upset with us," Marta added.

"I'm just bit confused, that's all. You're not a priest named Father O'Roarke. You're Luke Moore, a child psychologist, and this is your daughter Roberta Moore, and this is your wife, Marta Moore. Excuse me, Ma'am, Mrs. Moore. That right?" Tom pointed at each of us as he made the connections clear.

"Yep, that's all the eggs this hen can lay, Tom," I replied, back-sliding to my homespun clichés, which were the real Luke Moore.

"So, this isn't some kind of kinky game, is it? You guys aren't going to ask me to do something weird, are you?" Tom asked, a bit ruffled.

"No, no, Tom. I can understand why you might think something like that. The only weirdness here is my husband's insistence on telling stories, harmless stories, to complete strangers. He doesn't smoke, doesn't drink, doesn't do drugs, he doesn't even swear very much. His primary vice is spinning stories. Now, if you are worried at all, we can get your things out of the van, enjoy your lunch with or without us, and be on your way. Whatever makes you comfortable, Tom."

My wife, Marta, has a bartender's touch with people, making them comfortable with common sense and a kind, calming voice. Our daughter called her Joe the Guide, after a children's book character that made friends with every animal in the forest and every person in the village. She had been my guide to redemption, but was much more than that to me. She saved me. In the early days of our marriage, when I still drank three beers past my limit, I would sing her praises.

"I love my wife, she brings me no strife. I love my wife, she saved my life," I would warble off key and too loudly. Marta would laugh with my friends, but I meant every word. My ever-so-wise Marta is a tranquil, unassuming savior. Yes, she was stubborn and showed a flash of temper that scared us both. Early in our marriage, she could party with the best of the Lost Souls, matching my friends drink for drink. At age twenty-five, she announced to me on a Sunday morning while we drank coffee and read the morning *Free Press,* that she was an alcoholic, genetically predisposed, and that alcohol was no longer going to be part of her life. That was that. She threw herself into her job at Merrill Lynch, becoming a broker, and by the time she was thirty, I was convinced that she was going to make us rich. I was wrong. Another Sunday morning newspaper–and-caffeine session was interrupted by Marta's announcement that she was quitting her job, enrolling at Wayne State, and becoming a registered nurse. It was time to do something with her life that had meaning.

"Life doesn't promise tomorrows," she said. Her final term of nursing school, we learned she was pregnant, finally, with Roberta. She jumped on me in the bed at five in the morning, waving the blue strip from the home pregnancy test. "Luke, wake up! I'm going to have a baby. I have a child inside me. We did it!" Yes, we did, and we've been laughing and crying ever since.

Tom Lutac interrupted my reverie. "I think I'm fine. But, Mr. Moore, if you don't mind me saying so, that's one odd habit you have. I really thought you were a priest. You should have been an actor."

"I guess to some degree, I am a frustrated actor. But, Tom, even though I'm not a priest, I am interested in your story and your spiritual search. I have more than a little experience in picking myself up after a fall and finding God in unusual places. Let's keep that conversation going, if it's all right with you," I said.

"Fine with me, and since we're confessing our sins here, I haven't been completely candid with you. Maybe we can start from scratch," Tom replied.

"Ah, I suspected a little amplification, obfuscation, or stretching, but I wasn't sure which it was, or all three," I said.

"Luke, let's just enjoy our lunch now, and maybe have a real conversation. You and Tom can solve the mysteries of the universe once we get back in the car," Marta interrupted.

She was right, of course. Men do take themselves way too seriously on just about everything. Tom and I listened to Marta and
Roberta yak about this and that and, as I tend to do, I drifted back
in time. Knoxville Kate and I hadn't made it to Royal Oak yet.

Chapter 12

April 1973

Honey it don't matter, what you might have in your purse.
Darling I don't care, you could be a millionaire.
I don' need money, no, what I need now is a nurse.
I hurt everywhere, darlin,' I need intensive care.
So unless there's pills in your purse
What I really need right now is a nurse!
What he really needs right now is a nurse!
I need Band-Aids and gauze.
And the reason is just because.
All your lovin,' and your money, honey, just won't do.
Oh, you've got style, you got grace, big boobs and a real
pretty face.
But, darlin,' that's not what I need to pull me through.
What I really need is a nurse, ooh.
So honey, don't be jealous,
When she's sittin' on my bed.
I ain't after sex,
Just a little rub with phisohex.
Maybe in a year or two
I'll ask for you instead.

First I got to get some rest,
Don't worry babe, you're still the best.
It's just a matter of first things first
And what I really need right now is a nurse.

I stood in the shadow of the huge sign announcing Monroe, Michigan, as the birthplace of General George Custer, singing Martin Mull's classic song. Kate's arched eyebrow told me that she was thinking I was getting nuttier by the hour. Which was true. Spending hours on the side of the road waiting for something to happen other than watching every imaginable make, model, and year of car fly by, would seem to encourage an eccentric thought pattern. On the other hand, I guess you had to be an oddball to begin with to subject yourself to hitchhiking.

We were waiting for what we hoped was the last ride through Detroit to Royal Oak. It was 2:00 p.m., and we finally had made good time. I knew we were close enough to call a friend to pick us up, but for me, that was a last resort. I liked to make it into town on my own, although getting through Detroit posed a problem. Kate was sitting up on her bag after trying to lie down on the side of the road to take a nap. I gently, but firmly, asked her to sit up and look interested and presentable.

"Kate, if we don't look like we're working for a ride, it's tough to convince someone we're deserving. If we just sit on our bags with a sign, we look like what they think we are: lazy counter-culture slobs," I said.

"Well, maybe I feel like a lazy counter-culture slob. I'm hungry, I'm still hung over, and I don't give a goddamn that Georgie the Indian Killer Custer grew up in Monroe, Michigan. And I certainly don't care whether or not you need a nurse, big boobs or not," Kate replied.

"I know you're tired, Kate. You look as miserable as a bear with a sore heinie. If we don't get a ride soon, I'll call a friend to pick us up, okay?"

Kate sat up and appeared more interested.

Within minutes, a 1965 Ford Falcon without any recognizable color pulled over, swerving from the high-speed lane to the shoulder about fifty feet in front of us.

"It's Elvis!" I smiled and shook my head. "No one else has a car that looks like that and drives like a mad goat."

As the words "Who's Elvis?" left Kate's mouth, the front door of the Falcon opened and a compact man with a halo of curly hair surrounding a wide, smiling face leapt out.

Arms akimbo, he faced the two of us and yelled, "Moore Man! You are the Moore Man!" He opened his arms and strode toward Kate and me. Elvis and I embraced as he hooted.

"What in the world are you doing here, Luke? You just left a few weeks ago. Goddamn, it's good to see you anyway. I see you have very foxy chick companion. An introduction, please?"

He turned toward Kate and his brilliant eyes locked on hers.

I said, "Kate, this is Elvis. Well, actually his name is Matthew Muldoon. Matt—Elvis—this is Kate Brady, you may . . ."

"Hell, yes, I remember who she is. The Brady Bunch! We were in the same class together. Well, it is my honor to meet you again and to rescue you from this bad cad and get you safely through our fair city in my unsightly, yet reliable car." Elvis reached out and took Kate's arm, lifted the back of her hand to his lips, and kissed it gallantly.

I rolled my eyes, but Kate was still looking at Elvis's chameleonlike eyes. One eye was green and the other blue. Both seemed to change color, depending on the light. It was Elvis's most compelling physical feature, but his high-voltage energy could not be ignored, either. My slim hope of Kate ever finding interest in me floated away as I saw a smile in her eyes.

"Madame, my chariot is at your disposal," Elvis gestured grandly at the Bondo-covered, half-painted Falcon. "Luke, you hop in back; shotgun for this ride is reserved for Miss Brady" For the first time this trip, Kate sat in the front seat. She rolled down the passenger seat window and hung her elbow out into the humid Michigan air with a big grin.

He found an opening in traffic, gunned the six-cylinder engine, and moved the column stick shift quickly from the first through third. Then, after pushing the Jimmy Hendrix *Purple Haze* tape into the eight-track, pushing in the lighter, and pulling a cigarette from the pack above him in the visor, he reached into the small cooler on the floor and offered a Stroh's to Kate and me.

"I can't believe you found us, Elvis," I marveled. "What are you doing this far downriver?"

"Oh, I had a little delivery to make, a couple of bricks to Toledo," Elvis said.

Kate asked, "Are you in the construction industry, Elvis?"

Elvis and I laughed in unison. "No, ma'am, these bricks were specially made in Michoacán, Mexico, and they were a bit more expensive than your everyday, common brick. I assume the southern lady is okay to lay it all out to, isn't she Luke?" Elvis asked.

"She's cool. Kate, Elvis is an aspiring musician who is not above scoring an occasional bit of the weed to help finance his gigs. Is that right, Elvis?"

"Yes, indeed. I'm not a regular drug dealer, Kate. I just have a friend who, two or three times a year, brings some high-quality hemp up to Detroit, and I move it for him. No more than a couple of keys. Pot only, nothing more."

Kate smoked pot recreationally, and periodically bought the odd nickel bag or lid, keeping a small stash for a late night, after-study buzz. She wasn't nervous about holding her own pot, but a couple of kilos was over four pounds; more than 100 lids of pot. She had never seen that much pot before.

"You don't have that much with you now, do you?" Kate couldn't hide her anxiety.

"Nothing to worry about, Kate. All I have are these road buddies," Elvis said, pointing to the small cooler of beer. "I'm very careful and sober when I'm on a delivery," he told her. "Now, let's get to the important stuff. Why in the world would a beautiful woman like you travel with my never-had-a-date friend, Luke Moore? What's going on?"

To my surprise, Kate told my story, then hers. As she laid out the stories rather methodically, I watched Elvis occasionally look over at me in astonishment.

"My God," said Elvis, "that's un-fucking-real. Are you guys okay?"

We both nodded assents, but I could see the fatigue of grief in Kate's eyes. Repeating both stories recalled the pain. Kate and I sensed with dread that retelling the story when we reached Royal Oak would cause more than enough heartache to go around.

"Elvis, do me a favor. When we get home, can you explain this to everybody? I'm just getting—" I asked.

Elvis interrupted, "Done. But, man, that's the most heartbreaking story I've heard since…"

"Since the fire. I know, Elvis. It makes me wonder if I'm a magnet for bad karma."

A reprimanding glare crossed Kate's face. "That's not true and you know it, Luke. It was a blessing you were with my sister when she died. Don't you ever think otherwise."

She was right. That night caused a shift in my life. I had an amorphous promise to keep to Annette. And, absent the numerous hangovers, I felt a lightness that had been missing since I was a kid. I figured I would be a pretty good candidate for a religious conversion right about now. A screwed-up kid, jarred back to Jesus by a life-changing accident and death.

Hey, maybe I could be the priest my mother hoped I would become, until I couldn't memorize the Latin necessary to be an altar boy. Nope, I don't think even these earthshaking events are quite enough to drive me back to the fold. I plan on being angry at least until I'm thirty for having my life screwed up. And celibacy, up until Adell, is an affliction, not a goal.

Elvis interrupted my thoughts. "Let's get you guys back to Royal Oak. Luke, you staying at our place or going home?"

"We'll crash at the Vermont house with you, if it's okay."

"Hell, you never asked before, don't go getting manners because you're traveling with a beautiful girl."

"Thanks, Elvis."

"Why do they call you Elvis?" Kate asked.

"Good question," I responded. "Well, Matt, or Elvis here, as you might remember, has always been a wild-man entertainer. Do you remember when we did that Christmas pageant and our second-grade class sang, 'Glow, Little Glowworm' wearing those big paper bow ties in Day-Glo colors? At the end of the song, Matt got down on one knee and belted out a surprise rendition of 'Mammy.'"

"Yeah, I do remember that. Sister Dennis Margaret was laughing so hard, she was crying, but Sister Mary Therese looked like she swallowed a frog. Matt, you were a scream," said Kate.

"Yeah, well, he kept it up right through high school after you left. One summer night after our sophomore year, we somehow got hooked up with a running battle between the greasers who hung out at Peppy's—remember the burger joint in Ferndale?—and the bikers who hung out at the Red Barn across from the Detroit Zoo. God knows what we were doing in the middle of a gripe between those degenerates, but about fifteen of us landed up in the parking lot at Hedge's Wigwam, and the greasers were accusing us of throwing a milkshake at one of their cars. A few of the bikers showed up and started egging us on, except we didn't want to be egged on. We were basically partying jocks, and while we'd get in fights every now and again, we were wimps compared to the hardcore bikers and greasers. Well, when the chains and tire irons started appearing, we started freaking. Out of nowhere, Matt Muldoon shows up in this same Falcon, which had a color back then. He screeched to a stop, jumped out, and waded into the middle of this potential macho melee. But he was dressed up as Elvis, fresh from an Elvis-impersonation gig.

"Elvis had his hair slicked back, with the trademark lock hanging over his forehead, rhinestone black coat, and black shirt unbuttoned to the navel, and as he stood in the middle of the angry crowd, he said, 'What's shakin,' friends,' in a perfect Elvis imitation. We all froze, including the greasers and bikers, who were as flabbergasted as we were. Elvis walks up to the biggest badass-looking greaser and says, 'Looks like we might have a problem here, boys. But I'm not in the mood for kickin' some ass, so listen up. I'm going to give you all a special treat. Priscilla, darling, hand me my guitar.' He made this Elvis motion to this knockout blonde that was dressed like Priscilla Presley, sitting in the front seat of the Falcon. She stepped out of the car, gave Elvis his guitar, and he starts belting out "Hound Dog." We were all still standing there with our jaws hanging low, but Elvis is good, even if you didn't like Elvis. Before long, the greasers were singing along, and the beer got cracked out and passed around, and the fight was off. Eventually, the cops showed up and kicked us all out. Ever since then, it's been Elvis. Right, Elvis?"

"Call me whatever you like, dipshit. But enough talk, you two sit back and relax and listen to the jams. I need to psych up for my gig tonight." Elvis turned and winked at Kate, who smiled like a happy puppy. *Oh, Christ. Five minutes and he has her in his sights.*

Kate and I watched the skyline of Detroit rise above the highway bridge that crosses over the vast Rouge River industrial complex, the belching heartland of automotive manufacturing.

"It doesn't smell that bad," Kate said. "I can remember driving over this bridge when I was a little girl, and it smelled like a combination of backed-up toilet and my brothers' bedroom after they had the flu. Dad told me if the Rouge smelled bad, then times were good. He'd say, 'If the plants cough and color the sky with hues not normally seen on this earth, then people are working and spending money and times are good. If the skies are clear and you can breathe the air, then it's time to tighten up your pocketbook.' My dad had a way with words like that. I think that was one of the last times he was with us before he took off for good. It seems like a century ago. This feels strange, coming home again." Kate shrank back into her seat as she stared out over the metal landscape. Elvis and I had the uncommon good sense to let her be.

Downtown Detroit unfurled as we approached from the southeast on I-75. The Ambassador Bridge framed the skyline between Michigan and Canada. We viewed Windsor, one of the few places where Canada dips south of the United States. The sight ignited memories of the big city of Detroit.

Kate sat up and smiled when we passed Tiger Stadium. She excitedly told us a story of her mom taking the Brady kids to watch a Tigers ball game. Helen Brady had expected to buy the one-dollar bleacher tickets for her children and herself. Bleacher tickets were plentiful on a normal Tuesday night, but Mrs. Brady, not a sports fan, had picked a game in September when the Tigers were in a heated pennant race with the Yankees. The ballpark was sold out, and the Brady boys were almost in tears with disappointment. Their mother was undaunted, and within minutes, she was haggling with a scalper for five tickets, but the price was too high. A very old, hunched-over man with a polka-dotted bow tie watched the negotiations. Kate watched the old guy shuffle over to her mom and tug on her elbow. Helen Brady looked over, then down, and the old man produced five tickets.

"Happens I have some extras today. Put away your money, I can see your boys are Tiger fans. Of course, you'll have to sit with me." The old man took Helen Brady by the arm and walked her and the Brady family into the stadium, walking down, down, past the cheap seats, until they finally sat down in box seats two rows behind the Tigers dugout. Just about the best seats in the park.

"That's my best memory of Detroit," Kate said. "We couldn't afford to come downtown much."

The recollection invigorated Kate and she excitedly told us of other memories of Detroit, including watching the news about the summer of 1967 race riots that exploded and tore the town apart. She actually understood what a "blind pig" was when the newscaster used the term to describe the late-night police raid on an after-hours gambling joint that started the street violence and led to widespread destruction and burning of whole blocks, culminating with the arrival of the National Guard.

Her story stirred my own memories of the riots that split the city and spurred "white flight," in which neighborhoods changed hands in months, with whites heading for the suburbs and Jewish store owners burned out, never rebuilding. A beautiful city of homes started to crumble.

I was a fourteen-year-old in '67, with a summer janitor job stripping and waxing floors at the University of Detroit Prep, the premier Jesuit high school on 7 Mile Road, about a mile east of Livernois on Detroit's northwest side. Livernois was called "the Avenue of Fashion," a cluster of pricey retailers selling the finest haberdashery and women's clothing, shoes, jewelry, and furs. In the years before the riot, white flight to the suburbs was increasing from a trickle to an intermittent stream. As the white shoppers moved, a transition started on the avenue, as retailers started offering hats that appealed to the less conservative, black, upscale shopper. But the stores still catered to the white upper class that lived in nearby Palmer Woods, the exclusive Detroit Golf Club neighborhood. I told Kate and Elvis what happened to me that day.

"The day the riots began, I was just about finished with stripping a classroom floor with one of those big industrial circular scrubbers, when my boss came in and said, 'Hey, Moore, finish up quick and punch out. They're sending everybody home. The radio says there's some kind of civil disturbance going on.' Well, I didn't know a civil disturbance from a kosher hot dog, but a half-day off sounded good, so I put away my equipment and punched out. As usual, I walked up Outer Drive to Livernois, and along the way, I noticed the lights were off and the shops were closed, even though it was the middle of the day. My bus stop was close to the intersection of Livernois and Outer Drive, but my daily ritual was to attempt to hitchhike and save the bus money. A harbinger of things to come, I suppose.

"I was standing there with my thumb out for about fifteen minutes, looking down the avenue. I saw a bunch of people gathering in the middle of the street. I was thinking, *That's unusual,* when a brand-new gold Cadillac with those big fins on it pulled up next to me. There was an elderly black couple in the car, and the man leaned over from the driver's seat, almost in his wife's lap, and said to me, 'Son, what are you doing out here?' I told him I'd been sent home from work because of a civil disturbance. He snorted and roared, 'Civil disturbance my black bald head! There is a riot going on! Get in this car immediately!' I did what he said and sat in the backseat of the couple's Cadillac, which rode like a big boat as we sailed north to Royal Oak. The driver was a large, bald man with huge, black-rimmed glasses. He introduced himself and his wife as Mr. and Mrs. Washington. We talked, and I noticed Mr. Washington's wife acting nervously as we passed out of Detroit, north of 8 Mile and into the suburb of Ferndale, and finally into Royal Oak. She was tugging on her white plumed hat and looking over at her husband. Mr. Washington ignored her and asked me about my job and school and praised a good education and work ethic.

"When he dropped me off in front of my house, he said, 'Now, you get inside and stay there. You hear me, son?' I told him yes, sir, and thanked him for the ride. My mother rushed out the front door, and I watched the black couple drive away, Mr. Washington pulling on his hat to acknowledge my mom.

"I explained what had happened. My mom told me about the riots and said, 'Luke, you just witnessed real courage, the everyday kind of courage that makes me glad to be a human being. Dear, you know how we've talked about bigots and hate—how stupid and unreasonable it is for people to hate without reason or regret? Well, we live in Royal Oak, an all-white city that is like any other all-white city. It's all-white for a reason and wants to stay that way. So a lot of people would make life miserable for anyone black who even thinks of spending more than a minute here, other than to clean houses or garden or do other work. Black folks steer around Royal Oak and Birmingham and Clawson, even if it means going far out of their way. They know they can be pulled over for nothing, given a ticket, and sometimes even taken to the police station. The message is real clear. I didn't believe it until your father and I went to a Fraternal Order of Police party at the Elks Club and heard the cops talk about chasing the Negroes away—and their language wasn't that kind. Honey, those folks, on a day like this, when Detroit is going up in flames and the suburbs surrounding the city are loading their hunting rifles by the thousands, they deserve a medal of bravery. Don't you ever forget how people help people, even when they're afraid. And don't you ever think a bad thought about someone because they look different than you. You understand me, Luke?' Mom had such a passion for the truth. I'll never forget it." I finished and fell silent.

Elvis spoke up. "Luke, you remember that time your mom launched into us for playing 'niggerbaby?' I think we were only seven years old, and Tommy McGee and I were over playing at your house, and he showed us this new game they played in his neighborhood. He threw the ball up on the pitched roof of your garage and yelled 'niggerbaby,' and then we beat the tar out of each other to see who could catch the ball. It was my turn, and I yelled it out, and the next thing I know, I see your mom running like a fullback toward us, and her face was red, really red. I can tell she's mad, and she says, 'Matthew Muldoon, what did you just shout?' And I say, '*Niggerbaby,* Mrs. Moore.' 'Do you know what that word means, Mr. Muldoon?' I know I'm in big trouble now, because your mom called me Matthew and Mr. Muldoon! I don't have a clue what *niggerbaby* means, so I 'fessed up. 'No, ma'am, I don't know what it means.' 'I'm going to tell you, Matthew, Tommy, and Luke, that it is a vile, despicable way to refer to Negro children. I don't ever want to hear that word or any word close to it in my yard or in my presence, ever! I will not be raising hateful little bigots in my yard. Are we clear, boys?' You and me said, 'Yes, ma'am.' But Tommy said to your mom, 'Mrs. Moore, my daddy says *nigger* all the time. He says niggers are worse than kikes, and if either one ever shows their face our neighborhood, they'll be sorry.' Your mom says, 'Then your daddy is a fool, Tommy.' That was my first lesson about race, and your mom was a good teacher, Luke."

"Thanks, Elvis. She grew up in a mixed neighborhood in Detroit and had childhood friends that were black. Even when she moved to the suburbs, she always thought of herself as a Detroiter."

"When I moved to Knoxville, I told everyone we were from Detroit and proud of it," Kate said.

"Detroit's had a rough ride since you moved, Kate. It's a tough city, with a lot of great people. I do the same thing when I'm on the road. I tell people I'm from Detroit, the Motor City. Makes people think I'm tougher than I am."

We all went silent again as the Falcon slid through the submerged inner-city I-75, the twenty-foot cement walls hiding the decimated downtown as the road twisted due north and pointed us toward the suburbs. Royal Oak, ten miles north from the core of downtown Detroit and two miles from the northernmost border of 8 Mile Road, was close enough for the commute to downtown, which could be made via train. Woodward Avenue, the eight-lane main artery that splits Detroit in half, runs from the Detroit River through the humble, but respectable, suburbs of Ferndale, Royal Oak, and Berkley. Further north are the swanky cities of Birmingham and Bloomfield Hills.

Most of my friends' parents moved to Royal Oak in the 1950s and '60s for bigger backyards, newer schools, and a fresh start for their growing families. Thanks to an aggressive United Auto Workers union, auto workers were making great factory wages, overtime, and full health and retirement benefits. The emergence of suburbs downriver, east, west, and north of Detroit was the answer to a need for housing as an influx of workers flooded Detroit for the great factory jobs at General Motors, Ford, Chrysler, and their suppliers.

Kate and I stared out the Falcon's window as we exited I-75 at 11 Mile Road and turned east. The rows of south Royal Oak bungalows popped into view. The bungalows were designed identically, with a center entrance, a small living room to the left, and a smaller dining area to the right, with a small kitchen behind it. Through the living room, a short hallway led to a bathroom and two small bedrooms. *Small* and *bungalow* were synonyms. Stairs located past the bathroom led up to an attic that almost always was transformed into a large bedroom for the parents. The sum of the small rooms was less than a thousand square feet.

"Now I remember Royal Oak," Kate said.

We turned west on 11 Mile Road toward Vermont Street, where my lifelong friends Elvis, Mark McInerney, and John Parcell rented a three-bedroom bungalow. We had been friends since the first day of first grade, when Catholic school providence ordained that you stood in lines in alphabetical order. So it happened that McInerney, Moore, Muldoon, and Parcell were in uninterrupted order. If there had been a Newman or Olsen in our first-grade class, this would have been a different story. Since Catholic school required an enormous amount of time standing in line, we became tight quickly and firmly. We remained inseparable as each school year passed by.

When my house burned down, my three friends united to keep me from ruining my young life. In spite of their own creative

rowdiness, they knew I was out of control, and if they didn't inter-
cede, I was going to either implode or explode. They acted as a
counterweight to my episodes of binge drinking, vandalism, and
fights. They weren't saints. But compared to me they did appear
compos mentis.

They kept in close touch with my big sister, Ann, who became
the leader of my family after the fire. "Our boys," as Ann referred
to my friends, spent a lot of time at our rented house after the fire,
bringing meals and school supplies and canned goods from their
parents. It wasn't just me they helped. They kept an eye out for my
twin sisters, April and Angela, and particularly my little brother,
Donnie. They also were close enough to know when I fought with
my big sister, who struggled to control me. When I went off, the
boys took me to their homes to cool off. My troubles became a
point of common unity for Elvis, Mark, John, and their parents.

In the midst of my personal chaos, I knew I owed them all. I
didn't know how to tell them thank you. I didn't often think about
how much their friendship had saved me, and when I did, I was
usually standing on the side of the road, with plenty of time to tip-
toe through my emotions. We were companions in folly and had a
decade and a half of shared experiences at twenty years old.

Yet it was more than that. I guessed that it wasn't just the time
we spent together. We had seen each other disgustingly drunk,
frightened out of our minds from an escapade, hurt from a girl that
had ditched us, pumped up after a football game or a rock concert.
We lurched away from our parents and support systems by the
time we were thirteen. Yet our acts of charity and real friendship we
learned came from our parents and our upbringing. Even me.

This is how I figured things were, and I tried to find ways to
pay them back, even though I was perennially broke. But I knew
an emotional debt was mounting, even though I wasn't sure how
interest compounded on this kind of a loan.

When we graduated from high school, another social system
fell away as I saw classmates leave for college or take full-time,
good-paying factory jobs. I couldn't concentrate on anything more
than a day in advance. I argued with my sister Ann every day about
getting a job, getting drunk, and joining the ranks of adults.

After graduation, I began to disappear on hitchhiking trips for
months at a time. At the same time, my trio of friends moved into
the small house together on Vermont Street, which became my

haven after my trips. Even during this period, my friends never veered in their attention to me or my family. They would take turns checking on Ann, Angela, April, and Donnie while I was gone, shoveling snow, mowing the lawn, fixing the toilet. I wasn't given a free pass. Each of them took their turn trying to hold me accountable for my negligence after each trip.

In spite of our reckless behavior, we were inexorably marching toward adulthood. Since high school, my fights and drunken vandalism had all but disappeared. My friends were mostly working regularly. Renting the house on Vermont was a big step. A step forward and a step back. Along with my friends, we had discovered pot and the occasional potpourri of other drugs that had become widely available in the early seventies. Each of us wrestled with the effects of partying that included the combination of beer and drugs. We pushed a bit farther out on the edge. It was not a healthy development. But the rent check was due every month, so my friends dragged their butts out of bed, hangover or not, and made it to work, just like their dads.

I did wake up enough to realize that my sister Ann was my biggest supporter and that my bond with her, April, Angela, and my brother Donnie was stronger than the special wrath I held against my dad for wrecking our family. Whenever I was in Royal Oak, I visited our new home, usually after a reentry weekend at my friends' place. I worked hard at the rented Moore house and spent time with my sisters and brother, trying my best to develop new memories for our traumatized family.

While we all carried the millstone of our family story in our own fashion, we had a sense of humor about it all. It took me a while to adapt. My scarred younger brother kept his balance with his dark wit. At our first family dinner, after he finally came home after months in the University of Michigan Burn Center, he offered up this prayer: "Lord, I'm grateful I finally made it home and that my sisters and brother are here together with me to share this meal. And Lord, I ask your blessing on this house and my family—what's left of it, that is. I'm not complaining, Lord, but I would say that you've left us in a world of hurt with my mom dead and my dad in prison for killing her. It does seem like a bit of overkill on the sacrifice side of the ledger, Lord. No pun intended. You must have your reasons, and who am I to question you? I am praying that you give us some time to recover before the next challenge. And it wouldn't hurt if you could send some cash our way to pay some of the bills. Finally, Lord, I'm praying that Ann hasn't burnt my 'welcome home' dinner tonight, as that would be truly playing dirty pool! Amen."

Donnie picked up his bowed head with a big smile and winked at Ann. April, Angela, Ann, and I looked at each other, incredulous that our twelve-year-old brother could spill out that prayer. I didn't know whether to laugh or cry, and I saw my siblings didn't either. Ann started laughing first, even though her eyes were filled with tears, and we all joined in, Donnie laughing the loudest. Our precocious brother helped us take a big jump toward becoming a family again.

Elvis made the right-hand turn onto Vermont and pulled into his driveway. Mark and John were draped over cheap mesh lawn chairs on the tiny cement porch, long-neck Budweisers in hand. They laughed and whooped as they recognized me. We exchanged brother handshakes, pushes, shoves, and hugs on the front lawn.

"What in God's name is going on here? Where did you pick up this dredge of society and this outstanding-looking chick? I thought you were in Florida, Moore?" Mark asked, while releasing me from a headlock.

"Yeah, what the hell, Luke? We just restocked the refrigerator since the last time you left town," John laughed.

"Long story, amigos, long story," I sighed.

Elvis intervened. "Long and unbelievable, and it will wait. Gentlemen, let me introduce—"

"Kathleen Marie Brady, the girl who made me break my vow to be a bachelor forever," John Parcell said, interrupting Elvis. "Third grade, Sister Mary Leo's room, in the cloakroom, Kathleen Marie Brady stole my innocence," John continued.

"Stole your *what?* You convinced me to give you a kiss because you were so sad about your hamster dying. And Sister Mary Leo caught us, marking me as a harlot for the rest of the year. And then I found out you didn't even own a hamster! I remember you, John Parcell," Kate replied.

We all laughed as John tried to defend his third-grade honor without success. We poured inside the bungalow and opened the refrigerator for beers, assembling around the dining room table, chattering away a Friday evening.

John was a dietary assistant at Beaumont Hospital, the large, growing suburban hospital. He made $3.45 per hour and was frustrated that he was limited to providing appropriate dietary portions for the hospital's patients. He was an artist by vocation, but as the fifth of ten children, his parents had maintained a steady drumbeat of the importance of a secure job with benefits. He was the only scholastic achiever in the group and had completed two years of college before running out of tuition money. At six feet tall, solidly built with a chiseled chin, he was the handsome one of our group. He made us laugh easier and faster than anyone we knew. He was a natural mimic. His interpretation of life's day-to-day events boiled existence down to what really happened in people's lives. John was smart, good-looking and funny, yet buried underneath was a patch of insecurity that prevented him from seeing the potential that was so evident to us. His humility added another endearing quality.

Mark McInerny covered the dinette chair, leaning back, happy to be done with his long week inside the Royal Oak Post Office. Jobs at the post office were paying $6.40 an hour plus full benefits, a fortune in 1973. Mark was over six feet three, and his overgrown, black, curly hair added another two inches, to an already big, bear-like guy. When he smiled, his eyes crinkled. He was a calm guy until the "unknown beer" was drunk, and then he turned nasty. We called the trigger the "unknown beer" because one night it would be the eighth beer and the next night the twelfth. Mark could hold his alcohol remarkably well up until the trigger was pulled. We had learned to steer clear of him when a curled-lip, mean-spirited look that was dubbed "the snurl" appeared on his face.

The work pace at the post office was murderous, according to Mark. While unionized, the supervisors were notorious for their ability to keep the mail sorters on edge by enforcing nasty work rules. Mark was young and tough, but he worked his eight hours knowing, hoping, that this wasn't all the future held. But the present meant he held a good job with benefits, which was a beautiful thing for the third-born of seven children. His dad told him regularly he was blessed to be making so much money at such an early age. It was a mixed blessing.

The five of us sat around the dinette table, drinking beer, talking, and laughing. Kate was hanging on Elvis's every word, which wasn't surprising. Elvis had the gene, the pheromones, the laugh, and the eyes that immediately attracted women. Charisma. I did not have it and envied his natural ability. Elvis told a well-worn tale of one our misadventures, which we laughed at and added anecdotes to.

He held up his hand to us and said, "Mark and John, I have a serious story you should know. Luke and Annette have been through a real bummer of a time. It's kinda worn them out. Let me tell it to you."

Elvis told a condensed version of Annette Brady's death and the aftermath. Mark and John were agape.

Mark gasped, "Christ, Luke, even for you, that's—that's beyond comprehension. Kate, I'm—we're so sorry for your loss. You're welcome to stay here as long as you like."

"Or until you can't stand the sight or smell of us, whichever comes first," John said, deadpan, cutting off the morbidity of the moment.

"Thanks, you guys. I think," Kate replied.

It became very quiet in the small dining alcove on Vermont Avenue in Royal Oak, Michigan. It wasn't awkward, it was more like a moment of rest from the implausible story Kate and I had brought with us.

Mark interrupted the silence. "John, we haven't heard a story from you yet. What's the topic tonight, brother?"

John conjured up a pensive face, put his hand on his chin, and shook his head up and down slowly.

"Well, nothing much exciting has happened to me recently. However, I am willing to share the events of my week, if it will keep me in your good graces and keep a full beer in my hand."

"Give that man a beer!" Elvis hollered.

"Coming right up," Mark replied, and in an instant a cold can of Bud was sailing across the room toward John. In one motion he snagged the beer with his left hand, popped the tab, raised it to his mouth, and gulped the beer until it was half gone.

"Ah, that's the ticket. Keep 'em coming, Mark."

John put his hand over his mouth and let loose a theatrical belch that sounded like a walrus in heat. "Why excuse me, I have no idea where that came from."

"As I was saying: my week. I did have a wee bit of an accident at work last week. While demonstrating my new dance, which I call the "Freaky Deaky," for my fellow dietary department employees, I took a header on a wet spot in the hospital's tray-cleaning room and tweaked my knee. It was just bad enough for my boss, who we affectionately call "Miss Sweats-a-Lot" because of the sizeable pit rings that appear on her dietary supervisor uniform at the first sign of stress, to gurney me into the hospital's physical therapy clinic. She was worried about another workers' comp case, I guess.

"So every morning this past week, I spent my first two hours of work getting my left knee and leg massaged and iced by Sally 'Boob-a-licious' O'Hara. In addition, my therapy regime calls for a soak in a whirlpool tub, attended by none other than Howie 'Quick-Glance' Matuzak. Remember Howie from the St. Mary's football shower room? It went without saying that no self-respecting adolescent macho male would ever lower his field of vision below someone's neck in the showers. Not Howie. Man, he had the quickest glance in the entire Catholic League. And now this numb-nuts is running the whirlpool room. Let me tell you, his glance ain't quite so quick anymore."

John paused for dramatic effect and drained the can of beer. Another full beer flew through the air, repeating the previous ritual. John handed the latest empty can to Kate and in a dead-on John Wayne imitation said, "Here, little lady, hold on to this, while I save the women and children and finish this little old story.

"Anyway, did I mention that for most of this therapy session my privates were only barely covered by tiny white towel? Sally would ice me down, and I swear she and Howie were a team: one distracted me while the other copped a look. I'm not making this up. They were a freaking tag team! I wouldn't mind if it was just Sally. Her head may be shaped like a half-barrel of beer, but her breasts are like rockets. They were pointed right at me, like nuclear warheads, every time she rubbed my thigh—and by the way, she went way above my injured knee. I had to use all the powers of self-control I learned reading the CliffsNotes version of *Transcendental Meditation* to avoid flying my freak flag high, if you know what I mean.

"When I got done with the treatment, I had to meet with the clinic's doctor, a total cover-your-ass move, so I wouldn't file the workers' comp claim. He made me take some new vitamins that are supposed to speed the healing process. His explanation was quite technical and he asked me if I understood.

"I told him, 'Sure, Doc, the vitamins are like a team of very tiny folks who set up an off-site rehab center, right near the knee joint. They are a hardy little band of workers, and I see them as serious elves, elves in doctor jackets, with glasses, but still wearing green elf hats. In unison, they brush and clean the muscles and ligaments around the knee, giving them a good workout, sort of sprucing up the room around the knee, improving Mr. Knee's confidence. While they're working away, they sing this little ditty in their very best munchkin voices:

> *We are the Vitamin Elves,*
> *The Vitamin Elves, the Vitamin Elves*
> *We work all day to heal your knee,*
> *Heal your knee, heal your knee,*
> *But we don't get paid bupkus and that's not cool,*
> *So we might very well go on strike right now!*

'The Vitamin Elves are a lot like cheerleaders for the knee, except they don't have pom-poms and short skirts. Well, maybe more like unionized cheerleaders. Yeah, I think the Vitamin Elves concept is a good way to describe what's going on. What do you think, Doc?'

"Both of the Doc's eyebrows popped up into his forehead, a confused look crossed his face, and he told me he wasn't sure what to think about that. He also suggested that I might be a candidate for the hospital's new employee guidance counseling service. Which prompted the obvious question, 'Do I get out of work for that, too?' And that, my friends, is a week in the life of John Parcell." John took an exaggerated bow and we all clapped and hooted at his performance.

The moment erupted with Elvis jumping up and announcing, "C'mon, I'm playing at the Psychedelic Midway tonight. Let's get ready to rock!"

"What in God's name is that, a drug circus?" I asked.

John laughed and explained, "Well, my vagabond friend, you're going to find this hard to believe, but the Psychedelic Midway is the City of Royal Oak's attempt to provide wholesome teenage entertainment with a hip name and a headline band in a "safe" environment. That's what the posters are telling us. But I don't think they have a clue what's going to happen. I think it's pretty much a dream come true for us."

Elvis laughed louder and enlightened Kate and me further. "Yep, right in the heart of downtown Royal Oak, at the farmers market of all places, starting at 8:00 p.m. tonight, is the second part of a five-part concert series. Believe it or not, the Royal Oak Recreation Department has managed to book the hottest rock-and-roll talent in Detroit. And my band is going to open for Canned Heat, Mountain, the MC5, and the Bob Seger band—ain't that wild? Christ, Seger's 'Heavy Music' single is playing nationwide now. How the seersucker-suited Republicans in our hallowed city government became concert promoters is beyond me. But the word is out and the farmers market is going to howl tonight!"

I learned that the first Psychedelic Midway event, held two weeks earlier, was largely ignored by the town's young people, including my friends. Any event sponsored by the recreation department was by definition less than cool. But word moved fast about the great bands, and this night was turning into a mob scene at the farmers market, which normally acted as a weekend outlet for vegetable and fruit farmers to proffer their local produce along with other flea market offerings.

The opening act usually saw a sparse audience as it warmed up for the headliners. But not tonight. Elvis and his band had a strong local following, and the draw of name bands in our hometown filled the market by 7:30 p.m. with high school students, hippies, bikers, and jocks. We all crammed into the surreal setting of the farmers market, with a stage built up at one end and a large sign proclaiming the "Psychedelic Midway" framed paradoxically by a mural featuring a giant pumpkin, celery, and radishes on the back wall.

Elvis's band was named Retrograde, and he had four accomplished band members behind him. But Elvis was the show. He knew his audience and started strong with a set built around standard sixties rock anthems, including "Satisfaction" and "All Along the Watchtower"—but different enough from their originals to keep the crowd dancing.

He only had twenty-five minutes, so he moved from tune to tune fast and furiously, with the audience response growing as they danced by themselves, the custom of the day. A thousand people leaned in and grooved, and Elvis was the star. With one song to go, he stopped and asked the audience, "I need your help out there for a minute. I know it's way past Christmas, but I just love this song. So, let's finish this set with a little sing-along. This is a song you all know from Christmas caroling. It goes like this." The band stopped playing, and, microphone in hand; Elvis began singing a cappella.

> *Chestnuts roasting on an open fire,*
> *Jack Frost nipping on your nose,*
> *Yuletide carols being sung by a choir,*
> *And folks dressed up like Eskimos.*

"Come on, everybody, you know the words, join in. Sing along!" Elvis demanded.

Amazingly, many of the beered-up, half-stoned teenage crowd did just that. Even the few gnarly bikers and fully stoned hippies were humming the song. Elvis could pull off this kind of stunt.

He came down off the stage, mic in hand, and found Kate, who had moved close to the stage with Mark, John, and me. He cleared some space around himself and melodramatically, on one knee, sang directly to her.

Elvis sang the Christmas song on a sweaty April night in Michigan at the farmers market, doing his best to sing his way into her heart. It wasn't the first time he had used his act to woo an attractive woman. But in front of this big crowd, even for a hambone like Elvis, this was shooting the moon.

> *Everybody knows a turkey and some mistletoe,*
> *Help to make the season bright.*
> *Tiny tots with their eyes all aglow,*
> *Will find it hard to sleep tonight.*

> *They know that Santa's on his way;*
> *He's loaded lots of toys and goodies on his sleigh.*
> *And every mother's child is going to spy,*
> *To see if reindeer really know how to fly.*

And so I'm offering this simple phrase,
To kids from one to ninety-two,
Although its been said many times, many ways,
A very Merry Christmas to you.

He strode back onto the bandstand as the band broke out into a rock-and-roll version of the song with wailing guitars and a drum crescendo. This was Elvis's signature. Take a song that everybody knew from their childhood, sing it as a standard, and then, just as it becomes a little bit over-sentimental, hit them with a hard-driving, hard-rock version. It was a great, yet predictable, hook to end a set. The crowd roared as Elvis repeated the final chorus.

Kate was smiling, watching the show. Elvis looked directly at her, singing right to her. Finishing the song to wild applause, he pointed his finger at her and called into the microphone. "That one was for you, Kate Brady."

Kate blushed and laughed. John, Mark, and I rolled our eyes. *Another one bites the dust,* I thought.

"I see Elvis is a bit smitten with our visitor, eh, John?" Mark asked.

John didn't answer. He was thinking. He leaned over to me and shouted to us over the din, "You know, this sing-along thing is a good idea. But, if he used the right songs, changed the act a bit, he could get everybody singing. That would be cool."

"Or you could do it, John," I yelled back. He just smiled. John had given Elvis the idea for the sing-along and other ideas for the band. I knew from sharing a twelve-pack of Stroh's with him on the railroad tracks that John privately thought he could do stand-up comedy. He was a unique guy—could be spectacularly creative and yet very private and introspective. His ambition was a ticking insecurity bomb waiting to go off.

The cheering for Elvis and his band receded, the headline acts for the Psychedelic Midway set up quickly, and hard-driving rock pounded off the vegetable tables had been stood on end and pushed to the far walls of the building. The ceiling of the market started to fill with cigarette and pot smoke. Six packs and quarts of beer had been smuggled easily past the four auxiliary police officers who thought they were supposed to be chaperoning something more akin to a Boy Scout Jamboree.

Mark met up with his girlfriend Lois and led her by the hand back to us. He introduced her to Kate as Elvis found us at the back of the market, mini beer cooler in hand.

"Anybody need a Bud?" he asked.

We gave Elvis a hard time about the Christmas song, laughing at his dramatics. "Hey, it was John's idea, not mine," he replied.

"I don't remember suggesting you get down on one knee before this poor, unsuspecting southern girl and embarrass the living shit out of both of you."

"Okay, I'm an artist. I get to ad lib." Old friends patted Elvis on the back as Kate stood by reservedly.

He turned to her and said, "So, Kate, did you enjoy the set?"

Kate smiled and said, "You have lots of talent and energy, and you're not afraid to take risks. But if you keep pushing your voice like that, you'll be burnt out in three years."

My group of friends all laughed at the concise review. "Hey Elvis, this lady seems to know what she's talking about. She's not some groupie telling you how incredible you are!" Mark added.

Elvis grinned wryly and moved closer to Kate, taking her elbow and moving her away from his friends. "How do you know so much about voice?"

"From my mother," Kate replied.

"Then let's sit down and hear more about your mom." They found a picnic table outside the market, where Elvis learned about the Bradys, Tennessee, and the music business. By the end of the night, they were holding hands and laughing. Even the local groupies knew to leave Elvis alone.

The night rocked on as Bob Seger's band brought the thousand suburban teenagers to their feet; dancing, writhing, and screaming at what would be the last of the Psychedelic Midways. When the mayor of Royal Oak stopped by to see how the recreation department's teenage social was going and saw the sweat-soaked teenagers dancing wildly under a cloud of blue smoke, his gills turned green, as the local expression went. He saw his election prospects disappearing if these kids' parents, or worse yet, a *Daily Tribune* reporter, saw this craziness. The popularity of the Psychedelic Midway was completely unexpected and unwanted by the clueless organizers. The mayor rushed off to find someone to fire.

Around ten o'clock, I watched Kate and Elvis walk toward the parking lot together. The rest of us left the concert about an hour later and returned to the Vermont house. The faded Falcon was already in the driveway. We found Elvis's first-floor bedroom door shut. I assumed Elvis was successfully earning another notch on his carnal belt, which surprised me. I thought Kate was made of tougher stuff and at least would wait a couple of days before hopping into Elvis's bed. I was also jealous of my friend.

The rest of us drank beer and played pinochle until the game broke up and everyone silently found their bedrooms. I was left alone, drinking and chain-smoking and working out a plan. I had been in town one night and was ready to leave. I knew it wasn't going to be simple; I also needed some time at home after living in the Knoxville trauma chamber for close to three weeks. And while my trip to Florida had been aborted, my return to Royal Oak would be a welcome surprise to my family, especially Donnie. I could use this time to find a temporary job to both save some money for my next trip and to put some money in the family cookie jar. Any time I could spend around my family was good for all of us.

But I also knew I had places to go, people to see, and things to do. I didn't have an inkling where to begin. I knew that remaining in Royal Oak for long wasn't going to be part of the plan. When and where my mind wandered, my feet weren't far behind, and this visit was starting to feel like the end of the first part of this still-to-be-defined quest. *Onward and forward,* my restless soul was telling me, and, as usual, that was more of a general direction than a plan, and that uncertainty fired me up for the unknown excitement that most certainly lay ahead!

Chapter 13

September 2003

My twisted storytelling habit didn't scare off Tom Lutac, and he seemed reassured by Marta's straightforwardness. After lunch, we found our places back in the van, and I played Vivaldi's *Four Seasons* on the CD player as we drove northward wordlessly. I had replaced highbrow books with highbrow music to impress people, even my wife and daughter. Insecurities don't die, they mutate. I rationalized I was reliving my mom's love of classical music. It took years, but I was learning to remember and honor the best part of my family before the fire. As my own family life with Marta and Roberta took hold, I found poignant comfort in revisiting my childhood and certain points of joy. The good memories occluded Dad. The bad memories were Dad.

I leaned back, let my shoulders drop, and felt my body relax. Mom loved classical music, and *The Four Seasons* was her favorite recording. She would carefully pull the New York Philharmonic record out of its paper sleeve and delicately place it on the spindle of our record player.

"Listen to the genius of this music, Luke. It's heavenly," she would gush.

I pictured her in summer shorts, hair tied up and drinking lemonade, smiling at me. I slid a glance to Marta and she smiled, the look in her eyes a mirror on our years together and the battle of chasing the devils from my soul. I don't think I married my mom, but it was odd that Marta's diastema was reminiscent of Mom's chipped tooth.

Tom interrupted my reverie. "Mr. Moore, do you mind if I ask you how you became a psychologist?"

"That's a long story, Tom. The short answer is that in my wayward youth, I spent time with some abominably bad shrinks and counselors who had degrees up the yin-yang and not an ounce of common sense. When I finally found my feet a few years later and started attending community college, I found a psychology professor who changed my view on the profession. And here I am today."

"That's cool. I've spent time with shrinks. They were all assho— oops, excuse me, Mr. Moore. I didn't like them at all. Why did you get sent to the shrink?" Tom asked.

"Oh, nothing too much, just kid stuff," I answered.

"Well, thanks for answering my question," Tom said and turned back to his book.

I decided against taking Tom up on his offer to come clean about his story. He'd tell me when he was ready. But there was something about Tom that made me uneasy. He tipped his hand by telling me he had spent time with shrinks. Maybe he was too earnest. Or I could be overreacting. My sixth sense wasn't perfect, but damn near. I relaxed as the gentle hills of northern Michigan unfolded in front of me, a touch of fall color appearing in a few trees. I thought back.

My memory flashed to a time after the fire. It was a long and strange road that led to this point. Mom's death guillotined our family traditions. The loss of family rituals at age fifteen threw me off-kilter, and I didn't regain my balance easily. I compensated by running away from memories, good and bad. As I grew older and recovered, I could selectively seek out elements of the story and examine them. Through my training as a psychologist, I had become my own best and worst patient. Highway driving helped me work through the details again, some middle-aged-fuzzy and others frighteningly distinct

My nadir was not the night of the fire. That came when Dad was arrested a week later for the murder of my mother.

After the fire, a wave of community support had put money in Dad's pockets and provided two free motel rooms for him and my sisters to stay in. We were a feature story in the *Daily Tribune:* "Mom Lost in Fire, Royal Oak Rallies to Help Family" was the headline. But Ann, April, and Angela knew something was wrong. They watched Dad sit in a chair outside the motel room, smoking and drinking beer after beer, and yet he didn't seem to get drunk. Dad and the girls visited Donnie and me in the hospital each day. On Sunday morning, he sat in the waiting room of the hospital, chain-smoking while my sisters talked to me. Then there was a commotion, and through the glass wall, I saw the cops handcuffing Dad. He looked back at us with dull eyes. His skin was gray. He looked anguished and guilty. Two officers led him away.

Angela and April screamed, "What are you doing? What's going on? Where are you taking Dad?" There was an Oakland County social worker with the cop, who stayed and herded my twin sisters back into my room. Ann had not moved from my bedside.

I heard, "There's no easy way to say this. Your father has been arrested for the murder of your mother." I didn't hear anything after that.

Earlier that week, the state police arson squad had completed their work. A barmaid at Sid and Wally's bar started talking about my dad's drunken rages and his plan to burn the house for insurance money. The arson squad's evidence and the barmaid's story led to my dad's arrest, trial, conviction, and imprisonment for at least thirty years. And my journey from perdition to redemption began.

The days and weeks that followed kept adding nuggets of details that made the unbearable story more sordid and awful. The gambling, the insurance policy, bookies and their thugs. *The Tribune* blared the bad news one headline at a time.

Our family should have been obliterated when the social workers tried to farm out the kids. Donnie was desperately injured from his burns. I was recovering physically, but I was almost mute. I couldn't lift the blackness from my thoughts. April and Angela returned to high school as the trauma played out in front of them. It was like drowning over and over and over again.

Big sister Ann saved us. At twenty years old, she lived at home, working part-time as a waitress at the Suzie-Q and taking night classes at Oakland Community College. She had been our babysitter for as long as we could remember. But, nothing in her life prepared her or us for this epic disaster. Ann became indomitable, convincing first our family and then everyone around us to keep the family together.

The neighborhood, and church rallied around Ann. There was no help from Mom's only brother, living with his large family in West Virginia and struggling with his own day-to-day poverty. They sent single dollar bills with prayers—all they had to give. Dad's two sisters had disappeared from his life years ago.

Ann systematically found allies in St. Mary's, the Department of Social Services, the Salvation Army, neighbors, and the local newspaper. Father Mike Mitchell, the sixty-year-old pastor of St. Mary's, became her patron after she outlined her plan. He was a curmudgeon by nature and not an easy sell. Ann's strong will, confidence, and sensible plan won him over. He helped her commandeer the money and support needed to make a new start near our old neighborhood. Ann quit school and worked nights to buttress her income. With Social Security checks, Angela's and April's part-time jobs, my paper route money, and a stipend from the newly formed Roberta Moore Foundation, Ann paid the rent, bought groceries, and shopped at Kmart for essentials.

The twins were seniors in high school, and both volunteered to stay at home and work after graduation. But Angela's high test scores and 3.8 GPA won her a full ride to Michigan State, and April won a writing contest and scholarship to Kalamazoo College, an exclusive private school. Ann knew they both needed some independence of their own, and insisted they go. Her approval came with the condition that they both work and send money home monthly, no matter how little, and that they must come home every other weekend to help with Donnie's ongoing therapy and Sunday dinner. I was given my own individual marching orders, which I mostly ignored. Ann and April were troopers. I was a draft dodger.

Sunday dinner had been Mom's tradition. She made pot roast, roasted turkey or chicken, standing rib roast, and other main courses that came to life with four, five, and even six additional courses, and finished with intricate desserts like crème brûlée. Mom was a naturally gifted chef who learned to cook by watching and talking to chefs and the staff at the London Chop House, Detroit's finest restaurant. She worked as a waitress at the Chop House before she married my dad, a wine salesman who sold the lower-end wines to the Chop House's renowned wine cellar.

That's where our family story began: an Icelandic wine sales-man courting a Polish waitress. Dad talked about his unhappy past, especially after a few beers. Mom spoke fondly of her childhood. Years after the turmoil, I researched our family tree with Ann. We wrote letters and made phone calls to our distant relatives and learned the story of our ancestry. We talked to Mom's friends, who knew more about her troubled marriage than we ever would have guessed. We pieced our lineage together with a chronicle of how Dad went mad. Our investigation felt like finishing a crossword puzzle. It felt good, even though we weren't sure why. Our dad's history replayed like a black-and-white B movie. And Mom's was like an early color home movie.

Everything about Dad was a shade unusual, starting with his Icelandic-Irish heritage. His father, Emmet Moore, left Ireland in 1931 after a run-in with Irish gamblers in Dublin. He signed on as a mate on an ancient barge and headed to Reykjavik, Iceland. Being poor in Ireland in the 1930's could be desperate, but being Irish and poor in Reykjavik was colder, bleaker, and even more desperate. He kept financially afloat and in vodka by signing up with whaling and fishing boat excursions. He hated sea life and as a result worked only intermittently.

A tryst with a saloonkeeper's daughter resulted in a shotgun marriage, and although having a father-in-law in the saloon busi-ness was akin to being Icelandic royalty, he drank his way out of favor quickly. He continued to fish sporadically and without enthu-siasm. Three children and five years later, he found work fishing in Nova Scotia, Iceland's version of Florida. Dad was the youngest child of Emmet and Marie Moore. He was two years old when the family moved to Nova Scotia. Dad was named after his maternal grandfather, the saloon owner. His name was his only keepsake of Iceland.

Nova Scotia didn't improve Emmet Moore's work ethic or abil-ity to hold his liquor. A series of moves followed, each one leaving a trail of unpaid debts leading to a downward economic spiral end-ing in London, Ontario. He died at forty from a life lived badly. Dad's mother followed with lung cancer two years later. Trygvi was eighteen and on his own. His sisters had moved to the States as soon as they were able to save enough money for a fresh start.

Dad seemed to have escaped the darkness of his upbringing. He was smart, engaging and charming. A natural salesman, he was told. By his early twenties, he was selling beer and wine to party stores in metropolitan Detroit. When he met a lithe, quietly capable Roberta, she was managing her three-to-four martini-lunch customers at the exclusive London Chop House restaurant, and he was a top salesman for the General Wine Company.

The romance lasted for three years, when Mom told Dad that either a ring would be showing up on her finger very soon, or he would be seeking companionship elsewhere. Trygvi had been attentive and romantic during their extended courtship, but he was prone to moodiness and periods of disappearance in which Mom would not see him for weeks. At twenty-four, Mom had parlayed an entry-level waitress job at a Detroit breakfast nook into a series of progressively better-tipping jobs, ending at the Chop House, which could produce over fifty dollars in tips from her extended lunch shift. With the promise of a promotion to the elite dinner shift, she was at the top of her craft. She lived alone in a nice apartment in Palmer Park, an upscale Detroit neighborhood that catered to professionals and singles. Making more money than her father, a plumber by trade, she was taking a half-step up the economic ladder. But Mom was a planner, and her plan did not include becoming a successful but single thirty-year-old waitress. She envisioned marriage and children, mimicking the lives her girlfriends had begun, the norm for the 1950s. She loved Trygvi and had a substantial investment of precious time with him. His periodic erratic behavior worried her, but not enough to make her think about tossing him aside. It was with mixed feelings that she gave him the ultimatum.

Dad agreed almost immediately to her demand, and Roberta Wisnewski married Trygvi Moore in a small, but festive, wedding at St. Florian Church, her neighborhood parish in Hamtramck. What started with a marriage and ended in a murder was filled in between with a family raised in the 1950s and '60s by a loving, intelligent, and insightful mother who was wonderfully typical and likable, and by a moody father who doted on his wife and children, worked hard, and, apart from his interesting lineage, seemed to fit into suburban life. It might have been a life led happily and unremarkably except for a well-hidden, inherited time bomb: gambling.

It was sports betting that led to the unraveling of our family. Aside from the five-dollar sports bets on football, Mom never knew that Dad bet, much less that he had incrementally waded into the squalid world of bookies, betting on everything from ponies to greyhounds, basketball, and elections. He kept a separate bank account and for years was surprisingly lucky. At one point, the account balance was over five thousand dollars. It was his secret, abetted by his salesman's lifestyle.

Like most amateur gamblers, he hit a losing streak and then got careless, betting on long shots or fool's bets, like the over-under number in pro basketball games. From 1966 to the winter of 1968, the bank account was overdrawn and he went thirty thousand dollars down, betting to a ten-thousand-dollar limit with three bookies in Detroit, Lansing, and Toledo. When word inevitably leaked through the bookies' network that he had played their credit lines against each other, Dad discovered the dark side of bookies. He was beaten in January of 1968 and again in February, and reasonably feared for his life in March. Mom believed him when he told her he was mugged on the job after the first beating. When the policeman who delivered him to the hospital the second time took her aside and told her, gently but firmly, to wise up, she began to understand.

Dad was in morose denial, certain he could bet his way out of catastrophe. The second mortgage on the house was still unknown to Mom. He wouldn't talk to his wife about the beatings, but his fear was apparent. The bookies' enforcers were very good at their job; they told him the third time would be the last, and that it would go much more slowly and painfully. The life insurance policy on my mom became his only way out. His madness ruled and ruined us. My dad's date with earthly ruin and eternal damnation coincided with my baccalaureate in youthful debauchery, followed by my Master's degree in Catholic guilt and, eventually, my PhD in salvation.

That's how we came to our life without parents. We started calling Ann "Big Ann," in spite of her five foot two stature. She put her life on hold and held us together.

"Come on back, Luke," my wife Marta called from her front-seat perch. She knew where I was when the faraway gaze and tightened lips appeared.

"Here I am. Back safe and sound," I replied.

"Not likely. You look like you're about halfway through that daydream. Don't you think that a smart shrink like you could do something about that obsessive-compulsive tendency you have?" Marta said.

"I've found it's best to treat that demon carefully. Don't starve or overfeed the disorder, is the best policy," I said.

"Face it, Luke, you just love to obsess, and you ain't giving it up. So finish your daydream and come back and join us folks living in the here and now," she said.

"A daydream is a lot like a good story, Marta. You can't rush the ending."

"And a good daydream usually has some good sex involved, too. And daydreams may be where your love life is going, if you catch my drift."

"Good point. I'm thinking maybe it's possible to fast-forward a daydream," I replied.

I returned to the Lost Souls.

Chapter 14

April 1973

I woke up on the living room couch at the Vermont house with a sour head. A Psychedelic Midway hangover. I showered in the bathroom and noted for the hundredth time that the black-and-white checkerboard floor tiles were the same as in the bathroom in the house where I grew up.

I preferred baths, rather than showers. As a kid, I loved to sit in the bathtub Indian-style, close to the bath faucet, my hands open, cupping the hot water and splashing it on my knees, one at a time, back and forth, back and forth as the tub filled. When the water level reached my crossed knees, I would lean back in the large, white ceramic tub and let the hot water cover me.

The tub held the water's heat, and was solid and comforting. Water was a tonic for me. When I was small, I would float in the tub, letting the water lap up against my ears as I closed my eyes. Showers were for cleaning, baths were for relaxing before the day began. The tub in the Vermont house was ceramic, but far too scody to allow for a bath.

I scrounged a breakfast of frozen English muffins with grape jam and orange juice from the Frigidaire. My friends were generous in their support of my nomadic lifestyle, even while shaking their heads in disbelief that anyone would want to live this way. I thought back on their acts of friendship.

Whenever I needed a meal, a place to stay, beer, or a couple of bucks for a pack of cigarettes and a sixteen-ounce Pepsi, they were there. Yet they razzed me for my dissolute ways. They talked about my lack of a job and girlfriend. They called me a hobo and a bum, but I knew they had confidence that I would rebound. They considered my tragedy and accommodated me. In truth, they had known I was different from them even before the fire, but now it was easier to rationalize. It helped that I cleaned up after myself, worked—even if sporadically—and was a good party partner. As I steeped my tea in the kitchen, waiting for the aspirin to melt the fog, I wondered if we could stay friends for a lifetime. The friendships had rough edges. Binge drinking bouts brought out the worst in us.

We took on testing fate with a fresh fervor when we started high school; we explored teenage invincibility in a series of enthusiastic misadventures that included fast cars, beer, hitchhiking, pranks, camping, theft, light vandalism, sports, and pot smoking. We regularly tested our imagination and nerve. These testosterone-driven episodes taught us to trust and rely on each other for illogical support in our edgy quests.

By high school, there were upwards of fifteen to twenty boys gathering on weekends at St. Mary's parking lot for consensus-building sessions that would have made a business consultant proud. Our project was determining what havoc we might wreak on any given night. The group consisted of kids who attended St. Mary's, along with those that left or were kicked out and who now attended Dondero, the south side public high school. Others were from nearby Berkley and had attended Our Lady of La Salette Elementary School and found they enjoyed the recklessness.

The four of us had earned the nickname *the Lost Souls,* which became widely applied to anyone who hung together for the evening or weekend activities. Sister Maris Stella, our intimidating high school principal, had coined the label. John Parcell had engineered and engaged us in a plot that entailed super-gluing every classroom lock at St. Mary's. He thought it would be a good idea to get our high school reputation off to a good start. So, three weeks into our freshman year, we snuck back into school through an unlocked locker-room window and completed our mission, causing school to be cancelled the next morning when teachers found they couldn't get in their classrooms.

Within a half-hour of completing our caper, we were in our homes doing our homework, our alibi solid. But word leaked out, as it always did, and the four of us found ourselves seated in the principal's office the next morning, summoned by the omnipresent PA system.

Sister Maris Stella was at least six feet tall, and her habit hung on her gaunt frame like a ghost. When she smiled with either evil or good intentions, two spiny canine teeth appeared menacingly beneath her upper lip. The four of us sat on an ancient bench in her spartan office staring upward at the ghost of Christmas future. Sister Maris Stella laid out coldly all the trouble and cost the glue incident had caused.

"Boys, you might as well come clean with me. It will go much better for you. I know you're guilty, and guilty little sinners like you need to confess. Look at you. You have the names of the four blessed apostles: Matthew, Mark, Luke, and John. Stop stalling and confess. Now!"

She was a tough customer. But we were shameless little bastards. We'd been down this road before with our parents and elementary school teachers. If they had the goods on you, they didn't waste any time. You got busted. If they didn't, they ran the high-pressure game. We were not fazed.

"Golly gee whillikers, Sister. You're right. We do have the four apostles of the gospels' names. C'mon, fellas, if you know anything about this glue caper, we owe it to our school, to Principal Maris Stella and the four holy apostles to bring the culprits to justice. Are you with me?" Matthew Muldoon put his hand out, and, Three-Musketeers-style, we put ours on top.

"We're with you, Matt," we responded enthusiastically.

A hissing noise escaped Sister's throat, and she reached down and took hold of Matt's forearm with her skeletal fingers.

"It's going to be a very long four years of high school for boys like you who have lost their souls," Sister seethed. Her fingernails left five crescent marks on Matt's forearm.

"Lost Souls!" was our battle cry when we decided to create mayhem in our sedate suburb. We shouted "Lost Souls!" when we stole fifths of tequila and drove to Bald Mountain (a small hill in a state park north of Royal Oak) on a crystal-clear winter night for a moonlit snow football game, or when we "borrowed" enough Big Wheel plastic tricycles for a mass road rally race down Borgman

Hill in Huntington Woods. We cheered "Lost Souls!" when pipe bombs exploded in garbage cans or golf courses.

Elvis learned the fine art of making pipe bombs from the Fitzgerald brothers, who instructed him on how to very carefully stuff thousands of match heads into plumbing pipes. Blowing up garbage cans and mailboxes led to bolder planning. We eventually plotted to blow up the dam holding the small, man-made lake at the foot of Bald Mountain. I can't remember if it was a whiff of common sense or a car breaking down that prevented us from carrying out the plot.

Our communal lack of a risk-meter led to some incidents that could have ended badly. Twisting logic, our close calls made us more daring than cautious.

Let's see: if chasing each other in cars down a rural road, headlights off, at 70 miles an hour and shooting bottle rockets at each other didn't get us caught, hurt, or killed, then how about making the game include how many mailboxes you can knock over—not with the front bumper, stupid, but with a sharp turn at the last minute, catching the mailbox with the corner of the rear bumper . . . yeah, that should do it.

Most of the excursions and pranks were harmless, but the mix of independence, hormonal chutzpah, cars, beer, and pot fueled our imagination, diminished any fear of consequences, and led to greater risks.

In order to get fully away from parental and neighborhood restraints, we regularly began to drive north or into Canada for camping trips, canoeing adventures, and fishing-and-hunting treks that started out as a communion with the great outdoors and ended as proof that we would live forever.

An early spring canoe and fishing trip on the Pine River turned into a jousting match. Mark and Elvis challenged John and me to stand up in our canoes while heading down the swollen river's fastest rapids. As the canoes coursed downriver side-by-side, we pushed at each other with paddles until both canoes capsized. Our gear was in waterproof bags, but not idiot-proof, so they washed ashore a mile downriver, soaked. We spent the night huddled next to each other by the fire, trying to dry our clothes and sleeping bags. When John started shivering uncontrollably, Mark held him in his lap while Elvis and I draped him with the driest, warmest clothes until he finally warmed up. With his lips still quivering John, said, "I'm fine now."

Mark replied, "You're not fine until I satisfy my lust for you, sweetie!"

John leapt out of Mark's grasps, shouting, "You gross son of a bitch!"

We took a lot of chances, suffered minor to medium injuries, but survived and gained shared confidence and mutual stories.

Framed in the turbulent sixties, we were rebelling, but most of our parents didn't have an understanding of how much. With six, eight, ten, twelve kids or more, the parents had their hands very, very full. Parents taught their children good manners and discipline, reflecting both their own upbringing and the necessity of managing their large households. They also taught a work ethic through their own examples. Money was always short, but the wages from the factories, sales positions, or small businesses provided enough for all the essentials and even parochial school education, which they believed helped to pass on their own upbringing, including their deep faith in God and Catholicism.

God played a trick on our parents. Vatican II and its liberalization of generations of Catholic rituals changed the rules that had been strictly enforced. Changing the Mass from Latin to English and the many other theocratic changes meant nothing to us. What did matter was that Sister Regina Immaculata was renamed Sister Francine. She appeared on our first day of class in 1969, our sophomore year, without the high, starched, gleaming white coronet. The coronet was the nun's headdress, which arched a half-foot up above her forehead before descending down and cutting a deep line into her forehead that announced to all, particularly parochial school students, that this nun was fearsome and formidable. Now, the coronet was gone, replaced with a headdress that showed the entire forehead, including bangs! But it was worse than that. Sister Francine's habit was now cut just below the knees, not draped below her nun's black shoes. Nuns had legs!

The mystery that wreaked dread and awe was gone. Instead of a nun covered from head to toe in a black-and-white, forehead-scar-inducing costume of omnipresence, nuns became . . . people! What a huge mistake in judgment, at exactly the wrong time. Fear-instilled religion, a time-honored cultural tradition, evaporated for every student at St. Mary's and throughout the nation's parochial school system.

The Holy Roman Catholic Church had unwittingly unleashed a generation who not only asked why, but asked why not? With spirited vengeance, the generation struck out on their own into territory not defined by their parents, their church, or their older brothers and sisters. It was a culture quirk that drew us closer to each other. We experimented with unusual freedom in both the wildness of the sixties and the release from our religious traditions.

The transition wasn't pretty. Years of training and inculcation weren't relinquished without pain. We were betwixt and between in so many ways that finding our footing became complicated. We didn't have the benefit of an epiphany. And we weren't scared into routines and rituals anymore. We struck out on our own, and it deepened our dependence on each other, with one special exception. In spite of our parents' incredulity, they provided the security of family. As ridiculous as our behavior became, they loved us, and when it counted, unconditionally.

With all this new, shared common ground, the Lost Souls had a fair chance at keeping our friendships going strong. We only needed to keep alive and out of jail.

I shook myself out of my memories. After my borrowed breakfast, I took John's ten-speed bicycle and pedaled through Royal Oak toward home. My unpredictable lifestyle put a burden not only on my big sister, Ann, but on the twins and Donnie, who I knew looked up to me.

They still weren't happy that I chose to run fast and far away. Big Ann was my harshest critic and supporter, understanding that I was the linchpin and bridge between all of us because I had run away. Which they all wished they could do. Ann and I were on opposite ends of the magnetic poles. In spite of their disappointment with me, they knew I was dealing with our family imbroglio in my own way, no matter how unseemly it appeared. We were still a family.

I biked through downtown Royal Oak, detouring around the direct route home. Downtown Royal Oak was becoming an anachronism as the stores lost business to Oakland Mall. Riding through the downtown reminded me of being an unfettered kid. I remembered the Memorial Day parades, the hot fudge cream puff sundaes at Sanders, and the Santa Claus booth set up near the Washington

Theatre, now shuttered. Life was comfortable and uncomplicated then, and downtown, even in its deteriorating state, provided welcome memories.

Pedaling slowly, I passed by St. Mary's on Lafayette Street, the hulking 1917 building where I attended elementary school, and the 1926 building that housed St. Mary's high school. I rode onto my old *Detroit News* paper route, the largest in Royal Oak, tucked into a lower-rent area in the far southwest corner of town. I turned east and north onto Lincoln Avenue, bumped across the railroad tracks and glided down the gradual slope toward Lawson Street. I slowed down as I approached Lawson, as I always did when I was a kid returning home from St. Mary's or my paper route. I paused at the street corner and looked down the block where my family home had stood. I had not been down this block since the fire, unable to face the painful memory head-on. I knew the house had been razed after the fire.

Memories came to me of playing kickball in the street and tag in the backyards of my neighborhood friends. An image of my dad came to me. The handsome, dark-haired man turned and smiled. I remembered how much I had loved him. This I could not tolerate, and I pushed the image away. I had vowed to never think of him again. Let him rot in Jackson Prison and then burn in hell. I jumped back on the bike and pushed hard on the pedals of the bicycle, speeding away from Lawson Street and all the love and horror the block represented.

I pedaled through the south side of Royal Oak, stopping at a neighborhood bakery and party store on the way to Hoffman Avenue, turning south to reach the faded aluminum-sided bungalow across the street from Dondero Park where a Sunday morning softball game had begun. This was our rented home since the fire. The brakes squeaked as I stopped on the sidewalk in front of the house. I saw Big Ann reading at the dinette table. I entered the house through the side door and hopped up the two steps into the kitchen with a box of Hagelstein's Bakery day-olds and a brown sack filled with two subs from Rosina's, a twenty-four-hour pizzeria and party store.

Ann looked up from her poli-sci notes and said, "The prodigal brother is back again."

She stood up and walked into the kitchen as I opened the box of pastries on the kitchen counter. She hugged me tightly and awkwardly, from the side.

"I brought your favorites, Annie," I said, hugging back.

"C'mon, you lug, I'll make some coffee. Donnie and April are still sleeping. Go wake them up and we'll have a funky brunch of subs and doughnuts," Ann said.

I woke April, home for the weekend, with a verse of "You Are My Sunshine," along with a tug at her covers on the upper bunk in the first-floor bedroom.

She woke up quickly with, "You blockhead Luke, don't you know any other song?" I woke Donnie gently, who was sleeping on the lower bunk in the adjacent bedroom. When I was home, I slept in the upper bunk above him. "Who had the highest batting average from the 1968 World Series winning Detroit Tigers?" I asked, poking my little brother.

Donnie squirmed under his sheet, tilted his head toward me and answered, "Wayne Comer, one-for-one, batting average of one thousand."

"Right as usual, you sports brainiac," I replied, tousling his hair. "Subs for breakfast, little brother, up and at 'em."

"Rosina's?" Donnie added.

"Do you have to ask?" I said.

"All right!" Donnie said as he scrambled out of bed.

We sat at the used Formica dinette set and caught up on the past months since my last trip home. April talked about her college graduation the following January. Both April and Angela had stretched out their college stays by working nearly full-time in Kalamazoo and Michigan State. A boy was showing an interest in April and her writing. She talked excitedly and fast. It was clear her world was expanding quickly.

"Who's the lucky guy, April?" I asked.

"His name is Michael Berlin. He's smart, good looking, and he really likes me," April said.

"He treats you right, too?" I asked.

"Yes, big brother. He treats me fine. I told him I have this mean ogre for a brother who will beat the tar out of him if he gets out of line," April said.

"And that's the truth," I agreed.

Donnie didn't have as much to say; at thirteen years old, he juggled depression and joy. Unable to play his beloved baseball, basketball, and football, he had become the editor of the middle-school paper, the *Irish Eye*. There was no talk of his decreasing visits to the University of Michigan Burn Center or of girls, but Donnie's alternations between sad and happy seemed not unusual for a boy his age.

Ann was more animated than usual, talking about the employees at the Pancake House, her teachers at Oakland Community College, particularly a young sociology teacher named Thomas Kerr. He dined at the Pancake House often and left big tips in spite of his salary as lowly associate professor.

The mood at the table was light and bright, incongruous with my past weeks. I talked around the pathos and focused on Elvis at the Midway and anything else. We talked about Angela at MSU and her roommate troubles and achievement in the classroom. Yes, I told Donnie, I would be home for more than a couple of days. No, I wasn't staying for good. I wasn't ready to find a job in Royal Oak or apply for college yet. Maybe in the fall. I broke that tension by asking Donnie about opening day at Tiger Stadium.

"It's next Monday. Do you think we can go?" Donnie asked excitedly.

I looked at Ann, both of us knowing it meant skipping school. Ann smiled seriously and said, "If you can get tickets, Luke, I guess it's okay."

"All right, then, we can go downtown early and stand in line for bleacher seats," I said.

Ann's smile returned, and the easiness of the morning continued. We had found some sense of normalcy without Mom and Dad, even though our shared black past framed our lives with singed borders.

After breakfast, Donnie and I played catch in Dondero Park and talked sports, mostly the Tigers, school, girls—or lack of them—at St. Mary's and finally about his health and his treatments.

"It's not bad at all now. I go to the Beaumont burn ward for monthly check ups. Ann doesn't have to drive me to Ann Arbor anymore. The doctors are talking about one last graft and plastic surgery on my ear, so I don't look like a Martian anymore."

I knew better than to tell him it wasn't that bad. In some ways, Donnie handled his burns better than me, even though his arms, neck, and the back of his head up and around one ear were disfigured. "If you can make a request, I'd go for Daffy Duck—you remind me of Daffy. Well maybe not, maybe closer to Pluto. Yeah, ask the doc to make you look like Pluto!" I answered.

"You're crazy, Luke, I'm going for Fantastic Four, not some stupid Disney character. What are you thinking?"

We bantered for an hour in the field before walking across the street home. I played cards with Donnie until bedtime. I helped him apply the nightly ointment to his burns, a regimen I knew well. I walked Donnie into his bedroom and ruffled his hair at the door.

"Goodnight, Donnie. Sleep tight."

"Don't let the bedbugs bite," he called back, repeating the good-night line our mom and dad used long ago.

As I closed the door, Donnie asked, "Luke, when are you coming home for good?"

"I don't know, Donnie. I'm still pretty restless. But if you ever need me, I'll come home as fast as you call."

"I know, Luke."

I sat with my older sister at the dinette table. "Ann, we need to talk. You won't believe what happened." The Knoxville story spilled out. And while Ann's worry lines deepened, we talked into the night, a peaceful conversation. I think she finally understood she couldn't exorcise my strange devils; I would have to do it myself. When the conversation ended, she held me for so long, I gave up and hugged her back. I climbed into my upper bunk, knowing Donnie would be happy I was still there for him, and Ann's worries would be an ounce lighter.

It took two weeks before road itch took hold. I tried to convince myself that I could stay in Royal Oak longer, but as each day passed, the town started to close in on me again. I couldn't look down a street without a ghost leaping out and taking my breath away. I made sure to end most of my nights at my home. It was my home, but I had a difficult time even saying the word. Even though my sense of responsibility was twisted in a bunch, I did my best to be a good brother. I kept my promise to Donnie, and we traveled by bus downtown to the Tigers' opener. After waiting in line for an hour to buy two, one-dollar tickets, we made our way to the bleachers and had a great day in the sun. April and Angela came home on the same weekend so we could all be together. I did some serious listening that night. They were beginning to regain the glow I remembered both of them had when trying to impress Mom. Ann was full of advice, as usual, and maybe she watered the first seed of wisdom in me, as I didn't argue with her, but nodded, like I did when someone picked me up on the road. We were learning to be adults together, slowly.

I found a week of work with Mark McInerny's father, who owned a small remodeling company, which also waterproofed basements. Mr. McInerny was prototypical of most of my friends' dads. He worked his job hard and long, with little time for child-rearing, yet was a strong and positive influence by example. In spite of limited time with his kids after putting in ten- to twelve-hour days, he tried to find time after dinner for a game of "pickle." These games of trapping base-runners in a pickle resembled mass hysteria, as the game grew to ten, twelve, and even fifteen neighborhood and family kids racing back and forth between the bases, trying to avoid being tagged by Mr. McInerny and his oldest son, Mike. The game always landed up in sweaty bedlam, with a passel of red-faced kids huffing, puffing, and laughing until they were tagged out.

Every winter, Mr. McInerny built an ice rink in his backyard, standing in his snow-banked yard with a hose, spraying a mist on the initial two inches of a previously flooded rink, small ice droplets hanging from his nose. He lost two to three hours of badly needed sleep for two weeks until the requisite four inches of ice covered the backyard for a combination hockey and figure skating rink. He hung lights from the garage, and finally—finally—announced to his kids that the rink was complete and ready for skating. From the garage attic, he brought down a pile of used, beat-up brown hockey skates and white figure skates, and then sized up to matches as best he could for the seven sets of growing feet that belonged to his children. A trading session with neighbors resulted in skates for everybody. Mr. McInerny would turn the lights on for the first night, and stand back as the kids hit the ice. He shouted the rules as the chaos of midget Gordie Howes and Alex Delvecchios intermingled badly with miniature Peggy Flemings.

"Hockey on this half, skaters on the other half for the first half-hour. Then girls get the full rink a half-hour, then hockey players a half-hour. And no cheating on time, boys. You know I mean it!"

He placed a kitchen timer on the lawn chair next to the ice. Mrs. McInerny heated up a batch of hot chocolate with tiny marshmallows floating in it in the household's largest kettle, waiting for the half-hour changes. For his efforts, Mr. McInerny was revered, as best kids could revere a parent for creating the idyllic moments and memories of their suburbia. It softened the unbending daily household discipline and sometime remoteness created by long work hours and the demands of house, work, and marriage.

Mrs. McInerny led the large household in a never-ending cycle of cleaning, cooking, washing, nursing, and shopping, usually while pregnant with another child. Beleaguered but strong, Mrs. McInerny's small, slender, five-foot frame was almost always bent over to dress a child, take a load out of the washing machine, pick up clothes. She would occasionally stop, stand straight, arms crossed, and blow a strand of hair from her face, then exhale and smile over her compact world. Then she would grab the nearest child and start to dance and sing.

"Oh, Buffalo gal, won't ya come out tonight, come out tonight, and dance by the light of the moon!"

If it was a young child, they'd shriek with delight, while a nearby teenager might try to duck away before she grabbed them by the hand and made them dance.

"Skip backwards, Mom!" The girls cried out.

Of course, Rita McInerny performed her trademark dance move to the delight of the kids.

Mr. and Mrs. McInerny were my favorite parents, but all my friends' parents had complete commitment to their families. Divorce was nearly unknown in our circle, and while it was apparent that most of my friends' parents weren't Ozzie and Harriet, the marriages we saw endured and thrived. With so many kids, the households were far from perfect. Yet there were enough perfect memories to connect the tribe forever. As time went on, with such large families, inevitably one child or another ran into serious problems. The families closed ranks to help, often with success, sometimes not. My family was a part of this landscape, and that's why our disintegration pushed us front and center and in sharp juxtaposition to the rest of our surroundings.

We did our best to keep the parents from getting a peek inside how fast our teenage world was changing. This wasn't the era where a few reefers were smoked at jazz clubs by musicians; in the late sixties, marijuana was smuggled by the ton and becoming as accessible to teenagers as a "buyer" for beer. Mushrooms, peyote, LSD, downers, and uppers were all making appearances under the auspices of fun and entertainment. Our parents' idea of rebelling against their prewar parents consisted of backseat sex, early rock and roll, and drinking. While the music might have been foreign to them, our parents understood that drinking and hangovers were generational rites of passage.

A teenager of the early seventies quantum-leaped into rebellion, and could take a tab of LSD and ponder the inner workings of the universe by staring at a ladybug for hours until it finally looked up and pronounced the meaning of life. Except the ladybug was speaking Latin, which made a tripper wish he had paid more attention in Sister Marcella Margaret's class. Mix six beers and four joints in with the LSD, and the effects were likely to cause a three-day psychosis. A far cry from a parent dealing with a teenager's hangover.

Unless a kid went completely hippie, meaning rejecting everything a family offered, there was an uneasy truce between parents and their kids. Parents knew something was going on but couldn't quite put a finger on it. As long as they didn't get hit over the head with it (a drug bust or a breakdown), they kept one eye shut. The Lost Souls and our friends countered by striving hard to keep our brand-new culture as far away from home as possible, with the exception of long hair and acid rock, which parents could equate to Elvis and ducktail haircuts. This land of tension they understood.

Parents found jobs for their kids, and Mr. McInerny found me a job after his son Mark explained my need for temporary work. "Temporary job" was a head-shaking concept for Mr. McInerny, but he liked me enough to give me a week's work.

I was assigned trench digging next to a home's foundation, prepping for the waterproofing fix. It was a hard, dirty job, but at $2.50 an hour, I held out for five nine-hour days and made over a hundred dollars. Even after taxes, it was a small fortune. I gave Ann twenty-five dollars, mailed April and Angela five dollars each, and bought Donnie a used baseball encyclopedia for three dollars. The money also bought me a brand-new pair of black Converse All Stars, the newer and cooler low-cut style. The All Stars were a real luxury, and while I could never afford currently stylish clothes, new gym shoes were my one indulgence.

I also bought a case of cold Budweiser and took it over to the Vermont house on Friday night, surprising John, Mark, Elvis, and Kate. Elvis and Kate's romance was flourishing. Kate moved into

Vermont, an event Elvis had never allowed in his many short-lived trysts, and in direct contradiction to her commitment to Mrs. Brady to live with a family friend.

Elvis practiced his guitar in his bedroom as I sat with Kate at the dining room table, drinking beer. We talked about my plans to leave soon and head up north to the small town of Topinabee, about thirty miles south of the Mackinac Straits, where a small contingent of our Royal Oak friends had set up roost. Whispering, Kate told me that things were getting serious way too quickly with Elvis. She wanted to keep dating him, but not as an interloper at the Vermont house.

"I need some help here, Luke. I've never been a very good second fiddle, and Matt doesn't treat me that way. But he's so . . . so, I don't know what . . . contagious."

I laughed. "Contagious Elvis, that's a good one. It's clear you've caught Elvis fever. I don't know quite what to tell you, Kate. You know, he's been all over the map with women, but I gotta tell you, I've never seen him get attached to anyone like he is to you. He's a magnet for girls, and I guess you have to get used to that. But he's a good guy, and it's pretty clear you two have something different going on. I don't have any good advice but to let it ride and see where it takes you. Mark and John won't mind you staying here, but my guess is you'll need to find something to do pretty soon. I'm outta here on Monday. You're welcome to come, but I think this is where we part company, don't you?"

Kate leaned over and hugged me. "Luke, you know you will always be so important to me, but I'm going to stay and figure this out. I also need to decide the best way to explain this to my mother."

"Lie," I advised. "Lie like hell."

"That's been my strategy so far. But she's one phone call away from catching up to me," Kate said.

"Which is probably the best reason why I'm getting the hell out of Dodge. The wrath of Helen Brady will cut wide and deep," I replied.

"Yeah, I should go with you, if I was smart. No, I'm going to call her and tell her tomorrow or the next day. She'll freak out and then come back down to earth."

"Whew, good luck, Kate. This is definitely one of those rare times when being a good-for-nothing hitchhiker is a good thing. I'll be rooting for you from the highway," I said.

"Luke, I never asked you. How did you decide that thumbing all over the country was something you wanted to do? Did you just wake up one day and say, 'Yep, time to hit the road and live on apples and cream cheese?'"

"Doesn't everyone? Actually, my moment of clarity came after reading Kerouac's *On the Road* and *Siddhartha* back-to-back while on a camping trip on the Au Sable River. Sorry, Kate, that's absolute bullshit. The truth is that I was bonked out of my mind on beer and some kind of seedless pot called sinsemilla. I was in the midst of this completely debauched Memorial Day weekend celebrating our impending high school graduation. There were hundreds of teenagers intent on setting alcohol- and pot-ingesting records at the campground. I sat on the sandy, high banks of the river and pretended to read the two books given to me by Jackie Hewitt, the blonde, intellectual girlfriend of a friend from Berkley High School. She was yet another sexy, smart girl who I hoped to impress with my highbrow capabilities. It didn't work with her, either. While the weekend raged around me, I managed to ignore the tribe of lunatics that had the makings of becoming a coed *Lord of the Flies,* except the participants were too stoned to get organized.

"I did manage to finish a couple chapters of *Siddhartha* by firelight at 2:00 a.m. As I turned the pages, a resounding boom blasted through the river valley. John Parcell, who was lolling by the fire with Lois Martell, casually said, 'That would be the Fitzgerald brothers night fishing with M-80s.' I'm not sure what inspired my addled brain, but an idea settled in my head.

"'John, I know what I'm going to do. When I get home, I'm going to take off and see the country and find out if I have a soul worth saving. I gotta get the hell out of Royal Oak and get straight.'

"'You're just stoned, Moore. Where will you go and with what money?' Lois asked. 'What you need to do is get a job and stop behaving like an asshole.'

"'Gee, Lois, you really should work on your coyness. And thank you for your encouraging words and support.' If you don't know it yet, Lois would run you over if you don't fight back.

"'Luke, you can't just up and run away. Your family needs you. And as much as I would like to see the four Lost Souls lose a playmate, I do need someone to pick on.'

"'That's better, Lois. Now I see your soft and sensitive side. I know I'm not helping out at home. But, man, it's tough with your big sister ragging on you day and night. I need to get away, get a grip on something. I'm no good at home the way things are now.'"

I finished my explanation and Kate shook her head sardonically. "I guess I get it. I suppose hitchhiking is a better way to run away than doing heroin."

"I can see you're just about as sympathetic as Lois was," I said.

"I can't argue that. I like Lois. She's a no-bullshit kind of girl. I think we might get along."

"You might if you can pry her away from John. She's a chick with a plan."

"Well, I'm a chick without a plan. It sounds like a match."

"Amen, Kate."

Later in the evening, John and I teamed up against Elvis and Mark for a pinochle tournament while Kate read *The Screwtape Letters* by C. S. Lewis on the living room sofa. I had concluded that she was indeed a book snob, but smart enough to understand what she was reading. For the Lost Souls, it was a familiar scene: the case of beer and Jack in the Box super tacos disappeared as an LP played on Elvis's expensive Altec stereo system. Pink Floyd, Jethro Tull, Family, Moody Blues, and new jazz introductions played loudly enough that pinochle bids had to be shouted.

This was a comfortable and predictable routine for all of us. John and I won at pinochle, and we switched to euchre at midnight. Mark started getting angry at about his seventh beer, and by 2:00 a.m., a friendly wrestling match ended up with John and me pulling Mark off Elvis. Mark's snurl flared when Elvis made a jab at his masculinity, a comment that an hour earlier would have been laughed off. That ended the night. I landed on the couch, and everyone else in their respective bedrooms.

I listened to the sound of Elvis's bed posts and box spring rhythmically keeping time. *Goddamn him* was my last thought of the night.

* * *

By Saturday afternoon, we were all sobered up and watched the Tigers play the White Sox on Channel 4. Mark opened his first beer by the fourth inning. Elvis and John would wait another hour or two and drink in measured amounts until much later in the evening. I had the weakest stomach and rarely drank two days in a row. I couldn't handle the hangovers. Big Ann had invited us all over to dinner, so all of us were careful to nurse our buzzes.

We arrived at 5:00 p.m., an hour before dinner. Elvis and Kate drove over with Mark and me in the Falcon. John and Lois arrived in her brand-new 1972 Chevette. Ann greeted us with hugs as we tumbled through the door. She had known my friends and their families her entire life. She didn't kid herself; she knew we were mixing alcohol, pot, and risky behavior. She knew it was a bad mix and let us know it, even as we gave her the Eddie Haskell treatment: "Gee, Mrs. Cleaver, we wouldn't do anything as stupid as drink, drive, and smoke pot."

Kate and Lois volunteered to help in the kitchen. The Lost Souls lightly roughhoused with Donnie in the backyard. He worshipped my friends, especially Mark, who had been a three sport star at St. Mary's. We threw horseshoes until Ann called us in for dinner. The roasted chicken breasts with Shake 'n Bake stuffing, twice-baked potatoes, and tossed salad disappeared. The boys cleared the table and washed the dishes as their mothers had taught them, while Ann, Lois, and Kate sat in the backyard smoking Newport 100s.

Donnie and I sat side by side, knees touching, on the Salvation Army sofa in our tiny living room. He opened the mammoth 1966 baseball encyclopedia on his lap. We were all set to argue baseball.

"I'm telling you, Luke, Norm Cash is the one of the Tigers' all time best first basemen. Heck, hitting .361 in 1961 was awesome. And he's a darn good fielder."

"Donnie, you know you're nuts. Hank Greenberg is in the Hall of Fame, for God's sake. The closest Norm Cash is going to get to the Hall of Fame is introducing Al Kaline when they induct him after he retires," I retorted.

"Hey, Norm Cash isn't through with his career. I know he hasn't quite lived up to that 1961 season, but he's coming back. I know it."

We would go back and forth like this for hours.

We were interrupted by the exit of my friends. The dishes were washed and dried and the kitchen cleaned. Elvis, Mark, John, Lois, and Kate gathered with Ann in the living room, saying their good-byes. We bantered a minute before Elvis said, "Let's go, ladies and gentlemen, and leave this fine Moore family to a quiet evening. You're staying, right, Luke?"

"Yep, I have to school my misled little brother on who the greatest ballplayers of all time really are."

"Who are you kidding, Moore, Donnie knows more about baseball at his age than you'll know when you're fifty and over the hill," Mark said.

The whole group chimed in assent, bringing a beam to Donnie's face. Ann hugged each of them on the way out the door, telling them, "Keep safe, and you know what I mean."

I heard the car horns tap good-bye and the battle cry "Lost Souls Unite," but without me.

Donnie and I talked baseball well past his bedtime. The banter was our proxy for brotherly intimacy. Donnie knew I was leaving again, and it made him angry. We'd had a blowout about it a year prior. With tears in his eyes, he had asked me, "Why can't you just stay home and be my big brother?"

I didn't have a good answer for him then or now. I promised him that when I was home, I would be there for him. Since then I spent time with him every day I was home, and he appreciated it and didn't make a stink when I inevitably left again.

Finally, Ann said, "All right, jocks, it's time for the Einstein of baseball to go to bed."

Donnie yawned and didn't argue. I tucked him in a few moments later, sitting on the lower bunk and singing "You Are My Sunshine."

"Jeez, Luke, don't you think I'm getting a little old to be sung to sleep? And that song is for kids."

"Hey, you're still my little brother. And, Donnie, the song reminds me of Mom and when she used to sing it to both of us. It kind of keeps her alive for me. You mind?"

"No, Luke. I just wish I could remember her more. I do remember her singing and laughing when she put us to bed. I miss her, Luke."

"So do I, Donnie. I'll tell you what. When I'm home, I'll put you to bed and tell you Roberta Moore stories. That way you won't forget her and we can keep her stories fresh for both us. Okay? Did you know that Mom was a very fast runner when she was a kid? Just like you. Let me tell you the story."

Three stories later, Donnie was asleep, and I leaned ever and gave him a kiss on the top of this head. "Good night, little brother. Sleep tight."

I turned and saw Ann at the door, watching with her coffee cup in hand. "You're a good brother, Luke."

"Thanks, Ann. I'm trying to be good at something."

"Let's sit down and talk. We haven't done that for a while."

We sat in the living room and talked like friends. She was still flabbergasted at what had happened to me in Tennessee.

"I guess it shouldn't be a surprise that there's something different about you, Luke. You look different. Lighter, or there seems to be a glow around you. It's a good look."

"I feel different, too. Things are changing for me, Ann."

I hadn't told Ann or Kate or the Lost Souls about the promise. It lurked in my everyday thoughts. I didn't know what to do about the commitment to Annette, but she had told me not to worry, the time would come, and I would know what to do. Maybe it did change me. I was responsible for something now. And it reminded me that I had my own family.

We talked for an hour before Ann looked at her watch. "Oh, it's way past my bedtime. But I like having my brother back." She gave me our longest hug, finally letting me go and looking at me with moist eyes. "Somehow, we're going to make it as a family, aren't we, Luke?"

"Because of you, Ann. And it might not seem like it now, but I'll never forget what you've done for all of us."

"It's worth it, Luke."

That night I slept fitfully, and my morning dream featured an aging matador in the bullring, with a bull violently charging at his red cape. As the bull came closer, I could see the gray-haired, over-the-hill bullfighter was me. I woke up before the inescapable collision with a start, and thought I would be lucky to see middle age if I didn't change my life. I'm not sure it was luck, but the margin of error was very, very thin.

Chapter 15

September 2003

I listened to the rhythm of the van's tires meeting the pavement as I replayed the circuitous road map to my current life. I jumped back to the present when the reflective rectangular road sign greeted me: Indian River Next Exit.

I wanted to exit and take Marta and Roberta through the village, up Old Highway 27, over the Indian River, past Mullett Lake, and into Topinabee, to show them Tony Muldano's house. It would be a return to the scene of crimes and misdemeanors, rolled into a memory lane of a summer that changed everything. Marta would be kind and smile and be patient with me. But she didn't dwell on the past, good or bad, like I did. Roberta would be dismal with boredom, just like the last time I took us through these towns on our way to a Mackinac Island family vacation, years ago.

Instead, I said in a tour guide tone, "And now we're passing beautiful Indian River, home of the world's largest crucifix and some of the nuttiest squirrels you ever saw. Ha!"

My patient wife smiled with her eyes and reached over and let the flat of her palm settle on my thigh. Goosebumps met the follicles on my forearms. Decades after we met, Marta could still turn me inside out with a gesture. She's the reason I believed in God.

In the backseat, Roberta shook her head and said, "Dad, I've heard that squirrel story over a hundred times—not again."

"No prob, Bob. Although it never fails to amuse me," I replied.

"Dad, one thing's for sure, you'll never run out of your own stories that keep you thoroughly entertained," Roberta said.

"Why, thank you, sweetheart. I'll take that as a compliment."

Tom Lutac had risen from his road torpor and said, "Oh, we're in Indian River, not too far from the bridge now."

"Yep, we're about an hour from the top of the mitten. There's a rest area about ten minutes from here. Anybody need to stop before we cross the bridge?"

"I could use the restroom, Mr. Moore," Tom replied.

"That's fine, Tom. So, now that you've had a nap, would you mind telling us more about yourself? It's unusual to find hitchhikers anymore, car trouble or not."

"To tell the truth, I'm really not much for hitchhiking. It takes too long, and you never know what kind of crazy people will pick you up. Since you told me about your storytelling, I guess I should come clean with you, too. I really crashed my car, and I don't have the money to fix it. So I'm headed up north to the UP to visit my brother at Northern Michigan University in Marquette. He said I can stay with him until I find a job and get enough cash to fix my car," Tom said.

"I see. What about your family? Do you have other brothers or sisters? Where do your parents live?" I asked.

"No, no other sibs. My dad died when I was seven, and my mom lives in East Detroit. Works as a teacher. She's real good at it."

"I'm sure. Where does your mom teach?"

"Oh, well, right now she's between jobs. She hurt her back and isn't up to working yet."

"Yeah, it takes a while to get back on your feet from a back injury. I hope she heals up quickly," I said.

"Thank you, Mr. Moore. That's about it for me. Sorry about misleading you about the car trouble and going to college. I was just fibbing a bit."

"As you can tell, Tom, I'm guilty of that myself."

I asked Tom if he liked sports and our talk turned to noncontroversial opinion-swapping about the Red Wings' prospects that season. I knew now that Tom was a liar, not just a storyteller. He was quick on his feet, but not quick enough to fool an old bullshitter.

He had changed his story twice, and I still wasn't convinced. It was best to keep an eye on our belongings and generally be wary. My danger meter was not jumping, but it was turned on.

We passed by the Topinabee exit, and a few miles north, the minivan climbed to the crest of a gentle hill that presented a sweeping view of the top of the peninsula. It was early September, and the drive so far had revealed only a paintbrush or two of fall color. But autumn had visited this part of the state, and the maples had turned halfway already, the yellow tips contrasting against the green base of the leaves and the crisp blue of the northern sky. A steady wind from the north swayed the maples and shivered the pines.

It felt, more than looked, like a storm was a-brew.

Chapter 16

April 1973

M onday morning at ten o'clock, John Parcell and I stood on I-75, just past Clarkston, twelve miles north of Royal Oak, facing north. Having John at my side made this a unique occasion. Elvis and Mark had joined me for short hitchhiking jaunts during the last two years, but John was our responsible friend and had a girlfriend who could influence him, a sin for which he was regularly razzed. When I told my friends over a game of pinochle that I was leaving for up north in a few days for an undetermined time, John stunned us all by asking me if he could go along. If we were all surprised, his girlfriend, Lois Martel, was in shock. He told us he needed a the-hell-with-it break from his job at Beaumont Hospital. He called his alibi in on Monday morning, telling his boss he wanted to use personal days to visit his ailing grandmother.

John was normally reliable, hardworking, and predictable, and not one to step out on a ledge. He graduated from St. Mary's as the Class of 1971 Salutatorian through smarts and hard work. Unlike us, he did his homework and focused on his studies as part of a plan to go to college and get a good job. John's planning horizon extended beyond the next fifteen minutes.

He attended Michigan State University for two years, earning a 3.6 GPA in spite of too many party visits from the three of us. Now he was in the final months of a year off school to save enough money to go back and finish a degree in pre-law. His parents helped as best they could with college expenses, but not enough for John to make it back for his junior year, after his dad was laid off from Ford for six months.

John had a gift of making people laugh through his twisted observations of daily life. John's skills were shared with only his family and friends; outwardly, he seemed to have little ambition for the public entertaining Elvis pursued. His world was smaller and more stable. He thrived inside his world, finding time to paint watercolors of places he had never been, giving them to friends and family. Part of his stability was Lois, whom he had dated since they were in eighth grade. We all expected he would marry Lois after college, go to law school, and find a better-paying job than anybody we knew.

I was genuinely happy to have John as a partner for this short hop to northern Michigan. He was entertaining and likable, and one-on-one, he could make me laugh so hard my stomach would ache. We started off on a hot and humid early May morning, unusual but not unfamiliar for Michigan weather. Elvis had dropped us off an hour earlier, and we were starting to perspire and feel the initial impatience associated with getting the first ride. John was helping to kill time by describing the life and times of a female dragonfly that he had spotted in the grass just off the shoulder of the road.

"As you can see, Luke, the female dragonfly is a rapacious and militant creature. Watch her as she carefully dissects the hapless and helpless moth that she has mounted, and which she is voraciously ingesting. Oooh! She's separated the moth's body from its wings. She's taking off, moth in mouth, flying away to share her desiccated prey with her female offspring. It's well known that female dragonflies rule their world over their forlorn and enfeebled male mates. It's really a metaphor for life, my friend. The male dragonfly, in his entire splendor, is really just a pawn for the all-powerful female, who kills her mate with precision and purpose, satisfying not her hunger, but her quest for power and lust that is not and cannot be satiated!"

"John, you are a crazed lunatic! It's not the female dragonfly that mates and kills, it's the praying mantis!"

"That may be true, my friend, but you cannot deny the evolutionary facts. A million years ago, the Queen Dragonfly ruled the earth, and they will rule again! Mark my words!"

While we were stooped over examining insect biology, a 1966 VW bus pulled over and honked its tinny horn. "Hey, let's go, Darwin," I said, and we lifted our bags and made the weighted-down run toward the bus.

The driver was the quintessential Volkswagen van owner. His long blond hair was tied back in a ponytail, and his granny sunglasses barely hid his reddened, stoned eyes.

"Hey man, how they hanging?" he said as I opened the front door and John slid the side door open. He told us his name was Paul Malone, but said, "You can call me Wily, like the coyote, man."

I didn't bother to invent a *nom de plume,* figuring it would be wasted on a wasted Wily.

"I'm Luke, and this is John. We're headed up near Topinabee. Where you heading?"

"My men, I'm going to Rose City. My woman and her friends bought a twenty-acre piece of land and are starting an ashram. Lots of love, peace, yoga, serious weed action, and serious chicks. It's gonna be a happening, man."

"Cool, man," John chimed in from the backseat as Wily slowly eked the van onto I-75 from first gear to fourth over a mile of shoulder and highway. The faded, khaki 1964 van topped out at fifty-two miles per hour, about the same speed as Wily's mouth.

"Yeah, man, I ate two Betty Crocker fudge brownies with a serious infusion of Columbian red about two hours ago, took a hit of speed about an hour ago, and I'm flying high. I'll be ready to fire up a doobie momentarily, but if you guys want any speed or quaaludes, I've got plenty. I'd love to give it to you gratis, but I'm low on cashola, so it's a buck a hit for the speeders and two bucks for those 714 Rohrers. Them 'ludes will mellow you out seriously, my men. Man, I don't know why anyone would want to get wasted on booze when you can control the buzz so beautifully with these beautiful little pills, man. And if you guys are looking for some real adventure, well I got just the trick—window-fucking-pane Mr. Natural acid. LS–fucking-D, the real thing, that'll cost five bucks a hit, but you can split it and be riding that goddamn psychedelic rocket right up to the fucking moon, man!"

Wily didn't let up, and neither did his cornucopia of drug choices. Mescaline tablets, downers, Percocet, PCP, magic mushrooms, black mollies, peyote, Lebanese hashish, Oaxaca red bud and Acapulco gold bud. You name it—or even if we didn't know the name—he had it. Most dealers we knew specialized in pot, psychedelics, uppers, and downers. They usually had a personal stash of a variety of drugs, but Wily could provide quantities large and small across a broad spectrum of controlled and uncontrolled substances.

His speed patter didn't stop until we were near Flint. He reached in his pocket and pulled out a big spliff of his favorite blend of Colombian, combined with Californian sinsemilla, sprinkled with ground Afghani hash. After we smoked, neither Wily, John, nor I was capable of talking. It was a marvel Wily kept the VW bus between the lines.

Wily broke the silence as we passed the electronic sign just north of Flint that announced how many automobiles had been built to date in the United States in 1973. The last digit flashed a new number every six seconds; that's how fast they were building cars (which was a lot slower than past years, given the Arab oil embargo and accompanying recession). Even a stoner like Wily read enough of the newspaper to know that the economy in Michigan was bad. Flint was really suffering with the highest unemployment in the country, close to 20 percent, the highest since the Depression. Most of Wily's regular customers were on unemployment.

Wily pointed at the sign and said, "Shit, that's a lot of cars. You know, I used to work in the Chrysler plant in Highland Park. Goddamn worst place I ever set foot in. The pay was great, but man, we worked ten-hour shifts, six days a week in, pushin' the metal forward on that goddamn assembly line. It had to be a hundred degrees in that shithole plant. A real bummer in the summer.

Except that's where I found my first connections for my stash, man. I'd go out to the parking lot for lunch, and you could find every drug I could imagine. I got in way too deep back then, landed up snortin' smack in the back of my Road Runner. I'd throw a fuckin' wrench in the line so I could take a smack break in the john. I finally got caught and spent three months in rehab, paid for by Chrysler, of course. I had to get out of that scene, man. I left with the mother lode of connections, and it's a lot easier selling drugs than working in a factory. But the Man was onto my gig. I think one of my customers turned narc, so I'm taking my whole stash and moving up north to chill. There are a lot of hippies moving north, and I figure to get established as the main source with my old lady's farm as a good base of operations, man. Hey, you guys want a speeder?"

Wily held a prescription vial of white cross Dexedrine tablets out to John and me. That woke us from our pot-induced stupor.

I said, "No thanks, Wily, but I really could dig something to drink to get rid of this cotton mouth."

"No problem, the cooler in the backseat has some road buddies with your name on them," Wily said, as he popped two of the white crosses into his mouth. "Up, up, and away," Wily smiled.

"Hey, I'll take a couple of those, Wily," John chimed in, and pulled two bucks out of his wallet and passed them up to Wily, who pressed two small, white pills into John's hand.

John flipped them into his mouth, swallowing them with a gulp of his Budweiser road buddy. This took me aback. John would smoke pot with us, but usually avoided the indiscriminate drug use. I had my own standards, but I had set the bar fairly low. I did avoid uppers and downers from my past experiences that resulted in falling down stairs (downers) and days without sleep (speed).

I noticed that both Wily's and John's faces began to flush as the Dexedrine began to course its way through their systems. The music was loud in the van, and Wily was singing very loudly and badly along with Led Zeppelin. John vibrated and nibbled nervously on his lip. These guys were going to be fried by the time this ride ended.

The van plodded past Saginaw and more General Motors and supplier plants, reaching Zilwaukee just past noon. We approached and started to climb the incline of the Zilwaukee Bridge, spanning the Saginaw River. Our progress was stopped as a loud, electronic bell clanged and the drawbridge opened to allow immense barges carrying God knows what into the Great Lakes and the final factory destination. We had a panoramic view of opposing scenery on either side of the river. To the west, the river was lined with cement plants and other industrial ports. To the east, the broad river plain was undeveloped, and within two miles the river reached the Saginaw Bay, part of Lake Huron.

"I wonder what set of geniuses decided to put a drawbridge in the middle of an interstate highway?" John asked.

"Probably the motherfuckers who designed the Volaré. We're going to be here for a while. Luke, hand me beer," Wily said.

"Me too, Luke," John said.

I passed two Budweiser cans from the cooler.

John cracked his beer open. "Here we are, just a few hundred feet from being up north."

"This ain't up north. You're not up north until you get at least to West Branch. They even have a billboard that says, 'Welcome to West Branch, Gateway to the North,'" Wily said.

"No way. You're up north as soon as you cross the Zilwaukee Bridge. Look," John held the back of his hand to show the handy map of Michigan's Lower Peninsula we all carry with us. He drew an imaginary line across the back of his hand map. "Zilwaukee and this bridge are here. If you go due west to Lake Michigan, you form a base. South of this base is southern, lower Michigan. North of this line is up north. It's commonly accepted geography," John said.

"Common knowledge, my white ass. Up north starts at West Branch, or worst case, Clare."

The argument was on, and lasted a while. For some reason, this imaginary point of where "up north" Michigan began was a hotly debated issue leading nowhere. It was like arguing who was a better home-run hitter, Babe Ruth or Hank Aaron. I kept out of this fight, but did get a few laughs as the battle became animated. Somehow, the Upper Peninsula was drawn into the fight, with Wily demonstrating the shape of the "U.P.," as we called it, by holding up the back of his right hand as the mitten and the palm of his left hand held sideways, thumb up. He used his nose as pointer to show where he killed his first deer and then his first sexual experience with a hooker in Escanaba.

I drifted off into my own thoughts, remembering my first Michigan geography lesson. My mom read me a children's book named *Paddle to Sea*. It was standard kindergarten reading. The story was about a toy canoe—carved by an Indian in Canada—that was lost in a snowdrift. It found its way to Lake Superior in the snowmelt and miraculously made its way through the Great Lakes to the St. Lawrence Seaway and to the ocean before a grizzly freighter veteran rescued the little boat and it found its way back home. For most Michigan kids growing up in the 1950s, this book showed us the enormity of the Great Lakes' waterways.

I liked geography. As a kid, I loved peering through an ancient encyclopedia in our house and going from country to country, learning about the topography and the people. I was partial to my home state and learned a lot about it.

A reasonably informed Michigander could provide any number of geographical anecdotes about the state: Michigan has more miles of coastline than any other continental state, including California. There are over ten thousand inland lakes, second only to Minnesota. Lake Superior is the largest lake in the world. (The Caspian Sea is actually the largest lake in the world, but it's called a sea. It's so polluted you can barely call the water *water.* So, really, Lake Superior is the largest true lake in the world.) However, the largest lake in the United States is Lake Michigan (Lake Superior and Lake Huron are half in Canada).

It takes over twelve hours of driving from the southernmost border of Michigan and Ohio to reach the northernmost border at Ironwood, Michigan, and Wisconsin. Those two points could also be separated by as much as fifty degrees in temperature on some frigid U.P. nights in the Keweenaw Peninsula. It's a big state; it held a world of rough and wild nature in its upper half, and a gentle, often incomparable, beauty in the northern Lower Peninsula. The sunsets on Miller Hill in Leelanau County, if you're overlooking the glacial green water of the Glen Lakes and peering down on the sweeping Sleeping Bear Sand Dunes and the Manitou Islands, compare with those over California's magnificent coastline. "Up north" was a place where tens of thousands of factory workers owned a parcel of land, many lake-side properties with thirty-five to fifty feet of frontage, a small cottage, and a fishing boat. I knew a dozen families in Royal Oak who had cottages or fishing cabins, including the Muldoons. I had been a guest on numerous summer weekend getaways. In the history of the world's Midwest working class, this was about the apex of their working-class wealth, way past twenty acres and a mule.

But my state also contained one of the country's industrial armpits, and the good times were starting to creak. The term *Rust Belt* was coined in the newspapers as jobs started to flee our state. "Last one to leave, turn out the lights," wasn't funny in Michigan. Jobs were flushed out of the state to Mexico and elsewhere. It wasn't just a slogan when our neighbors lost jobs and had to pull their kids out of St. Mary's because they couldn't afford the tuition.

There were still many great-paying jobs in the plants at the base of the big mitten, in cities like Detroit, Flint, Saginaw, Battle Creek, Kalamazoo, and Grand Rapids. But a trend had started southward, and it was a one-way road. The auto companies were building cars that didn't hold together, like the Volaré. Not even Ricardo Montalbán's singing commercials could convince the American public it was a car worth owning. Michigan was the last bastion of big American cars, but the assembly workers weren't proud of the cars they were building. Before national pundits snobbishly, although accurately, described the demise of the auto industry and America's industrial might, the factory worker knew it already. The car designs that eventually hit their stamping machines and assembly lines were inbred with poor quality. The workplace atmosphere reeked, causing a slow, simmering anger. The irony wasn't lost on many. While smashing a Toyota with a sledgehammer at a radio station promotion, autoworkers arrived in rusting Vegas and Pintos.

The bell clanged again, and the bridge roadway lowered into place; we crossed the Saginaw River into John's version of "up north." Wily and John had switched gears into sports arguments, and, while that was my specialty, competing with two hopped-up guys on Dexedrine didn't seem like much fun. I looked out the window at the low-lying farmland that spread out past the Zilwaukee Bridge and Bay City. The van chugged off the expressway at the Pinconning exit and into a combination gas station and cheese store, selling Pinconning cheese, Michigan's answer to medium-mild Wisconsin cheddar. It was my idea to stop for gas and cheese. I was getting a headache listening to Wiley sing. Also, about two years ago, I had been picked up by Wally Hepner, who owned the establishment he named Hepner's Villa. Wally was also the chief cheerleader for "Pinconning Cheese, America's Best," his own superlative marketing tag line.

"Cheese, my friend, cheese," Wally had told me. "Just say the word a few times. Just like the cameraman says, just 'say cheese'! Now add Pin-con-ning. It's natural, sounds like a doorbell chime or Avon calling. Pin-con-ning, Pin-con-ning, Pinconning Cheese! And yes, my young friend, it tastes as good as it sounds!"

I was hitching south from Indian River when Wally had picked me up in Gaylord, 110 miles north of Hepner's Villa, just as it was getting dark. He let me fill up on cheese products and told me I could pitch my pup tent behind the store. Wally was one of my favorite road characters. He had no experience picking up hitchhikers, but he picked me up and figured it was just the right thing to do to help me out a bit. I don't know why it surprised me that every part of the country had a Wally Hepner-type character: decent, God-fearing people who took the most basic lessons of Jesus and found a way to practice them in everyday life. And they wanted nothing in return. They made up for the repulsive creeps and skulkers. Wally Hepner was a good example of an optimist.

In return for Wally's hospitality, I cleaned up the litter in the Villa parking lot and emptied the garbage cans into the Dumpster before getting back on the highway just past dawn. Since then, whenever I came through Pinconning, I would try to stop and see Wally. Upon seeing me, he would guffaw loudly and retell the story about what a considerate, honest young man I was, instead of the scruffy, near-hippie I appeared to be. I regretted I had told Wally my name was Bubba Luke, a community college student with a mild stutter and a penchant for medium Pinconning and Ritz crackers. Sometimes my stories escaped out of my mouth before I could stop myself.

Wily pumped gas into his van while John and I made our way into the Cheese Shoppe side of the store. I asked for Wally, but he was golfing. I was disappointed. No free cheese.

John responded to the matronly cashier's question, "How are you on this fine day, young man?"

He let loose with barrage of speed-induced information on how exactly he was doing on this fine day. "Well, ma'am, that's a very good question. I am actually in a very agitated, but still satisfying, state of mind. I'm wired, mired, and fired up. I'm escaping my humdrum life, maybe for a few days, maybe forever. I don't know. We'll have to see. I'm alternately confused and seeing with startling clarity on this fine day. On this fine day—"

I interrupted, seeing the alarmed look on the cashier's face. "Shut up, John." I grabbed him by the elbow and started moving him toward the van.

Wily was in a deep conversation at the pump with a couple of townies wearing Pinconning High School varsity jackets. Wily was shaking hands with one of the jocks as John and I joined them.

"Okay, bro, we got a deal. Hold on, I need to talk to my buds here." Wily turned to us and said, "Change of plans. I think I have a quantity sale brewing here. I'm going to follow these young studleys here and conduct some business. If you want to come, I could use some backup. I'll make it worth your while, but I'm guessing we're talking on at least a couple of hours."

While John was busy chewing his lip, I told Wily, "Thanks, Wily, but I think we'll just move on up the road. But are you sure you're going to be okay alone? Those guys look harmless enough, but this isn't exactly hippie-friendly territory. And I'm sure they have a lot of friends with varsity jackets."

Wily smiled. "Thanks for the concern, but I'll keep the exchange of goods for cash limited to those two dudes. We only do business in a wide-open space, and if they decide to get cute, they can deal with my friends here." He reached under the van's driver seat and pulled out two handguns, showing them surreptitiously to John and me. "Meet my friends Smith and Wesson and their German pal, Mr. Luger. I don't think those boys can give me any trouble I can't handle with my associates here. I may look like a laid-back hippie, but make no mistake, I'm a professional drug dealer, and if somebody fucks with me, they will regret it."

Wily's tone, demeanor, and appearance darkened considerably as he spoke. It freaked the shit out of us.

John stuttered, "O-okay, Wily, g-good luck with your deal, and thanks for the ride and speed, weed, and beer."

"No problem, dude, here's a couple of speeders for the road. You seem to have a groove going on." We gave Wily a brother's handshake and unloaded our packs hurriedly. We walked toward the highway entrance, watching as Wily turned the van eastward on a rural highway with the two townies following behind him in a pickup truck with a gun rack.

"Jesus, that Wily was one crazed dude," John's face looked distorted and worried.

"Yeah, John, he was time bomb waiting to go off. I'm glad we weren't around to get hit by the shrapnel."

"No shit, dude! You're right, he is going to blow up. Maybe a case of spontaneous combustion. You ever hear of that Luke? How a guy will just be sitting in his easy chair, drinking a beer and watching a football game, and the next thing you know, poof! He's gone. All that's left is just a pile of ashes and the fillings from his teeth. And maybe a wedding ring if he was married. Or maybe a watch, too. Or any other jewelry. Oh, he might leave some eyeglasses behind, too."

John continued on for five more minutes describing the peculiarities that might be associated with a man combusting in his easy chair. He kept on like this for ten minutes. I finally grabbed him by the shoulders and shouted, "John, please stop, you're killing me here. You just have to shut up for a minute!"

John said, "I'd like to Lukey, yes, I'd really like to, but it's like a giant reel-to-reel tape player inside my head moving at fast-forward. It's just a never-ending tape of stories, songs, colors, and ideas that have to get out! And out they will come, my friend. I can't stop them, and neither can you! These tapes were meant to be played, and now is their time! If you can't listen, I'll just walk on down the road a piece and get out of earshot. I'll be lonely down there, yes, and I'll be a lonely, lonely man, singing my own only lonely, sorry, unheard, unloved, and under-understood song, but it's okay. It's only lonely John, standing on the side of the highway singing . . ."

And he broke into his lonely-guy variation of "Ain't No Sunshine."

> *Ain't no sunshine when I'm gone*
> *It's not warm when I'm away*
> *Ain't no sunshine when I'm gone*
> *And I'm always gone too long*
> *Anytime I go away*
> *Wonder this time where I'm gone*
> *Wonder if I'm gonna stay*
> *Ain't no sunshine when I'm gone*
> *And this house just ain't no home*
> *Anytime I go away*
> *And I know, I know, I know, I kno-o-o-o-w . . .*
> *Gotta leave this young thing alone*
> *Anytime I go away*

I watched as John sang at full volume to the intermittent cars whizzing past. There was no stopping him, so I joined in.

> *Ain't no sunshine when we're gone*
> *Only darkness everyday*
> *Ain't no sunshine when we're gone*
> *And this house just ain't no home*
> *Anytime we go . . . away!*

"This is so great," John shouted. "I've never really let go like this and it is *so* unbelievable!"

"Okay, John, I can see you're having fun, but let's remember to cool it when we get picked up."

"That's not a problem, Big Luke, and that appears to be just about now." John turned as a boxy 1956 Checker pulled over slowly, almost a mile ahead of us. It wasn't a Checker Cab, but a limited-production deviation that Checker Motors, located in Kalamazoo, had produced in the mid-fifties, hoping to develop a consumer product beyond their cab market. Unfortunately, the product looked almost identical to the fortress-like Checker Cab; it was a safe, reliable, and incredibly ugly vehicle didn't click with car buyers. The few that were sold lasted forever and continued to be seen like apparitions, usually in rural Michigan.

When we reached the silver-gray Checker, I was surprised to see two diminutive, silver-haired ladies sitting in the front seat. I hadn't been picked up by many old ladies.

"Hello there, boys, now you hop right in, and we'll get on our way," the elderly woman sitting in the passenger seat called out through her half-open window.

We scrambled into the backseat that was spacious enough to hold us and our bags comfortably. The two ladies both turned around, and it was clear from their profiles they were sisters. Oddly, they were both dressed identically, in white outfits with black trim.

"Thank you so much for stopping to pick us up," I said quickly, worried what the souped-up John might say. "It's unusual that two lovely ladies would be gracious enough to stop for us. I can assure you we are reliable and respectful, and more than grateful for your generosity. My name is Walter Williams, and my traveling companion here is my brother William Williams, but we call him Will. And I'm guessing that you two must be sisters, maybe even twin sisters, aren't you?"

The two ladies started giggling and then laughing loudly. "Oh, we're sisters, all right. I'm Sister Jean Rosina, and she's Sister Rose Margaret, sisters in piety and humility, and retired members of the Dominican Order, you silly boy," the driver said.

Lowering her voice, she continued, "We're nuns, boys, and the look on your faces tells me that you both went to Catholic schools. So let's cut the crap and be honest. Think you can handle that, boys?" Her laughter faded until all that remained was a thin, stern smile that reminded me of several nuns from St. Mary's. Sister Jean Rosina turned forward and stepped on the gas, spinning gravel from the shoulder as the heavy-duty V-8 cranked up and pulled the Checker out into the road.

John and I caught each other's glance, not exactly sure of what we had just walked into when the lecture started. Sister Rose, the passenger, was gentle, yet as direct as her partner.

"Now, boys, it's clear those aren't your real names, and starting with a lie, even a white lie, is simply a bad habit. One you can both do without. Let's get back on track—tell me your names and a short oral report on where you're from and why you are standing out on the side of this road. You there, stop biting your lip and begin."

John let his lip go from his front teeth and wiped the sweat from his brow with his sleeve. "Ma'am, I mean Sister, do you mind if I roll down the window? I'm getting pretty warm—"

Sister Jean cut him off. "Just keep the windows closed. If you're warm, just turn on those little fans behind you. Sister Rose will give you some water from our little cooler we keep up here. If you're on your best behavior, there are sandwiches to go around for lunch later. Now begin, young man."

"You got us, Sister. My friend here gave you fake names, all right. I'm John Parcell, and this is Luke Moore. And I took drugs today."

I hid my face with a hand. John was going to let it rip, and there was nothing I could do but watch.

John managed to keep himself under a semblance of control as his story spilled out. It was more like a confession, a side of John I barely knew. He earnestly wanted to perform as an artist, but was afraid. His fear prevented him from trying out for high school plays and musicals or joining the choir or showing his art to any but a limited few. He told of his insecurity and feeling of inferiority in the face of a talent like Elvis, and his resentment was obvious. He talked about the confines of family and school. *Christ, he's completely spilling the beans,* I thought. *But I know him better now.* John, thankfully, skipped details of drug use and finished with, "I'm aching to break out of this rut I'm in. I feel like the mold is hardening into cement."

"Very good, young man. That was honest and true, and you were respectful enough to avoid any seamy details that might offend two retired sisters like Sister Jean and me. And you can see you've calmed down quite a bit, and your sweating has stopped. You're quite comfortable now, aren't you?"

"Yes, Sister, I am." John reclined in the seat and closed his eyes. He seemed almost serene, except his eyelids were rapidly fluttering.

Sister Jean's eyes settled on me. I knew what was next and was anxious because this ride had turned out so strangely. I quickly analyzed what was wrong: two nuns do not pick up hitchhikers. The rolled-up windows and stifling air circulated by the tiny fans made it hard to breathe. I thought, *These nuns act like they know us, like they have a right to grill us and give us the third degree. They don't look familiar, but it seems like I know them from somewhere.*

The whole scene reminded me of a recurring dream from my childhood. Whenever I found myself in a lot of trouble, like getting a one-day suspension from school for counterfeiting milk tickets used in the cafeteria, I would go to sleep at night hoping to wake up and find out my life was really a dream. I dreamed about the details of this parallel life which starred me as a great, untroubled kid. At the end of the dream, my parallel persona would start to unravel, and it usually ended with me being chased by a variety of scary characters into a dead-end chasm. My only escape was to jump, which I always did. Upon jumping, I found I could fly. It wasn't a graceful Peter Pan or powerful Superman kind of flight. I ran hard, pumping my arms and legs furiously to avoid hitting the ground. Eventually, with the bad guys at my heels, I climbed through air just above telephone poles and trees to escape. Waking up in a fog, I didn't know if my dream life was real, or if I had to face the music with my mom about the suspension or whatever pickle I was currently dodging. That moment of entrapment between two worlds was what this car ride felt like.

"So, young man, I'm eager to hear your story, your real story. You seem to have so much pain those eyes," Sister Jean said.

The afternoon sun was streaming through the windshield so brightly, I had to squint to bring the nuns into focus.

Exhaling deeply, I told them, "Sisters, I hate to disappoint you, but I'm not going to tell you a story. No disrespect meant, but it's really none of your business."

The light seemed to intensify, bouncing off the marble-like foreheads of the good sisters as they looked at each other, their profiles illuminated, smiling.

Sister Rose said, "Now that makes some sense, young man. Your privacy is important, and I can tell you have good manners. Our job is to allow for confession, which can do the soul good when confession is a self-revelation. Your friend, John, needed it, as you could tell."

I looked over and saw John was asleep, looking peaceful. Sister Rose continued, "You need some help, but I think you'll be finding it soon. In the meantime, you need to keep out of harm's way. You might consider being thoughtful about all the risks you take. I know you're young and strong, with a quick mind and quick feet. But if you insist on dodging arrows and freight trains daily, you simply increase your odds of really hurting yourself and those who around you who care for you. Do you understand me?"

Sister Rose's voice had softened, and I was overcome with heaviness. I could barely keep my eyes open, fighting off the bright light and warmth in the car.

"I think so, Sister."

I felt myself falling asleep. I was pulled back to when Mom would tuck me into bed and sing until I was sound asleep. As I fell into sleep, I could hear Mom singing a bedtime song, her hand stroking my forehead, like she was right there.

John and I both slept until we heard Sister Rose's voice, gently, then stronger, calling us. "Boys, we're almost there. Come on, boys, wake up, wake up." We looked at each other in the backseat quizzically, wondering what had happened. I saw the gentle, rolling hills of the northern half of Michigan and knew the good sisters had covered some ground.

"How long have we been asleep, Sisters?" John asked.

"I'd say you boys have been dreaming for well over an hour. We'll be in Indian River in about a half an hour. That's our first stop. We didn't want to dump you on the side of the road, so it's rise and shine and give God his glory, glory!" Sister Rose announced.

"Boy, that's great, Sister Rose. We're headed to Topinabee and we're hoping to get there before dark. Are you stopping in Indian River to visit the big cross?" I asked.

"Absolutely, no self-respecting Catholic would miss the opportunity to view the largest wooden crucifix in the world. Or, for that matter, the Mystery Spot!" Sister Rose cackled.

"Or the Call of the Wild museum!" chirped Sister Jean.

"How about that Snake and Snail Hall of Fame in Grayling!" John laughed.

Sister Rose echoed, "Absolutely, it's our Christian duty to visit, along with the world's largest ball of yarn in Roscommon."

"Not to mention the world's largest rosary made out of pine cones in St. Helen's!" I added.

"St. Helen's, yes, there's a blessed city—I think the largest collection of tuning forks can also be found there!" John said.

As they bantered, I thought, *This is so strange—what was that freshman year vocab word?—so . . . ethereal.*

John kept the sisters entertained with a series of Catholic school stories that the nuns could appreciate. He made all of us laugh.

Sister Jean interrupted the stories. "Now, boys, we're going to be in Indian River in a few minutes. I know your destination is Topinabee, but I want you to consider coming to the big cross and visiting God with us for a few minutes. It's only a short drive from the exit. We'll have you on your way by 7:00 p.m."

I said, "Gee, Sister, we'd love to, but we really need to meet up with our friends."

Sister Rose said, "So you can go out and drink and raise Cain and probably Abel? Well, that just is not a good enough excuse. I think it's a fair enough bargain to give you this ride in exchange for this small pilgrimage, don't you?" Her eyes narrowed and her brow furrowed again. I knew this was a battle I wasn't going to win without being rude, and I was in debt for the ride, no matter how bizarre.

"It's all right with me. You okay, John?" I said. John nodded.

The mood lightened again, and we chatted as the Checker reached Indian River and exited off I-75. Within two miles, we reached the Catholic shrine, called the Cross in the Woods. John, Sister Rose, Sister Jean, and I left the parked Checker and walked to the large wooden placards explaining the shrine. John and I stood behind the sisters. They couldn't have been four and a half feet tall. Here we were at the big cross with two midget nuns who were driving an ancient cab. This was like the one Fellini movie I had seen by mistake.

The big cross story began in the late 1950s, as explained by the wooden signs. A Catholic priest living in northern Michigan was inspired by the story of a sixteenth-century, converted Indian girl who left handmade wood crucifixes wherever her travels took her. Kateri Tekakwitha was converted by Jesuits after her parents died of smallpox. She was shunned by her Mohawk tribe, went to live with a Catholic mission, and died at age 24 after establishing a reputation as the Johnny Appleseed of crucifixes. For her troubles, she was given "Blessed" status by the Catholic Church, a title just below sainthood.

A pious-looking guide also announced the various stops at the shrine, including the outdoor Stations of the Cross and the world's largest Nun Doll Store. "No wisecracks about the doll store, boys." Sister Jean looked over her shoulder and faked a grin at us.

Alright, Sister, but is it okay if we just go see the big cross? I know you're interested in spending some time here, but we really need to be on our way," I asked."

"We're interested in spending some time here with *you.* So let's go visit the cross and we'll be on our way," Sister Rose said.

We walked down the trail, two near-dwarf nuns leading us toward the big cross. I saw John's forehead wrinkle up in a headache, right frontal lobe throbbing. He reached into his jeans pocks and pulled out a hit of speed Wily had given him and furtively pitched it at the garbage can. The white pill with a cross on it landed on the remnant of peanut butter jelly sandwich. A black squirrel clambered up the side of the large garbage can, picked up the PB and J crust, munched on it, then took the white pill half covered in peanut butter in his tiny paws, and nibbled on that, too.

I whispered to John, who saw the squirrel munching on the peanut-butter covered speed, "Oh, Christ, a hopped-up squirrel. That's not right."

John put his hand to his throbbing forehead. "He's going to have bad headache when he comes down."

The path circled down through a grove of large, red pines into a grotto revealing the cross. It was immense. With our necks craned back, we looked up at the Marshall Fredericks bronze sculpture of Jesus affixed on the 55-foot-tall redwood crucifix. Jesus's face stared mournfully, painfully, down on us, framed by a green ring of treetops. The looming crucifix was contrasted by the dark blue sky at dusk, with passing clouds picking up the first hint of pink from a sunset beginning on an unseen horizon. Our unlikely foursome stood and stared, oblivious to both the devout tourists crawling up the stone stairway, praying at each step in mumbling undertones, and the chatty families armed with Instamatic cameras.

A grandmotherly tourist asked, "Did you save enough film for the big cross, Herb?"

Sister Jean pointed up past Jesus's head, where dusky clouds had opened up just enough to let a spray of light touch the top of the crucifix, giving the crown of thorns a muted illumination, and said, "There's where God must live."

I heard her, but couldn't believe my ears. That's what Annette had told me.

"What did you say, Sister?" I asked. My head was reeling.

"You heard me, Luke," she replied. Sister Rose turned to John and me.

"Boys, can't you see the majesty of God, inspired by the hand of art, surrounded by nature in the midst of God's children? It's all so imperfectly perfect. The lesson is simple. You have to remember to look, take the time to find your inspiration, your God. Have your fun, but as you move forward through life, remember to take the time to seek your true path. Your relationship with the spiritual world, with God, is yours and yours alone. When you reach and find the moment where you see divinity and it touches you, God will become personal. You deserve that joy."

Sister Jean continued, "That about wraps it up, boys. I think Sister Rose and I have said about all we want to hear! Let's get you to Topinabee."

The nuns both giggled, and they took both of us by our elbows and pointed us back to the parking lot. We sat in the back of the Checker silently as Sister Jean slowly pulled out of the parking spot. As the car started to move, a crowd of big cross visitors were streaming from the narrow path, walking fast, trotting, and some running to their cars. Sister Jean braked the car and watched the crowd grow. A middle-aged couple reached the end of the parking lot near the Checker. A balding, perspiring man fumbled for his car key.

Sister Jean rolled down her window and asked the man, "Sir, what's going on?"

"Ma'am, it's the darnedest thing, but there's a mad squirrel running amok at the big cross! I watched the darn thing hopping from Catholic to Baptist to Methodist who were making their prayer vigil on the Stairway to Jesus. That dang squirrel was jumping from back to back right up to the cross, and then he ran straight up the cross so fast, all you could make out is a blur of fur! Then he started doing laps around the crown of thorns, top to bottom and back up again. Then the critter launched himself like he was Rocky the

Flying Squirrel off Jesus's crown of thorns onto a priest's chest! The priest fainted, and the squirrel leapt onto a lady's hat, then onto a blind man's buttocks—excuse the expression, ma'am—and the blind man ran around trying to knock the squirrel off his buttocks with his white cane, and finally the squirrel jumped off and scrambled up the big cross again, holding tight to the Savior's nose and shaking like a leaf. People were panicking and running in all different directions by this time, and I high-tailed it out of there with my missus. Some people are saying it's some kinda sign from God—that God is trying to tell us something through this squirrel. A group of them stayed at the cross. They're praying the rosary right now. Me and the missus just thought that squirrel was crazier than my Uncle Mort, who's been in a VA hospital for 20 years!"

Sister Jean replied, "Well, I'll be! God does sometimes work in strange ways. Bless you, sir."

John and I looked at each other, trying to figure out whether to laugh or cry.

We drove the ten miles to Topinabee in easy conversation. It was a nice drive at dusk as we sailed through downtown Indian River and between the expansive twin Burt and Mullett Lakes on Old 27. Our friend Tony Muldano lived in a house on a hill just off the main drag in Topinabee. I directed Sister Jean where to pull off the two-lane highway, close enough to Tony's house for us to walk.

"Well, young men, this is the end of our day together. Good luck in your lives, and remember what you learned today. You're good boys, and we have high hopes for you," Sister Jean said as Sister Rose smiled.

"Thank you, Sisters. I'm not sure about what happened today, but thank you for your kindness. Where are you off to tonight?" John asked.

"Oh, we old nuns have plenty of places we call home. We'll be partying in Mackinaw City before you know it, young man!"

"I believe it, Sister. Good night and travel safely." John climbed out of the car, pulling his duffel bag along with him. I lingered for a minute, fiddling with my backpack. I looked up at the sisters, both smiling at me.

"Sisters, what . . . who are you, really? I mean, this has been a very different ride and experience. I mean, nuns never pick up hitchhikers, do they? And, Sister Jean, when you told me, 'That's where God lives,' well, I had someone tell me that not too long ago. Who exactly are you, and what are you doing out on the road picking up guys like us?"

Sister Rose patted, and then held, my hand that rested on the front seat. "Luke, you'll figure it out. We're just so happy we could spend some time with you, maybe help you and your stubborn self to see the world in a different way. Before long, you'll be able to see around corners. Now, good-night and Godspeed."

Sister Jean turned and smiled. "Luke, we're just a couple of old nuns trying to save a few lost souls!" She winked at me and laughed.

As I opened the car door, headlights from an approaching car filled the Checker, and through the bright light I saw something change in their faces. I left the car, calling back, "Thank you both. I won't forget you."

"We know you won't!" called Sister Rose as Sister Jean pulled out onto the highway.

I stood and watched the car disappear before turning to see John looking up the hill toward Tony's cabin. Standing on the cabin's porch, watching the sunset blend into twilight over Mullett Lake, was a comely young woman, and even in the waning light, it was apparent she was stunningly beautiful.

John nudged me and pointed up the hill. "Luke, is that some apparition sent by the nuns?"

I sighed, "After today, I'd believe just about anything." We reached for our bags and walked up the hill, the night's first stars appearing above us.

Chapter 17

September 2003

I pulled into the last rest area in the Lower Peninsula and parked the minivan among the gray-haired tourists who waited until after Labor Day, when kids were back to school, before venturing out on fall color tours. Tom slid back the van's door, and Roberta followed him toward the new bathroom building that featured indoor plumbing. Marta was a chapter away from finishing her book, and she could get persnickety if I interrupted her as she wound down with a favorite story. At my peril, I did it anyway.

"Marta, why do you think they call these places rest areas? Hardly anybody rests here. I mean, look, nine out of ten people just leave their car, stretch their arms above their head, and go take a leak. Look, just like that old guy there, that's the stretch I'm talking about. All right, there's a few people having lunch on the picnic table, and the dog run is in use. But think about it, who wants to rest at a place meant for dogs and people to pee and poop? Doesn't make sense, does it? And if you do rest too long, or fall asleep, you can get a ticket. It would make more sense to call these relieve-yourself areas or take-a-stretch-and-pee areas. Use something more accurately descriptive. What do you think, Marta? Am I onto something, or am I over-thinking this whole shebang?"

No response. I waited until she looked up from her book. "Do you know who would use this line of logic?"

I smiled because it was obvious. "Yeah, good old John Parcell. I was just thinking about him. You know, we hitchhiked this stretch of road . . . of course you do. I miss him. I miss all of them."

"I know you do, dear. It will be a very good thing when we see them again. Now, is there anything else you want to talk about before I finish reading the last eighteen pages of this book?"

"Just one more thing, Marta. I'm getting a vibe off our young fellow traveler. Might be nothing, but he's not playing it straight with us. He's not a storyteller, either. He's just not telling the truth, and I'm not sure why. It's not strong enough to worry about, but if I change the itinerary, stay with me, okay?"

"You know I will, Luke. This is your field of play. But if you get a stronger feeling, we dump him like a load of coal, right?"

"Faster than that, my dear."

Tom and Roberta walked back toward the van and stepped back in.

"All set, you two?" I asked.

"Yes, sir, Mr. Moore," Tom replied

"Yes, Dad, I'm ready to make it to the UP I'm going to be a Yooper once we cross the bridge, eh?"

"We'll see, sweetie. It might take more than a term of school in the U.P. to get the accent on the right syl-*la*-ble, don't you know?"

Everyone settled back into their seats, and I accelerated fast to merge from the rest area back onto I-75. I pushed the van up to seventy-eight miles an hour, less than ten over the speed limit, making a fair bet against a speeding ticket in my future. I passed a Saturn with a white-haired driver in the high-speed lane, and just as I set the cruise control, a canary-yellow Corvette pulled up fast behind me. There was a string of cars traveling below seventy in the right-hand lane, so I punched the accelerator to pass them, planning to get out of the way of the Corvette pronto. I hit eighty-two miles per hour as we passed under a highway bridge. The state trooper was hidden just past the bridge.

"Damn!" I said as I finished passing the slower cars and merged right. The state police car's flashing lights were already on as it rolled off the shoulder in fast pursuit. My heart went staccato. Surprise police cars with flashing lights had induced a variety of anxiety responses since the summer of 1973, when a squadron surrounded me.

The Corvette behind me reacted too late, the middle-aged driver roaring by. The cop passed me and was on the Corvette's tail in a minute. I double-sighed and started to relax as the Corvette and trooper pulled over in tandem.

"Thought he was after you, huh, Dad? You look like you saw a ghost. You've never had a ticket, have you, Dad?"

"No tickets. Just a bad experience in my delinquent youth. I've told you the story before. It wasn't far from here. It was a bad end to a great summer."

"I've heard the don't-do-drugs version, but never the true story. How about you tell us the grown-up version? You've told me the children's fable variation enough times," Roberta said.

I looked over at Marta. She peered over her reading glasses.

"Our daughter is eighteen years old and off to college. I think she can handle it."

"Well, I do have a hard time turning down a willing and trapped audience, a storyteller's dream come true. I'll give you the slightly varnished account, instead of the fully lacquered rendering. Now, where to begin?"

Tom Lutac chimed in. "At the beginning, Mr. Moore. Always at the beginning."

The zinger made us all smile.

Chapter 18

April 1973

This was my second trip to Tony Muldano's place. As John and I trudged up the hill, I was grateful Tony was another gracious friend. I knew we could drop in without any notice and be welcome. John and I knew Tony from first grade. While we were busy playing sports, he learned how to hunt, fish, and thrive in the woods with his dad. We went to the same school for twelve years, and as our circle began leaving for weekend camping trips, we connected and became friends.

Tony was handsome, but he fought to keep his weight under control, which fluctuated up in the winter and down during summer and hunting season. Two weeks after our high school graduation, he'd moved to Topinabee to work in a family friend's tavern. Since the Roy family had moved north to Topinabee five years prior and bought the Breakers Bar, they had been host to Tony and his family many times. Tony's dream was to live where he could reach unspoiled country in minutes, not hours.

Within a month, Tony taught himself how to short-order cook masterfully. He developed a new clientele for the tavern, including a faithful breakfast trade that came to see him juggle pancakes and French toast, or over-easy eggs, four, six, eight at a time.

On the weekends, the Breakers hosted local bands, mostly country-and-western dance groups. When Glen Reed and his Hoedowners lost their drummer to his third DUI, Tony learned the drumming basics in a week and stepped in the following weekend. Within two months, he convinced the Roys to book the rock-and-roll band and immediately doubled the weekend beer intake. Before the end of the summer, he had moved to lead guitar, his thick fingers finding a home on the fret board. On a return visit to Royal Oak, he welcomed visitors to Topinabee. John and I were part of a regular stream of Lost Souls looking for a party up north.

The cabin in Topinabee was in a spectacular setting overlooking Mullett Lake, which, in spite of its ignominious name, is one of Michigan's largest and most beautiful lakes. In addition to the natural beauty of the lake and the usual recreational boating, swimming, and fishing, it was renowned for its huge sturgeons, which were speared during the ice-fishing season with large, Poseidon-like tridents. The record sturgeon speared was over six feet, killed by a seventy-six-year-old Topinabee native known as Otis.

Tony reveled in the man-oriented outdoor activities northern Michigan offered, and became skilled at taking brown trout from the Sturgeon River. The locals did not warm easily to city interlopers finding their favorite fishing and hunting spots. But Tony was a big, gregarious guy, and even the natives found him likable. That's how he became the perfect guide and entry point for the parade of city kids that came to stay at his cabin on the hill. The only pimple on Tony's butt was his landlady, Mavis Morton. She thought she had fleeced the city kid, charging him three hundred dollars a month, a hundred dollars over market, for her deceased parents' home, which was in dire need of maintenance. Originally a charming one-bedroom rustic cabin built in the 1920s, the house had been remodeled and enlarged in a haphazard manner that eliminated the appeal, with the exception of the view.

What Mavis hadn't counted on was Tony subletting the extra two bedrooms, the basement, and the front porch, in addition to allowing weekend visitors to pitch tents in the backyard. Tony was amused by the chaos; Mavis was not. She would show up unannounced at odd hours, striding into the kitchen through the back door and berating Tony for having too many people in the house, the mess in the kitchen sink, or anything else that struck her. She would work herself into a rage, her voice rising and shaking along with her three chins. Tony patiently listened and lied to Mavis that the mess would be cleaned up and the visitors would be leaving soon. She would have evicted Tony, except the unmarried, loveless Mavis had a crush on him.

I knew all this from my last visit to Tony's place, which had lasted three weeks, a lifetime of staying in one place during my travels. I wasn't sure where this stop was going to lead. I figured I was good for a week, including the upcoming weekend with John.

He had entertained me all day and was still chattering on as we reached the top of the hill. The girl we saw from the bottom of the hill was still standing outside the cabin's porch, viewing the sunset's denouement. She was dressed in a simple, white linen dress, cinched at her waist and unbuttoned at the top to reveal a tanned chest and a hint of cleavage. Her long, brown hair fell past her shoulders.

We reached the top of the hill and porch, and John was off to the races. "Hi, I'm John Parcell, and this is Luke Moore. We're friends of Tony's. Is he home? Can we come in? What's your name?"

"My, you're full of questions. That's not good. My name is Sydney Smolinski, and don't call me Syd. It's Sydney. Come on in."

As we followed Sydney through the front porch, I noticed she walked with a pronounced limp. We entered the living room, the largest in the house. The entirety of the décor was early Kmart and late Salvation Army. Two card tables pushed together acted as a dining room table, surrounded by lawn chairs and battered folding chairs. A sofa, the only upholstered furniture in the house, was covered with an Army surplus blanket and faced a black-and-white TV. In front of the TV was another card table, with Tony and three locals sitting and playing euchre, smoking giant cigars, the blue smoke filling the room. Tony turned and saw us.

"Parcell! Moore!" he boomed.

Tony pushed back his chair and grabbed me into a bear hug, picking me up off the floor and parading me through the living room. "I've got myself a jive-ass city dude here!" He dropped me on the sofa and seized John. "City dude number two!" He threw John on top of me and then jumped on top of both us, pounding at us with harmless punches.

We rolled onto the floor, wrestling until one of the card players yelled, "Okay, homos, that's enough touchy-feely, we're in the middle of a goddamn game here."

Tony scrambled to his feet and into his high school wrestling position. "I'm way too much for these wimps," he said, sweat dripping from his forehead. "It's great to see you, boys. John, I'd never guessed you'd make it up here. Your old lady let loose of the gonads, eh?"

"Lois sends her regards, Tony," John answered.

Tony introduced the card players, who were also his bandmates. They had nicknames that didn't seem to match their appearances. The piano player, Tiny, was average size. The bass player, Smiley, didn't; his expressionless, closed mouth was framed by an oversized handlebar mustache. The drummer's moniker, Rock, could have been used to describe the massive head on top of his thin frame, but it was a stretch. "And I see you met our groupie, Sydney," Tony finished.

"In your wildest dreams, Tony," Sydney retorted.

"No, really, Sydney is good people. She's from downstate, too, from the beautiful downriver city of Wyandotte. She's permanently screwed up like the rest of us, a good Catholic girl. Ain't that right, Sydney?"

"Absolutely. My life has been a binge and purge of sin and guilt, guilt and sin. It's a revolving door of feeling good and then feeling bad about feeling good. Some days I sin so much I feel guilty about feeling guilty, the ultimate Catholic paradox."

Tony shouted, "Well, boys, welcome to Topinabee. My home is your home, unless my landlady comes in, then you're staying someplace else, capisce? You're welcome to stay a week. After that, if there's an empty room, you start paying rent and chip in for expenses. You guys ought to be starving! I've got some special award-winning Muldano venison chili cooking on the stove. Hot enough to burn the hair off your legs. You eat, I'll finish this game, and then we can catch up. Sydney, would you be so kind to show these boys the kitchen?"

"Sure, Tony, that's my goal in life: to feed and care for your friends. After they're done eating, I'll make sure to take care of their sexual fantasies. This way, boys, to food and kinky sex!"

She gestured grandly to the kitchen and then led us to the well-used kitchen with a sink littered with two days of dishes and a four-gallon pot of chili bubbling on the stove. In the brighter light of the kitchen, John and I simultaneously noticed that Sydney was missing three fingers on her left hand, with only the index finger and thumb remaining. It made her hand permanently look like she had a gun, ready to shoot. She noticed our observation, frowned, shook her head, and reached for a knitted purse on the kitchen counter. She pulled out a stack of three-by-five cards held by a rubber band. She peeled two cards out with her right hand and handed one each to John and me. We were both flummoxed as we read her preprinted explanation of her missing fingers and more.

> You noticed and stared, and I'm tired of explaining, so read this and DON'T ASK ME ANY QUESTIONS! I repeat, DON'T ASK ME ANY QUESTIONS.
>
> I lost my fingers and my foot (in case you didn't notice that yet) in a water-skiing accident. I was practicing for a competition on Burt Lake when a drunken idiot turned his boat right into my wake. I fell and my left foot hit the propeller first, followed by my hand. The prop slashed my foot so badly it had to be amputated and then tore my fingers off. (Turn card over)

As instructed, John and I turned the card over and it read:

> I lost the foot below the ankle. I wear a prosthesis, aka fake foot, which is why I wear these unfashionable shoes. I still ski competitively, and other than idiots staring at me and asking me stupid questions, I am just fine, thank you. That's it. DON'T ASK ANY QUESTIONS!

John muttered, "What the hell." I was wordless. Sydney acted nonchalantly, standing at the stove ladling chili with a coffee cup into a bowl. John walked over next to her and said, "Sydney, I just have one question."

She roared, "What in God's name is wrong with you? Can't you read? I said no questions! What can be clearer than that? For two years I've had to explain again and again. It's really none of your goddamn business anyway—"

John put a hand on Sydney's shoulder and interrupted her. "I just want to know if there are any oyster crackers to go with this chili." Sydney's face went from a florid red to crimson embarrassed, "Yes . . . yes, up in the cabinet over the fridge." She grabbed a spoon and huffed into the living room.

"That wasn't very nice, John," I said.

"I just couldn't help myself, Luke, it was the perfect set-up. And she deserved it. I mean, c'mon, she limps and has fingers missing. People are going to be curious. I have to admit, that card she hands out is a hoot. You never can tell about a strong-minded girl like that. I'm thinking that calling her out gives me an outside shot that she's going to like me after all. Although I'm not betting on a positive result."

"No shit, Sherlock," I agreed.

Sydney reappeared at the kitchen door, "I forgot my chili."

We stared at our feet. "I guess I deserved that," she half-smiled. John looked up with a shamefaced grin to see Sydney's smile turn sideways.

"That doesn't mean you are not a complete asshole, John Parcell. Christ, you just made me feel like Charlie Brown when Lucy pulled that damn football right out from under him. Nice guy!"

John replied, "I'm really sorry."

She cut him off. "Don't start. Let's eat hot chili and drink cold beer, okay?"

"Sounds good," I said.

"Hey, Luke, you may want to use Sydney's three-by-five card approach. Only you'd need a stack three inches high to tell your tale of woe," John laughed.

I rolled my eyes, and Sydney said, "Oh, good, another sordid story. I'd love to lose my 'That's so sad' title!"

We sat at the makeshift table and scarfed chili, talked, and listened to the euchre players mindlessly describe each hand, blow-by-blow, interrupted by whoops and yells, countered by curses and expletives at every euchre, loner, or bonehead play.

John and I spent the summer living in Tony Muldano's house in Topinabee. Within a week, we both had jobs, John as a short-order cook at Christopher's in Indian River. I found a seasonal job with the Department of Natural Resources, picking up garbage at the seven state forest campgrounds scattered across Emmet County. I loved the job. I drove over a hundred miles a day in a shiny DNR truck, and about every ten miles, I would hit a crest in the road and see a glittering lake vista, or a pair of hawks circling, or deer whose white tails would pop up, frozen by surprise for a second, before bounding off. It was a true change of scenery, as I kept the job all summer, breaking my job longevity record by weeks. I managed to save some money and send small amounts of cash to Ann and Donnie. For John, not returning to Royal Oak was viewed as temporary insanity, and I bore partial brunt for his bad decision. His parents couldn't comprehend what had possessed John, and his longtime girlfriend, Lois, became temporarily possessed, driving immediately to Indian River and demanding John return home. But John had left the reservation and wasn't going back anytime soon.

I was surprised by John's decision and resolve. In a heartbeat, he gave up a girlfriend, peace with his parents, a job, and his next term at college—darn near most of his life—for an unsettled life in Topinabee as a short-order cook. I wasn't sure if I liked the competition for chief screw-up.

Unlike me, John had a new plan. It started with Sydney, who, halfway through the summer, started to laugh at his patter and then fell for him. John also performed a stand-up comedy routine, first at the Breakers Bar, where Tony Muldano managed and hosted a Monday night open-mic night. By the end of the summer, he earned his first money as a comedian at the Wigwam in Afton. The summer's applause changed his life.

My summer was a pleasant version of limbo. I wasn't getting anywhere fast, but I wasn't backpedaling either. I made new friends who enjoyed the same bad habits I did. But I never missed a day of work: the routine of supporting myself and the outdoor recreation were satisfying.

I kept in touch with my family, Kate, Elvis, Mark, and even Lois, via letters and postcards. I missed them, but didn't venture downstate all summer, a sure sign that I was teetering toward some type of normalcy. The peacefulness didn't last long.

Near the end of summer, on a late August Saturday evening, John, Sydney, and I planned to meet Tony at the Indian River Inn in advance of a giant party that was planned at Slim Perkins's place about six miles east of Indian River. Labor Day was approaching, and the college students would soon be returning to school. The summer season ended at Labor Day, and nearly everyone worked double shifts to keep the tourists in gas, food, suntan oil, souvenirs, film, and fudge.

An Indian River tradition had developed the weekend before Labor Day over the last four years. Slim's Dome Party was an old-fashioned field party: pig roast, roasted corn, keg beer, including a pot-luck and an outdoor stage with bands that played for pork and beer and a hundred dollars. The cost was ten bucks per person, and Slim had hosted four hundred people the previous year, clearing sixteen hundred dollars after expenses.

Slim had built a geodesic dome as a home on the eighty acres he bought with the earnings he made from his firewood business, established in high school. Although Slim's hair was long, and he grew pot and lived in a geodesic dome, he wasn't a sixties hippie. His politics were rural conservative, stay-the-hell-out-of-my-life. He accommodated the college students who worked the summer tourist jobs, but had a thinly disguised disdain for the tourists who were his customers.

Thanks to Tony, Slim's Dome Party had the reputation as the "biggest, baddest-ass blowout pig roast in Michigan." Sydney, John, and I were drinking Cokes at the Indian River Inn when Tony joined us. "You ready to party, northern Michigan style?" Tony asked. He ordered a beer and put a quarter in the coin slot for the pool table.

Suddenly, the side door of the bar opened and two men rushed Tony, grabbing his arms and pushing his head and upper torso down on the table. Nearly everyone in the room knew Tony, and stood up in unison to help him as he struggled against his attackers. Tony yelled, "What the hell?" into the green felt of the pool table. But John and I stood back and laughed. It was a Lost Soul ambush.

"'What the hell? What the hell?' Is that all you have to say, Muldano?" The duo let go of Tony's arms and sprang back. He leapt off the pool table and turned to find Elvis and Mark laughing, but rapidly being surrounded by the young crowd in the bar.

"Elvis, Mark, you assholes!" Tony saw the bar crowd closing in on his friends and raised his hands. "You guys, it's okay. These guys are my buds, believe it or not. Meet Elvis and Mark, a couple of Lost Souls from the big, bad city down below."

He grabbed Elvis's and Mark's heads in the crooks of his elbows and pulled them tight. John and I jumped out of our seats and enveloped the three of them. We laughed and hugged as the bar crowd dispersed.

Kate and Lois stood just inside the bar door.

Tony noticed Lois and said, "Lois, good God, it's great to see you." He strode over and gave her a big hug. "And you will just have to be Kate Brady. I can barely remember what you look like, but you are a sight for this northern kid's sore eyes. Oh, man, you two chicks are beautiful."

Tony grabbed Lois and Kate by the elbows and joined us in the middle of the bar. We hugged and jabbered until John put some tables and chairs together for us. Kate held me a few seconds.

"It's good to see you, Luke Moore. I've been missing you since you left me alone in Royal Oak."

"You too, Kate. I'm glad you made it up to my new stomping grounds."

"Seems like your pals and I had to come and make sure you and John are alive and kicking in the North Country."

It could have been an uncomfortable reunion with Lois's arrival, but Mark McInerny had called John a week earlier with the plans. "Well, old pal, you won't believe this, but Lois and I have hit it off. I mean really hit it off. I just want you to know. And that flyer you sent us on this Dome Party next weekend? We decided to make the trip. Lois and me, and Elvis and Kate. Think you can handle that, John? It'll be cool, right?"

John and Mark had talked on the phone and sorted out the situation with Lois and Sydney. They agreed it was an odd set of circumstances, but Mark was happy to be with Lois, Lois was happy with Mark, and John was happy for both of them. Particularly, since his plan to woo Sydney was working.

I watched as Sydney met Lois, and they gave each other a tentative hug. It was strange to see Lois lean into Mark while John stood behind Sydney, close enough to signify they were together.

Elvis eased the tension by saying, "Jesus, it's Bob and Carol and Ted and Alice. I feel like I'm in a goddamn soap opera!"

It was also strange to see Elvis dote on Kate. They sat next to me with their hands interlocked. Elvis paid more attention to Kate than the rest of us. That was a first. Kate looked terrific, and I told her so.

"Well, thank you, Luke. I feel great. And I do appreciate you answering my letters, even if every response was on a postcard featuring Indian River's big cross."

"Tony had about a hundred of those cards, and postage is cheaper with postcards," I replied.

"However you did it, I'm glad you stayed in touch," Kate said.

Tony stood up and said, "Okay, enough, let's get this show on the road. To the Dome!"

We touched our Coke and beer bottles together and toasted, "To the Dome!"

Tony's pickup and Mark's Chevelle bounced us along the back roads to the Dome. We turned right through a passage created by a stand of pines, and the party came into view. There was a variety of tents, ranging from two-man pup tents to larger, multi-colored tents, set up in a semi-circle around a homemade stage and dance floor next to the Dome. A rockabilly band named the Sturgeon River Boys was playing to a large group of mostly male youths doing the rural half-jam dance step, which consisted of moving only the upper body. Tony led our group over to a card table where Slim Perkins was collecting ten-dollar bills and marking each of us with a "Dome" stamp.

We all paid and made our way to the beer tent, eager to grab our beer cups and find a table at the food tent. The first spit-roasted pig was already carved and served with firepot-baked potatoes, roasted corn, and warm, homemade applesauce sprinkled with fresh cinnamon. Wendy, Slim's wife, prepared the food. Desserts were pot luck, and a large picnic table was laden with specialties by the young women. Tony grabbed a plate of food and made his way to the stage.

I sat at a picnic table with my oldest friends. We ate, drank, and laughed as the party built and raged outside the tent. It was unsettling to see the three couples—Lois and Mark, Elvis and Kate, and John and Sydney—touching each others' arms and hands playfully and lovingly. I didn't have to say much, as everyone was talking loudly above the music. Kate caught my eye and winked. Man, these were good friends, but I was still the odd man out. We split up as the night progressed, making new friends by sharing a joint or a puff of pipe.

By midnight, Slim announced from the bandstand that the paying customer count had reached 442, a new Dome record. The hard-packed dirt dance floor was jammed, while the night's best band, the Windchill Factor, riffed through an Allman Brothers set. We dispersed from the food tent. Relatively sober, I felt that ache in my gut that usually called me back to the road. I watched as the throng danced and sweated. I knew what most of the guys were thinking: *I hope like hell I find somebody in my sleeping bag at night's end, and that she won't make me cringe when I wake up with the inevitable hairy hangover in the morning.* It was obvious that the mix of beer, hormones, and music was overwhelming respectable inhibitions. Pheromones were gaining ground. I could sense the night was going to get messy in some way. These many young people teetering into intoxication would turn raucous and produce some memorable moments of fun and pain. How many of the night's couplings were going to result in passing on venereal diseases?

The latest scourge of free love was herpes. This little virus was permanent. Hell, the clap was a bummer, but at least you could get shots and chase it away. I remembered Adell's description of the various forms of VD that lasted a week or forever. A thought crept into my head: how many coital sleeping bags would be the beginning of the end of sexual freedom for the glistening youths of summer? But no one was thinking of that now. For the partiers, the night was filled with sweet, immortal youth, and what they lacked in perspective they overcame with mass exuberance.

I shook reality from my head and watched John dance with Sydney. He was a good dancer: he spun and twirled Sydney into his arms. She was graceful, even with a missing foot. I knew she was falling for my friend, and that made me happy. They finished the dance swaying in each other's arms as the band ended their set.

Tony was on the stage urging the crowd on. "Let's let those guys know how much we appreciate them. C'mon, let's hear it for the Windchill Factor."

Nearly all the 442 paid youths, plus the Perkins family and the twenty or so ne'er-do-wells who snuck in (and less the eight teenagers passed out from drinking apple Boones Farm wine) yelled, clapped, and whistled their approval.

As Tony wound down the applause, he spotted John and Sydney. "John," he called through the mic, "how about it, you have a song in mind to kick this bad boy into high gear? Whaddya say?"

John looked at Sydney, who had had other plans, but she said, "Go for it, John."

"All right, but only if you come up with me."

He led Sydney by the hand as she gently protested, but the part of the crowd that knew him called for John.

Tony exhorted the rest, "Ladies and gentlemen, natives and fudgies, summer worker bees, tonight, direct from the Breakers, a summer institution, let me introduce the man with a story and a song, John Parcell!"

John pulled himself up on the stage with a hand from Tony and took the mic. During the last three months, John had parlayed the "open mic night" at the Breakers into an event drawing standing-room-only crowds. Word had spread about John's off-the-wall stories, which found a way to touch both oldsters and teenagers. He had introduced a closing sing-along that was popular with inebriated tongues at the bar.

"All right, everybody! It's time for audience participation. One song, brothers and sisters. I'll get it started, and Tony will take it from there," John shouted into the microphone.

Imagine me and you I do
I think about you day and night
It's only right
To think about the girl you love
And hold her tight
So happy together
If I should call you up, invest a dime
And you say you belong to me
And ease my mind
Imagine how the world could be
So very fine
So happy together
I can't see me lovin' nobody but you
For all my life
Me and you and you and me

No matter how they toss the dice
It had to be
The only one for me is you
And you for me
So happy together
I can't see me lovin' nobody but you
For all my life
When you're with me baby the skies'll be blue
For all my life

Everyone in the crowd knew the words. Filled with beer and youth, we bellowed out the end of summer.

Me and you and you and me
No matter how they toss the dice
It had to be
The only one for me is you
And you for me
So happy together
Me and you and you and me
No matter how they toss the dice
It had to be
The only one for me is you
And you for me
So happy together
So happy together
How is the weather
So happy together
We're happy together
So happy together
Happy together
So happy together
So happy together!

The crowd roared. John shouted into the microphone, "That's it for tonight, folks. There's still some serious drinking to be done as we take one last run at this fantastic, ass-kickin', earth-shakin', knee-knockin' summer of bliss in northern Michigan! Let's party on and remember our friends. And please, please be happy together!"

The crowd roared approval. Tony pushed an eight-track into the stereo system that boomed "Yours Is No Disgrace" by Yes. The crowd slowly moved to the beer and food tents or off to their makeshift campsites. The Royal Oak gang mobbed John when he jumped off the stage.

"I had no goddamned idea you could do that, John. What the hell!" Elvis roared.

"Who stole my friend John Parcell? Where have you put him, you lousy bastard!" Mark yelled and pounded John's back.

Kate told John he was terrific. Lois pulled him close, kissed him on the cheek and whispered into his ear. I thought that maybe this was all working out for the best.

I cajoled my friends to head out to the campsite. Sydney and I had set up our camp in a meadow a few hundred yards away from the party. I had loaded Sydney's car before we left Indian River and slipped away during the party and set up our camp. I had also scrounged up two large beer coolers: one to keep beer cold and to avoid multiple trips to the beer tent, and the other with fixings for pork sandwiches and breakfast for the morning, including powdered doughnuts. I dug out a fire pit and bought a night's supply of Slim's discounted seasoned hardwood. My friends settled into the camp quickly. Mark and Elvis built a fire, and we soon were lounging around the flames, sitting in cheap lawn chairs and wrapped in blankets, toasting marshmallows.

Elvis reviewed his band's tours on the Holiday Inn circuit in Ohio and Indiana. He was on the road from Wednesday through Saturday, and since the local groupies were now off the table, he was getting bored and lonely.

Kate laughed and said, "Yeah, so my loyal boyfriend convinced me to go on the road with him. I had couple days off my new job on the Fourth of July weekend, so I found myself in Fort Wayne, Indiana, listening to my sweetie play the same set four nights in row. It was kinda fun to watch Elvis fend off the budding groupies. And as much as I love spending time with you, Elvis, it was the most boring four days of my life. So, we have learned that absence really does make the heart grow fonder."

"And you weren't very happy when I finally found the right answer to keep those Indiana chicks from asking me out," Elvis said.

"No kidding. Telling those girls I was the head groupie for the band was not a term of endearment," Kate replied.

"But it did work," Elvis said.

"I'll give you that, and only that, Elvis. And with my career as head groupie ended, I was lucky enough to find out that Lois was looking for a roommate so she could move out of her parents' house. We found a nice, cheap, two-bedroom flat in Ferndale. And we like each other and have been talking about how we aren't really sure why we need men after all," Kate said.

"Amen to that, sister," Lois agreed and raised her beer cup toward Kate.

"Although, for some unknown reason we have been double dating with Elvis and Mark all summer. I guess they provide some light entertainment," Kate finished.

"Amen again." Lois raised her cup again.

"Hey, Elvis, I think we have the makings of pretty good gigolos, don't you think?" Mark said.

I stood up and raised my glass. "I'm stepping in here, because it's getting way too thick. I'm just glad you're all here and looking pretty damn happy. I'm glad you could see a little bit of why John and I have stayed here all summer. I'm glad that Tony took us two vagrants in and that we met Sydney and that John has cut loose and started getting up on stage. Here's to us and being glad. A toast to my friends, old and new!

"Lost Souls!" Elvis yelled.

"Lost Souls!" we rejoined.

We continued talking, catching up on the summer and the changes we didn't expect. I listened to the stories, some new, some old, and considered how we were growing up even as we fought it. The flames of the fire flickered and retreated into the pulsating coals.

Kate had found work at the YMCA as a program director for the summer youth program.

"I can't believe that the attention span of ten-year-old kids is about six seconds. And unfortunately, my teenage counselors aren't much better. I found if I just keep everybody busy playing kickball, running races, sculpting blobs of clay into ashtrays for their moms and dads, and generally exhaust them, everybody leaves at the end of the day tired and happy."

Kate was a natural at the job and found it balanced her young love affair with Elvis.

Lois had started working as a dental technician after completing a two-year course at Oakland Community College. The pay was adequate, the hours regular, and the job secure; tartar was not going away, and the UAW medical plans paid for teeth cleaning.

I knew Lois was tough and strong, but her breakup with John was a singularly huge defeat in her fairy-tale plan: secure a loving husband with a good job, two kids, a cottage up north, and enough money to help out her parents, who were hurting financially since a plant accident landed her dad on disability.

While turning to Mark might have appeared as a fast rebound relationship, she had also known Mark since grade school, and out of the group of friends, he was the calmest and steadiest. Mark was the least adventurous of the Lost Souls. Of the four friends, he could see a good life with a good wife and lots of children and an ice rink in the backyard. I knew they were a good fit.

Mark told me he found himself lonely this summer with both John and me up north and Elvis on the road. He was an expert at the one-night stand, but that was beginning to bore him.

He leaned over to me and said, "I never would have guessed that Lois and I would get together. I'll tell you, she just calms me down. And man, Luke, she is a hottie. Look at that figure!"

In my opinion, everybody involved in their new romances was darn accommodating, because everybody was getting laid regularly. Except me. As the night turned late, the embers of the fire were just bright enough to illuminate our faces as we told our summer stories. The current tales devolved into our past, shared histrionics, which I embellished and then Mark, Elvis, and John corrected.

Sydney interrupted one of my stories. "For a bunch of young guys, you sure like to trip down memory lane, don't you?"

"Yeah, you guys sound like my dad and his war buddies, but they're all old men in their forties," Lois said.

"I guess it's just guy gossip. You boys are like old ladies in a sewing circle," Kate laughed.

"That would be us," I answered.

"Hey Luke, did you ever find that girl from Cincinnati?" Kate asked.

"Marta?" I answered. "No luck. She told me she was going to be at the Wycamp Lake State Forest Campground on the Fourth of July weekend. Tony lent me his truck to drive up. I found a ranger who pulled her campsite permit, but he said there was a big party that got out of hand and ended in a fight. The campers had cleared out the day before. I was a day late."

"That's probably for the best, Luke," Kate said.

"Easy for you to say, love-struck," I said, and pushed Kate.

My friends had all settled back into easy conversation over the fire. Sydney leaned over and whispered into John's ear. He stood up and she took his hand and led him away from the campfire, guiding him through a grove of red pines to her tent, just under the canopy of an ancient willow tree. They walked quietly, hand-in-hand, to the clearing, until Sydney turned and smiled upward into John's face, glistening from the heat of the fire. I nudged Kate. We watched John and Sydney's silhouettes in the early autumn moonlight.

"There's a happy man," Kate said.

"It's been a big summer for John. I'm happy for him," I replied.

Lois and Mark had retreated to a corner of the Perkins acreage with sleeping bags and U.S. Army shelter halves, courtesy of Mr. McInerny's garage attic. Kate and I sat next to each other in the lawn chairs. Elvis was a few yards away from the fire, snoozing on top of his sleeping bag, his hands behind his head for a pillow. Kate and I laughed at the sleep-talking coming from Elvis. He had done this since he was a little boy. Mark and I discovered it on our first sleepover in the McInernys' backyard. Elvis would talk softly, but clearly, just as he entered sleep, tailing off as he fell deeper into his dreams.

We listened to him and snickered until he slept soundly, and then watched the fire as I poked at the logs, creating orange flickers.

"All right, it's late. We've had a few beers, everyone's gone, let's have ourselves a little heart-to-heart," Kate said. "Thanks for being a good letter-reader this summer. I needed to pour my soul out to somebody, and, well, you were the lucky reader. I really appreciate you listening and writing back with encouragement. You're a real friend, Luke. Thank you."

Kate reached over and put her hand on top of mine and looked me directly in the eyes. "Luke, we belong to two really screwed-up families. I thought my family's history was pathetic, and then I learned about your situation." Kate cringed. "Oh, I didn't mean it like that."

I laughed. "Ha, Kate. No problem. You are right on. Right-goddamn-on. Both of our histories are pathetic. Funny, though,

I'm feeling less pathetic this summer. And Christ, Kate, at least your mom bounced back, and look at your family now."

"I'm not complaining, Luke. But the money and all the good things my mom has done is just the surface. Everyone in my family has been affected by Dad leaving us, let alone for another man. It's like we have these emotional twitches just below the surface of our everyday lives. And then Annette, the sanest of all, dies. I mean, goddamn, goddamnit!"

I sighed, "I know, it's screwed up. It's like living with a cut that won't quite heal. I think that's why I keep on the road and away from home. I keep waiting for the damn cut to finally heal and just leave a scar that reminds me of the pain."

"I'm with you, Luke. I really didn't have the guts to leave before Annette died. Then you showed up. I just had to get away from the bullshit that comes with being a Prescott, let alone being a Brady. It's not just the money, either, it's the whole kit and caboodle, as my mom would say. Everyone in Knoxville knows our family's history. You can't escape the whispers or even the taunts. I can't remember how many times I heard, 'Your dad's a flaming faggot!'"

"Yeah, I can remember at a high school basketball game I played in, the guy I was guarding kept telling me, 'Your dad's a jailbird, and that's where you'll end up.' He kept it up the whole game."

"What did you do?" Kate asked.

"I kept my cool, but near the end of the game, I lined him up from about mid-court and caught him at the baseline and gave him one of my best ever football cross body blocks. He went down like a clump of sod. I got kicked out of the game, but I didn't care."

"We're a melancholy pair, aren't we, Luke?" Kate said, patting my hand.

"Yeah, we are. But you know, Kate, I'm still pretty sure there's a happy ending up ahead. Or at least a happy middle. I guess that would make me an optimist, eh?"

I stared into the fire, noticing my dwindling marshmallow stick. Kate put her head on my shoulder. The fire embers were more coal than flame as we sat together silently, two improbable friends with two impossible stories. Our bond ran deep, and I knew we would share a kinship for a long time. Maybe a lifetime.

Kate yawned long, patting her mouth with her hand. "I should collect Elvis and get some sleep, Luke. It has to be past three."

I didn't respond. I heard a familiar sound.

"Do you hear that sound, Kate?" I asked.

"What sound?"

"I've heard this before. It's driving me nuts. I feel it more than hear it. It's like it's subsonic, or something. I heard it when those troopers kicked us off the highway in Kentucky, before the big accident. I also heard it in the field where Annette died. It's weird. You sure you can't hear it, Kate?"

"Sorry, Luke. I don't hear anything."

Kate stood up, gave me kiss on the cheek, and walked over to wake Elvis. I leaned back in my lawn chair, looking up at the clouds playing off the light of the blue moon. The sound had retreated, but now I heard something different. I looked past the fire and field between me and the Dome. The field suddenly lit up. At first, I saw a sea of bobbing headlights and then a cloud of red and blue, spinning police car lights blasted into the meadow. I jolted up, unbelieving. My drunken mind was having a tough time registering what a herd of police cars hurtling through a field at 3:00 a.m. meant. It hit me hard. "Jesus Christ. It's a bust. It's a bust! They're busting the Dome party!"

I turned and ran toward Kate and Elvis. "It's the cops! A whole bunch of cops! We gotta get out of here! Now! Leave everything and follow me!"

Elvis focused quickly when he heard the words *cops* and *bust* in the same breath. He jumped up, grabbing his sleeping bag. I took Kate's hand and grabbed Elvis's elbow and said, "Leave the bag! Get outta here, quick! There must be a hundred cops out there!"

I looked over my shoulder as we ran, and saw the field aglow with the twirling red and blue lights, almost washing out the countless blinding headlights.

We sprinted up to the rise of the hill that was the highest ground on the property, away from the rush of cops. From our perch, we could see Slim's field dotted with tents and dwindling fires. Most of the kids were asleep or too sloshed to move quickly—easy catches by the time the police cars roared up to the main body of the party.

Elvis said, "Shit, we need to find everybody and get the hell out of here."

Too late. I turned and saw three county sheriff cars screaming toward us from the back of Slim Perkins's property. They must have entered in the back gate. "That's all she wrote, folks," I said. If you have pot on you, now's the time to dump it!"

"I don't," said Kate.

"Damn," Elvis said. He reached into the inside pocket of his denim jacket and pulled out a lid of pot with three pre-rolled joints enclosed in the baggy with the loose pot. He quickly put his hands behind his back and emptied the contents, stepping forward at the same time. It was too late. The lead patrol car skidded to stop. The deputy sheriff in the passenger seat had the spotlight focused on Elvis, and the driver was out of the car and on Elvis in an instant.

"You, young man, show your hands. Now!"

Elvis put his hands, palms up, at his side. The two deputies rushed at us, one scanning the ground behind us with a flashlight.

"Bingo," he said as the light danced on the three joints. In seconds, the deputy had Elvis turned around, snapping handcuffs on his wrists.

"Young man, you now have a real problem," the deputy announced solemnly. The other two cars had come to a less dramatic stop, and one of the four deputies called to Kate and me.

"All right, young man, let's put your hands on the car. Young lady, I want you to empty every single one of your pockets out."

Oh, God, no. My skin went cold: I started to sweat. I remembered the gram of hashish that Mark had given me, buried in my front jean pocket for safekeeping. While the cops watched Kate empty her pockets, I slipped two fingers into my jeans and pulled out the small, foil wrapped hash and let it drop to the ground. Only Kate noticed. But before I could step on the foil wrapper or kick it under the car, a deputy grabbed me by the belt and pulled me backwards away from Kate.

"Okay. Your turn, hotshot," the deputy said, and I emptied my pockets. Barely looking down, Kate moved her foot and stepped on the foil packet. After my pockets had been turned inside out, a deputy directed me away from Kate toward the second police car. The deputies wanted to talk with us separately about Elvis, to determine if we could be convinced to snitch on him or anybody else they busted.

A deputy told Kate, "Young lady, I want you to answer a few questions for us. Just step away from the car."

As he moved her away from the car, his flashlight traced over the foil encasing the hashish. "Hold on there a minute, sister. What's this?" He reached down and picked up the foil packet, opened it, and held it up to his nose. "Sweet mother of God, this is not incense. Is this yours, young lady? You only get one chance to tell me the truth." Kate's face went white. She tried to swallow, but she was scared dry.

"Yes, officer. It's mine."

The trooper shook his head. "Damn, little lady, we're going to have to take you in."

He led her to the same car where Elvis sat in the backseat with his head slumped forward, his hands handcuffed behind his back. The deputy opened the door, and before Kate could get in, he said, "Regulations, put your hands out."

Kate extended her wrists, her face contorted, trying to hold back her tears. The cuffs closed, and I thought, *She's luckier than Elvis—her cuffs aren't behind her back.* The deputy gently put his hand on top of Kate's head as he eased her into the backseat next to Elvis.

The series of events reeled past me in a jarring blur. But not so fast that I didn't realize Kate was taking the fall for me. Idiot, chicken-shit me was only thinking that I hadn't been caught and my, wasn't Kate lucky her arms weren't cuffed behind her back. *I am a complete asshole.*

The deputies' car bounced past me with Kate and Elvis looking at me with tight-lipped fear and frantic eyes.

I said, "Hey, what's going on? Where are they taking them?"

A deputy questioning closest to me said, "You're lucky you weren't carrying any contraband. Those two are in for a heap of trouble. And if you don't cooperate, you're headed for the same kind of trouble. Make this simple. Where did your friends get the dope? Do they have any more stashed? Are they dealers?"

My head started to pound. I was terrified and rabid with anger at myself and at these shit-heads cops for trying to make me a snitch. I thought about telling them the hashish was mine, not Kate's, but I rationalized that wasn't going to help either one of us.

"I don't even know those two people. I'm here on my own, and I haven't done anything wrong."

"We'll see about that, son."

Am I Judas Iscariot or Peter denying Jesus? Or just a simpleton asshole?

Without cuffs, I was put in the backseat of one of the cars, and we drove slowly through Slim Perkins's back twenty acres, meeting the crowd of police cars near the Dome. There were close to a dozen cop cars assembled, from the state police, Emmet County, Cheboygan County, and Petoskey City Police.

"Holy cow," I said softly.

"Yeah, holy cow is right," a deputy replied.

"Pretty impressive display of law enforcement isn't it, son?" Deputy Hollister said. "You picked the wrong party tonight. We figured we could clear out about half the dope dealers and potheads in the Emmet County by raiding this party. Not to mention busting Slim's ass for those five acres of mary-wanna he's cultivating in the middle of the pine stand in the back forty. Oh, yeah, there will be hell to pay by the time this night turns into morning."

Deputy Sheriff Hollister was right. At least as far as the Lost Souls were concerned. The cops were bluffing me, but after an hour of standing with my fellow disheveled arrestees, they still ticketed me for disorderly conduct and told me to find a ride home. I didn't argue. As I stood in the field observing the other drunk or hung-over hellions sober up to bad news, I felt a tap on my shoulder. It was Mark and Lois looking as bedraggled as possums at noon. They hadn't run. They peeked out of their tent after hearing the commotion caused by the armada of arriving cops, and watched the chaos develop. The cops chased after the kids like they were herding cats. They finally detained over ninety scared and tired partiers sitting in chairs on and around the pig roast tent. Mark and Lois were among them.

Lois was near tears. "Luke, they arrested Elvis and Kate. I saw them in the tent earlier. We just got tickets. Have you seen John and Sydney or Tony? Luke, I just want to go home."

I put my arm around her and said, "I know, Lois. I haven't seen those guys yet. Maybe they ran and made it out. Let's wait a little while longer, and if no one turns up, we'll leave in Mark's car."

"Luke, man. I'm glad we weren't holding. Them dudes are going to jail," Mark said, and pointed to the temporary booking station the cops had set up in Slim's food tent.

The cops sorted the offenders into two groups: those who had been caught with any amount of dope or paraphernalia, and those who had dumped their stash fast enough or were drug-free. The law enforcement strategy was straightforward. Like me, everybody without drugs was written a ticket for disorderly conduct and released. Mark and Lois and I fit into this category. It turned out the cops didn't much care if the tickets were enforceable. The raid was about instilling the fear of God into the county's youth about drug use. The remaining two dozen or so scruffy youths were piled into police cars and a state police paddy wagon for processing in Petoskey.

We watched as Slim Perkins was taken alone in a state police car, his wife Wendy wailing and finally cursing the police as they pulled away.

"You fucking pigs! It's just weed, man. We weren't doing anybody any harm. You come in here like the fucking gestapo."

She didn't have any support from the disconsolate, ragtag group being ticketed. The police ignored her. Some just smiled. They had known about Slim's patch of marijuana for several weeks, from a Petoskey pot seller turned snitch they had busted earlier in the summer. The deputies determined this coordinated raid would scare the hell out of the good kids and move the drug dealers down the road and out of the county. They were right on both counts.

The cops also had assembled a pile of drugs they had recovered from the teenagers dumping their stashes. They had a high stack of baggies of pot, vials of speed, quaaludes, blocks of hash broken into grams, pink pills marketed as mescaline, and a large bag of frozen psilocybin mushrooms found in a cooler. I walked as far as the deputies would let me, looking for John and Sydney. I played the repentant sinner with two of the deputies to find out what was going to happen next to anyone caught with drugs. Tony suddenly appeared with a blanket over his shoulders and a ticket in his hand.

"What a nightmare. Anybody see Elvis and Kate? What about John and Sydney? Christ, I was passed out with some lovely little lady when I heard the sirens. I stood up buck naked and a cop car pulled right up to our tent. Freaked the shit out of me. So, where the hell is everybody?"

I told him that Elvis and Kate had been caught with pot.

Mark said, "Yeah, they're over on the side of the Dome with everybody else that got busted. I tried to go over and see them, but no dice. What the hell are we going to do?"

"Something doesn't jive with Kate. She barely smoked pot. I can't imagine she was holding any," Mark said.

"She didn't. She took the fall for me. And I didn't do a god-damn thing to stop her. I gotta make this right now," I said, and started to walk toward the police cars.

I was surprised when Lois stepped in front of me.

"No, you're not going anywhere, Luke. That would be stupid, not brave. They'd just bust you, too. Kate's stuck, and if it's of her own accord, there's nothing you can do about it."

"She's right, Luke. Let's just get the hell out of here and figure out what to do next," Tony said.

I knew I was a spineless wretch, but I went along. The second time in an hour that I could have, should have stepped in and spoken up for my friend.

Maybe I'm a combo of St. Peter and Judas.

Tony, Mark, Lois, and I walked toward Tony's truck and Mark's car and saw a line of cars waiting to exit Slim's freshly mowed field. The cops were searching cars before they were allowed to leave. I jumped into the truck, and Mark and Lois trailed us to the search point. The cops gave us a half-hearted look over, figuring after this dramatic bust, we'd have to be dumber than potash to try and leave with drugs. Both of our vehicles drove out of the Dome's parking lot slowly. Tony turned off the side of the road about a mile up. Mark pulled up alongside of him. Lois was in the passenger seat crying. I rolled down the window of Tony's truck.

"Jesus, this is bad news," Mark called out.

"Yeah," I said. "But we need to get Elvis and Kate out of jail before we fold up our tents. I talked to one of the cops. They have a judge waiting to do arraignments in Petoskey this morning. He'll set bail at the arraignment. The cop said he wasn't sure, but bail could be anywhere from two hundred to a thousand dollars. Let's go back to your house, Tony, and see how much money we can raise quick. And hope we find John and Sydney."

"All right, Luke, you're right. Let's keep our shit together until we get them safe. Man, oh, man," Tony muttered as he pulled away.

John and Sydney were already at Tony's house when we arrived. They hadn't slept and didn't know what had happened at the field since the police arrived. They looked like tired raccoons.

"John, Sydney, how the hell did you make it back here?" Tony asked.

"We were still up talking when we saw the cop cars. We ran like hell and hid in the woods for a couple of hours and got eaten alive by mosquitoes. We finally followed some two-track roads that Sydney knew back to Indian River and then caught a ride from the *Detroit Free Press* delivery guy back to Topinabee. Where's Elvis? And Kate?"

"They popped Elvis and Kate," I said. "They're on their way to jail. We need bail money. Right away."

"Oh, shit! What in the hell happened out there last night?" John asked.

"It's a long story that's gonna get lots longer if we can't bail them out this morning. How much money can we come up with here?" I asked.

I didn't have the goombahs to tell my friends that Kate had taken the fall for me. Mark did it for me.

"She's a righteous woman. Don't worry about it, Moore. She knew what she was doing," Tony said.

I felt like the tortured dog that I was.

We opened our wallets and dug into pockets and glove boxes. The total was 106 dollars and change.

"This isn't going to do it," Tony said.

"Yeah, you're right. Look, I can get one advance on my paycheck, but not this morning," I said.

Tony interjected, "Let's make a deal. We all commit to a hundred dollars each. I know it's a lot, but that would give us six hundred bucks. I think the Roys will front me that much. But we all promise to give it back within two weeks. Will that work?"

"Yes, yeah, let's do it," we all agreed.

We planned to meet at Lee and Carl's restaurant in an hour. We would do one-minute showers, grab some doughnuts and juice, see if we could scrounge any more cash, and rush to Petoskey. Tony and I woke Mrs. Roy by pounding on the door of their house behind the Breakers. She listened to Tony's plea with a frown. But with few questions, she came through for us, lending five hundred dollars in cash.

"Oh, Tony, you boys just never believed you'd get caught. This is a hard lesson. You're all good boys, but you'd better learn something from this," Mrs. Roy said.

"Yes, ma'am," Tony said, head bowed.

"Now, you listen to me. Get going and get that wild Elvis and that Brady girl out of jail. I'm going to call John Miller in Royal Oak. He's a good lawyer with a lot of political connections. I'll see if he can help at all."

"Thank you, Mrs. Roy. We'll repay every cent. You can count on it."

"You bet I will, Mr. Muldano."

John Miller was a graduate of St. Mary's and a very successful lawyer. He was fifteen years older than the Lost Souls, but was a close family friend of the Roys.' He had been an assistant prosecutor in Oakland County before starting his own law firm.

Mrs. Roy caught him eating breakfast. "Hi, John. It's Mrs. Roy from Topinabee. It's been awhile. John, we need your help." Mrs. Roy waved us away with a shake of her head and a thin smile.

We arrived at Emmet County Courthouse in Petoskey looking better than we felt. Doughnuts had soaked up the alcohol, peppermint patties took the heat off our breath, and coffee strengthened our edginess. We decided to leave Lois and Sydney in Indian River to raise more bail money, so the courthouse reconnaissance and strategy was left to John, Mark, and me. The courtroom was half-filled with the besotted arrestees sitting in their pew-like seats, waiting their turn to be arraigned by Judge Sterling. The judge sported a longish, off-white mane of hair and a beet-red face, topped off with a bad case of rosacea that mottled his large nose.

Judge Sterling was both angry and satisfied. Happy because he was going to clean up this hornet nest of dope-smoking hippies, and angry because it was the weekend and it was going to take all morning and half the afternoon to finish the job. He looked at his watch with exasperation and lit a fire under the young assistant prosecutor's rear end.

"Prosecutor Adams, the county is very grateful you and your law enforcement colleagues have collaborated to help us rid this great county of drugs. Now I just need you to keep the paperwork moving and get these alleged criminals in front of this bench. Pronto!"

"Yes, sir, Judge Sterling," Prosecutor Adams answered.

We sat in the last row of the courtroom listening to the arraignments. Mark pointed out Elvis and Kate sitting next to each other in the second row. Elvis glanced back and saw us, touched Kate, and motioned his head slightly to the rear of the courthouse. She looked back and they both smiled grimly. It was the first sign of good news they had encountered since the Dome.

The arraignments moved fast. Elvis and Kate were near the middle of the pack.

John leaned over to us and said, "It looks like anyone busted with more than a couple of joints is getting bail set at five grand. The rest are getting a five-hundred-dollar bail. Does anyone know how much dope Elvis had on him?"

Mark answered, "Shit, I don't know for sure. Elvis told me he was running low on pot. I sure hope so."

Tony said, "Look, I'm going to see what I can find out in the courthouse about all this shit and talk to the bail bondsmen. I'm not sure the 780 dollars we have is going to get the job done."

We nodded and continued to listen to Judge Sterling efficiently process the frightened youths in front of him. Prosecutor Adams called the next defendant. "Your Honor, Mr. Paul Malone from Warren, Michigan, is next. This is our most significant offender in this operation. Mr. Malone was arrested with almost eight ounces of marijuana in his possession. In addition, we confiscated one hundred tablets of Dexedrine and twenty tabs of what we believe our labs will tell us is LSD."

Judge Sterling harrumphed and said, "Mr. Malone, you are clearly a drug pusher. You came into our county with your cornucopia of drugs expecting to profit at the expense of our young people and our citizens. I don't know what your recommendation for bail is, Mr. Adams, but I expect it to be high."

"Excuse me, Your Honor. I'm sorry to interrupt," Prosecutor Adams said quickly, "but that was just the drugs we found in his possession. We later searched his van, and I'd like to read the list of drugs and paraphernalia found."

The judge's expression hardened, and his eyes blazed. As the prosecutor began listing the drugs and quantities, John elbowed me hard. "Jesus Christ, Luke. Isn't that Wily? It is him, isn't it?"

I looked ahead at the man standing with his back half-turned to us. "Oh, my God, I think you're right, John. Listen to that list of dope. Damn, that's about the same list we heard from him when he picked us up," I said.

"You guys know him?" Mark asked.

John gave Mark a shortened version of our van ride with Wily on our hitchhike to Indian River.

The prosecutor finished his list, and then said to the judge, "Your Honor, we also found two unregistered pistols under the driver's seat in Mr. Malone's van. We are also investigating the shooting of a suspected drug dealer in April this year near Pinconning, Michigan. The victim was shot in the kneecaps in an apparent drug deal gone awry. Judge Sterling, we recommend bond set for one million dollars for Mr. Malone."

John and I were flabbergasted. We looked at each other with widened eyes, shaking our heads.

Mark interrupted our reverie. "You know, I saw this guy pull his van into the Dome and set up shop. He was selling shit out of that van like it was an ice cream truck."

"I never saw him at the Dome. But John and I knew he was a crazed dude."

"Yeah, I think we knew that, but not crazy enough to shoot someone!" John replied.

"Bond recommendation accepted. One million dollars." Judge Sterling slammed his gavel down. The judge's reddened nose seemed to glisten as he leaned forward and scowled at Paul 'Wily' Malone.

"I am looking forward to your trial, Mr. Malone."

We watched as a deputy guided a defeated Wily toward the side door leading to the county jail.

Mark whispered to us, "That judge is mean and getting meaner. And it looks like Elvis and Kate are getting close to their turn. I sure as shit hope we have enough dough for their bail."

We watched and waited, and just as Tony returned from the hallway, the bailiff called Kate Brady's name.

Tony pushed into the seat next to me and quietly said, "Good news. I can sign over the title of my truck to the bail bondsman for another thousand bucks. That oughta put us over the top, don't you think?"

I wasn't listening to Tony. I only heard the prosecutor call out the charge against Kate.

"Your Honor, the defendant, Kate Brady, currently residing in Royal Oak, Michigan, has been charged with possession of a controlled substance, in this case, a small amount of hashish, a little less than half a gram."

Can't let this happen. I stood up and pushed my way past Tony's knees into the courtroom's main aisle.

"Where you going, Luke?" Tony asked under his breath.

I didn't answer, because I knew if anyone stopped me, I would lose my nerve again. I walked quickly toward the front of the lacquered oak railing separating the court spectators from the participants.

"Your Honor! Your Honor!" I bellowed, surprising myself at the volume and depth of my voice. I pushed my way through a swinging gate that led to the court proper.

I heard John call out, "Oh, shit, Luke, don't do it."

I started talking fast, "Your Honor, this wasn't Kate's hashish. It was mine. She's not guilty, I am."

A court deputy started toward me, but Judge Sterling stopped him.

"Hold on there for a minute, officer, let the boy speak."

But before I could begin, Prosecutor Adams interrupted.

"Your Honor, can I approach?"

Judge Sterling looked puzzled, but motioned him toward the bench. They had a short, quiet conversation. The judge nodded his head in assent and the prosecutor returned to his table.

"All right, you two, approach the bench. I want to have a little talk with you. That's right. You, Miss Brady, and you, too, young man."

Ashen-faced, Kate and I stood in front of Judge Sterling, looking up at his bulbous red nose.

He leaned down and in an imperious voice us, "Now, this is an interesting situation. I have one young lady who appears ready to take the blame for her boyfriend, and then the boyfriend gets religion."

I butted in, "Sir, Kate's not my girlfriend."

Judge Sterling's face became redder. "Don't interrupt me again, ever. Are we clear on that?"

"Yes, sir," I said, feeling the color leave my face.

"Now, where was I? Oh, yes, the two of you are ready to accept justice for each other. I don't see much of that anymore. Now, who's guilty? And no more cover-ups."

I said, "It was mine, Your Honor."

"And who are you?" the judge asked.

"Luke Moore, sir. From Royal Oak, Michigan."

Judge Sterling sat back a little. "And that's where you reside also, Miss Brady?"

Kate nodded her head, too frightened to talk.

"And you're both familiar with St. Mary's Parish, aren't you?"

I stammered, "Yes, sir. That's where we went to school. How did you know that?"

"Son, fortunately for her, Miss Brady has received a very fine recommendation from a friend of this court, Mr. John Miller. Seems Mr. Miller is a parishioner of St. Mary's and was asked to make a call on behalf of Miss Brady. It also appears that Mr. Miller went to the University of Michigan Law School with Prosecutor Adams here. And I just happen to be a Wolverine alumnus myself. With the character reference Miss Brady has received, and with your confession, I am inclined to believe she does not belong with the rest of the drug-infested riffraff in jail. Therefore, I am dismissing the charges against Miss Kate Brady."

The judge slammed down the gavel.

Kate had not said a word since her arraignment had begun. She swallowed hard, and then spoke up clearly.

"Thank you, Your Honor. I just want to say that Luke Moore doesn't deserve to go to jail. He's a good person who's been to hell and back, and he deserves a chance. Please, Your Honor, give him a chance."

Judge Sterling frowned and said, "Is that why you claimed the hashish was yours, Miss Brady?"

Kate thought for a second. "Yes, Your Honor."

"I will consider your entreaty, young lady. Now please move to the prosecutor's table and fill out the forms for your release." The judge pointed a long, arthritic finger toward Prosecutor Adams.

"Yes, sir. And thank you. But Your Honor, may I mention one more thing? I'd also like to put in a good word for Matthew Muldoon, our friend who—"

Judge Sterling interrupted, "Miss Brady, you are finished here!"

Kate's chin slumped, and she walked away smoldering.

"Now, Mr. Prosecutor. I believe Matthew Muldoon is up next, isn't he? Approach the bench, Mr. Muldoon" the judge ordered.

Elvis, accompanied by the prosecutor, walked up and stood next to me. He was smiling that winning Elvis grin, but I could see his forehead was beaded with sweat.

"Now Mr. Muldoon, your case is a little more complicated. You, too, have a recommendation from Mr. Miller, but I'm inclined to believe you are not as innocent, in more ways than one, as Miss Brady. And you, Mr. Moore, you do not have a recommendation from Mr. Miller. Of course, he isn't aware of your Johnny-come-lately confession. But I like chivalry. Too damn little of it these days. Here's what we're going to do."

Elvis and I listened as the judge sentenced us to a one-week work detail at the Michigan State University farm near Cross Village, known as Camp Muck. In addition, we were hit with one year's probation, with our records to be expunged if we managed to avoid doing anything else stupid. We were directed to a table for a paperwork session with the clerk to the assistant prosecutor. Moments later, we were free to go. Kate was off the hook completely. Elvis and I had to report on Monday morning to the work-release program for a week of manual labor. Hands filled with paperwork, we walked quickly away, as Prosecutor Adams called out, "Listen up, Moore, Muldoon, and Miss Brady. You are now officially in debt to Mr. John Miller. You get in any more trouble of any kind, and you will be in jail. And if it involves drugs, we'll be throwing away the key. We clear on that?"

We answered in unison, "Yes, sir."

"Look, I know you're not bad kids and you come from good families, or John Miller wouldn't vouch for you. I know you kids think smoking a joint isn't a big deal, and maybe downstate, you're close to right. But up here, you're just another druggie. Enough said. Keep your noses clean and fly straight out of here. We see you again, and you'll see a jail cell. And you make sure to thank John and tell him he owes me one.

I stepped up and shook Mr. Adams's hand. "Thank you, sir. We won't forget what you and Mr. Miller did for us."

We walked silently down the middle aisle of the cavernous courtroom, the oak-slat floor creaking under our feet, gaining speed as we hit the courtroom door. Lois and Sydney arrived just as we rushed out of the courtroom with John, Mark, and Tony in pursuit. We spilled out onto the courthouse steps together.

"What the heck happened in there?" John asked.

"Let's get the hell out of here and then we can explain it," Elvis said, moving fast down the sidewalk with his arm around Kate.

"Excellent idea," I said. I put my arms around John's and Mark's shoulders and lifted myself up between them.

We hurried into the municipal parking lot next to the red brick courthouse. Elvis picked Kate up and let out a cathartic yell. "Yeeehaaaw! We're out, Kate. We made it. We're not going to jail. We're not going to the hoosegow!"

I had been in some serious pickles with the Lost Souls and had more than a few run-ins with the police. But none of us had ever been arrested and faced actual jail time. The hugging and back-pounding in the parking lot was relief and disbelief for most of us.

"The Lost Souls did it again," Elvis cried out. That brought silence from the rest of the group.

Lois was direct. "Elvis, you just came within an inch of finding out what the inside of a jail looked like. Yeah, you got away with it, mostly. But you only have so many lives, Elvis."

"She's right," Kate said.

The four of us stood together facing two formidable women.

"Of course, you're right," Elvis said. "We are the luckiest guys on the earth. Let us enjoy that for a few minutes before we remember how completely scared shitless we were. Look, I'm still shaking." He held out a trembling hand.

"And, Kate," I said, "why in the hell did you take the blame for me? That was dumb as dirt."

Kate shook her head, "Well, it seemed like the right thing to do at the time, but I started to change my mind when Elvis and I were cuffed in the police car. Luke, you have no idea how frightened I was sitting next to Elvis, the cops talking about Hanging Judge Sterling who was going to give us a one-way trip to Jackson Prison. I almost peed my pants. Then they took us to a small room in the police station."

Elvis chimed in, "Yeah, we were there for about a half–hour, and I was freaking out. I couldn't believe Kate had any pot on her anyway. I had to pry it out of her that it was my gram of hash that I had given to Luke. At first I was pissed at you, Luke, but as Kate said, it was my hash in the first place. I was freaking out that this was my fault."

"It wasn't your fault, Elvis, I should have stepped up," I said.

"Maybe so, Luke, but fate is fate. It was my stash, and you standing up in the courtroom is good enough for me. Better to get religion late than not to have it at all. You did all right, Luke."

It was slight consolation for me.

"When they put us in the holding room, Kate started to freak out. She was crying and telling me should we never do drugs again." Elvis said.

"I won't," Kate interjected.

"Yeah, well, all I could think was the room was bugged, and kept telling Kate, 'shut up, please, they'll use all this against us.' Then they came and took our fingerprints and mug shots," Elvis said.

Kate continued, "I've never been more mortified in my life. All I'm thinking about now is what's going to happen when my mom finds out."

Elvis concluded, "This was the scariest freaking night of my life."

We all joined in talking, telling, and retelling our individual tales of the night, building a story to be told and retold as we shouldered life's burdens and lost our nine lives, one by one. I was a half-hearted participant. I couldn't shake the guilt of letting Kate take the fall for me. It ate at me.

As we moved to their cars for the ride back to the Indian River, Kate grabbed me and held me tight. "Friends for life now, right, Luke?" she said.

"I'll never forget what you did for me, Kate."

"It'll all even out over time, is my guess," she replied.

We met at the Breakers for burgers and to thank Mrs. Roy and pay our debt. We pleaded with her to keep the incident quiet. She agreed and gave Kate a hug. Kate didn't relish telling about her close call to her mother. I knew the shelf life of this secret was about one week before it leaked south to Knoxville.

I was both relieved and tormented, which, sadly, was not an unusual combination of sentiments for me. I finally stood up and was counted as a friend in the courtroom, but only after I had betrayed a friend. I had no one to help me make decisions. I had fallen and then picked myself back up. I wasn't proud of myself. My dad would have denied his family or friends, and I realized that trait was an unbearable part of me.

On the other hand, I was like my mom: I had found my footing and told the truth. Who was I going to be? Which way would I turn at this crossroad? I had struggled with how to keep my promise to Annette, but it was obvious it wasn't going to happen while I was hanging out in Indian River. I was going to have to figure out a solution, or at a least a direction. This was the impetus for taking control of my life. At least it sounded good. I was always a sprinter when it came to taking action in my screwed-up life: fast out of the gate, but usually flaming out after the first one hundred yards.

We spent the afternoon talking about plans for the autumn and following year. Kate was going back to school in two weeks at the University of Detroit, intent on getting an education degree with a double major in economics, her ambition emerging. She even had Elvis talking about how long he could keep playing the bar circuit. I could see Mrs. Brady in her as she talked encouragingly about Elvis's first studio sessions as a rhythm guitar and backup singer for Motown.

Mark and Lois were content to return to Royal Oak and their love affair. John and Sydney were considering a move to Chicago, where Sydney's parents lived. John was thinking about all the clubs where he might find work, and Sydney knew she could find work in the big city. Tony wasn't going anywhere. He enjoyed all the seasons Indian River offered. It was his home.

I was quiet, enjoying the conversation. I was thinking about finding work in Florida, where our friend Vincent Delgado and his family had moved five years ago. That would send me in the right direction to solve the puzzle of my languishing promise to Annette Brady.

As evening approached, it was obvious we all wanted to put the weekend behind us. Mark, Lois, and Kate had the car packed for Royal Oak. In all our laughing and pushing outside the Breakers, we had a different look in our eyes. We should have felt more invincible. Hell, we got away with a slap on the wrist. But maybe we knew we were nearing the end of our nine lives. For the first time, I noticed their faces looked older and tired.

We said good-bye to Kate, Lois, and Mark. Lois slid onto the bench seat of Mark's metallic green 396 Chevelle coupe. Mark tucked his arm around her, his hand settling on her hip. Elvis reached through the window and kissed Kate.

"I'll see you in a week, darling," Elvis shouted as the car bounced down the two tracks. Sand dust rose up behind the car, clouding the tail lights. Summer was over.

Chapter 19

September 2003

D ad, it sounds like you and your friends were regular little drug fiends. And I sure don't remember the part where Kate takes the blame for you. At least you did the right thing in the end. You told me you were wild, not a complete hellion. Don't you think all your rants to me and my friends about drug use—or, heck, even drinking beer—is a little holier-than-thou? I mean, c'mon, Dad!"

My daughter wasn't taking the high road here, even though I had sanitized the story for teenage daughter consumption.

"Roberta, it's like this: you're eighteen, and as best I know, you've managed to keep yourself from a mistake that could drown you. That was the goal. I would have to agree with you that along the way my parenting may have been over-the-top and self-righteous. I just didn't want you to have to repeat the stupidity of my early years. So, I did what I thought I had to do."

"Dad, for a guy who helps kids find their way out of some pretty big holes, it's just dopey to think I'm immune from growing up. Let's face it, you grew up with brick-loaded baggage compared to my life with you and Mom. You need to relax—don't worry so much. I'm no dummy, but I'm not a saint, either. You just try too hard, Dad."

Eighteen years of parental overcompensating down the drain with one little speech.

"But, Dad, you didn't finish the story. I've always wanted to hear the real story how you found Mom. Not the fairy-tale version," Roberta said.

"Roberta, it wasn't Cinderella," Marta interjected, "but it was a fairy tale for me and your dad. Tell her the story, dear. This one, I'll never get tired of hearing."

"All right, then, I'll give it a whirl. Tom, you bored to tears yet?" I said.

"No, I'm fine, Mr. Moore. I gotta tell you, I've never really met a family quite like yours. The stories are cool with me. Go for it."

"You know, there have been so many so-called coincidences in my life, I have faith that you can learn how to catch the winds of fate and let them blow you in the right direction. It was right here on this stretch of road, just about thirty years ago, that I was on the way to meet Marta Czechowski, and I didn't even know it. With a little diversion called Camp Muck, I went from feeling lower than a gnat's navel to finding soul-stirring love. I was tired of being alone, challenging life like a matador who had lost his nerve. I was damn unhappy, and just a few miles up the road, across a bridge, into a boat, and onto an island, was the rest of my life."

Marta put her hand on my forearm and smiled. "Dear, we'll be in Wisconsin if you don't get to the story."

"Enough, you say? As I said, with a little detour to Camp Muck, I was on my way."

Chapter 20

September 1973

C amp Muck was a week-long nightmare. Far too early on Monday morning, Tony gave Elvis and me a ride to the MSU farm for our week of legal repentance. The farm was an hour northwest of Indian River, just south of Cross Village. It covered two hundred acres and almost surrounded Wycamp Lake. We waved good-bye to Tony at 6:45 a.m., and walked into the Quonset hut labeled "Headquarters." There were six other young men sitting on a bench, and I recognized one of them, Todd Michaels, as a regular at the Indian River Inn. We nodded at each other as a short, block-like uniformed man with a brush cut barged into the building and started barking.

"Listen up and listen up good, men. This detail is a work detail. W-O-R-K, work, D-E-T-A-I-L, detail. Work detail. This one week of work is just one step away from jail. You will work and work hard for seven days. If anyone does not follow the rules I set out for you, or lollygags in the slightest, I assure you Judge Sterling will fry your sorry white asses. I am Frank Polaski, Emmet County's Youth Adjudication Program Officer. My word is law for the next week."

Frank Polaski worked the eight of us from 7:00 a.m. to 7:00 p.m., pulling ten acres of cornstalk remnants out of the bog that had been planted to test marsh production for a hybrid corn program. It rained every day for the week we were there, making the low-lying corn patch a swamp. Walking in our knee-length, camp-issued rubber boots was debilitating; the suction of the black muck held fast onto our feet. I woke up the first night with cramps from my toes to my thighs.

Elvis and I fell in with Todd Michaels, who had also been arrested at the Dome. Todd's father was a wealthy real estate investor from Columbus, Ohio, and owned one of the largest homes on Burt Lake. Todd called his dad with his one phone call, and the best lawyer in Petoskey was in the courtroom representing Todd within an hour. He received the same Muck Farm sentence as Elvis and me.

At age twenty-four, Todd was four years older than Elvis and me. It was clear he was a confused, spoiled rich kid who hadn't grown up. He had been living in Indian River for the summer at his parents' Burt Lake "cottage," a twelve-room estate with a boat house and tennis courts. He was still two semesters away from graduating from a small private college in Ohio. The week was well beyond the hardest work he had ever contemplated, let alone undertook, and he was hurting. We took him under our wing at the farm and helped him make it through the week.

When we were released from the work camp the following Sunday, sore, tired, and five pounds lighter, Todd gave us a ride to Topinabee in his brand-new 1973 Dodge Ram pickup truck. He told us that he wanted to "party hearty" after our hell week. Elvis wanted nothing to do with Todd, partying, or even with me after our week of mosquitoes and swamp work. Elvis was headed back to Royal Oak that evening with Tony to join Kate. Our good-byes were tired and brief as he met Tony for his ride at the Indian River Inn. Todd and I went inside for beer. After five Michelobs, he pestered me to take a hitchhiking trip with him.

"Luke, I'm twenty-four years old and a hitchhiking virgin. Let's split somewhere." I was on my fifth beer when Todd said he would pay for a hotel and all expenses for a trip to Mackinac Island, with the condition we had to hitchhike. In my world, that was a vacation. With a five-beer buzz, it was easy to agree.

For me, a hitchhike this short was a waste of time, but Todd had insisted. Monday midmorning, we sauntered down the entrance ramp at Indian River toward northbound I-75 with light backpacks. This was going to be a luxury adventure, according to Todd. I was already regretting my beer-induced agreement. I figured it was one last sojourn before I returned home to Royal Oak and came up with a plan to keep my promise to Annette.

Todd and I would hitchhike the sixty miles past Mackinaw City, across the world's longest suspension bridge to St. Ignace, and take a ferry boat to fusty, stuck-in-time Mackinac Island.

"Todd, we're less than an hour from the bridge. For the last time, please, let's get your truck and drive. This is nuts," I implored as we reached the main highway.

"C'mon, Luke, humor me. If we don't get a ride in a half-hour, I'll go get the truck. Fair enough?"

"Fair enough," I replied, and we sat on our bags on the shoulder of the road, Todd's bright-red, brand-new backpack in sharp contrast to my worn-out canvas bag.

I could see Todd was uneasy standing behind me as I took my habitual position, foot touching the highway, thumb out. Todd mimicked me, but stood three feet off the road, inching backward after the first station wagon blew by at eighty, a gust of air pushing us back. Traffic was a light, but steady, parade of late-summer vacationers and empty-nesters who knew the North Country would soon be desolate and relaxed. To most of the motoring tourists, we were invisible.

Fifteen minutes turned into a half-hour. Todd bought another half-hour with a bribe for a beer at the Grand Hotel, the elegant and imposing resort hotel that connected yesterday's island grandeur with the wealthiest visitors.

Another half-hour passed, and a car finally stopped, but it was Sydney and John, who, passing by on the overpass on their way to Afton, saw the chatting hitchhikers and couldn't resist shooting a few barbs at us. As Sydney's rusted 1964 Fiat sedan pulled up, Todd was at first joyous. "Yeah, here we go, the first ride. C'mon Luke . . . aw, shit, it's Sydney."

"Hey, boys," John called from the passenger window as he pulled alongside, "out for a Sunday—I mean, Monday stroll? A nature walk on I-75, perhaps? Trying to identify the various animal roadkill? Or perhaps you're mapping the local highway flora and fauna?" he continued before I interrupted.

"Shut up and unlock the back doors, you moron. You're taking us up to the Topinabee exit," I said.

Todd protested, "Hey, Luke, c'mon, this can't be our first ride. We know these guys. It's just not right."

"Todd, the first rule of hitchhiking is 'never look a gift ride in the mouth,'" I answered.

"What the hell does that mean?" Todd asked.

"I don't have a clue, just get in the goddamn car and let's move on down the road."

Sydney and John laughed as Todd and I argued for the six minutes it took to drive to the next exit. We were still arguing as we hopped out of the car, slammed the doors, and walked down the Topinabee/M-27 ramp. As we reached the highway, a recent model Cadillac, the first car in sight, slowed down and stopped seventy-five feet in front of us. I trotted to the Cadillac with Todd in pursuit. We were laughing now.

The power window on the passenger side opened. I peered in to see a silver-maned man with an expensive, large cowboy hat set atop his very large head.

"Where you boys headed?" he asked.

"Just over the bridge, sir," I replied.

"Then I think you're in business," the driver replied.

I opened the heavy door and held the seat back for Todd to enter. Before pulling back onto the highway, the driver leaned over and offered his huge hand to shake. "I'm Dr. William Blunt, from Reynoldsville, Ohio, the tomato capital of the Midwest. I'm pleased to meet you, young man."

His large hand covered mine in a gentle and firm shake. As the doctor leaned forward, his hat moved down on his forehead and then back in place, like he had muscles in his temples that controlled the hat.

I replied, "I'm pleased to meet you, too, Dr. Blunt. I'm Leroy Love, and this is my friend Todd Michaels." Dr. Blunt leaned over the seat and shook hands with Todd.

The eight-cylinder, 484-cubic-inch engine roared as the doctor punched the accelerator. He explained he was a retired surgeon in Reynoldsburg, his wife's hometown. He met his wife, a nurse, in a floating triage hospital ship on the English Channel. Their job was to try and piece back together soldiers who were badly injured during the Allies' advance through France after D-Day, and ferry them back to England.

"I did some hitchhiking before the war and before medical school. I was working as a journeyman oil field worker in West Texas. I'm a pretty big guy and felt pretty comfortable that I could handle most trouble that came my way."

Dr. Blunt was returning to his hometown of Calumet, located in the Keweenaw Peninsula, a starkly beautiful peninsula jutting into Lake Superior. The copper mining heydays were long gone, but the small towns on the Keweenaw were home to the hardiest residents in Michigan. The peninsula was held captive by subfreezing, often below-zero-degree temperatures and constant lake-effect snow from October through April. Real summer only lasted for six to eight weeks. Half that time, the mosquito and black fly hatches made it impossible to go outside.

"Foolhardy to try and live up there. I left at seventeen, but my brother stayed on, and he passed away last week. Never married, but somehow, he managed to save enough to have an estate to settle. Then there's the matter of a supposed bastard son, maybe more than one. I don't have a clue what to do about that!"

He was getting pretty heated up: a "therapy driver." The doctor needed to pour out his soul, and what better listeners than a couple of poor slobs fresh off the highway? I played the therapy drivers one of two ways. Either sit quietly and listen with some pretension of interest, or jump right in and possibly arouse additional consternation and probably some lively entertainment.

I chose option one and sat silently, but attentive to Dr. Blunt, adding the occasional but necessary conversational interjections. "No kidding!" "That's a shame." "You got a point there!" Dr. Blunt's crescendo of complaints built and then ebbed while his huge hands gripped the steering wheel tightly at eleven and one o'clock. After thirty minutes of monologue, he breathed a loud sigh over the top of the steering wheel, arched his back, and then settled back into the car seat.

"Boys, how about a fine cigar? Young man, there's a box of Havana's finest in the top of that suitcase. Just open it up and let's start a-puffin'!"

As the Cadillac reached the top of the rise on I-75, revealing the Straits of Mackinac and the glistening bridge, I was "a-puffin'" away on an eight-inch cigar, blue smoke pushing against the inside of the windshield before sliding off in both directions, leaving the car through the slightly opened side window vents. I was ensconced in the enormous, upholstered, adjustable twelve-way seats of the Cadillac, listening to *Frank Sinatra's Greatest Hits* through the doctor's premium stereo system. This was first-class hitchhiking.

Dr. Blunt paid the toll for the Mackinac Bridge and exhaled from the stub of his cigar. "Breathtaking."

"Sure is," I concurred.

The bridge's steel suspension cables shot gracefully upward from the roadway, attached to the two giant pillars positioned equidistant from each other in the middle of the straits. The steel strands reminded me of harp strings. As the Cadillac cruised over the bridge, the afternoon sun cast vertical shadows rapidly across the car. The blue water was two hundred feet below and shimmering bright from the sunlight.

Todd who had been silent most of the trip, said, "This must be why God intended man to build things. This bridge fits so perfectly here."

I thought that was modestly insightful for a dope-smoking, spoiled rich kid.

When we reached the other side of the bridge, the doctor was kind enough to make the short detour off the main highway and deposit us at the ferry docks, where he bid us good-bye.

We boarded Arnold's Ferry, one of three ferry providers to Mackinac Island, and bounced across Lake Huron for the twenty-two minute boat ride to the Mackinac Island ferry dock. Our fellow passengers were mostly empty-nester tourists. Perhaps some had passed Todd and me on the highway. The boat sliced through the lake's waves while Todd and I stood by the railing and watched the island come in focus. This late in the year, the weather was dry and clear. The color of Lake Huron ranged from aquamarine to the deepest hue of blue, depending on the water's depth. It reminded me of the National Geographic pictures of the Caribbean I thumbed through in our family dentist's waiting room. As we pulled up to the dock, we could see the sea of bicycles on Main Street. Even though it was past the summer season, the streets were still busy with camera-toting tourists in Bermuda shorts, providing stark contrast to the turn-of-the-century town we approached.

The Arnold Line boat pulled up to an immense wooden pier that served the ferry trade, and which shared the harbor with a marina that moored dozens of sleek sailboats and motor yachts. Gliding into the pier, I could vividly remember my family vacation to the island years ago.

The harbor opened up into the picturesque, old-time downtown. No gas or electric-powered vehicles were allowed on the island.

The horse-drawn carriages littered the street with "road apples," obstacles for the hundreds of rented bicycles pedaled by the island's visitors. I remembered the numerous fudge shops where the term *fudgies,* referring to tourists, was born. To the west of the town, a road led up a hill where the Victorian mansions were perched, and behind them the Grand Hotel cast its elegant shadow.

Todd and I strolled into the heart of downtown to the Chippewa Hotel. Todd had partied on Mackinac Island frequently. The Chippewa was also the home of the Pink Pony Saloon, a notoriously wild hub of island nightlife.

The Chippewa was in need of a general refurbishment, but was still listed as a three-star hotel in the AAA guide, mainly on the strength of its past reputation. The hotel was filled with semi-celebrity, colorful guests, some of whom arrived on the sailboats and motor yachts we passed in the marina. We checked into a third-floor room, stuffy before the windows were opened to the lake breezes. There were no air-conditioned rooms on the island; the cool effect of lake breezes making it unnecessary except for only a very few days of the tourist season.

We unpacked our bags and entered the Pink Pony Bar, named for the oversized pink carousel pony mounted on the back wall behind a long, curved bar. We avoided the exotic umbrella drinks that were the bar's specialties, settling for two Molsons. Two hamburgers and four lagers apiece later, we buddied up to a well-tanned and well-coifed foursome: two couples in their fifties who were guests at the Grand Hotel. They invited us to join their table, where we drank and laughed into the late afternoon. The men were semi-retired from their sales rep business, which employed hobbled ex-professional athletes to peddle stamped steel parts to larger automotive suppliers.

The business had been successful for over two decades, and they had recently turned the business over to one of their sons, who thought spending half his time on the golf course was going to sell more stampings. One of the wives, an attractive silver-haired woman who had spent far too much time in the sun, glanced at her watch. She announced with a smile that pushed her leathered face into a mass of tan wrinkles that it was time for martinis at sunset on "the porch at the Gra-a-a-a-nd!"

Outside the Pink Pony, our group pushed into a horse-drawn taxi and clopped down Main Street singing a badly sung rendition of "Danny Boy." I followed my normal formal form and drank more slowly than Todd and our newfound friends. I pushed back into the cart's seat and drifted off, listening to the clip-clop of the horse's shoes beneath the singing in our cart. The absurdity of the scene sank in as I watched the walking, bicycling, and horse-drawn tourists shopping, arguing, and enjoying their vacations to various degrees. I was out of place in this cart. I didn't mind, but it was a reminder I didn't really have a place, and that my wandering led to situations like this on a regular basis. I sometimes thought that this life was leading me someplace special, that I was being designated by God or some superior force to deal with the absurd life I lived. Someday, finally, my true mission of greatness would be revealed. Alternately, I thought I was a ne'er-do-well, and my life was going down the tubes. Hero or goat, nothing in between. The cart passed through downtown and pulled uphill, pointed to the Grand Hotel, illuminated by the soft, late summer sunlight.

My companions were boisterous as we reached the long, steep promenade leading to the hotel. I joined in as we finished a chorus of "What Do You Do with a Drunken Sailor" at the disembarkation point of the hotel's broad stairway, the midpoint of the Great Porch. The imposing, top-hatted bellman greeted us with solemnity. I detected a sneer under his top hat as we walked up the green-carpeted stairs and steered left onto the porch. We found a table surrounded by white wicker chairs.

As we settled in, one of our hosts exclaimed, "My boys, you are just going to love the Grand Hotel martinis. And lucky you, because as our guests, you didn't even have to pay the five-dollar tourist tariff to visit this unmatchable spot!"

The table laughed, including Todd. I smiled tightly, watching the day tourists walk the porch gingerly. I was more akin to the day-trippers in mustard-stained T-shirts than to my newfound companions in autumn sport coats.

"Ah, a waitress approaches!" Todd proclaimed.

I saw a tall, uniformed young woman, her blonde hair tied up away from her face, tray in hand and order-pad tucked into a white apron. Her long legs reached into her waitress skirt. The fading, orange sunlight bathed her face, causing her to squint slightly as she approached the table. I recognized her immediately.

"Marta?" I asked incredulously.

Her face blanked for just an instant. "Luke?"

The table silenced. I was flummoxed and transfixed by Marta's smile, which caused creases at her eyes. She didn't appear confused at all. Actually, *flummoxed* is just a fancy word for completely freaked out. I learned that having one's heart stuck in one's throat was not just a metaphor. Several thousand of my pores opened up to a cold sweat. After what seemed like an interminable, uncomfortable pause, I managed to find my manners and stand up.

She grabbed both my hands and said, "Luke, it's Luke Moore, right? I didn't think I would ever see you again. But you recognized me, didn't you? What a trip to see you sitting on the porch of the Grand Hotel! You must have done pretty well for yourself, or robbed a bank since I dropped you on the side of the road outside Cincinnati."

With my legs wobbling, I pressed for a reply.

"No . . . no bank robberies and no money, just happened to meet some people kind enough to buy a few drinks for a stranger. And, yeah, I recognized you. You made quite an impression. I was hoping I would see you again. You know, I did keep your note with your vacation plans and tried to find you at Wycamp Lake.

Marta's face darkened. "That was a very bad week and the end of a very bad relationship."

Todd interrupted our conversation. "Excuse me, Luke, but can you introduce us to your friend, who also happens to be our waitress?"

The rest of the group at the table chimed in, asking what the reunion was all about. Marta dropped my hands, smiled at the table, and told a genteel version of our chance meeting in Cincinnati. My well-to-do companions guffawed in disbelief, saying things like, "How about that!" and "Can you believe this!"

"Well, don't this beat all? Let's have some martinis and celebrate," one of the foursome said.

"I think I can handle that order, sir. Give me a minute with this young man, and I will be back with the best martinis on the island," Marta said.

She pulled me away from the table, holding my hand tightly.

"Isn't this a trip? You and I finding each other. I'm not sure how or why you're hanging with the Geritol crowd. You a gigolo now, Luke? Ha, I'm just kidding. I have to finish my shift, but after that I'd love to catch up with you. Are you staying here?" Marta asked.

"God, no, I'm the poor hitchhiker, if you remember. And I don't think I'm a gigolo. At least, nobody's asked so far. It's a long story, but I'm staying at the Chippewa Hotel in a room Todd is paying for." I pointed toward Todd at the table.

"I'd like to hear the story. This is crazy that we ran into each other like this. I'd really like to buy you a beer after my shift ends at ten tonight. I hope you're free."

"I'd like that. I'm really along for the ride with this group. It will be interesting catching up with you," I said.

"Interesting, huh? I'm betting on a lot more than interesting. You know, Luke Moore, I remember our conversation in my Volkswagen. Something happened there. I'll meet you at the Pink Pony inside the Chippewa at about ten thirty. I'll be all yours, then. Okay?"

I nodded. Marta squeezed my hand a little tighter, leaned forward, and kissed me half on my lips and cheek. She made a girlish turn, and her uniform skirt swished upward, revealing those extended, tanned legs that produced a purr through my nose to the back of my throat. My heart started pounding and beads of perspiration formed on my upper lip. She bounced away to fetch the drinks, and flashed a bright smile back at me that tightened my chest even more. I was speechless.

My good fortune gave me an unexpected rush of anxiety and hope. I had failed to find her at the camp, been too late, and here she was: gorgeous, sexy, and maybe, just maybe, making a play for me. Or at least, that's what seemed apparent. I was too preoccupied with turning into a bowl of oatmeal to trust my instincts. I really wasn't interested in sitting with Todd and four drunken oldsters. But I wanted to at least watch Marta, see her work, and remind myself that this was real and good. Did she really say I was all hers, after her shift? Maybe she meant "all ears."

I was still numb, but found a way to leave the table, reach Marta with a tray of drinks, gently touch her arm, and tell her I would see her soon.

I walked past the formal doorman and gave him the nod, which was oddly returned, and I strode down the hotel's promenade, hands in my jean pockets. There was still pink in the western sky. The Mackinac Bridge was illuminated by thousands of small lights outlining the graceful spans. As I walked downhill onto Main Street, alive with the island's nightlife, I marveled at this twist of fate. This could be another turning point. I was going to get the girl, and she would be The One. It would help if I could get my heart rate somewhere below its current hummingbird pace.

I showered in the room at the Chippewa and put on my clean, faded polo shirt. Brushing my wet hair back, I took a deep breath, assessing myself in the bathroom mirror. *Keep calm,* I told myself, but my heart was pounding out of my chest. I lay back on the bed, my head cradled by the oversized hotel pillow. Closing my eyes, I took deep, meditative breaths and tried to calm down. It didn't work. I read the tourist magazines on the nightstand and practiced deep breathing again. I looked at the small hotel clock for the hundredth time. It was nearly ten thirty. My heart thundered again.

I can do this. I made my way downstairs through the hotel lobby and the archway connected to the Pink Pony bar. The bar was nearly filled and loud with the din of well-lit tourists, mixed with the sound system blaring Weather Report's "Birdland." I found a seat at the bar, and by the time I ordered a Budweiser, Marta had entered the bar from the street entrance. She had let down her blonde hair, which touched her bare shoulders. She was wearing a white, sleeveless cotton dress that praised her bronzed shoulders. Her face beamed as she smiled in recognition. I took in her full breasts and curved hips, accentuated by the dress as she moved through the crowded bar toward me. There was no point trying to stop the arrhythmia. Droplets of sweat formed on my forehead, back, and underarms as she reached me and, for the second time, enveloped me in a full hug.

"Luke, I can't believe we found each other. This is so great and weird. What a trip!" She was so close, and it terrified me. This was the moment I had waited my short lifetime for. *Don't blow it, Luke. What's the right next move?*

I managed to tell her, "I never forgot you, Marta Czechowski. To tell you the truth, I'm terrified that I'm sitting here, talking to you. I tried to find you this summer, but I just missed you at Wycamp Lake. Even though we only met that one time, I don't know, I felt we connected, and I thought it might be great if we met again and then, then to meet you at the Grand Hotel. It's remarkable. I don't quite know what to say, but I guess I'm babbling on here. . . ."

Marta laughed. "Why don't we start by getting a couple of beers, and we can get reacquainted, Luke?"

I offered Marta my bar seat and ordered her a beer. We talked over the music, close to each other, catching up from our last meeting in her Volkswagen. At one point, she took a bar napkin and wiped the sweat off my forehead, not missing a stride in our conversation and not mentioning or even appearing to notice that I looked like a cat that was caught in the rain.

I learned that she had been camping with girlfriends at Wycamp, and that her husband had showed up, and that his penchant for drinking and drugs had led to an ugly scene, including money and pot disappearing from a girlfriend's purse. The next morning, he was gone, and so was her vacation money. It was a replay of a year of bad scenes. She was not going to return to the already-ruined relationship. She called her mother and arranged for her lease, phone, and utilities to be transferred into her husband's name. She borrowed money from her friends and made her way to Mackinac Island after learning that summer jobs were plentiful for skilled waitresses. With savings of three hundred dollars, her next trip was to Cincinnati, where she would file for a divorce. From there, she was seriously thinking about joining some friends who were leaving for Florida for the winter season.

I could see this was one hard-working, well-organized, tough, hurting chick. I told her about my summer, and then we recounted our conversation in the VW bug on I-75.

"I remember everything you told me, Luke, and I loved how open you were with me. I always hoped we would meet again, and here we are."

She placed her hand on my forearm and squeezed gently, leaned down from the bar stool, and kissed me with her full lips in a soft and friendly entreaty. I returned the kiss with patience I didn't have, and our lips lingered, matching each other beautifully.

"That was nice, Luke Moore, better than the grand conversation. Now, tell me, do you dance?"

"Not well, but I'm game."

Marta took my hand and led me to the dance floor in the back of the bar. The jukebox was playing Irving Berlin's "Always." The crowded dance floor of couples was intertwined with each other, swaying. I put my arms around Marta, worrying about my perspiration-soaked polo shirt. She put her arms around me. She looked directly at me, into me, with her hazel eyes, centered with shining, blue starbursts. I was melting, in more ways than one.

"Sorry about the sweat, Marta." She nuzzled in closely, resting her head in my shoulder, her warm nose on my neck. I could feel her breath on the back of my neck as we swayed almost in time with the music. I started to unwind. I didn't realize I could be enthralled and relax at the same time.

"Don't worry, Luke. I like the way you smell." My anxiety disappeared as the final refrain of the song played.

> *Not for just an hour,*
> *Not for just a day,*
> *Not for just a year,*
> *But always.*

We made love with our clothes on that first night. She was perfect for me. I knew this after only a few hours with her. Lust gave way to love as pheromones and hormones did their work, and the lightness in my chest, where my soul had been lost for so long, led me into unsullied territory. I had never embraced a woman for so long and with fervor and hope. My lips had never sought and found partner lips I could kiss for hours, exploring and finding deeply, delved passion. And talking in tongues was not just a Pentecostal ritual. I held Marta's head in both my hands, my fingers and thumbs learning the ridges of her occipital and temporal bones as I looked past her smiling eyes.

The only undressing of the night was freeing the top two buttons of Marta's linen dress to admire the tan line of her full cleavage, which I traced with my nose and lips. I'm a cleavage man. I even like the sound of the word. The sight and scent of the upper half of Marta's breasts led to a mantra-like moan that rumbled from my breastbone through my throat.

"Calm down there, tiger," Marta said.

I put my head on my elbow and smiled down on her. "I can wait."

"I know. And I appreciate it."

And so the night went. Marta settled her head into my shoulder and neck and fell into an easy rhythm of sleep. I stared at the ceiling and hummed the lyrics: "Try to remember a kind of September." I knew this was a September night I would never forget.

Chapter 21

September 2003

I finished my one-true-love story in a line of cars approaching the toll booth to the Upper Peninsula. I glanced into the rearview mirror, surprised to see a bemused smile on Roberta's face. Our passenger, Tom Lutac, appeared more amazed than my daughter. Knowing how children at any age react to the slightest reference that their parents might have sex, I romanticized the end of the evening and skipped over other details that weren't necessary for anybody's daughter to know. I also wasn't particularly eager to disclose that we made love, even without coitus, after just a hello and howdy-do, either. Parenting is riddled with hopeful hypocrisy.

I also didn't relate that after our first night together, this hungry tiger met a yearning tigress. She released me. And we devoured each other. Thirty years later, Marta would suggest a connubial roll in the hay by asking if I was interested in another "night of untold positions." Although at our age, "untold" would have to be downgraded to a "night of tenuous positions." Or even more accurately, "a night of positions that won't cause leg cramps."

I made sure while telling our story that I kept one eye on Marta, watching for expressions I'd learned over the years that she approved of my version. I saw amusement as she watched Roberta's reaction, but behind her eyes, I could see hidden tears rising as she saw our history with our daughter was changing on this very day.

"Dad, that adaptation is lot more truthful than the *Reader's Digest* version you've been telling me for years," Roberta interrupted. "But I have a confession. I've heard this story before. The last time your Lost Soul buddies were in town—it must have been when I was about twelve or thirteen—that crazy Mr. Parcell pulled me aside and asked me if I wanted to know the real Luke Moore. I said of course, and he told the real version of Mom and you. Then he made me swear I would never tell you or Mom or my teeth would fall out. Even Mr. McDermott, who I saw all the time, had a few beers that night and told me a story about you guys. I hope my teeth don't fall out telling you this."

"No surprises, then, huh? What a letdown. I'll kill those guys when we see them after we drop you off," I said.

"Your version is more colorful and detailed than theirs. But, Dad, they loved telling those stories to me. Mr. Parcell told me, 'I never thought the day would come when I would be talking to a kid of Luke Moore's. Your dad's life was one far-fetched story after another. And here he is married, to Marta, for Christ's sake. With a teenage daughter. God bless you, young Roberta, and God bless that lucky son of a bitch that's your dad. It's a life that's damn near impossible to believe.' I wasn't exactly sure what he was talking about at the time, but I got it over time. I'll cut you some slack, Dad, because, excusing my language, you are one lucky son of a bitch!"

That made all us laugh, although my laughter was bittersweet. Here I was driving down memory lane and simultaneously driving toward the destination where I would lose my beautiful, young, and wise daughter to the big, bad world of college and life beyond my treasured family. I had prepared for this day, yet I was completely unequipped to let her go. Family and my family of friends were the bridge to my life of contentment. Without them, I careened toward tragedy. The lifeline started with Ann, April, Angela, Donnie, then the Lost Souls, and, in our few moments of luminous revelation, Annette, followed by Kate and Helen Brady. In an excruciating full circle of lessons, I learned that life was always about family. My psychology education and experience had taught me to deal with the real world of human problems, but life wasn't that straightforward. In the world of the unexplained, where my history lived, there was more. Life is infuriating, magical, and completely unpredictable. Family is the pathway and training ground to coping and then enjoying all that came down the road. The nature of life is filled with gains and losses. Family is the wholesome context to enjoy the gains and weather the losses. The ethereal cosmic hum was a harbinger of the forces that family could marshal to protect its own. See, I knew how to rationalize and even take a stab at explaining the mysteries of family love. But, damn, my daughter was hours from walking away from the eighteen-year-old nest Marta and I had built for her. I was hurting.

I paid the toll and drove out onto the main bridge. A brace of Great Lakes air cooled me through my open window. The touch of the breeze from the Straits of Mackinac matched the water's aquamarine hues, spread out below the bridge. I wished I had a cigar.

Chapter 22

September 1973

S ilence became a friend to Marta and me once we talked ourselves out. We chattered nonstop from the night in the Pink Pony through the following three weeks that led us off Mackinac Island and back to Topinabee. We learned to be quiet together on long walks or sitting next to each other reading.

While our personalities were strikingly different, we were both decisive. Maybe a better word was impulsive. I remembered a very old nun taught a boys' ninth grade seminar on human sexuality; beforehand, we adolescents laughed at the lunacy of a nun teaching sex ed. Three hours later, we'd learned more about the biology of sex and its relationship to love than all of our previous combined knowledge. This prune of a nun was the Dale Carnegie of sex education. She told us that the difference between impulsive and mature sexual activity was the difference between being a child and adult. Then, to keep the point Catholic, she told us our impulses would lead to pregnancy and social disease, and mature decisiveness would lead to love, marriage, and God. She had us right up to that point. Who could think of God when your johnson was pointing north?

The season ended at the Grand Hotel, and Marta left her job a week earlier than planned. I stayed on the island for two days with her in the dorm-style housing offered to seasonal workers. Todd

Michaels had found his own set of parties, and I finally caught up with him drinking his lunch at the Pink Pony. He smiled when I told him I wasn't going back to the mainland with him the next morning as we had planned.

"Well, at least I had one day of hitchhiking, even if it was only one ride. I don't think I'm cut out to stand out there by myself. I think I'll call and get somebody from Indian River to pick me up. If you two are interested, stop by tonight, and I'll buy you two a beer."

That was the last time I saw Todd Michaels. Marta and I never made it back to the Pink Pony.

Three days later, we left the island, the water plume from the ferryboat spraying behind us. Life moved fast for us from the beginning. I was accustomed to picking up on a moment's notice: so was Marta.

We drove to Topinabee from Mackinaw City where Marta's VW Bug was parked. Tony was happy to take us in as we formulated a plan: head south to complete unfinished business. We decided to make our way to Marta's home in Cincinnati, visit her mother, close her bank account, collect a few of her belongings from her mother's apartment, file divorce papers, and drive to Florida. Marta was willing to risk adventure with me. This seemed like a big leap to faith, considering my circumstances and the short term of our relationship.

Meanwhile, we partied with John and Sydney, who remained in Indian River, through the autumn color season. They considered alternatives for the winter, including Miami, Chicago, or Detroit.

Marta fit in with my friends, who would have cut a wide swath for just about any woman who might be a match for me. As it was, she was a genuine person with an earthy, open personality. She might offend by asking a question better left unasked, but without guile or bad intentions, so the moment was overlooked quickly without any lingering mortification.

We found walking to be an inexpensive courting exercise. I showed her the hiking trails through the Pigeon River Forest and the sandy beaches and bluffs on Lake Michigan near Cross Village. We poured out our life stories, dreams, fears, and ambitions to each other. Conversation came freely, and we didn't argue. After the torrent of life experiences slowed, we found comfort in each other.

In mid-September, Marta and I hitchhiked to the Vermont House. Marta had sold her repair-hungry VW for $250 and a backpack. I had sent Big Ann a letter telling her about Marta and imagined her reaction to reading that I had fallen in love. The letter did not include details of Marta's failed marriage. No need to put sugar in the gas tank quite yet. Ann invited us to dinner the next night.

Our first visit with Kate didn't go as well. We met Kate and Elvis at the Four Green Fields pub, where she cornered me in the back of the bar. Over the din of Irish music, Kate reminded me that Marta was married, and it didn't make it any better that the guy was a jerk.

"There's trouble ahead with her," Kate sternly told me.

"Kate, I don't doubt you, but there's trouble ahead with me, too."

"Look, Luke," Kate hissed, "don't let the first woman to give you steady sex lead you around like a little puppy. You're better than that! You don't know a thing about this woman, other than she's married to a loser and helped out a down-on-her-luck waitress living in a smarmy apartment with a jelly-head roommate! It's not just about living in the moment, Luke. This girl and her no-good husband can lead you somewhere you don't want to go. Can't you see that, Luke?"

I was taken aback by Kate's outburst.

"Kate, I'm thankful for your concern, and I agree I don't know exactly where this is going, but I think I can handle it. And, Kate, I'm falling in love, or at least I'm pretty sure that's what's going on here."

"You moron! You're not falling in love; you're just getting laid regularly! Grow up!"

Kate stomped and pushed the restroom door open with her shoulder, oblivious to the men's room sign until she saw a drunk pissing into the sink. She turned and ran out to hoots. She glared at me as she found the right door into the ladies' room. I waited outside for her; I knew Kate well enough to feel certain that her know-it-all gene would soon be overcome by her kindness. I bummed a Virginia Slim menthol from an elderly woman waiting to use the pay phone. The sweet menthol taste hit the back of my throat and made me grimace. I finished the cigarette regardless. Kate emerged from the restroom as I ground the butt into a puddle of beer on the floor.

Kate pointed a finger at me, saying, "Okay, I said too much about your girlfriend, but I worry about you."

"You're just jealous, eh, Kate?" I said.

"Yeah, right," Kate replied. I locked arms with her and led her back to the bar room and stage. The crowd was standing and singing along. Marta stood on stage with the balding lead singer of the Four Rovers, belting out "The Black Velvet Band" with gusto.

"Oh, great, another performer," Kate moaned to me.

"Let me get to know her, Luke. She must have something going for you to have fallen so hard."

"She does, Kate, she does," I answered. The band played on past last call and came down into the audience to jam with Elvis, Marta, and musicians who frequented the pub. They played and sang every Irish tune they knew. Kate Brady finally felt the effects of the many black and tans she had drunk. She jumped up on her chair and led the group in a sloppy version of "The Black Velvet Band."

We didn't reach the Vermont House until after 4:00 a.m. We sat on the front porch talking until the full moon fell and first light appeared. "That's all for me. That was a good night," Elvis declared. He took Kate by the hand and led her inside. Marta nestled close to me and concurred, "This really was a good night, Luke. I could get used to a lot of good nights."

"Me, too," I said.

The dinner with Ann and Donnie was as I expected: nervous at first, relaxed by the end of the evening. Ann was ever-so-polite in her grilling of Marta, who managed to avoid telling of her current marriage without lying. I think Ann saw the look in my eyes and thought maybe this was the beginning of something, anything, positive for me. Marta scored easy points with Donnie by knowing about the Cincinnati Reds and the Big Red Machine. We sat at the dinette table and played Michigan Rummy past Donnie's bedtime. After saying good night to Donnie, I emerged from his bedroom to see Marta and Ann on the couch turning pages of a family photo album. The album, like the few family pictures around the house, was filled with photos taken after the fire. All of the Moore family memorabilia was lost when our home went up in flames. We didn't have a single picture of our mom. The house on Hoffman was straining to be our new home. It was a long-term building project. That night, playing cards and watching Ann and Marta, it felt a little more like home.

I told Ann about our plans to go south, first to Atlanta, and then Florida to find work. As expected, she worried. She also insisted, "While you're in Royal Oak, this is your home. You don't need to camp out at Elvis and Mark's." That meant me bunking with Donnie as usual and Marta staying in April and Angela's room as a guest. I wasn't about to fight with Big Ann about the separate quarters, and Marta played along.

We lived at the Moore home for a week. Ann and Marta cooked together each night, and by the middle of the week, she told Ann about her busted marriage. It didn't matter. Ann liked Marta's easy manner, and as she learned more about her and how she worked her way out of a hardscrabble past, a certain respect was earned. I think Marta reminded her of Mom.

Ann tried to persuade me that we could live in Royal Oak, but she knew it was a lost argument. Marta was a better listener. We sat on the front porch one evening, and Marta explained to Ann that she would enjoy coming back to Royal Oak after getting her life in order in Cincinnati and maybe making some good money in Florida in the winter.

"I know Luke has avoided coming back and living in Royal Oak, or even sitting still in one place for long. He's still so angry about what happened to your family. Give us a few months. I think I can help him. I know we just met, but I love your brother, even the mixed-up, angry part of him. We need to sort things out in my life and his, and then figure out where home should be. I don't intend to be a wanderer or a wanderer's gal pal for long."

How could I not love this woman? In an ever-so-direct and succinct way, she told Ann and me how it was.

Angela and April came home for the weekend, and the four girls bonded easily, spending a lot of time around the dinette table with coffee, leaving Donnie and me out of their sorority. During our week together, I showered Donnie with time and attention. His pencil drawings of sports figures had caught a teacher's eye, and she gave him free private art lessons. I marveled at the drawings and watercolors covering the walls of his room. He was good and beginning to understand his talent. He smiled knowingly when I complimented his work.

I persuaded my three sisters, Marta, and Kate to attend a Tigers game with Donnie and me. We borrowed a neighbors' station wagon, piled in, and toured downtown to Tiger Stadium. None of the girls had any interest in sports, so they didn't mind when I tipped an usher a couple of bucks in the second inning and then slid into unoccupied front-row, upper-deck, box seats closer to the field with Donnie. My dad had taught me the art of tipping an usher at my first Tigers' game when I was eight years old. Not much of a legacy.

I talked baseball with Donnie, who was hunched over the box seat railing, rooting hard for a late-inning Tigers rally. It was a cloudy, cool, late September afternoon at the ballpark. The green grass of the outfield contrasted against the blue stadium seats and walls. Looking over Donnie's shoulder, twenty rows behind us, I could see the girls laughing and talking. I grinned and watched the lovely women, two of whom I had known for less than six months, and thought of the strange circumstances that had brought us all together.

Donnie cheered loudly as pinch-hitter Gates Brown connected and the sharp crack of the bat brought me back to the game in time to see the baseball arc into the right field reserved seats—a two-run homer to put the Tigers up by one, heading into the ninth inning. Donnie and I high-fived and hugged.

Dark clouds had been moving fast above the stadium, west to east, and low thunder answered the home run. The thick humidity broke into a downpour, quickly drenching Donnie and me before we reached the girls, who were dry under the stadium's canopy. We sat for an hour waiting for the rain to clear until the game was called. We walked through the rain to the station wagon. Donnie, Marta, and I wedged ourselves into the far backseat, soggy and chatting as Ann drove toward Woodward Avenue, stopping at Lafayette Coney Island for chili dogs. It was a family night for our eccentric troop, and as close to home as I had been in years.

Two days later, Marta and I were off to Marta's hometown of Cincinnati.

At 9:30 a.m., Marta and I hugged Elvis and Kate good-bye over the front seats of the Falcon. "Here you go again, man. But I'm guessing your luck's going to improve with your foxy new hitchhiking partner," Elvis laughed.

"It wasn't so many months ago it was me that was the foxy lady. But I notice Marta isn't wearing any funny-looking hats. What gives?" Kate asked.

"I haven't raised that subject yet," I said as we grunted out of the backseat with our bags.

"I've learned quickly that taking fashion advice from Luke is a bad idea. I'm not sure there is such a thing as Fashion for the Road Warrior," Marta replied.

"You are so right. I was a naive Road Virgin, and I let this nut dress me in a Gilligan's Island hat," Kate said.

"Luke, sounds to me like these ladies have no appreciation for your sense of style," Elvis said.

"I agree, although I have no style or sense, as we both know. I do think this would be a good time to head on down the road," I replied.

Marta and I picked up our bags and Kate closed the car door.

"Travel safe. And remember to always come home," Elvis called.

"I'll miss you, again." Kate called to me through the open window as Elvis pulled away.

I waved. *Here I go again, but this time with Marta.*

Cars whisked by at the Allen Road ramp, my favorite drop-off point when hitchhiking south. The downriver communities of Taylor, Allen Park, Trenton, Wyandotte, and Southgate were filled with honest, hardworking, hard-drinking autoworkers whose roots were in the rural south. They were often the children of the original five-dollar-a-day workers Ford employed in the 1930s. Their children were securing jobs in the GM, Chrysler, and Ford plants and the numerous metal-bending shops supplying the auto industry. They favored the heavy rock of Ted Nugent, Grand Funk Railroad, MC5, Canned Heat, and Savoy Brown, yet a country station still filled one of the buttons on the car radios.

Southgate was far enough past Detroit's city center, and the younger downriver drivers didn't have a problem picking up hitch-hikers, especially the young drivers of muscle cars who pulled over with music blaring, cigarette smoke pouring out of the car, and a half-pack of Marlboros rolled up in their T-shirt sleeve. They greeted hitchhikers with "Hey, man, where you headed? I can give you a ride to Flat Rock. Hop in, man." The rides were usually short; the downriver cruising range stopped at Monroe, but occasionally,

I caught a ride as far as Toledo. Downriver was the other side of the world for me when I was growing up in Royal Oak, but the straightforwardness and reliable generosity of those picking me up reminded me of my friends on the opposite side of Detroit.

We waited patiently, Marta positioned in my shadow. We were quiet, thumbs out. We stood for over two hours on Allen Road. Marta broke the silence several times, first gingerly inquiring and finally mildly complaining about how long it was taking to snag the first ride out of Detroit.

"I know you explained this to me, but when do you just figure today's not a good day to hitchhike and turn around and go home?" Marta asked.

"I never really thought about stopping. We'll get a ride. I always do. Sometimes it takes longer," I replied.

"How long? What's the longest you ever waited, Luke?"

"Well, the longest I ever waited here, or trying to get out of Detroit, was probably four or five hours. But, remember I told you about Banff Park near Calgary, and how the mountains were so stunning? The hitchhike out there started out like a wet kiss on the end of a hot fist, as Firesign Theatre would say, and ended up like a waterslide, fun-filled and with a happy ending. I was traveling with Jimmy Colombo, and we decided to take the scenic route to Banff, thumbing up through northern Michigan, the U.P., and into Minnesota, and finally Canada, before heading west. It was pretty scenery, but took forever to hitchhike. We waited two, three hours a bunch of times. After making our way north into Canada, we waited twelve hours on the Trans-Canada Highway just outside Brandon, Saskatchewan, before finally getting a ride. Twelve of the longest hours of my life. We were out there with at least fifty other hitchhikers, and the pickings were slim. Canada is much friendlier to hitchhikers, which is the good news. The bad news is there are too damn many of us. When our last ride dropped us off in Brandon, we couldn't believe the line of hitchhikers. There must have been fifty of them ahead of us. We got at the end of the line and in two hours, only six or seven hitchhikers were picked up. A hippie couple in front of us told us about the youth hostel a mile down the road, and we decided to pack it in for the night. The hostel network in Canada is government subsidized, so it was really cheap. For a buck, you got one of thirteen mattresses in a dilapidated cabin and a cold breakfast in the morning. Jimmy and I were bushed, so after swapping lies with some Canadians from Quebec City, a Swedish couple, and two California surfer dudes, we crashed.

"Sometime in the middle of the night, one of the Quebec Canadians jumped off his mattress, and in a French accent, yelled 'Crabs! CRABS! CRABS! CRA-A-A-BS!' In an instant, everyone was up and grabbing their sleeping bags and running outside. Jimmy and I sat up, not having a clue what the hell was going on. Jimmy said, 'Crabs, here in the middle of Canada? I thought crabs came from the ocean.' 'Yeah, me, too,' I said. A guy had come back into the cabin to pick up something he left behind, and Jimmy said, 'Hey, what's with the crabs call? What's going on?' 'Crabs, man, you know crabs, scabies, bedbugs, you know, the little rascals that love to work their way up your legs . . . ' 'Oh, shit,' Jimmy cried, 'bedbugs! Let's get the hell out of here, Moore!' We ran outside with our stuff, and the rest of the group was already spread out on picnic tables and on the ground, trying to get back to sleep.

"Jimmy said, 'It's 2:00 a.m., buddy. We might as well go to the highway and try to get a head start on the line.' We walked to the road where ten diehards had stayed out all night trying to get the hell out of Brandon. We got in line and waited and waited. Even in summer, the Saskatchewan nights are cold, and before long we stepped into our sleeping bags and pulled them up to our chins just like the ten guys in front of us. We looked like a dozen multicolored vertical caterpillars. A car would come by every ten minutes or so, and only the lead caterpillar would unleash his thumb to try and get a ride. Some guys had destination signs taped or pinned to their sleeping bags spelling out their hopes to get to Regina, Vancouver, anywhere west. By daybreak only two of the dozen caterpillars had been picked up, and I saw a 'road first' for me. Caterpillar number nine hopped over the highway to the other side and started hitchhiking east in the opposite direction. The crazy thing was, he got a ride in the first ten minutes!"

Marta interrupted my soliloquy. "Wait a minute. You can't stand here and tell me these stories like I'm a Sunday school teacher. I've seen you in action, Mark Twain, and this caterpillar business is completely unbelievable. You can spin your yarns on some other unsuspecting soul!"

"Marta, listen, this stuff happened. You spend enough time out on the road and you wouldn't believe what happens in the world.

The old saw that truth is stranger than fiction is gospel. Look at my eyes. Could I lie to you?"

"No, but you could spin a story out of thin air, Luke Moore."

"Okay, there's a little embellishment here and there, but only to benefit you, the eager listener."

Marta rolled her eyes, which I took as assent to continue.

"It was pretty bleak out there, and by ten in the morning, we were hungry, tired, and pretty cranky. Jimmy made a run to the gas station on the four corners where Trans-Canada crossed a north-south highway and came back and introduced me to a road meal staple I've used a lot since. It consisted of two apples, two oranges juices, and two four-ounce, silver-foil-covered packages of Philadelphia Cream Cheese. He took a bite of the apple followed by a bite of cream cheese and chewed them together down to the apple core and the last sliver of cream cheese. It sure beat my regular road diet of Paydays and Pepsis.

"Finally, by noon, there were only four hitchhikers in front of us! Traffic had picked up a bit, and a gnarly guy in a pickup put four guys in the back of his truck. So, we're standing there a couple more hours and we're finally number one in line. I'm looking southbound toward Minnesota on the north-south road, where very little traffic had been coming from, and I see this little green Datsun slowing to a stop at the intersection's blinking light. I said, 'Hey, Jimmy, doesn't that look like Austin's car?' Jimmy laughed and said, 'Yep, what's the odds of finding a lime-green Datsun like Austin's out here?' The car stopped at the intersection and slowly turned left on the Trans-Canada in front of us. Jimmy's jaw dropped, and he said, 'Holy Christ, it is Austin! Austin Goddamn Andres!'

"The passenger in the car was asleep, and as the Datsun completed its turn and started to accelerate, it was parallel to us for an instant, but Jimmy was up and running alongside the car, yelling, 'Austin, Austin, save us, Austin, for Christ's sake, if there is anything holy in this world, pull over! A-a-a-austin!' Austin had that road zombie look going on, but this wild-eyed, screaming hitchhiker jolted him awake, and his passenger opened his eyes, blinking, just as the car sped past Jimmy. Jimmy fell to his knees and started getting road religion. 'Please God, Please God, Please God, Please God,' he repeated over and over. About fifty feet ahead, the Datsun's brake lights came on, and the car pulled over on the shoulder of the road. We scrambled out of our caterpillar costumes, picked up our bags, and ran as fast as we could to the Datsun, where Austin Andres and his passenger Jim Purtell got out of the car.

"Long story short, they saved us. Austin and Jim were two years older than us, much cooler, and fully employed. We were sure they debated leaving us, but Jimmy's older brother was in their class at St. Mary's, so they felt a tinge of pity. Jim stepped out of the Datsun and sized up Jimmy and me, giving us a sardonic look that was vintage Purtell. 'Austin, we only have one choice. We take Colombo and leave Moore to wither and slowly die in this godforsaken, foreign wasteland. Or we could bungee-cord him to the luggage rack and bring him along. Whaddya think, Austin?'

"Austin had a kind heart, but also believed that Jimmy and I were lowlife wastrels. 'It's not like we have a choice, stuff them in.' The problem was that their vacation-bound Datsun was completely filled with their gear, and stuffing us in was no easy feat. When the car merged onto the highway, all four of us were packed in like sardines.

"They gave us a ride over one thousand miles of nothingness. I mean, there is nothing between Brandon and where the Rockies leap out of the prairie. We would have died out there. To boot, I only had twenty-four dollars to my name. By the time we left them a week later, they had taken us to Banff Provincial Park, which I think I told you was the most beautiful place I've ever been, through Glacier Park in Montana, and finally to Yellowstone. They gave us a hard time about being worthless leeches, but, when they left, I still had nineteen bucks. They paid for just about everything! So the answer to your question: that twelve hours was the longest I ever waited for a ride, and the fifteen hundred miles with Austin and Jim Purtell was the longest ride I ever had!"

"You are asking me to believe that you went from a vermin infestation to a caterpillar imitation to being picked up in the middle of the Canadian prairie by two guys you went to high school with?"

"Yes, and if Austin, Jim Purtell, or Jimmy were here, they would verify all the mostly true facts. I couldn't make this up."

"Yes, you could! I refuse to believe this story without verification, and I will remain unconvinced until I meet any of the characters in this cockamamie story."

We argued back and forth until we noticed a powder-blue Malibu with a white vinyl roof had pulled over in front of us.

"Hey, a ride! It's an omen. I must be telling the truth! Let's go," I shouted as we chased the car like two crazy dogs.

Marta waited to step into the backseat of the two-door car as I paused with the door open to assess the driver. I pegged his age as somewhere in his early thirties, driving a nice car, fashionably long hair, but not a hippie, dark sunglasses hiding his eyes. The driver didn't send off any negative or hostile signals, so I pushed back the front seat for Marta to enter the car and thanked the driver for picking us up.

I sat in the front seat and leaned over and offered the driver a handshake saying, "I'm Larry Wallegolla, and this is my wife, Wendy Wallegolla. Pleased to meet you."

"Hey, Wendy and Larry, my name is Larry, too, Larry Lavalier. Where you two headed today?" He looked over his shoulder and, seeing a small opening in traffic, stomped on the accelerator.

"Cincinnati, Larry. How far you headed?"

"My friends, today is your lucky day. Miami is my destination, so Cincinnati—the home of Little Kings Cream Ale, the Big Red Machine, Skyline chili, the city formerly known as Porkopolis—is gonna be no problem, no problem at all."

Larry Lavalier picked up the conversation seamlessly and moved right on to telling his personal background, beginning with the present and proceeding in dizzying detail to describe the previous two years of his life. I knew the supersonic patter of someone on speed, and I reflected back to the summer hitchhike with John. Larry didn't stop for fifteen minutes, all the while driving at a constant eighty-eight miles per hour. I was usually unconcerned about high speed drivers, but I didn't know about Marta. I glanced over my shoulder and saw Marta relaxed in the backseat, almost nodding off.

Larry was a college professor of mathematics at Michigan State University and, if he were to be believed, a wunderkind of sorts. He told of his gift for seeing math problems solved on a television screen inside his head. He had parlayed his skill into a research and teaching position at MSU two years ago, but this fall he had connived his way into a one-year research position at the University of Miami. The way Larry described it, he was using his superior skills to beat the academic system and get the best teaching position possible at the earliest possible age. I finally saw an opening to engage Larry when he started in about his passion for running.

"I love running. I run at least five miles a day, seven days a week. And that's down from ten miles a day. Last month I ran in the Seattle Marathon," Larry announced, gesticulating wildly, often with both hands off the steering wheel.

He took a sip of the sixteen-ounce Mountain Dew between his legs when I blurted, "Hey, I'm a runner, too. I run track for Northern Michigan University. But I'm transferring to the University of Cincinnati because they're giving me a full track scholarship. I had a partial scholarship at Northern Michigan for my freshman and sophomore year, but Cincinnati offered me the full ride, and I'm taking it."

Larry tilted his head down and looked over the top of his sunglasses at me, revealing bloodshot and questioning eyes. "Really? What distance do you run?"

"Mostly middle distance, half mile, mile," I replied.

"Really? And you say you ran track at Northern Michigan for two years? You were there in 1972 and '73, right?" Larry asked.

"Yeah, I red-shirted my freshman year and ran varsity last year. It's pretty tough training in Marquette, you know. The fall is pretty short, and running in the cold weather was a drag." I continued lying about my experience at NMU for a couple of minutes while Larry removed his sunglasses, nodded, and grinned slyly, driving at exactly eighty-eight miles per hour.

"That's really interesting. Larry, what did you say your last name was?"

"Wallegolla, Larry Wallegolla," I replied.

"That is interesting, and funny, too. You see, Larry Wallegolla, I taught at Northern Michigan University in 1972. I guess I didn't quite get to that part of my story, did I? In fact, Larry Wallegolla, I was the assistant coach for the Wildcats track team during my short stay there. And, for the life of me, I can't remember a middle distance runner named Larry Wallegolla, or, for that matter, anybody that remotely resembled you! Now, I must admit that I was regularly ingesting several controlled substances at that time, because, yes, indeed, the weather in Marquette was monstrously bad, as you pointed out, Larry. But, I'm certain, yes, oh, so sure, that I would have remembered an ever so artful and creative, shall I say, storyteller, such as *you*, Larry Wallegolla!" he shouted.

Damn! I couldn't believe it. I had been caught for the first time since I hit the road two years ago! I was flabbergasted. My skin turned clammy as Marta's low, swelling laughter rolled over into the front seat of the car. Larry and I turned our heads. Marta was laughing so hard she was gasping for air, pounding her knees with her hands. Larry burst into laughter, cackling at first and then hooting, pounding his hands on the steering wheel, maintaining exactly eighty-eight miles per hour.

Marta's laughter finally subsided enough to say, "Well, fellas, that is one helluva way to get to know each other and start off a long ride together. Larry, it's time for some truth telling. My traveling partner is a storyteller extraordinaire and really can't help himself. My name is not Wendy Wallegolla. It's Marta Czechowski, and your front seat partner is Luke Moore. Luke, tell Larry your real story, which is really out of this world anyway. I think you owe him that. What are the odds that you could get caught so, so red-handed! Unbelievable!"

"Okay, okay. Larry, I'm sorry for my fabrication. You may wish to believe my fiction after you hear my real story, but here it goes," I replied, shamefaced.

"I'll be the judge of that!" Larry said.

I told my story. Larry interrupted with an occasional "No shit," "Oh, man," and "Whew!" By mid-Ohio, Marta had told her story, and then Larry talked about his childhood, pedestrian by comparison. We were fast friends by Dayton, when Larry suggested that maybe we might want to continue on with him to Florida. "Listen, you guys, you said you wanted to head down to the warm weather anyway. I could use the company and help driving. As you can probably tell, I'm flying a bit high on speeders, but to tell you the truth, I don't like to get this wired. I can help you out on expenses. This is a paid trip, and I'll be able to save on hotels if we drive straight through. I figure we could be in Miami in twenty hours or so. Whaddya think, are you interested in a really long ride?"

"Larry, that's a very generous offer, but Marta and I are just getting started together, and we need to take care of a few things in Cincinnati. It's going to take us a day or two, right Marta?"

"Yeah, Larry, I need to spend some time with my mother. It's probably not going to work out. But you're more than welcome to take a break in Cincinnati. If you want to spend the night, I'm sure that's all right. We're just not quite ready to get to Florida right this minute," Marta said.

Larry was disappointed, but said, "No problem. I'll get you to your mother's house and maybe grab some Skyline chili and then head out."

He drove the hour from Dayton to Cincinnati. At his request, I entertained him with a list of aliases and accompanying road stories. It killed time, and soon we were entering Cincinnati just past rush hour. Marta directed Larry west on Thirteenth Street and north on Vine, past Findlay Market and, according to Marta, the first grocery store started by Barney Kroger in 1912. Marta's mother's house was located in the part of town known as the Over-the-Rhine district. The section was the original settling place for the largely German immigrants who settled in Cincinnati to work in the burgeoning slaughterhouse industry. Marta wrinkled her nose when she described the nasty business of turning pigs into bacon and pork chops that provided fetid, steady employment for thousands of immigrant workers.

Over-the-Rhine was an "entry" neighborhood, and as the decades passed, southern blacks and Appalachian transplants mixed with the remaining Germans. It was a vibrant slum. Marta's mother lived in the second story of a flat that resembled her pock-marked past. Three divorces and alcoholism had led her down a bitter road. But she had kicked her bad marrying and drinking habits a decade prior and lived alone, sober and strong, working as the manager and chief waitress of Karen's Kafe. Her wages and tips sustained a minimum standard of living for a forty-four-year-old woman, and the dignity of providing for herself and helping out her only child.

Larry snaked the Malibu through the lively streets of Over-the-Rhine, onto Race Street, past the Emmanuel Gym, and parked in front of a red brick building between a Laundromat and an astrology and tarot card storefront. Marta's stories had prepared me for the neighborhood. Larry seemed relaxed as we made our way up the stairs to Lila Herman's flat.

Marta used her key to open the door, knocking loudly as she entered. "Momma, it's Marta, I'm home!" Larry and I followed Marta into the small foyer, through a tiny kitchenette, and into the large living room area where Marta's mother Lila was sleeping on the sofa. Marta kneeled quietly, saying, "Mom, it's Marta. Wake up, Mom."

Lila's eyes fluttered and opened, recognizing her daughter with a smile. "Marta, Marta, my dear. How good to see you." She noticed

Larry and Luke and sat up on the couch. "One of these young men must be Luke," she said. "Luke Moore, correct? The young man that you wrote so fondly about in your letters, am I right?"

I stepped forward next to Marta and said, "Yes, ma'am. I'm Luke Moore. I'm very happy to meet you."

Marta's mother pushed herself upright into a sitting position and pushed back her gray-streaked, auburn hair. "Well, I'm glad to meet you, too, Luke. You'll have to excuse my appearance. I'm not feeling all that well right now. Now, who is this other gentlemen you're with?"

Marta explained how we had made our way to Cincinnati. Lila pushed her afghan off her knees, stood unsteadily, and insisted that her daughter and friends have something to eat.

"You boys just sit right here and let my daughter and me make you a proper meal," Lila said. She took Marta by the elbow and ushered her into the kitchen. Larry and I settled uneasily into the two worn chairs facing an ancient black-and-white television set while Marta and Lila prepared dinner.

The smell of sautéed hamburger, onions, and peppers blended with the canned laughter of *Hogan's Heroes*. We were on our third beer when the sounds of conversation in the kitchen changed to the low tones of Marta crying. Larry and I didn't know what to do. I finally entered the small kitchen and saw Marta and her mother seated at the two-chair table. Marta's face was in her hands, her head on her mother's shoulder. Lila stroked her daughter's hair. "Don't worry, Marta, it's going to be okay. It's going to be all right." I stood awkward and mute.

Marta raised her face to me and said, "It's cancer, Luke. My mom has cancer. She's really sick."

Lila calmed her daughter. "Marta, I've got a good doc, and thank God I bought that insurance policy from the newspaper in 1967. It's gonna cost me most of my savings, but after the first thousand dollars, the insurance pays for almost everything. I have two nurse's aides who come here to help me after I get my treatment. I'm not sure who to believe, but I'm told I can beat this kind of cancer, which I'd rather not talk about in front of these boys." Larry joined us around the kitchen table. "Now, you boys, I'm sorry you have to see us carrying on this way. I want you to go down to the corner and buy yourselves some beer." She stood up and took three dollars from her purse on the kitchen counter. "Let me and my Marta sort this out and finish making you some dinner."

We were relieved to be out of the emotional tension in the apartment. As we left, we heard Marta ask, "Mom, why didn't you write and tell me?"

Lila replied, "There's nothing you can do to cure me, honey, and you've got a life to live."

Larry and I took our time, stopping to smoke two cigarettes before climbing the stairs to the apartment. We entered with somber faces, but heard singing in the kitchen. Marta stood at the stove. Her face still mottled from crying, she was stirring a large pot of spaghetti sauce while singing "Tell Him" along with her mother.

"There, that feels better doesn't it?" Lila soothed.

"Yes, it does, Mom," Marta replied as she produced a bottle opener.

Shortly, the small table was filled with a simple, flavorful, and filling meal. A votive candle provided ambience for a remarkable dinner, lighthearted and peppered with questions directed to the men at the table: our past, present, and future. Lila's quiet courage was gracefully present as she steered away from her illness.

"So, Larry, where will all this math lead you to? You can really see the problems solved in your head? How did you figure out this is what you wanted to do with your life? And, Luke, how long do you think you'll keep this wandering life going? When you get to Florida, what kind of job will you look for? Out of all the places you've traveled, where did you like the best? Why?"

Lila listened to the answers carefully and then asked more questions. She seemed genuinely curious about two young men whose lives were well outside the definition of her experience, which encompassed her job at the diner, her apartment, and her daughter's life. The questions lasted well past the first twelve pack, when Lila grew tired.

"This has been a grand night. I have enjoyed the conversation. I think you young people have had too many Little Kings for any driving tonight, so you two can share the pullout sofa. It's not a bad place to sleep for one night. Marta can sleep in my room, but we'll be up early. My home nurses will be here at 8:00 a.m. Wait till you meet them! They are a hoot!" Lila laughed. Marta walked her mother to her room.

Marta rejoined us at the table and told us about her mother's cancer: lymphoma. Marta knew it was bad, but treatable, because they had caught it early. Her tears began again. I held her closely.

The entire evening was an emotional roller coaster none of us could have anticipated. Larry sat slumped at the table, surrounded by little green beer bottles. The amphetamines had worn away, and his red-rimmed eyes filled with sadness. He shook his head and lowly said, "Larry Wallegolla."

Marta asked, "What did you say?"

"Larry Wallegolla," he repeated, still shaking his head and smiling slightly. "Larry Wallegolla."

Marta giggled through her tears, and a snot bubble formed at her left nostril, which made her giggle and snort as the bubble popped. She wiped her face with a napkin and mimicked Larry, "Larry Wallegolla." The two of them repeated the name together, "Larry Wallegolla, Larry Wallegolla."

I joined the chant until it reached a ridiculous crescendo: "Larry Wallegolla, Larry Wallegolla, Larry Wallegolla, *Larry Wallegolla!*"

"We'll wake your mom," I hushed. We disintegrated into laughter. "What the hell was that all about?" I asked.

"I don't have a clue, but it's a fitting end to very, very long day," Larry answered. "I'm off to sleep. I'm going to have to leave tomorrow. But if there's anything I can do before I go, just name it."

"Thanks, Larry. You've been great today. We can talk tomorrow. I need to figure this out with Marta."

Marta stood up and kissed Larry on the cheek, "You're a doll, Larry."

Marta and I talked for an hour, tossing possibilities back and forth. She was adamant that her place was with her mother and mine was on the road south. I wouldn't hear of it. I would not be separated from Marta so soon and in the midst of crisis.

"Luke, I understand why you want to stay, and I love you for it. But that's about you and this is about my mom. You have to understand we have been each other's only lifeline all of my life. The years my mom drank were pretty bad for me and for her. At one point, it got so horrible I went to live at a friend's house to get away from her and my son-of-a-bitch stepfather, an asshole if ever there was one. I was scared and hurt. Within a week, my mom showed up, and we sat on the front steps of my friend's house and talked it out. It's not easy getting out of a bad, bad marriage when you have nothing of your own and a drinking problem on your back. That day, my mom promised me she would find a way to stop drinking and somehow find a place of her own. She started attending AA meetings that evening, and found a job waitressing the next day. Her shithead husband slapped her around for getting a job, but she put up with it. She saved a little and borrowed a little, and six months later, I left my friend's house with my duffel bag and moved into this apartment with my mom. That was ten years ago. I was just a little girl. My mom kept her promise and hasn't had a drink since. I managed to get through high school with good grades and even started college, which makes my mom proud. I guess I picked up one bad habit and landed up marrying the wrong guy. That's a mistake I will never make again.

"There's a special bond between us, and don't take this the wrong way, but you're just going to be in the way. I need to figure out what's going on with my mom and help her through it. It's a little early in our relationship to understand exactly where we'll end up, but I know I want to be with you. But not right now. I want you to leave with Larry tomorrow and go to Florida. As soon as you get an address, you write me, a lot. And I'll write back. I promise. There's a future for us, but I have to take care of the here and now first. Do you understand, Luke?"

My head was in my hands. "Yeah, I do, but I wish I didn't. It's just not fair, but I guess your mom being sick isn't fair. You're sure there's no other way? I could work here and find another place to live. I could—"

Marta interrupted, putting a finger up to my lips. "Hush, Luke. We both know this is the right thing. You go with Larry tomorrow morning. But for tonight, I know a place up on the roof where we can sleep that will be a lot more fun than curling up next to Larry on the pullout sofa."

Marta led me out the living room window onto the fire escape where we climbed up to the roof, blankets and pillow in hand. I held Marta under the Cincinnati moonlight, with neon signs fluttering on and off below as the sounds of inner-city nightlife ended. "I love you, Marta, and I'm not going to lose you."

"I know, Luke, I know. And I love you, too." We made love on the rooftop until the morning delivery trucks interrupted the night. We slept for barely an hour before Marta rustled me awake.

* * *

In the morning, Lila was back on the sofa, Marta and I were drinking coffee in the kitchen, and Larry was showering, when the nurse's aides arrived at 8:00 a.m., knocking an elaborate rhythm on the apartment door, announcing themselves.

"That will be Glenn and Gilbert. Let them in, Marta," Lila called out. Marta opened the door to reveal two identical twin male nurse's aides.

"Oho, who do we have here? This must be Marta, Lila's beau-u-u-u-tiful daughter. Am I right? Or am I right? You are so cute, dear! How about a big hug for Glennski here. That's my name, sweetie, Glenn Schweitzer. Schweitzer as in Dr. Schweitzer, the humanitarian doctor."

Glenn's brother pushed him out of the way with a gentle hip check. "Move, over, Glenn, and let Gilbert in to meet this glorious girl. Marta, I'm Gilbert Standish. I'm Glenn's brother, but I changed my name to reflect my personality. Glenn, you're right, she is so adorable. Now, who is this cute-as-a-button boy? Marta's boyfriend, I'm betting? Bringing him home to mother already? He must be special. Now, enough about you two, where is that troublemaker mother of yours? There she is! Lila, how are you doing today, darling?"

The boisterous duo danced into the living room with their medical bags and began fawning over Lila, taking her blood pressure and asking questions while writing answers. They were dramatic, yet professional, in their nursing approach. Lila was clearly uplifted, entertained, and distracted while they gathered information. They had Lila laughing when Larry emerged from the bathroom shower.

"Well, well, well, what do we have here, Lila Herman? A very handsome, lithe, and, I'm sure, agile Adonis, sashaying out of your bedroom bath? What surprises lurk in the life of our Lila!" Gilbert squealed.

Glenn leapt up from his perch on the sofa almost into Larry's arms. "Li-la! Look at this hunk of man! Where have you been hiding him! He is just scrumptious. What is your name, sailor?"

Larry started to move backward toward the bedroom door, but Glenn had already locked arms with him and firmly led him back into the room. "Larry. I'm Larry Lavalier," he said, recovering a bit. "You must be Lila's nurses."

"Nurse's aides, actually, although Glenn is considering nursing school. I have different aspirations. I'm enrolled at the University of Cincinnati Architecture School. I want to build really, really big skyscrapers someday. Larry, do you like really, really big sky-scrapers?"

Larry was back on the defensive now, and stammered, "Sure, but—but, uh, right now I think I need some coffee."

"Okay, honey, let's get you some coffee while we find out how long Lila has been hiding this hunk of a boyfriend," Glenn said.

Lila giggled, "Oh, Glenn, you're such a card. Now, cut that out with Marta's friend." Lila introduced the nurse's aides to Larry and me as we found refuge at the kitchen table. Glenn and Gilbert finished Lila's exam and talked to Lila and Marta about Lila's upcoming radiation treatments and side effects. They maintained their lighthearted approach, only becoming earnest when insisting Lila keep her strength up during the treatments by eating well and resting.

Marta announced her plans to remain at home. She would coordinate her mom's treatments and work Lila's shifts at Kate's Kafe. She told her mom that I was leaving with Larry to take care of care of some unfinished business. Lila protested weakly, but was relieved, as were Glenn and Gilbert. "Oh, goody, goody, goody, Marta is going to be a big help, Lila! This is good news!" Gilbert proclaimed.

Larry and I overheard the conversations in the living room. I whispered, "Those two fruits are too much, eh, Larry? I think they have a thing for you. Did you see the way Glenn was ogling you? I'd watch out for those joy boys if I were you."

Before Larry could respond, Gilbert and Glenn stood at the kitchen table, glaring at me. "Fruits, Mr. Moore? Is that what we are? A couple of pineapples, perhaps? A bit light in our loafers, so to speak? What if we are . . . queers, raging faggots, ho-mo-sex-u-als? Is that a problem?" Gilbert glared.

I could feel my face and neck flushing crimson, fumbling to make amends. "Hey, I didn't mean anything. I mean, you are who you are, right?"

"That's right, sweetie, we are not what we seem to be," Gilbert chimed in.

"All right guys, I'm sorry I spoke out of turn."

"It's more than that, Luke. Whether we're queer or not, you don't have the right to insult us," Glenn retorted.

Gilbert said, "That's enough, Glenn, the boy said he would try to remember . . . a kind of September, when grass was green and grain was yellow . . ." Gilbert started to sing the theme song from *The Fantasticks*. The song was unsettling to me. "Try to Remember" was a favorite song of my mother's. When I thought of her, I would usually hum or sing the first few lines. His song choice was too close to home for me. Glenn joined in a duet under the kitchen archway, and the two sang enthusiastically, with arms locked, in a Gilbert and Sullivan falsetto. The singing aides finished the song with a crescendo, much to Marta and Lila's delight.

I smiled tightly, too afraid to say anything that might unleash another torrent from Glenn and Gilbert. I thought, *Jesus Christ, my life's turning into a goddamn musical. And what is going on with these two fairies? They jumped in on me a bit too fast and hard. I could care less if they're gay, just stay away from me.* I had limited exposure to homosexuals growing up. Even though gay road cruisers and predators were overrepresented on the highway, my experiences with homosexuals on the road were mainly innocuous. Most of the sex-seeking men who picked me up were considerate and cautious in leading up to a hint of "the question," trying to discern if I had homosexual tendencies or curiosity. I became good at reading the innuendos and signals and learned how to respond in a non-threatening way that made it clear I wasn't interested, but still grateful for their ride. I only had two experiences in which a hand landed up on my thigh—in both instances, my quick request to be let out of the car was never denied. However, I did worry about traveling through Georgia and the Okefenokee Swamp when I thought about Burt Reynolds and his pals in the movie *Deliverance* facing the backwoods advances of gap-toothed, inbred men of strange sexual persuasion. The line from the movie, "Squeal, squeal like a pig!" instilled fear in a generation of male suburban moviegoers.

Glenn and Gilbert were animated and friendly again as they packed up their medical paraphernalia and gave Lila and Marta hugs. Lila pulled home-canned tomatoes from a shelf and insisted that they take a case of mason jars with them.

"Luke, will you carry this case down for Gilbert and Glenn?" Lila asked.

I lifted the case and started down the stairway with Glenn and Gilbert. They pushed open the security door leading to the street. I followed them out into the bright morning sun. The sunshine made me squint as a bright light surrounded Gilbert and Glenn. I felt disoriented and dizzy. My feet felt the vibration before I heard the rumbling, low sound again. I recognized it this time. The first time I'd heard it was the night Annette showed me where God lived before she died. And then I'd heard it again hitchhiking with Kate outside of Cincinnati when the strange cops had chased us off the highway, and once more at the Dome just before the bust.

Glenn turned, looked at me, and steadied me by the elbow. "Whoa, Luke, you look like you saw a ghost," Glenn said.

"Can you hear that? That sound? I can feel this pulsating, low sound. Like it's coming from somewhere deep in the earth. Can you hear it?" I asked.

"Oh, you must mean the *dung-chen*. I'm not surprised you can hear it. It seems those with the most trouble can hear the earth's frequencies. Pay attention to those cosmic hums, Luke Moore," Gilbert said.

I felt seasick and didn't understand Gilbert. My knees buckled slightly, and Gilbert and Glenn each took one of my arms and guided me down the street. Glenn said, "You see, Luke, we all need some help now and then. You never know where it might come from. You have someone watching over you all the time, and that someone might be little old angels named Gilbert and Glenn." Glenn's voice had turned decidedly deeper and his brow furrowed, narrowing his dark blue eyes as he took the case from me.

"You're headed in the right direction, young man. Marta is the right one for you. Don't lose her. She asked you to leave now, so you leave. But you write her every day. Every day, you hear me?" Glenn finished.

"Okay, then, sweetie, on your way. Be good and be safe. We'll be looking after Marta and Lila and be praying over you!" Gilbert said, back in character.

My legs returned to me as quickly as they had left. "Thank you, Gilbert. Thank you, Glenn. I don't know who the heck you guys are, but I'm hearing you. I'm used to meeting a lot of different people, but I've been having some damn odd encounters with people giving me warnings or advice. You two, two nuns, a couple of cops. What's going on?"

"You'll figure it out, young Luke. Now we're on our way," Glenn answered.

"Well, hey, I am sorry for the fruit comment. But you guys act... different."

Gilbert laughed. "Oh, Luke, you still don't get it! It just doesn't matter! But to set the record straight, I'm married with two kids. A happy hetero. Now, Glenn, he's definitely a horse of different color. A fruit of the first order, queer as a—"

Glenn interrupted, "Gilbert, you are so full of shit. Luke, the answer is, it's none of your business!" He turned and laughed and they hopped in their yellow Pinto and sped off, the bright light ricocheting off the yellow paint.

I shook my head. "This is freaking me out."

I made my way back to Lila's apartment and found Larry at the kitchen table, his packed bag next to him on the floor. "Ready to go, Larry?" I asked.

"Yeah, Luke, it's time to get moving. You still coming?"

Marta entered the kitchen with my packed bag. "Yes, he's going. I want you to be careful driving, Larry. I can't believe you haven't been ticketed in Ohio. The Smokies are pretty tough here. But they're even tougher in Kentucky and Tennessee, so you watch out, okay?"

"We'll be fine, Marta. Thanks for the place to stay. And I'm really sorry about your mom. I'll take care of the storyteller. You take care of your mother. Tell Lila I said good-bye and thank you. Luke, I'll be in the car when you're ready to go," Larry said.

Marta leaned forward and gave Larry a kiss on the cheek and a hug. "Bye, Larry. Just remember one thing: Wallegolla!"

Larry chuckled. "I will." He returned the hug and made his way down the stairs.

"Where's your mom?" I asked Marta.

"She's sleeping. She said to say good-bye and give you this." Marta held out a brown, cloth scapular from the Sisters of Mount Carmel. "I told Mom you're a fallen-away Catholic, but she really likes you, Luke, and wanted you to take something with you, for protection. She's not big on hitchhiking." She reached up and hung the cloth scapular necklace around my neck. "Mom reminded me if you die with a blessed scapular on, your soul is automatically in a state of grace and you go straight to heaven."

"I know, you don't even have to pass Go to collect. Hey, I'm not going to look a gift pass to heaven in the mouth. Thank your mom for me. But I do feel like a loser. Your mom is worried about me getting bumped off on the highway. I'm being booted out the door by the girl I love, and Glenn and Gilbert ream me out for being a raging bigot."

"Well, you're my loser, Luke Moore, and I love you." She threw her arms around me. "C'mon, let's get you downstairs before Larry decides to leave you with all this drama and goes to Florida by himself."

I didn't want to let Marta go as we embraced by Larry's Malibu. After several desperate kisses, Marta pulled away from me. "This isn't getting any easier, Luke. Time to go."

"All right, Marta, I'll write every day. You let me know the minute I can come back and be with you. Promise?"

"I promise," Marta called as I plopped down on the Malibu's front seat. Larry pulled away. Marta waved with one hand. I watched her face, weary with life, as we pulled away. I did love her.

"Luke, I have to tell you. I never in a million years expected this trip to turn out like this," Larry said.

"Me neither, Larry, me neither."

Chapter 23

September 2003

I steered our minivan past the southern tollbooths and onto Mackinac Bridge. I started to pick up speed as we approached the main body of the bridge where the suspension cables met the roadway. Brake lights started to light up in sequence from the vehicles in front of us. I tapped my brakes as traffic came to a halt. We sat for almost ten minutes before my hyperactive drive started kicking in, which coincided with my left eyebrow beginning to twitch. I turned to Marta, and before I could utter a word, she said, "Go find out what's going on, Luke."

"Good idea, dear. I'll be right back."

I walked forward until I reached a pickup truck with a CB antenna. The driver, whose window was rolled down, was talking into the CB. "Yeah, that's ten-four on that. Looks like we'll be here awhile."

I nodded at the driver, who was wearing a weathered John Deere hat and mustard-stained T-shirt that didn't quite cover his beer- and fast-food belly. He nodded back, knowing what I was after. "Gonna be a while, pal. They had a car break down about halfway across the bridge and then some dipstick hit that car. They're sending a tow truck from the other side of the bridge, but they think it will be an hour."

"That stinks. Guess there's nothing we can do but sit it out."

"That's right, pal. Good time for a nap."

"You got that right. Thanks for the info, good buddy," I said.

He gave me a two-finger salute off the bill of the John Deere cap. I traipsed back to the car and eased back into my captain's chair, explaining the situation to Marta. Roberta and Tom snoozed in the backseat. "Take the man's advice and relax and have a nap. There's nothing you can do to change this, no matter how hard you worry, scheme, or fret."

"That's not easy for me, Marta. I live to worry, scheme, and fret."

"I know, Luke. Take a nap."

I positioned the power seat to my liking and leaned my head back into the headrest. My thoughts drifted to all the characters I met out on the road, or just off the road. The real-life Larry Lavalier, and the surreal Glenn and Gilbert. There were dozens of characters, when I thought about it. I started going over the faces and names from my first trip in 1971. It was like counting sheep jumping over a fence. Mike, the sales rep, my very first ride. Albert, the alcoholic salesman who constantly hacked up phlegm from his five-pack-a-day habit. Stewie, the custodian, who offered to let me sleep in his school if I would go to a drive-in movie with him. My skin crawled after that ride. Porter, the black magician who bought my lunch at a diner in Kentucky where magicians hung out and practiced their tricks. Mr. Joseph, a Lebanese immigrant who was moving to Detroit to open a grocery store. I could remember a lot of them. So many rides. So many stories. I slipped off into a siesta of memories that were mine alone.

Chapter 24

September 1973

Larry Lavalier and I drove down I-75 with the windows rolled down and a moist, morning Kentucky breeze whipping through our hair. My forearm cradled the windowsill, my weary eyes reflected in the side-view mirror. There was a trace of peace rattling around my usual wry expression. I thought back over the past few months and worried and marveled again at how my fate seemed to move into both calm and turgid waters. Living by my wits, thinking on my feet, making rapid adjustments, was second nature to me. Leaving while Marta stayed behind was troublesome but, I had to admit, liberating. I loved Marta and would have stayed in Cincinnati if she gave even the slightest hint of wanting me to. But the thought of actual, day-to-day living with Marta and her deathly ill mother was consterning. Departing with Larry was best for all of us. I had already crafted a plan that included a stopover in Knoxville to visit with the Bradys, and then on to Miami to meet up with the Delgado brothers.

The Delgados were Cuban immigrants who resided in Royal Oak for five years before the winters proved to be too much for the family patriarch. I had made friends with them and kept in contact with Vincent Delgado, third of seven Delgado brothers, through letters, and had visited him in Miami on my first hitchhiking trip after high school graduation. We had played football and basketball together our freshman and sophomore years at St. Mary's. Sports had been the link that bridged our vast cultural differences. After a long Cuban-Italian engagement, Vincent was set to be married in eighteen months and had asked me to stand up in the wedding. I had not met Vincent's fiancée, Maria, and hoped that this unannounced visit wouldn't leave a poor impression. I had a bad habit: I was an incorrigible surpriser. I knew it was bad manners, but I regularly showed up unannounced and unexpected at friends' houses, dorms, or workplaces. I wasn't always welcome, even by my closest friends. John Parcell almost beat the shit out of me when I showed up for the second time in three months at his dorm room window after 2:00 a.m., creating a *coitus interruptus* with Lois both times. A very angry and naked John opened the window to his first-floor dorm room and shouted, "You asshole!" Lois wasn't pleased either. But they let me sleep on the floor anyway.

All this passed through my mind, mile by mile, as we pulled farther away from Cincinnati, through Kentucky, and across the Tennessee border. I couldn't reconcile the contradictory contentment of being back on my own, on the road, with the angst of leaving a real, first love behind. Settling back in my seat, I let out a deep breath and looked ahead through the Malibu's windshield. The green mile markers shot past every forty seconds, reflecting Larry's constant eighty-eight miles per hour.

"Time for a buzz, Luke?" Larry interrupted the silence as we crossed into Tennessee.

"Sounds good," I replied.

Larry reached into the console, produced a pre-rolled spliff, and lit it on the car's cigarette lighter. We toked in silence. I hadn't smoked pot in weeks, and Larry's Colombian gold was potent. The buzz did not mellow me; rather, a hint of paranoia crept into the nether parts of my mind. Since the Dome bust, I had reconsidered the efficacy of smoking pot and whether it was worth it. I rarely paid for pot, but it was still a habit that wasn't moving me forward. The piquant taste of the smoke hit the back of my throat. I liked to wash it back with a cold beer and wait for the effects of both to reach my usually thrashing thoughts and calm me down. But the effect was getting old.

I took another deep hit, closed my eyes and reflected back, remembering the two larger-than-life policemen who had inadvertently helped Kate and me avert the truck explosion. I remembered the two nuns on the way to Indian River and Lila's nurse's aides, Glenn and Gilbert.

Were they all linked? Why? I looked up and noticed we were approaching the spot in central Tennessee where I had held Annette in my arms. I remembered what she had said to me and the promise I made. I could almost see life draining out of Annette as she lay limp in my lap that night.

She was serene and purposeful when she told me, "I'm dying. I believe in God, and His spirit is going to let me finish my work. Listen to me. After I'm gone, somehow I will need you to help me. You'll know when I reach out to you. When I do, promise me that you will listen and finish what I've started. It's our secret, a secret you have to keep alone after I die. Promise me, Luke Moore. You're my angel on earth, and I'll be your angel in heaven. Promise me!" she gasped.

I remembered making the promise as the blue shadow light from the emerging full moon covered Annette, as she died under my shuddering sobs. The ground and sky rumbled that night, the first time I felt and heard the earth talking to me.

It had been months since Annette died, and if she was trying to reach me, I hadn't heard her. Were the cops, the nuns, and the nurse's aides the messengers? I couldn't recall a message, but there was a similarity, a continuity, to each of those strange encounters. My buzzed brain was firing through all sorts of possibilities. Were these angels? Was one of them Annette reincarnated? Thinking back, the cops, the nuns, and the nurse's aides all acted like they knew me and were intent on giving me advice. There didn't seem to be a message, only timely warnings and counsel and concern. What was going on?

Hell, I was raised a Catholic, and miracles and saints were everyday fodder. But my Catholicism went up in smoke with my soul the night my mother died. Now I dabbled with the hip, culturally popular flavor-of-the month spiritual explorations found on college campuses—transcendental meditation, Buddhism, other eastern religions, and meditative techniques—which, when combined with hallucinogenic drugs like peyote and psilocybin mushrooms, caused temporary profoundness. This was followed by further confusion. I had taken a Kundalini yoga class, although the very flexible and beautiful teacher was the main attraction of the course. Angels, reincarnation, and messages from the dead should have been out-of-bounds for my cynical and scarred self. Yet, deep inside, I couldn't kick out the possibility. The possibility of what eluded me.

Thinking back, I was fairly certain I hadn't heard any specific message or request that might be connected to Annette from the eccentric road characters. Maybe I needed to pay a little closer attention to all things strange and unconventional. I hadn't gotten much right over the last few years, but least I could try to fulfill Annette's last wish. I hadn't told anyone, not even Kate, about the secret promise. I told Marta that I had unfinished business with the accident, and she let the subject lie. As Larry's Malibu cut through the Tennessee foothills, I reminded myself that this was a promise I was going to keep.

As I saw the first road sign for Knoxville, I reminded Larry about my visit to Knoxville in March. I couldn't pass through the city without stopping and visiting Helen Brady. I knew she would give me holy hell for helping Kate lie about our trip to Royal Oak. I deserved that, and Mrs. Brady deserved a visit. After the night in Cincinnati, I doubted Larry was interested in another visit with strangers, Luke Moore style, but I encouraged him to join me nonetheless.

He turned to me, reclined in his bucket seat, left arm hanging out the window, right hand guiding the steering wheel at six o'clock. "My newly found friend, I think I'll take you up on that. This trip has been a far cry from what I expected. As anxious as I am to make it to Miami, you seem to keep leading me into some pretty wild shit. This isn't necessarily the most fun I've ever had, but it sure is . . . different. I think I'll stay with you one more night and see what happens. After that, who knows?"

We cruised into Knoxville to the sounds of Van Morrison, Woodstock, and The Who's *Who's Next*. I directed Larry to parking near the student union at U.T. We ate a late lunch in the cafeteria, where I called Helen Brady. She was animated on the phone and insisted we come over immediately.

The powder-blue Malibu made the slow turn into the tony neighborhood and finally stopped halfway into the Brady circular driveway.

"Is this all right to park here?" Larry asked.

"I think we're fine," I said, watching the massive oak front door open. Mrs. Brady stood framed in the doorway of the formidable southern home. Larry followed my lead to Helen. She was formally dressed in a stylish, conservative pastel yellow suit, which accented her tan face and perfectly coiffed auburn hair. Helen held me tightly before pulling back, still holding my arms and looking directly at me.

"Luke! I was hoping you were going to stop. Kate called me just today and told me you're back on the road. Come inside and introduce me to your friend and tell me the whole story."

Larry, Helen, and I sat at the kitchen table and talked, sipping sweetened Tennessee tea and eating small sandwiches prepared by Helen Brady's maid, cook, and companion, Esther Short. Eventually, Esther joined us. Before long, we were playing pinochle with the mismatched matrons; one white and wealthy, and one black and working-class. Before Helen helped Esther reclaim her life, Esther was an almost catatonically depressed woman, who had lost two sons to random shootings in the increasingly violent Knoxville projects.

Late afternoon evolved into evening, and a pinochle contest developed, with Larry and me teaming up against Helen and Esther. We played in the card room, at an old mahogany card table lined with leather armrests and equipped with cup holders. A couple of quick wins by the women turned into a best-of-seven-game challenge, which Esther and Helen accepted. By eleven o'clock, we had consumed pizza and Chinese take-out and we were all heavily watered with Glenmorangie Scotch whisky. Any early light-heartedness had turned into an intense, spirited battle to win the spontaneous tournament. Larry and I tied the series at 3–3 and came from behind to win the fourth and deciding game. Larry whooped as he played the last card for the win.

"Oh, I'm sorry, that's rude," Larry apologized.

Mrs. Brady said, "I bet that feels good." Esther threw her last card onto the table in disgust.

With the exultation over, the booze was clawing at me. I was dead tired.

Helen announced with a hint of a slur, "I am pie-eyed and fit to be tied. This was a great evening, gentlemen and Esther, but I must say it did not end the way I intended. I will swallow my pride with silent bitterness, remaining a gracious loser to you highly skilled and very lucky northerners. Here's to Luke and Larry, victors over the great dames of the South!"

She raised her brandy snifter to us and we collectively clinked our glasses and drained the last of the scotch. Setting the glasses on the table, we teetered into goodnight hugs. Esther showed Larry to a guest bedroom suite on the first floor. I helped Helen clear the ashtrays, snifters, and remains of the night into the kitchen.

"We'll clean the rest of this mess tomorrow, Luke," Helen said. "I know it's late and we're more than a bit snookered, but let's sit and talk for a few minutes before we sleep. It's been quiet around here lately with all my children out living their own lives, and I want to see how you're doing."

"Not a problem, Mrs. Brady," I said, and we made our way to Helen's office, formerly her father's. She had changed the décor of the room to reflect her lighter sense of style, but the dark rosewood paneling and large partners' desk retained a hint of her father's stern formality. We sat in two large, green leather chairs, a single Baldwin lamp on a library table providing muted light.

"Mrs. Brady, I know you have to be angry with me for that hitchhike to Royal Oak with Kate." I figured maybe the booze would fog Mrs. Brady's reaction.

"Oh, that would be a wild understatement, Luke." Her eyes narrowed and bored into me. "We're going to let that go for tonight, but you're fortunate that I hold my daughter responsible for her own actions. I want to talk about how my daughter is doing now. I need some firsthand information."

With that, the questions and worries of a parent festooned me.

"Let's start with Kate, Luke. How is she really doing? Do you think Elvis is good for her? Does she ever talk about Annette? How is she dealing with that loss? I am still crushed. I walk around like a zombie most mornings. By the afternoon, I can usually get a few things done. Annette was such a treasure. I know you didn't know her at all. And the funeral and wake didn't really do justice to her soul. I knew we all tried to capture her in our testimonials, but we were in such a state of shock. She was so complicated, so deep for a girl her age. She was far from perfect, and Lord knows she tried my patience and challenged me in so many ways. I was beginning to appreciate how special she was when she died."

Mrs. Brady was talking fast and more animated than I had ever seen her. "Oh, my, I'm off to the races, aren't I, Luke? Oh, my."

I could see her eyes begin to glisten, but she closed them for a few seconds, composing herself before continuing. "Did you know about the year she spent in Miami with her father? She moved in with her dad just after she graduated from high school, against my wishes. She told me she understood the pain he had caused all of us, but she knew he needed to be a part of our lives, and she could be a bridge. That's exactly how she put it: 'I can be a bridge to the past, Mom. It may not be a pleasant past, but it's our history, and Dad is part of me, part of all of us. I'm not leaving you, I just need to help Dad and complete a broken circle. I love you, Mom, and I'll love you even more while I'm in Miami with Dad.' And she was right, Luke. I couldn't fathom the healing she began. The Prescott family secrets run deep, and the pain and hurt caused by my father weren't as easily overcome as I thought. I try my best to right wrongs with the wealth I inherited. But the human toll of decades of greed and power can't be undone just with pregnancy clinics, recreation, and drug counseling programs. Annette saw that and knew the real healing happened one-on-one, with those who suffered and were hated. It's such a story, Luke, what Annette did, the pain she was trying to relieve with her love. She was an angel, Luke, a beautiful, flawed, and determined angel. I loved her so very much, so much . . ."

Helen's shoulders shook, and when the tears followed, her embroidered hankie had a hard time keeping up with the flood. I reached forward from my chair and took her hands. After a few minutes, she composed herself and laughed through her sorrow. "Oh, Luke, I'm so sorry for pouring my troubles to you. But there's a bond between us."

"It's okay, Mrs. Brady. I've been thinking about Annette lately, and I think she's still in the healing business. I'd like to get to know more about her. I like hearing about her."

"You are a dear soul, Luke. All right, let me tell you about my beautiful daughter."

She talked into the night. I listened and learned, especially about Mr. Brady.

Life had not been easy for Curtis Brady after he had deserted his family. He had come to grips with his homosexuality, finding a partner in Miami and a career, of sorts, running a semi-closeted jazz club in downtown Miami Beach that catered to the homosexual community. Being queer in the 1960s wasn't easy, but Miami was just bohemian enough to allow for a careful gathering place that was frequented by lovers of all persuasions, including the rich and powerful who happened to be homosexual.

Mr. Brady had been less successful in dealing with his guilt, encouraged by his Catholic upbringing, over leaving a struggling family behind in Michigan. His family's move to Knoxville and the improvement in their financial condition didn't help to ease the guilt.

Curtis Brady was a functioning alcoholic and periodically fought off incapacitating rounds of depression. His introduction to casual marijuana use, followed by cocaine, exacerbated his emotional paralysis and ruined his health. Annette had written letters to her dad in 1968, and came to live with him in 1969. She quickly understood how dire her father's condition was, and with the help of her dad's lover and housemate, Martin Lane, cajoled, challenged, and finally demanded that Curtis Brady get help.

Annette aided Curtis's four-week dry-out in a New Orleans clinic when she stepped in to manage La Bohème, her father's nightclub. Martin Lane was an accountant in a regional firm and had never before been involved in the nightclub's operations. Curtis Brady had insisted upon this arrangement, wanting to keep his personal and business life separate. Annette rescued La Bohème's books from her father's disheveled office at the club and took them to Martin. The financial picture was as precarious as her father's health. Annette asked Martin for a crash course in analyzing a financial statement. They determined that while the debts were daunting, the club wasn't that far from making a profit. During the month of Curtis's absence, Annette begged and pleaded with creditors, winning some price concessions and an extension of payment terms. With Martin's help, she tightened the cash flow management at the club; free drinks and food were reduced with stubborn, yet cheerful, insistence.

The turning point for the club was Annette's involvement with the entertainment. Her first appeals to agents for reduced rates were met with derision. Then she started to open main acts herself, accompanied by a talented, unknown piano player. Her singing touched the regular audience immediately, and word spread around Miami quickly about the angelic voice of the owner's daughter. The club started to fill up early. The local bands and the more prominent out-of-state bands listened to her as they waited to play, astonished by her natural singing style, whether singing jazz standards or musical theater songs from *West Side Story, Oklahoma,* and *Porgy and Bess.*

After the month of drying out, Curtis Brady returned to Miami on a Friday night, stopping first at La Bohème. He stood in the back of the crowded room and watched as his daughter sat on a bar stool in front of the microphone, next to a light-skinned black piano player, singing "Summertime." A rush of chills covered him as his daughter sang, reminding him of Helen, of all he had lost. Yet, there was a glimmer of hope. Radiance surrounded his beautiful daughter and reached out to him. Annette Brady sang. A future returned to her father.

Annette lived in Miami for one year, long enough to see the nightclub thrive and her father learn to stay clean and sober. Her attempts to shepherd reconciliations between her siblings and father were met with coldness in Knoxville. Finally, her brother, Matt, agreed and visited. Even though the visit was awkward, it was a beginning. Annette's singing brought offers to perform in larger venues in other cities, but she declined, content to work in her father's club, meeting and playing with established jazz legends like McCoy Tyner, Rahsaan Roland Kirk (who played six horns at one time), and Joe Sample, and highlighted by a visit from Miles Davis. The club also began showcasing young fusion talent like Chick Corea, Weather Report, and the John McLaughlin Trio. It was an exciting and fulfilling year for Annette and Curtis Brady, as they grew closer through music and companionship. When the year drew to an end, she announced she was moving back to Knoxville. Curtis felt the heaviness of depression reaching out again, but he fought it off. He wanted her happiness to follow.

Martin had been brought in as a partner in the club, and his button-down business style meshed with Curtis's easiness in working with the musicians. Annette's absence would create a void, but he was healing, and with Martin's help, he felt like he could survive and thrive. For the first time in his life, he felt almost whole and able to cope with the anguish he had caused and endured. *What a marvel,* he thought. His young daughter had been able to assess his bleak life, determine what needed to be done, and then execute a plan that, while difficult, was realistic and achievable. On the day she left, he told her as much, thanking her for his life.

She smiled and laughed. "Dad, I'm not going to lie to you. After you left, I hated you, as only the granddaughter of Walter Prescott could hate. That lasted for years. When I was fourteen, I had an experience that opened my soul. I went to church for a choir practice. It was canceled at the last minute, and I stood in the choir loft alone. I decided to practice my solo, and really let loose. I thought if there was a God, my song was going to be heard. I had my doubts about God, which I kept to myself. I'm singing as full as I can, even improvising the melody to hit some high notes. As I sang, I could hear—actually, more like feel—that I was being accompanied by the most beautiful bass voice I had ever heard. The voice completely surrounded me. I closed my eyes and reached a place I had never been to before. I don't know how long I sang, and when I opened my eyes, I could hear the remnants of the bass voice, like a giant tuning fork's last vibration. I was at peace for the first time in my life. It was a great gift to receive at fourteen. I walked out of that church and started living for today and tomorrow, instead of yesterday. Loving you was a big hill to climb. After our time together, I can see me in you. I know you've been in pain. You're my father, and this year has been a salve to both our wounds. I love you, Dad."

Helen Brady took a deep breath. It was a painful story for her to repeat.

"I learned all this about Annette from Curtis at her funeral. It was the first conversation of substance I had with my ex-husband in years. Which, of course, is what Annette would have wanted. That's what's so remarkable about my daughter, Luke. She saw with such clarity that the pain we suffered also clouded our ability to hope. Even though my children and I found stability and strength through our travails together, we were missing a part of our past that allowed us to find real happiness. Annette changed that, and slowly, we have all begun to strengthen and set out on our own. Family provides the cornerstone, and then it's up to us to go forward on our own."

I was touched that Mrs. Brady would let me see so deeply inside her family. "Mrs. Brady, I don't know what to say. That's just an incredible story and an eye-opener for me. I'm sitting here, half numb from drinking, and you're telling me a story about your life, completely truthful, and I can't help but think that it's meant for me, too. Could it be that Annette reached out and touched me through you? I have to confess, Mrs. Brady, more happened the night Annette died than I told you. I can't—I can't tell you everything, because I promised. But I'm sure, more than ever now, that Annette isn't done with opening doors. I'm getting chills just listening to you, and, even more than that, I'm starting to believe that I'm just about ready to start living again. Don't know how, or really even why, but something's happening. Something's happening." I slumped back in my seat, drained.

"Dear, what are you telling me? You have a secret about Annette that you can't tell her mother? Are you sure about that, Luke?" Mrs. Brady wasn't relaxed anymore. She was coiled, wanting an answer.

"I'm sorry, Mrs. Brady, but I don't think it's time, or right. I can tell you this. What Annette told me hasn't happened yet, and when it does, I promise you'll be the first to know. Will you please let me leave it at that?"

Helen was poised in her chair and didn't speak for a moment. Finally, she said, "All right, Luke, I won't press you any further tonight. But you have my full attention now, and where you go from here, and for that matter, your final destination. Do we understand each other, young man?"

"Yes, ma'am, we do," I said.

Helen relaxed a bit and said, "You've had a tough life, but you've fought back. I like you a lot. I think you're so—to tell the truth, confused. You are so full of life and bright and creative, and in spite of your family's troubles, you were raised right. Polite, well mannered, and honest, even though I understand your storytelling suspends belief, if you know what I mean. But I do need to tell you something about Annette. She always had a mysterious side. She didn't always tell us everything that was going on in her life. When she was in Miami, she developed this relationship with the mulatto fellow I mentioned. He was involved with Curtis's club. Annette mentioned him once, and her eyes lit up, but then she changed the subject. I'm still not sure exactly what her relationship was with this man. Come to think of it, Curtis was especially close-mouthed about him, also. Apparently, they were a perfect match when they performed together. He played marvelously, and was completely comfortable with Annette taking center stage. I know she kept in contact with him after she left Miami, but I still don't know how she found him and what she saw in him.

"I saw him at the church for Annette's funeral mass, sitting in the back. I remember our eyes met. He smiled and then looked away too quickly. I saw him talking to Curtis after the funeral on the church steps before we left for the cemetery. Later, I asked Curtis who he was, and Curtis also looked away and mumbled that he was Annette's piano player at the club. The following day, when Curtis and I had our heart-to-heart talk, I told him that after Annette had returned from Miami, I had learned that she had been in contact with this fellow. His name was Gerard Lafleur. I tried to bring it up with Annette, but she was unusually evasive, giving me cause for concern. Curtis told me they had become close in Miami, like others who Annette had touched at La Bohème. I left it at that, but several months later, I had a dream. Annette was sitting on a piano bench next to a piano player, and she was singing "Ave Maria," a favorite song of ours. I couldn't see the piano player, but suddenly he turned and looked at Annette and smiled that same smile I saw in the back of the church. I didn't recognize him, but the smile seemed so familiar. It was quite eerie, and I woke up in a start. I didn't know what it meant, or why I'm remembering it now. Oh, well, as I said, there was mystery in my daughter's life, and you've sparked a memory. That's probably all it is."

Helen slumped back in her chair, feeling her age and the long night. "All right, Luke, I've done all the talking I can do tonight. I started with inquiring how my other beautiful daughter is doing in Royal Oak. Before we go to sleep, tell me about Kate and her life. I know she completely ignored her commitment to me, and we had a big argument, but she's my daughter, and I can't stay angry forever. I do want the straight story from you. I know how close you are with your friend Elvis, but I want the truth, no stories."

"I promise, Mrs. Brady," I said. "Even though I lived in Indian River this summer and they were in Royal Oak, we all kept in touch, and I think I know how she's doing. I can tell you that even though Kate is quiet about it, the loss of Annette hurts her every day. I can see the pain in her face. She plays through it, but it's always there."

I gave Mrs. Brady the rundown on Kate's new life. Kate had been smart enough to carve out her own niche in Royal Oak, moving in with Lois and not chasing after Elvis's gigs in small-town Holiday Inns. Elvis was head-over-heels in love—attentive, respectful, and faithful to a woman in a way my friends and I had never seen before. Over six months had passed since he sang to her at the Psychedelic Midway, and Elvis doted on Kate like they were an old married couple. Mark McInerny had told me that they seemed like they had known each other their whole lives. He recounted a night out at a local pub where the performing band asked Elvis to join in a set, which Elvis always accepted. That night he declined, offering no excuses, just telling the lead singer he was with his lady.

They argued, but Elvis listened. Kate told Elvis he needed to organize and plan his career and life. Elvis believed in the benefits of spontaneity and living life for the moment. They loved each other for the opposite traits they brought each other. They compromised in their relationship, not really knowing they were making changes. Kate, in her well-ordered way, knew that, over the long haul, it would be difficult to make a life the way they currently lived and loved. But for now, she had a life filled with passion, excitement, and unpredictability. And she loved Elvis for it. She balanced her life with her work and school, planning beyond her lover and her friends in Royal Oak.

I told Helen that, from all accounts, Kate seemed genuinely happy. Of course, I left out any mention of the fiasco at the Dome. I did tell Helen about my last conversation with Elvis before leaving Royal Oak.

"Elvis told me that he waited his whole life to meet someone like Kate. He told me, 'She's smart. She knows exactly who she is and exactly who I am. I don't bullshit her, and she sure doesn't bullshit me. It's not about me being some local rock-and-roll stud. She knows I'm not the smartest guy in the world, but she knows I have some talent, and goddamn it, she holds me accountable. I know it may look like she's leading me around by a ring on my nose, but it's not like that at all. Kate knows I need to sing and perform, and the travel and the groupies are part of it all. Now that she's part of my life, the partying and free loving chicks aren't important anymore. Can you believe that?'

"That's the most mature thing I ever heard from Elvis, or from any of my friends. I don't know where the two of them will end up, but so far, it seems like a wonderful thing. You know, after years of wild fun, it seems like my friends and me aren't such Lost Souls anymore," I concluded.

Helen Brady's eyelids fluttered, and I wasn't sure she heard me. "Mrs. Brady?"

"Yes, dear, that's a good report. I wish I had enough stamina to find out where and what you're up to next, but it will have to wait.

I'm afraid I can't stay up a moment longer. Now, help this woman to her room." I held Mrs. Brady's elbow and led her up the grand staircase to her bedroom. She gently pulled my cheek down to her lips and gave me a kiss and full hug. "You can use the guest room at the end of the hall, Luke. Esther has already put your bag in the room. Now, goodnight and sweet dreams. And thank you for a fulfilling evening. You're a gem."

"Thank you, Mrs. Brady, and sweet dreams to you, too."

I dropped onto the large canopied bed and put my arms behind my head, propping up on the down-filled pillows covered with frilly fringed slipcases. I thought about the Brady women, stitched onto me like a hidden tattoo. I thought about Marta. I was drunk and out of gas, but I made a promise to write every day. My old bag was next to the bed. I reached down and pulled open the flap where I kept my tablet. The note was short and inchoate. A commitment kept.

Staring at the ceiling, I thought about how the Brady women had given me hope. They had lived through tough times, and, while a quirk of ancestry changed their financial condition, they had to fight their way through the ugliness of life, like me and, for that matter, Marta. There had to be some goodness to hold onto, or life became a rolling train wreck, piling up at each station down the track. It dawned on me that I spent a lot of time staring at ceilings and having ridiculously serious musings. *I'm no stranger to being peculiar,* I thought, and fell asleep.

Larry woke me up at 8:30 a.m., anxious to get back on the road. "Luke, we've got to get moving. I called my new boss in Miami, and they want me down there for an orientation of new professors by tomorrow evening. I thought I could blow it off, but he made a big deal about it, and I can't afford to get on this guy's bad side right off the bat. We can make it if we leave now and drive straight through."

I rolled over and moaned, hugging my pillow, hoping Larry would go away.

"C'mon, bud, I need you to help me drive. Whaddya say?" Larry pleaded, lightly shaking my shoulder.

"Oh, man, I am a mess." I pushed myself up on my elbows. My eyes hurt, a sure sign this was a bad one.

"Oh, yeah, you are a mess, but you can do it. Take a shower and come downstairs. Esther has breakfast ready, and you can sleep the first shift. C'mon, Luke, you can do it," Larry begged again.

I swung my legs onto the floor and held my head. "Yeah, I can make it. Give me a few minutes, I'll be right down."

The bathroom in the guest room had a walk-in, huge, multi-head shower system that shot water chest and thigh high. Buffeted by water in all directions, I mustered a smile through my headache. Who would have thought I would be a welcome guest in this grand house? I knew I would be welcome to enjoy the luxury and hospitality the Brady home provided. But I knew guest status would wear off fast. I turned off the water and stepped out into the steamy, spacious bathroom. A wall of full-length mirrors, partially clouded by mist, reflected my naked, disfigured body.

God, I am ugly. I turned slowly and looked over my shoulder at the angry welts, reddened by the hot water. *No matter where I go, I'm always going to be this ugly abomination,* I thought.

I rarely reviewed my body and the fire's scars. It was depressing and reminded me that not only the scars would be with me every day of my life, but so would the shit-pot full of terror and revulsion. I hated my father and myself. I could block out the loathing day-to-day, but it always returned. Mom's natural optimism had a place in me, saving me from tilting off into hell and keeping me muddling around in purgatory. I saw more of Mom in my sisters, Ann, April, and Angela. Pillars of Optimism. And Donnie—there was tough little kid. Clothes only hid part of his scars. He kept his devils to himself and the shrink he visited at Catholic Social Services.

I had visited a psychologist, also, at Ann's insistence. She drove me and sat in the waiting room to make sure I didn't bolt. The shrink looked like a Poindexter, and even I knew that working at the Catholic Social Services was at the bottom of the psychologist barrel. I sat in a chair across the desk from this nimrod, and he pushed a notebook toward me with his most serious face. He opened it up dramatically. His name was Dr. Rood.

"Now, Luke, I want you to look at these pictures very carefully and tell me the first thing that comes to your mind. Don't think about it—just tell me the first impression you have, no matter how crazy you may think it is."

I looked at an inkblot picture. *For Christ's sake, even I know what the hell a Rorschach test is. So, he thinks I'm crazy. I'll give him crazy.* I remembered the *Mad Magazine* edition that featured psychologists. *Ha!*

I told him, "That one reminds me of my mother."

"Really!" The bespectacled old goat couldn't contain his enthusiasm.

"Yes, sir, that picture reminds me of my mother."

He stood up from his chair and flipped the page to another inkblot.

"This looks like my mother, but when she was much younger."

"Really! A younger version of your mother," Doctor Rood commented anxiously. He fumbled with the plastic-covered pictures as he excitedly tried to turn to the next page. Another inkblot appeared.

"What about this picture, Luke?"

"That's either my mother or my grandmother, I'm not sure."

"Hmmm. Luke, I think that's all the pictures we need to look at right now, but I think we're going to need to spend much more time going over this again."

The guy had a line of sweat just above his lip. He rubbed his hands together a little too gleefully. *What a putz,* I thought.

"Now, if you'll just wait here a minute, I'd like to talk to your sister for a minute before we schedule our next appointment."

The psychologist hurried around his desk and walked into the small waiting room where Ann sat reading an ancient *National Geographic.* He talked in a forced whisper, but he had left the door open, and I could hear most of what he said.

" . . . very unusual, highly unusual, quite an interesting case. Seeing one's mother in all of the pictures is highly revealing. The correlation to mother is indicative of a very deep problem."

I heard Ann say, "Doctor, you're saying he told you all of the pictures were of his mother?"

"Yes, and one of his grandmother!"

"And you believe him?" Ann replied.

"Well, of course, his reaction was immediate," Dr. Rood said.

"I hate to break this to you, sir, but Luke never met his grand-mother. He's just telling you a story." Ann stood up pushed open the door, and called out to me, "Okay, wise guy, let's go."

We scurried out of the Catholic Social Services office and took two steps a time down the dark stairwell. Dr. Rood called after us, "Please, please, we must set up another appointment. Your brother needs help."

Ann and I rushed down the stairs together and pushed out into the early evening light. "You need help, Luke, but that guy may need it more. I don't know whether to whack you or hug you."

Ann grabbed me and held me tight, tickling me until I laughed with her. She was right, I needed help. I just wasn't ready to accept it yet.

The scars were my constant reminder that my troubles were inside and out. But now, I had Marta, a beautiful woman who somehow overlooked my body and even my darkened soul. This put a different spin on things for me. I had something to look forward to.

I toweled myself dry and shaved, brushed my damp hair, and put on a clean T-shirt and jeans. I took a deep breath and looked in the mirror and said aloud to myself, "Luke Moore, look ahead. You are blessed and cursed. The blessings outweigh the curse. Survive and thrive. Survive and thrive." I exhaled and hoped my self-pre-scribed pep talk would stick.

Downstairs, I found Esther smiling over a hot breakfast of scrambled eggs, French toast, bacon, sausage, and coffee.

"Luke, you look like death warmed over. Sit down and get something in your stomach," Esther said.

I sat down to breakfast and read the *Knoxville Herald,* which Esther placed next to me. Before long, I was at the front door of the Brady manor with Larry and Esther. "Mrs. Brady is not going to be happy that you left without saying good-bye, although she's not going to be awake anytime soon. She drank more last night than I've seen her drink since I've known her," Esther said.

"I know, Esther. Please tell her I really appreciate her hospitality, and tell her I wish I could have visited longer, but Larry needs to get to Miami. I owe him, big time. And most importantly, tell her that our talk last night gave me a clue to solve a problem. All right?"

Esther shrugged and said, "Mr. Moore, I'll tell her, but she'll still be agitated. You mean a lot to her, and don't you forget it.

Don't you worry, though, I'll make it right. You and Larry be careful, you hear? I packed you a lunch and dinner in this cooler." She gave both Larry and me a hug, and called out as we descended the front steps, "You boys were lucky you won last night, don't you know! Mrs. Brady and I are expecting a rematch. The Lord knows we are better pinochle players than you Yankees!"

Larry laughed and said, "Yes, ma'am, we know we're lucky, and God willing, we'll be back to defend our title as the best damn pinochle players in Knoxville, Tennessee!"

I wondered through my hangover if Annette had heard my cosmic hum in the choir loft as she sang to God, many years ago. There seemed to be a lot of spirituality swirling around my otherwise godless life. I had always hoped to save being born again until I found myself in a really big jam. My pragmatic instincts told me it was a waste to throw away the experience on something trivial. But my life had been turned upside-down. Suffering from a bad case of heartburn of the soul, I'd been years into a cycle of self-destruction, and then, suddenly, otherworldly signals like deathbed promises, cosmic hums, and characters right out of *Man of LaMancha* start showing up, imparting strange and unsolicited advice. Maybe I was in the middle of a big jam and didn't know it. Christ, God could be right around the freaking corner!

Apparently, not quite that close. My headache and nervous system were still a wreck, and deep car sleep seemed to be the only certainty on the horizon. Nevertheless, the stop at the Brady house was revealing for me. I knew for certain now that a visit with Curtis Brady was the next step to keeping my pledge. And finding the piano player might be the linchpin to the promise. I closed my eyes and hugged the door of Larry's car as we drove south.

Chapter 25

September 2003

I tried unsuccessfully to relax while stuck on the entryway to the Mackinac Bridge. Instead, I twitched. We were hundreds of miles away from a city, and I was miffed about this traffic jam. I made three trips to my new good buddy with the CB for accident updates. He finally informed me and a host of other high-strung types that the tow truck had finally completed its mission and the roadblock was being lifted. I sat in the van, massaging the steering wheel, waiting for traffic to start moving. How did I ever manage to stand on the side of the road for hours? What did I think about?

I closed my eyes and leaned back, when a familiar, black thought covered my mind and my stomach recoiled. It was my dad again. Trygvi Moore, back to haunt me. The apparition always appeared the same way: a daydream was interrupted by a flare of coruscation followed by a blanket of murky gray. My dad's face hurtled forward from the grayness at blinding speed. I couldn't recognize the image at first, but I knew what was coming. The figure struck like an ice-cream headache, right between the eyes and shooting to the temples. It was a holograph of my dad, handcuffed, led away by the police. He turned his head, chin down, and looked at all of us, his eyes dim and soulless. He mouthed words I couldn't understand. I strained to listen, but there was no sound. I forced my eyes open, and he was gone.

The residue of these episodes was the psychological equivalent of food poisoning. Loathing, vengeance, and fear fomented into thick bile in my psyche. The toxin was debilitating, but I knew the way out. Eyes closed again. The images of Roberta's birth, Marta extending the baby-filled blanket to me for the first time, the cherub's face squinting at me. Playing catch with Donnie. My mom blowing a kiss to me as I left for school. Any one of these memories would work. The vitriol would recede, seeping away more slowly than it arrived.

"Luke, Luke." I heard Marta's concerned voice.

I faked a smile. "I'm fine, dear. Not so bad this time."

Traffic started to move. I started the minivan and shifted to drive. Marta handed me a Kleenex, and I patted the sweat beads off my forehead. Roberta stirred from her sleep as we moved forward. I like watching my traits in her.

"Are we there yet, Dad?" she asked me with a sheepish smile.

"We're here, but we're not quite there." I gave Roberta my standard reply, which was as old as she was.

"How long from here to there?" Her Abbott.

"You can't get here from there, but it's about two hours from here to there." My Costello.

"Then we're neither here nor there." Roberta finished our routine.

Good outweighed evil.

Chapter 26

September 1973

I half-slept in the fully reclined front bucket seat through the Great Smoky Mountain foothills, missing the signs for the Lookout Mountain chairlift, Gem City, World of Fireworks, and other tourist attractions that beckoned to highway travelers. I didn't wake until after Larry eased the Malibu through the long series of winding downhill miles leading to the gently rolling hills of southern Tennessee. I woke up to the car slowing and odd mechanical noises coming from under the car's hood. The thousands of miles of traveling in strange passenger seats had tuned my ear to notice the change in an automobile's pace. Larry had a worried expression on his face.

"What's up, Larry?"

"Something's not right. Sounds like the transmission is slipping. I'm going to slow down a bit and see how she goes."

I adjusted my seat upright and listened as the car cruised at an unnatural forty-five miles an hour. Other cars whipped past the Malibu as the car lurched forward, losing speed before lurching again.

Larry saw the exit sign for Riceville in one mile and said, "Shit, motherfucker, I think the transmission is shot. I'm pulling off. Maybe we'll get lucky and it's just a fluid leak. Goddamn it!" Larry steered the car onto the off-ramp and into a Shell gas station. "This is not good, stuck in the middle of nowhere, with a shot-to-shit transmission. Not good. Maybe somebody in this godforsaken gas station can tell us where an honest car mechanic can be found. Fat chance!"

Larry opened the car door and started for the gas station, which did not have a mechanic's bay attached to it. I pushed back into the car seat and closed my eyes, catching a catnap, waiting for Larry's return with hopeful news. There was nothing I could add with my nonexistent mechanical skills.

Twenty minutes later, Larry tapped me on the shoulder, waking me. "Well, bud, it's like this. The only garage that has a chance to look at the car is fifty miles back toward Knoxville. I called the garage and they're sending a tow truck. They can't even look at the car until tomorrow, and if it needs parts, it will take another day to get them. With good luck, it will be Thursday before it'll be ready to go. With bad luck, who knows? I can't wait that long. So here's the deal. I'm going to drop the car off at the garage, then pay some yahoo fifty bucks to drive me back to Knoxville, and I'll take a plane to Miami. I can get a flight out tonight. It's going to cost me a goddamn fortune, and then I'll have to fly back to pick up my car. But I gotta do it, man. You can come with me, and I'll get you back to the Bradys' house. But I'm afraid this ride south is busted."

I knew my trip with Larry was over. "That's all right, Larry. I'm really sorry about your car. I wish there was something I could do to help. I'm just going to keep heading south, if you don't mind."

"Yeah, I figured as much. Sorry it had to end this way. You're a real interesting cat, Luke. Let me give you my address in Miami, and I can give you a place to shack up when you get there," Larry said.

"That's cool, Larry. I'll give you my sister's address in Royal Oak. If we don't meet up in Miami, she knows how to find me," I replied. We exchanged addresses. I pulled my bag out of the backseat. "Larry, thanks for everything. You are a generous and righteous dude. I hope we see each other again. We'll have some stories to tell."

We gripped each other's hands in a brother handshake.

"That we will, my man. That we will. You take care of yourself on the road, all right?" Larry said.

"No problem, I'm right at home out here."

As I started walking up the ramp, Larry called out, "Hey, bro, let me give you some traveling cash."

I looked back and smiled, "You've done more than enough already, Larry. I'm fine with my cash. Just wish me luck that I get a ride before your tow truck comes."

"Right on, Luke. I'm predicting you get a ride from a tasty blonde in a halter top before you know it!" Larry called.

"It's good to dream," I called back.

I stood at the top of the ramp with no cars in sight. I performed a roadside stretching ritual, a form of highway yoga I used to loosen up and kill time on low-traffic highways. It helped to clear my mind. I was almost glad to be alone again.

The traffic was intermittent on the cloudy, humid Tennessee afternoon. I beckoned each car with habitual earnestness, but my thoughts drifted back to Marta and her mother, Annette and Mrs. Brady. I didn't often spend time looking backward. Usually my road solitude focused on the future. I made up scenarios that included Larry's halter-topped blondes and rich travelers who wanted to become patrons of a vagabond hitchhiker like myself. It kept my mind busy and hopeful that I would win the hitchhiker's lottery. More likely was the ride from traveling salesmen or other gritty characters. My dream ended like it had so many times before, when a pickup started to slow as it passed and pulled over a hundred feet behind me. I hustled to the door of a 1961 Chevy truck with more blue smoke pouring out its tailpipe than was natural.

"You can only open the door from the inside," the pickup truck's driver called out. I reached inside the open passenger-side window and pulled the latch open under the watchful eye of an old mutt that looked like it mostly favored a collie.

I threw my bag in the bed of the truck and hopped next to the dog onto the truck seat patched with gray duct tape. I guessed the driver to be at least seventy years old, diminutive and wiry. He had two seat cushions under his rear end and one behind his back, which barely sat him tall enough and close enough to reach the pedals and see above the steering wheel. A tan, battered, wide-brimmed cowboy hat with a tall feather tucked into the hatband sat smartly on his head, contrasting with his deeply lined, tanned face.

"Hey, partner. Where ya headed today?" he asked me with a toothy smile. He maneuvered the column stick shift into first gear and depressed the well-worn clutch pedal.

"Miami, Florida, sir. How about you?" I replied as the truck slowly chugged through first, second, and into third gear and onto the highway.

"Well, I'm headed south, as you can see, but not quite that far, no sirree. But I can get you down the road a piece, that's for sure. God willing, and if this old truck here can muster another good day's drive, I can get you through Chattanooga and into the great state of Georgia, yes-sirree-bob, that's a real possibility, God willing. I'm not forgetting the manners my mother taught me, so let me introduce you to me and mine. I'm Charles Abraham Whitefeather, and this old hound dog is Michael, and this here truck is Rufus. My friends and enemies know me as Chattahoochee Charlie. Born and raised in the Chattahoochee Forest, the prettiest part of Georgia, I'm close to a full-blooded Cherokee Indian. And a great friend to those who treat me right, and the damnedest, foulest enemy to those that cross my path, yes-sirree-bob! Now, who do I have the pleasure of meeting?"

I extended my hand over Michael and told Charlie, in a bogus brogue, "I'm William Fitzroy Fitzwillow, full-blooded Irishman from the County Killarney, most recently living in the Corktown district of the Motor City, Detroit, Michigan, United States of America. My friends call me Fitzwilly for short, and my enemies are few and far between. I'm pleased to meet you, that's for sure!"

Charlie made a face and said, "And I'm pleased to meet you, young gent. Although if you have few enemies, you must not have very strong opinions, or you don't drink very much, which isn't a very Irish manner in my experience, either way you look at it."

"Well, yes, that's the truth, Mr. Whitefeather, but I learned at an early age from my grandmother, Rosie O'Grady Fitzwillow, that drinking is the undoing of the Irish, and I've heeded her words, not like my father and my nine brothers, who have a taste for the evil sauce and a proclivity for fisticuffs, leading to enough enemies for the whole clan, don't you know." I was laying it on thick, in spite of my experience with Larry Lavalier. I couldn't help myself, and figured the odds favored my fiction in spite of my inconsistent Irish accent.

"I hear your words, young Fitzwilly, and agree with your grandmother, who sounds like a fine, Christian woman, like my mother, Violet Whitefeather, God bless her Christian soul. I wish I would have listened to her more as a young man. It would have saved me from a world of woe. But, what's done is done, and I'm living a life closer to the Lord with my wild years long behind me. Now I travel the straight and narrow with my dog, Michael, named after the top angel himself. After years of raising holy hell, I finally found the right road and quit the bottle, cold turkey. That was close to twenty years ago, yes-sirree-bob. I found myself in a fight I wasn't looking for in a bar in Chattanooga. Left me with this nasty reminder."

Charlie turned his face full toward me and showed a scar running from his left ear down to his neck bone. "A busted beer bottle from an Indian-hatin' redneck helped show me the way to sobriety. I just about bled to death on that barroom floor. Somehow I lived, and I haven't had a drink or been in a fight since. Not that it's been an easy road. I lived a life of sin and depravity, and I'll tell you, it was wild and woolly. I ran through moonshine, women, and song like they was tap water. Thought I had it made, yes, I did. I was wrong about that, top of the world to fighting in bars. It was an ugly slide."

Michael nuzzled his snout into my lap as Charlie told his story. The old truck puttered at fifty miles an hour in the slow lane of I-75 toward the state line.

Charlie grew up in a farm in northern Georgia, bordering the Chattahoochee Forest. The farm was established by his grandparents, full-blooded Cherokee Indians, in 1910. His grandfather saved enough money as a logger to buy ninety acres of rock-infested, over-forested land for one hundred dollars. The Cherokee Indians ran the Creek Indians out of northern Georgia in the early 1800s, and the Cherokee were chased out by the U.S. government in the late 1830s in a forced march to Oklahoma, the infamous Trail of Tears. The exodus killed over half the Cherokee before they arrived in Oklahoma.

Charlie's family returned back to their native Chattahoochee in the 1880s. While Indians were not well received in northern Georgia, Thomas Whitefeather weathered rural hate and insults, eventually earning grudging accommodation from his neighbors by buying a ten-acre plot of land and removing tons of rock from his barren property, making productive farmland. Charlie's father, Joseph, was the firstborn of nine children, five of whom lived, all boys who found their way to owning a series of twenty- to forty-acre farms in Catoosa County, within a day's walk to their father's original homestead. Joseph married a mixed-blood fourteen-year-old girl, Elvira, in an arranged marriage.

Charlie was the firstborn son of Joseph and Elvira, who lost six of their nine children. He was groomed to be a farmer, but he showed a real aptitude for winning horse races on the dirt tracks in northern Georgia. Because of his size and talent, he became a sought-after jockey, beginning with county fair races in Chattanooga and Nashville. Charlie's win-loss ratio was over 20 percent, and eventually, he made his way to horse racing's major-league venues in Lexington and Louisville, Kentucky. He reached his apex in 1939, winning a Kentucky Derby mount. His horse, Heather Broom, started well and led at the halfway point of the race, but faded in the stretch, coming in third, to show. While climbing horse racing's ladder, he learned how to drink and squander his money. His win-loss ratio slipped quickly, and he followed the same trail back to state and county fairs. Along the way, he suffered a string of injuries, falling from horses, breaking bones, and snapping tendons, that ended his racing career in 1947. A truly broken man, he found work as a groom and horse walker, but mostly he drank until the bar fight in 1953 that left him with a gash he saw every day in the mirror.

Charlie found God while watching fireworks in Macon, Georgia, on the Fourth of July, 1959. "Fitzwilly, I was sitting on a stump minding my own business, and the sky was lit up with fireworks when I heard the call. 'Jesus loves you,' I heard loud and clear. It made me get off that stump and look skyward. 'Jesus loves you,' I heard again, clear as a bell ringing! I've followed the straight and narrow from that day on. Saved my earthly life and my eternal soul. I found good, honest work ever since. Found me a God-fearing woman in '63, and we have a good life in Industrial City, Georgia. We were too old to have children, but my family took me back into the fold after I sobered up, and I have twenty-one nieces, nephews, and great-nieces and -nephews, a blessing each and every one of them. I run short-haul loads to wherever they need to go in old Rufus here. Just delivered some tractor parts in Bossville, just before I picked you up. So, tell me, young man, you say you're a sober man, but has the Lord entered your life?"

I knew it was of little use to do anything but agree with a born-again ride. "Yes, sir, Mr. Whitefeather. All the saints in heaven above are my witness that Jesus is my savior and my guide. I have to tell you, sir, that the temptations are many, but whenever I get the devil urges, I pray to the Lord and beg him to release me from my sinful inclinations."

Charlie Chattahoochee agreed, "Amen, amen, hallelujah! Let's say a prayer together, Brother Fitzwilly." He reached his tiny, grizzled hand across Michael. I grasped it and listened to Charlie's earnest and well-practiced prayer.

Over a hundred miles, I gave Charlie a good story about how I was traveling to meet with my older brother, Seamus Fitzwillow, who had promised that there was a sales position in a furniture store waiting for me. Our time together passed easily through Chattanooga and across the Georgia state line. I pried Charlie for jockey stories that he was happy to tell, and I learned about the racing game, storing the tales for future use.

Industrial City was about forty miles south of the Georgia–Tennessee border and five miles east of I-75 on Highway 136. As we approached the exit, Charlie asked me if I would consider joining him and his wife, Imogene, for dinner and a place to stay for the night. It was four o'clock in the afternoon, and I seriously considered the hospitality. But I declined the offer, not willing to continue the Irish and Christian act outside the confines of the old truck. I still wanted some time on my own to think. I figured that with some luck, I could make Atlanta's outskirts, one hundred miles away, by dusk, and possibly make it through the metropolis by nightfall. It wasn't necessarily the wisest course, because it entailed night hitchhiking through central and southern Georgia, not the friendliest stretch of road for hitchhikers. But I felt like I was on a roll with the ride from Charlie, so I chose to push my luck. I said good-bye to Charlie and Michael and started my walk up the ramp with Charlie's blessing.

"Let the power of Jesus guide you, Fitzwilly," he called out the window.

The shoulder of the road was stained with rain-washed remnants of the famed red Georgia clay that made up the surrounding hillsides. I remembered my first hitchhike through Georgia in 1971. As a novice hitchhiker, I carried a large army surplus duffel bag. It was stuffed with too many clothes, books, and food, and a brass fireplace poker I carried for protection in case any *Deliverance*-type characters emerged from the brush or in pickup trucks. The bag weighed close to sixty pounds, and my tennis shoes and bag became stained from the red dust through the long state. My trip preparations back then included stereotypical fear of southern rednecks with nothing better to do than harass hippie hitchhikers.

I never had to take the poker out of the bag, and although an empty beer can or two was tossed at me, I never had any trouble in Georgia. I was picked up by a few drivers named Bubba with Confederate flags and rifle racks mounted on their trucks' rear windows. But I found that, other than their accent, they were the same as the other younger, blue-collar workers who picked me up in every part of the country I thumbed through.

I waited over an hour before a salesman from Calhoun gave me a twenty-mile ride. That set the pattern for the evening. An hour went by, and then a short ride. I made it to the outskirts of southern Atlanta just as the sun set. I had to thumb through Atlanta's sprawl in the dark. I had hitchhiked through Atlanta four times before, and it was never easy. Twice, the Fulton County sheriffs had forced me off the main highway and back to the top of the ramp to wait for the thin volume of cars entering the freeway. They were neither kind nor understanding, and made it clear that if they found me up the highway again, I would spend the night in jail with a fine I couldn't afford. One time, I had unwisely taken a ride that let me off in downtown Atlanta; I had to walk six miles with a heavy bag to a spot south of the city.

This time, I was located just north of the city and outside the newly constructed ring road, I-675. Traffic was heavy, too heavy, and I waited for three hours with no luck. My last meal had been with Charlie, who had shared his road meal of hard salami and warm cheddar cheese, sliced with a hunting knife, and coffee from the cup covering his thermos. I took out a Payday candy bar and my water-filled bota bag, a deerskin-covered wine pouch that had gained popularity as a drink container at rock concerts, and sat down next to my bag. My sister April had given me the bota bag, a prized possession, as a birthday present the previous year. I pulled back the wrapper of the peanut-covered candy bar and slowly consumed it, savoring the caramel as it melted in my mouth, and then chewing the peanuts. It satiated my hunger, but I knew if this bad luck held, I was going to be hungry in another hour.

There was only one gas station at the bottom of the ramp, and its light flickered off at 11:00 p.m. I didn't wear a watch. I didn't like jewelry, and couldn't afford one anyway. I also knew watches and jewelry attracted thieves. I liked to keep time by my own internal clock, watching the sun in different seasons and knowing what time it was within five or ten minutes. It was a point of pride.

I finished the Payday and took a swig from the half-empty bota bag. This was the hard part of hitchhiking. Prospects for rides were shallow, and a combination of day-old perspiration and road dust was ripening on me. It had been a long day begun with a hangover. I couldn't sit for long, but my back and legs were tired from hours of standing. I also knew that if a ride didn't materialize soon, I would have to find a place to curl up and sleep for a couple of hours. I rubbed my hands over my face and through my hair, and picked myself up for another stab at getting a ride, asking myself for a reserve of energy to pull a ride in and help me out of road doldrums. During these times, loneliness overcame optimism, and only the experience of knowing a ride would eventually appear defeated despair.

I had acquired tricks to help, which included singing. I would sing in my deep, radio-announcer voice, but for the life of me I couldn't hold a tune unless I was singing alongside someone who could. As a result, my roadside sonatas were hopelessly off-key. I also suffered lyric dyslexia, remembering the first few lines of hundreds of songs and forgot the remainder. As a result, I sang the five songs I had managed to memorize through sheer force of repetition. "Ain't No Sunshine When You're Gone," "You Are My Sunshine," "Heart-Of-My-Heart," "Try to Remember," and "What I Really Need Right Now Is a Nurse" were my repertoire.

As midnight approached on I-75, traffic slowed and my fatigue grew heavier. I decided to sleep underneath the overpass bridge a hundred feet in front of me that carried the local east-west traffic. I had done this close to two dozen times during my years of hitchhiking. It was a last resort, because it was always an uncomfortable and unsatisfying rest. I was disconsolate as I dragged my knapsack toward the bridge, still beckoning rides with my thumb, hoping for a reprieve. Once under the bridge, I climbed up the angled cement until I reached the three-foot horizontal ledge that was under every interstate bridge. The roadway was just three feet above, and every car that passed over the bridge shook it gently. Late at night the vibrations were infrequent, depending on how close a town was to the bridge. This close to Atlanta was the worst, with bar revelers and other late-night travelers crossing the bridge every other minute until the wee hours of the morning, when traffic slowed to a vehicle every twenty or thirty minutes. Sitting cross-legged, my head barely clearing the bottom of the road above, I pulled out a thin, wool Marine Corps surplus blanket from my bag. It was large enough to provide a layer between the cool cement and me. I curled in the fetal position and wrapped the blanket around my body, trapping my body heat. I used my bag as a poor excuse for a pillow. I was so road weary, I nodded off faster than I expected. The rhythm of the cars whooshing through the bridge below me and the rumbling of cars above pulsed a cadence that lulled me to sleep. I slept fitfully, in and out of dreams. I was dehydrated, so I didn't have to urinate, another complication to road sleep that resulted in either peeing down the cement incline or stepping outside the bridge to pee on the grass, out of view of passing cars. An inopportune urge for a bowel movement truly complicated life on the road, but was, thankfully, not a problem this night.

The hours passed, and I woke as the first light of morning crept under the bridge. This was the worst time. I was hungry. My mouth was parched, my teeth were gritty, and I was pungent. Bone-tired, I had to move my stiff and aching body. I wondered if this was what getting old felt like. I sat up slowly, folded my blanket, and thought about making my way to the gas station at the bottom of the ramp. My internal clock told me it was only 5:00 a.m., and, likely, the gas station didn't open until 6:00 or 7:00 a.m., if I was lucky. I decided to attempt to drift back into the last pleasant dream of the short night: Marta and me on Burt Lake beach. The hour passed slowly. Finally, I shook off the lethargy and repacked my bag, ducking the roadway above my head. I crawled out from under the bridge to the road above it. It was never easy being a hitchhiker at a gas station. The owners or employees looked at me as a nonpaying interloper, at best. This was where charm was tested severely. As I walked toward the Sinclair station, I saw an attendant gassing up a car, indicating the station had opened early for business. I tucked in my T-shirt and pushed back my hair. I had been chased from gas stations infrequently, but the threat always existed. In the best case, there would be a young employee opening a station who would have some sympathy for a glib, yet polite, hitchhiker. If I could persuade the gas station attendant to fork over the restroom key, I was in luck. I could use the rarely or barely cleaned restroom to take a sink bath. If it all worked out perfectly, I could shit, shave, wash, brush my teeth, put on a clean shirt, and be on my way, as refreshed as a person could be after sleeping under a highway bridge.

That's not exactly how it worked out on this day. While the gas station attendant, an old guy, gassed up an early traveler at the pump, I sneaked into the station and pulled the restroom key attached to a dirty block of wood from its hook and made my way to the rest room outside the station. The attendant didn't notice until I was in the door. A few minutes later, he was pounding on the door, telling me only paying customers could use the restroom. There was a lock on the door, so I ignored him. After several fist poundings, I opened the door, smiled at the attendant and handed him the key.

"Thank you for your hospitality, sir. It is greatly appreciated." I smiled. He mumbled something unflattering as he marched back into the station.

I took this as an opportunity to chat up the driver of the Plymouth station wagon at a gas pump. When he said he was going north, I didn't belabor the conversation. I had mixed success getting rides at gas stations and truck stops. It was a different skill than standing at the side of the road. I couldn't jump right into asking for a ride; a connection of some kind was necessary, such as latching onto something, like noticing a Michigan license plate, or one of those bumper stickers announcing an attraction, like *Mystery Spot, Mackinac Island,* or *I Survived the Everglades.* At my dismal rung in life, it was tough for me to look down on anyone. But for the life of me, the purchase and display of tourist bumper stickers eluded my sensibilities. After visiting the Mystery Spot, why would anyone want to provide free advertising? I guess even the poorest church mouse could rustle up snobbery over someone else.

Usually, drivers averted my searching eyes as soon as they saw the knapsack. Truckers were more direct—that *No Riders* sign mean just that, buddy, no riders! These were truckers who drove for a fleet, and their companies insisted on no hitchhikers, a rule rarely broken. Independent ma–and-pa operators were more open, but still had insurance policies that forbade riders.

It was one of those truckers who saw me as I trudged up the on-ramp. The truck was making a left turn on the ramp, and I heard the sound of an air brake, so I turned and walked backward with my thumb out. The eighteen-wheeler was in first gear and slowed to a stop in the middle of the on-ramp. The driver's head was barely visible through the open passenger window of the truck's cab. "Hey there, how far you going?"

I stepped up on the small ladder leading to the cab and said, "Florida, but any ride past Atlanta would be appreciated."

"Okay, pal, I'm headed to Worthville. I can get you as far as Blacksville, about twenty miles south of Atlanta, before I turn off," the driver called out.

I hoisted myself up into the cab and met Bill Stickley, a Findlay, Ohio-based trucker wearing a John Deere hat. "Been out long, fella?"

"Yeah, I couldn't catch a ride last night, so I caught a little shut-eye under the bridge. Thanks for stopping. You ended a dry spell," I said.

Bill smiled and nodded his head.

"Been there. Used to thumb a bit in my earlier days, so I try to help out if the guy looks harmless enough. I usually steer clear of hitchhikers, unless they're chicks who want some action, know what I mean?" Bill winked.

I winced internally, but enthusiastically shot back, "Hell, yes."

"I get a lot of action out here on the road. Chicks dig me, know what I mean? Chicks like us real men in the big rigs, know what I mean? I give it to 'em good, and they always leave a satisfied customer, know what I mean?"

"Yes, sir, I do," I replied, knowing the fewer words the better with guys like Bill. I knew this was going to be a long tour of listening to Bill's sexual fantasies. It would be difficult to be a good listener. All I wanted to do was sit back in the shock-absorbing seat in the air-conditioned cab, and sleep. Bill did take the time to offer me a cup of coffee and a cigarette, which I gladly accepted. I wasn't a regular smoker, but I usually kept a pack of cigarettes in my bag for very long roadside waits.

The coffee and Lucky Strike gave me a helluva head buzz, and the accompanying lightheadedness made his blather easier to tune out. Eventually, I did my best head nod, falling into a dream state as my head bobbled up and down, eyes half open, half-listening to Bill and occasionally looking over at the right time and saying, "Yes, sir," or "No shit."

Bill never stopped talking about his conquests. "Then there was this sweet chick with the biggest titties you ever laid eyes on. Oh, yeah, she wanted me bad, all right, and I wasn't going to let her down, know what I mean?"

I snapped out of my trance about ten minutes before the Blacksville exit. I had developed a sixth sense about when a ride was about to end, even if I was in a deep sleep. Bill didn't even notice, still on a roll.

"Those twins told me they had never met a man like me before and wanted to know when we were going to meet up for another round, know what I mean?"

I was tempted to tell him what was really on my mind, but demurred, like I always did, not wanting to end a ride prematurely. But the cartoon bubble above my head said, "Bill, you are a complete asshole who hasn't been laid for free in years. You are a lying, contemptible sack of shit with no redeeming qualities except you picked me up and gave me a cup of coffee and smoke in exchange for me sitting here trapped, listening to your babbling train of fabrications."

But my voice said, "Yes, sir, Bill. You have a way with the ladies, don't you?"

"That's for sure, that is for fucking sure!" Bill agreed.

I departed the truck somewhat grateful I didn't have to waste a lie of my own on the self-absorbed twinkie. As I stepped away from the truck and watched it ease through the first of its seven gears onto the highway, I noticed another hitchhiker standing in the prime spot at the top of the on-ramp. Road etiquette dictated that the most recent hitchhiker on the scene should stop and exchange pleasantries with the first in line, and then walk a hundred or so yards past and wait until his turn. Some ill-mannered hitchhikers would act oblivious to the first hitchhiker and stand in front of them, or, slightly less rude, stand at the bottom of the on-ramp and try to pick off drivers entering the freeway. I was not shy about letting those impetuous hitchhikers know the rules of the road. Occasionally, it led to heated words, and, while I wasn't physically imposing, I usually managed to gain my rightful place in line, even if it meant walking in front of the hitchhiker by a hundred yards.

I walked up to the tall, tanned, relatively well-groomed hitchhiker, and introduced myself. The young man was about my age and returned the introduction. "Hey, bro, glad to meet you. I'm Paul Taylor from Racine, Wisconsin. I'm headed down to Tallahassee to hook up with my girlfriend who goes to Florida State. Where you headed?"

I told him my name and destination. He asked, "Hey, you want some company? We can thumb together if you want. You seem cool."

I thought about it for a second and agreed. It was tougher hitching tandem, but the odds evened out given my second position if I declined.

"Sounds good. You been out here long?" I asked.

We exchanged histories as we set up to hitchhike. Paul told me about his trip from Chicago, where his father lived, and how he was taking a semester off college at the University of Wisconsin in Madison, to "sow some wild oats."

Shorter than Paul, I stood a few feet in front of him, beckoning for an early morning ride. We didn't have to wait long. A 1971 red two-door Cutlass pulled over with two long-haired young men occupying the car's bucket seats.

The passenger opened his door, leapt out of the front seat, and called out, "Hey, y'all, let's go. We're gonna be late for work."

The driver also exited his seat and hurried to open the trunk as Paul and I approached. "Put your bags in, boys, we gotta move!"

We put our bags in and clambered into the backseat. The driver and his friend hurried into the car, slammed their doors, and the car screamed back onto the highway.

"We're only going to Jenkinsburg, boys. We're on a construction crew down there, and we're running late. Where you boys headed?" the driver asked.

Paul said, "Miami, Florida, but thanks for the ride."

"Yeah, no problema. We've been out there hitchhiking before, right, Ralph? Last year, before we hit pay dirt with this steady construction gig, we had a piece-of-shit car that was lucky to get us anywhere, so we used to thumb over to Anniston, Alabama, to visit Ralph's girlfriend. Made that trip six times until Ralph broke up with her. Ralph bought this car last month, and that's the end of our hitchhiking days, right, Ralph?"

Ralph, a husky man with shoulder-length blond hair, said, "Yep." The passenger laughed and said, "That's Ralph, a man of few words. I'm Todd. You boys want some doughnuts?" He passed a box of Dunkin' Donuts back to me.

Paul and I introduced ourselves while eating the glazed doughnuts and licking our fingers. Paul picked up the conversation while I took a catnap, grateful for the opportunity to sleep without paying attention. The tandem hitchhike was working out.

We waited only fifteen minutes before we were picked up by a peanut farmer from Griffith. Another short wait skipped us to Popes Ferry, just north of Macon.

We set up again with me in front. "Hey, Luke, you're good luck. We're moving right along."

"It's not me, Paul. We've got some good chemistry working here. Let's hope our luck holds."

"You got that—knock on nylon," Paul said, tapping his knuckles on his backpack.

I smiled, remembering we were in the middle of the Deep South; Confederate flag license plates and gun racks were a common sight on cars and trucks passing by. Some people in this part of the country still harbored deep-seated resentment about the war over states' rights and remembered Sherman's March like it was yesterday. My travels through central Georgia had taught me that rednecks did exist, but generally the kids my age were more interested in the Allman Brothers than kicking some Yankee's ass. It made sense to prevent a conversation from drifting into the Civil War or civil rights. There were good people down here picking up hitchhikers, but there was a thin veneer of accommodation to Yankee hitchhikers that could explode into generations of inculcated resentment.

The morning heat bounced off the asphalt and hard-packed red clay roadside as we waited for our next ride. A 1970 Mercury Comet station wagon puttered in the slow lane at what appeared to be just above the forty-five miles per hour minimum speed allowed on interstate highways. It passed Paul and me slowly enough that we were able to see the male driver and his female passenger fairly well. We used our smiles and wagging thumbs to reel over the car to the side of the road. We ran the short sprint to the vehicle.

I reached the car first, and said to the middle-aged woman in the passenger seat, "Thank you for stopping, ma'am. Should we put our bags in the back?"

The woman remained silent. The driver, a man with thinning gray hair, spoke up. "That would be fine. Just lift the hatch and throw your bags on in."

The car pulled slowly off the shoulder onto the highway as the driver introduced himself. "Gentleman, my name is Jesse and this here is Brunette. We're on a leisurely drive down this ol' highway and are pleased to have a little company. Now, who do we have the pleasure of picking up?"

We introduced ourselves with our destination, and Jesse, in turn, spoke of some vague spot south. Midway through his monologue, Jesse asked if we wanted to quench our thirst with a cold one and passed two Budweisers back to Paul and me.

As Jesse talked, I noticed that Brunette sat motionless in the front seat. I reckoned she had to be forty, maybe forty-five years old, a few years younger than Jesse. Her red hair was poufed up above her forehead, and her white face showed pancake makeup and red lipstick that almost matched her hair. Brunette stared straight ahead, her face expressionless, at least from what I could see from my seat behind the driver.

I caught half of Jesse's blabber as we finished our beers. I opened the second can and took a long drink. It was just too early to get buzzed, so I warmed the can between my legs.

My attention snapped alert when Jesse inquired, "Now, boys, at your age, I'm guessing that you have a healthy interest in naked women, don't you?"

Paul's lanky frame was sprawled over the backseat of the station wagon. He laughed and said, "Sure, Jesse, we love naked ladies."

"Well, I thought so, and since we're all comrades in travel, I thought you might enjoy some of these girlie magazines I keep handy for boys like you." Jesse nervously reached under his seat, came up with two magazines, and passed them back to us.

I was no stranger to pornography, but I was aghast at what Jesse handed me. The pictures were vivid and crass. This was way beyond *Playboy* magazines and even the crudely made porno films I had witnessed at bachelor parties. This was explicit pornography. I looked up at Brunette, motionless as a statue, and then over at Paul.

"Holy shit, Jesse, this is some hot shit! Look at this, Luke," he said, holding up a picture of a man and woman in a very uncomfortable position.

My gut started to ripple: I felt queasy. It wasn't just the pornography. It was the imperturbable Brunette, the beers, the smooth-talking Jesse that disturbed my hitchhiker's instincts. It was clear Paul didn't have the same feelings as he chuckled, turning the pages of his magazine.

A sense of trouble escalated as Jesse exited I-75, saying, "They're working on the highway up ahead, boys, so I'm taking the scenic detour."

Abruptly, we were on a two-lane highway, still driving south, but in a rural area of central Georgia, bypassing Macon completely. Jesse was still talking, his conversation steering toward the benefits of "girlie magazines" and then gesturing toward Brunette, who was a "sweet woman, a woman with needs, like all women," and how he couldn't satisfy her properly, and "if the right young man was willing and able, it made all the sense in the world to let nature take its course. Don't you agree, boys?"

I chimed in quickly, the hair on the back of my neck standing up, a reminder that this situation wasn't just leading to trouble, we were right in the middle of it.

"Jeez, Jesse, I hear what you're saying, but I'm a God-fearing Christian with a fiancée waiting for me in Ohio. It just wouldn't seem right to go where I think you're suggesting. I'm not meaning any offense to anyone, if you know what I mean," I said nervously.

Paul just continued to chortle as he paged through the outrageous pictures. I listened intently for the deep rumble that had preceded every unpredictable situation since the night Annette died.

"That's just fine, young man, don't you worry your young head for one minute. I was just making a suggestion. Now, if you don't mind, I need to fill up my gas tank and stretch my legs. My old knees are feeling a bit hinky today," Jesse said as he pulled off into a Sinclair gas station.

There were a few gas pumps next to a tiny hut, typical for the middle of nowhere, which was where we were.

As the station wagon stopped at the pump, Jesse said, "Brunette, I expect you'll be needing the ladies' room." Without a word, Brunette opened the passenger door and, in a ladylike manner, pivoted her body out of the open door, stood up, straightened her dress, and walked with a wiggle that bordered on a waggle, to the ladies room. I thought that she wasn't unattractive, not slender, not fat . . . just middle-aged, like a lot of my friends' moms.

As I watched her walk to the ladies' room, Jesse said, "Boys, like I told you, Brunette is a woman with needs, just like any other woman. And I can't cut the mustard. That's another story, for another time. I can see you boys have good intentions, so we'll just let sleeping dogs lie." Jesse stepped out of the car, stretched, and watched as a grizzled gas attendant filled up the Comet.

I whispered to Paul, "Jesus Christ, we should we get the hell out of here."

Paul replied, "Shit, Luke, what are you worried about? They're harmless. You worry too much. Relax and enjoy the ride."

I was not consoled. I fidgeted in the backseat, trying to figure out if it was best to get out in the middle of nowhere and make my way back to I-75, or to weather the storm and stay with what was emerging as a band of wackos. Jesse paid for the fill-up as Brunette wiggle-waggled back from the restroom to the station wagon. I decided that, because I was with Paul, there was at least some strength in numbers.

Soon, we were back on the two-lane highway, heading south into an increasingly remote area of Georgia. Before long, there was nothing but a forest of red pines on either side of the road. Jesse offered Paul and me another beer, which I declined and Paul accepted. Jesse was talking about what a beautiful sunny Georgia day it was, and suddenly switched gears.

"Boys, I don't want to press the issue, but I want to ask you one more time if you have an interest in satisfying my Brunette here. She is a one-of-a-kind woman, and she will treat you right as rain. What say you, boys, any takers?"

Words stuck in my throat and before I could retrieve them, Paul chimed in, "Oh, what the hell. Sure, I'll do it with Brunette!"

I couldn't believe what I had heard, but before I formulated a response, Jesse pulled abruptly off the road onto a two-track trail that appeared between the red pines. The station wagon bounced along the road. I seriously considered jumping out by opening the car door and rolling into the tall grass next to the trail. Before I could make up my mind, weighing the injuries I might get leaping out of a station wagon traveling at thirty miles an hour, leaving my bag in the car, and what to do if I managed a safe landing, Jesse slowed the car to a stop in a meadow.

He said, "This will do just fine. Paul, why don't you escort Miss Brunette up over that little hill and take care of your business. Luke and I will wait here for you and get to know each other a little better."

Brunette exited the car with a blanket she took from the front seat and silently walked toward the hill ahead of Paul, who was closing the distance with his lanky strides. Jesse turned to me and smiled. I was scared white. Every hair follicle on my body was alert, a sensation I felt just before my fear and flight instinct kicked in.

"Luke, my boy, there's nothing to worry about. You can relax. My intentions are completely honorable. I just can't satisfy Brunette, which is a great cause of pain to me. So I try to find someone who can. You can't fault me for that, can you? I promise you that when those two have taken care of business, I'll have you back on the highway, lickety-split. If you'd like, we can get out of the car, have a beer, and enjoy this day."

Old Jesse was smooth, but I was unconvinced. I thought about running as fast and as far as I could, but then I would be careening around the backwoods of Georgia. My memory revisited the scene in *Deliverance* with Ned Beatty, belt around his neck, being told to "Squeal, squeal like a pig!" It had always been an abstract fear. But now I was in Georgia!

While this middle-aged pimp of sorts didn't seem harmless, he had a story that made some sense, as strange as the situation had become. I caught my breath and relaxed enough to say, "Sure, Jesse, sure."

We both stepped out of the Comet station wagon and sat on a knoll by the side of the dirt road with the grasshoppers. Jesse pulled his wallet out of his pants pocket and eagerly showed me his driver's license.

"See here, Luke, my name is Jesse Thaddeus Wilkins. A resident of East Juliette, Georgia. But that's just a slice of my story. I've been all over the world, fought in WWII and on the Korean peninsula. The military was my life for over thirty years. I've been involved in military intelligence at the highest levels, and even though I'm officially retired, you're never out of the Company. I still get the occasional assignment from my friends in the CIA. You're in good hands, Luke. This business with Brunette is not easy or simple. I've been with the gal for right about ten years, and let it suffice to say we've been in some sticky wickets together. Before I met her, I was lower than whale shit. I suffered some on-the-job injuries I'd rather not go into, and that leads me to take some extraordinary measures to keep her happy. Which is what leads us to this fine day in the woods of Georgia. I can see you're nervous as a cat, but as I said, when we're done here, I'll get you safe and sound back on the highway with a story you and Paul can tell for the rest of your lives. You all right with this, son?"

I shrugged and said, "Yeah, sure, Jesse. You're right, I'm not just nervous, I'm scared shitless. But you seem cool enough. I'm wondering, if you don't mind me asking, how do you figure out who to pick up and make sure things don't, you know, get out of hand?"

"That's a good question, Luke. I am not indiscriminate with whom I choose for Brunette. I've spent a lifetime reading people, and I made sure I only pick up clean-looking young men like yourself. No hippies, drunks, or other riffraff. After I get them in the car, I size 'em up and make a decision. Brunette has a say, of course, and she gives me the nod if she likes the look of our passengers. As far as trouble, I pretty much have that handled with my old friend." Jesse pulled up his shirt and revealed a silver handgun tucked into his pants.

Please don't ask me to squeal like a pig. Sweat formed and rolled in beads off my forehead.

"Yeah, that should take care of any problems, which you aren't going to have with Paul or me," I said, half an octave higher than my normal tone. Jesse laughed and patted me on the back.

"Now, don't start worrying again. C'mon, now, sit up. You're hunched over like a greyhound making love to a football. I know you're a gentleman, that's easy to see. Your friend is a bit of a rogue, but harmless, and he's got a tiger by the tail with Brunette."

I carried on a conversation as amicably as a frightened hitch-hiker could, given that I was talking to a purported CIA agent with a gun in his belt while waiting for my traveling companion to screw a mute, middle-aged redhead named Brunette. More likely than not, I was passing time with a psychopath who was a full bubble off center and would maim and mutilate us before having his way with us. I gulped and hoped.

Twenty minutes or so passed, and Brunette and Paul emerged from over the hill where they had obviously copulated. Brunette sashayed unsteadily on the red dirt in her low heels, with Paul catching up, blanket in hand, brushing bits of grass from his hair.

Jesse sprung up and exclaimed "All righty then, let's get this show on the road." With that, the four of us found our respective seats in the station wagon. I noticed the scapular Marta's mom had given me was hanging outside my shirt. I reached up and massaged it, breathing slightly easier. Jesse steered his station wagon in a broad U-turn back out of the trail, keeping a steady stream of patter about the beauty of the Georgia landscape, the weather, college football, and other topical subjects with no references to sex with Brunette or pornography or what had just transpired. Before long, Jesse found an east-west country road that crossed over I-75.

"Sorry there's no on-ramp here boys, but this should still be a good spot for you. You're almost twenty miles south of Macon. Perry is just a few miles south of here. You can get your bags and go with God." We exited, stepped toward the rear window of the station wagon, and took our bags out. Paul walked up to the open passenger window, leaned in, and gave Brunette a peck on the cheek.

"Thank you, ma'am," he said. Brunette smiled, and keeping in character, never said a word. Jesse called out, "Thank you, boys. God bless and good luck on the road." He tooted the horn and slowly pulled away.

We watched as they pulled away. "Jesus Christ, that was the wildest thing that ever happened to me!" Paul exclaimed. "And that Brunette, she may have been old and plain, but Christ almighty could she screw! She never said a single word, but she was all over me. She was like a wild animal, she—"

I interrupted, "*Jesus Christ* is right, Paul, what in the hell were you thinking? That crazy bastard Jesse is sitting with me telling about his CIA exploits with a pistol stuck in his pants. You're screwin' a middle-aged lady who has God-knows-what diseases, while I'm sitting with a goddamn maniac who panders his girlfriend or wife or whatever on unsuspecting hitchhikers. If I was you, Paul, I'd be scrubbing my dick with some Borax before you meet up with your girlfriend in Tallahassee. All I want to know is what in God's name were you thinking?"

Paul laughed a deep belly laugh. "Aw, c'mon, Luke. It was a lark, a once-in-a-lifetime opportunity. I just thought, *What the hell.* It was a desperate old man who couldn't get it up and a nympho old maid who needed some loving. They seemed harmless enough. Shit, I can't believe Jesse had a gun. That's kinda scary!"

"No shit, Sherlock."

We picked up our bags and walked down the incline from the road and onto I-75 in silence, my lead again.

"Hey, I don't think I caught VD or anything. Old Brunette came equipped with rubbers. She had three kinds to choose from, those kind you find in the gas station restroom: Purple Passion, Mr. Big, and Triple Studded for Pleasure, I shit you not!"

I couldn't help myself and laughed out loud. "You asshole, Paul."

"I picked Mr. Big, of course. Actually, I picked the Triple Studded for Pleasure. I was a bit worried about Mr. Big not fitting!" Paul continued.

I put my hand up and said, "Stop, Paul, no more details, please!"

"Okay, but you're missing out on a real good story. You know, Luke, I'm going to college to learn how to be a writer. This is just the kind of stuff you need to write about. Hell, for all the time you've been out on the road, you must have a shitload of stories to tell. Maybe you ought to be a writer."

"Yeah, you're right, that's a helluva story we just lived through, with the emphasis on living. I think you'll have to write the stories; I'm just a road warrior, bullshit artist."

We kibitzed for a while, thumbs out as cars passed them by; then we fell quiet.

"What the hell was that fluorescent red hair on top of Brunette's head all about?" Paul asked. I doubled over in laughter.

"And why did Brunette never say a single word? Was she really a mute? I'll tell you this, she did have a tongue, but the noises she made sounded like she was from another planet, no shit!"

"Paul, enough! I do not want to have nightmares with sound effects of you and Brunette doing the nasty!"

"Okay, okay, Luke, but we didn't do nothing that would top those magazines old Jesse gave us. And by the way, I just happened to purloin one of those skin mags, if you're interested."

"Paul, you are something else. Let's just try to focus our attention on getting a ride and away from those wild oats you've just sowed. Damn, the visual of you and Brunette, it's killing me!"

"No problem, buddy. So, how about them Detroit Tigers?"

We talked for a half-hour more, not discussing Jesse and Brunette again. We had a whale of a story. Twenty minutes later, a salesman in a Bonneville picked us up. We heard about his success selling replacement tractor parts throughout his south and southeast states territory. A boring ride was a welcome relief.

It was nearing 7:00 p.m. and we had enjoyed a series of short waits and short rides that put us past Valdosta and just a few miles north of the Florida border. The terrain had flattened out, and the beginning of evening had begun to cool the sun-baked road. We had splurged on a lunch at a Howard Johnson's motel and restaurant in the town of Adel, Georgia, which, of course, reminded me of Adell. We laughed a lot over hamburgers. Paul had the morals of an alley cat, but he was a likable guy with an easy way about him.

We picked up another ride from a hippie couple from Gaines-ville, our longest ride so far, and well past I-10. We sat cramped in the backseat of the 1969 Rambler, bags on our laps. The two hippies were named Peter and Sue, a.k.a. Truth and Spirit. I wasn't paying attention and didn't know which name went with whom. They were true flower children, peppering their conversation with: "Man, isn't life beautiful?" "Yeah, groovy, man." "Outta sight, man." "Do you have any weed? No? Bummer, man."

The I-10 intersection came up quickly, and Truth and Spirit asked where the best spot was to let Paul off. I advised a quarter mile before the exit was about right, and the driver eased the Rambler into the shoulder. Paul pulled himself up, opened the door, and pushed the seat back, climbing out of the car.

"Thanks so much, Spirit and Truth. Keep on keeping on."

Paul looked into the backseat at me and shook his head while he smiled. "Well, partner, this is it. It's been real, very real. Thanks for everything."

I reached out for his hand through the window and Paul met me with a brother handshake. As he closed the door behind him, I called out, "Remember the Triple Studded Mr. Big!"

Paul laughed and shot back, "Brunette forever!"

"Right on!" I yelled as the Rambler's copilot closed the door and the Rambler pulled back onto I-75. I pushed my bag onto the seat Paul had vacated, and looked out the back window as he raised his fist in a salute. I turned my attention to Peter and Sue, hoping I could convince them to let me stay the night with them at the commune in Gainesville. I didn't relish another night hitchhiking episode, and a road dinner of granola mix, fresh fruit, and papaya juice was looking mighty attractive, given the alternative.

My head nestled nicely into the middle of the Rambler's backseat. I was missing Marta—missing the smell on the back of her neck, her full lips opening up to a broad smile punctuated by her ever-so-slightly-gap-toothed smile. I missed her touch, easy laugh, and how she fit into the crook of my elbow in the afterglow of making love. *What an idiot I was to leave.*

Sinking deeper, I thought of Ann and Donnie and how they could use my help. I cringed thinking of how little time I had spent with April and Angela since they had left for college. *What was wrong with me?*

After the Jesse and Brunette incident with Paul Taylor, I missed the Lost Souls. *How long could I keep running away and hold onto their friendships?*

Real life was seeping into my thoughts. I measured the trade offs of family, friends, and life in one place against the freedom of the road. *Can I rebuild my life?*

The Rambler cruised south, and my thoughts tossed back and forth.

I fell asleep in the backseat of Truth and Spirit's Rambler as wisps of smoke floated past me from the small incense burner sitting on the dashboard. I didn't wake until I felt Spirit's gentle touch on my shoulder. I looked up, startled, at the beaming, freckled face, framed by braided pigtails.

"Hey, brother, this is where we have to let you out." I sat up and rubbed my face.

Truth told me, "Hey, man, we took you past Gainesville a few miles to give you a head start to Miami. You were sleeping like a log, and we didn't want to wake you. Spirit put together a little something for you."

She handed me a brown bag and said, "A little trail mix and some of my homemade yogurt, I hope you like it, bro."

Too late to lead them into taking me to Gainesville, but I was grateful for their kooky generosity.

"Thanks, you guys, for going out of your way and for the food. Good karma is coming your way," I said, opening the back door and dropping my bag on the shoulder of the road. Truth and Spirit beamed.

"Right on, brother!" they exclaimed together.

As they pulled away, I flashed them the peace sign and they both saluted me with a "power to the people" fist in the air. It didn't take much effort to be nice to someone.

I was past the mid-sized city of Gainesville, standing at the Rochelle exit. It was late afternoon, and the air was sticky and hot. The nap had refreshed me, but I was thirsty and in need of a bathroom. I spied a Speedway station at the top of the ramp. I strapped on my knapsack and walked to the station and bought a box of Junior Mints, a bag of pretzels, a bag of almonds, and sixteen-ounce Pepsi before asking for the key to the restroom. It hadn't been cleaned recently. A small wastebasket overflowed with crumpled paper towels. The toilet seat was up, urine splattered everywhere. There were no paper towels so I took a few sheets of toilet paper and gingerly pulled the seat down, which was paint-chipped and splattered with dried piss and God knew what else. I let out a breath and lined the top of the seat with toilet paper before taking care of business. *There's nothing adventurous or romantic about living this way.* I washed up as best I could in a grungy sink with the remnant of a bar of Lava that was surprisingly usable.

Whistling "Zip-a-Dee-Do-Dah," I tried to cheer myself up at the bottom of the ramp. I had skimmed a map in the gas station and knew it was over three hundred miles to Miami. There was no chance of making it tonight. I envisioned that, with luck, I could make it past Orlando and then splurge on a cheap motel room for the night. I wasn't looking forward to another night under a highway bridge. Florida was a mixed bag for hitchhiking. The Florida state troopers were tough on road thumbing, and the local police could be downright nasty. But the highways were straight and flat, making visibility easy. It was warm, too warm, and after dusk the mosquitoes could get bad. There were plenty of rest areas, where it was sometimes easier than at gas stations to make contact with travelers and con a ride. But they could also be conclaves for deviants on the prowl. In my previous two trips through Florida, I had never waited more than three hours to get a ride and had been chased off the road by the police only twice. My calculations complete, I stood and worked the steady traffic, replaying old high school football games in my head, remembering some of my few shining moments, like two interceptions against St. Lawrence. It comforted me, and I reflected on how much I enjoyed high school at St. Mary's. The small school seemed to stifle me when I was there, but remembering back now, it was so comfortable and cozy. Everyone knew me and my story. I was treated gently in spite of my burgeoning rebellion. Standing in the heat of the Florida night, I wondered what in the hell I was doing so far from home.

Road doubt visited me again, and my thoughts raced from high school, to Marta, to my mom, to Donnie. I second-guessed the decisions I had made for the thousandth time. If only I had stayed in Royal Oak, worked a job, gone to college, and found some semblance of normal life. But then there would be no Marta, no adventure, no challenge—and yet, no shit-strewn bathrooms, nights under highway bridges, and stomach cramps from gas station snack food as a dietary staple. I remembered what John Parcell had told me one night after I returned from a trip out west, telling John about the fun and peril of the road.

"Luke, it seems to me you must really enjoy living on the knife's edge. But, man, it must be tough standing up there blowing in the wind, hoping you don't fall off."

The truth was, I did fall off on nights like this. The emptiness and loneliness collapsed around me. I shuddered and tried to shake off the gloom. I focused on Marta, a first real love. Lovely, tall, broad-smiled Marta, who, unbelievably, had offered her love to me. The reminder of her in my arms and the swiftness of our commitment were reassuring, overriding my haunting anxiety about ever being loved. If I could be loved, then I could love back—but that love could be violently wrenched out of my heart again, leaving me with worse than nothing. I would have to revisit the desolation created when Mom died. I would have to think about my dad again, my version of a chute straight to hell.

I fought off that lousy place, held Marta in my mind's eye, and found my way back to the knife's edge. I believed my strength was my ability to find hope in the future, and Marta provided a look forward that held great possibilities. I imagined a life five, ten, fifteen years ahead with her. I would have a job as a successful traveling salesman; Marta would be a teacher or maybe a nurse. We would have three children in one of those nice colonial homes with four bedrooms in north Royal Oak. Marta and the kids would rush to the front door to hug me and greet me upon my return from places across the country. I'd bring the kids commemorative spoons and T-shirts and snow globes from the places I traveled. I would bring home flowers for the love of my life. She would hold me, bouquet still in hand, her free hand working its way up my back to my head, her fingers running through my hair. She would pull her head back to look me in the eyes before opening her lips to create a sensual, but loving, cradle to kiss.

"Never waste a kiss," she would say. Each kiss had meaning.

We would eat dinner as a family, and then I would play catch with my son. In the winter, I'd freeze our big backyard like Mr. McInerny and watch my daughter skate pirouettes under the floodlights from the kitchen window, my arms around my wife. *It can happen this way.*

I stood outside Gainesville on the highway as afternoon disappeared into evening. I was all right. I solicited rides with renewed strength and wooed and willed a Buick Riviera to the side of the road. *Yeah! I can make things happen. I can control my destiny. Yes! I am all right. This is living.*

I ran to the big blue car and opened the door to greet the large-beaked driver wearing a white straw Panama hat. "Thanks for stopping. I'm Mortimer Molesky," I said as I sat on the white leather seat and extended my hand to the driver.

Chapter 27

September 2003

I slid the CD that held "Luke Moore's Greatest Hits" into the CD player. I knew the order of the songs. "Try to Remember" was exactly the old-hat selection appropriate for the ride across the bridge. I loved the sappy musicals, like *The Fantastiks* and *Fiddler on the Roof,* that were Mom's favorites. No matter that *The Fantastiks* featured a fake rape and *Fiddler* was about nineteenth-century Russian Jews. The stories are about strong-minded daughters and the timeless fight of love with their parents.

> *Try to remember a kind of September*
> *When life was slow and oh, so mellow.*
> *Try to remember a kind of September*
> *When grass was green and grain was yellow.*
> *Try to remember the kind of September*
> *When you were a tender and callow fellow.*
> *Try to remember, and if you remember, then follow.*

When I was a tender and callow fellow, so many character-building Septembers ago, I used to believe the adage "what doesn't kill you makes you stronger." My current philosophy is "what doesn't kill you, doesn't kill you." And a healthy dose of luck is worth a lot in life. As the Lost Souls and I made it into our thirties, we used to count up the stories where we could have died. There were ten. We would laugh about our luck. After we became parents, the tenor of our story-fests changed. We were aghast—what the hell we had done? Shit, what if our kids turned out like us, but weren't blessed with our good fortune? And what if they were cursed with our lack of common sense? I'd be damned if some kid of mine was going to sleep under a highway bridge.

The Upper Peninsula spread out before us as I remembered a different kind of September. Our hitchhiking passenger stretched and woke. It was time to leave Tom Lutac behind to travel west to his supposed destination of Marquette. I glanced in the rearview mirror and saw him fidgeting with his backpack as we exited the bridge. I saw the glimmer of a blade. My guts tightened and the rumbling began.

I followed the exit off the bridge toward St. Ignace. Two miles up the road, I pulled sharply into the rest area for travelers coming off or onto the bridge just past the ramp.

"Tom, this is where we part ways. I can let you off here, or if you want, I'll take you up a mile or so onto Highway 2 to get you started. Will that work for you?"

"A mile or two up the road would be great, Mr. Moore. That will work fine. Just fine."

If he was nervous, it didn't show.

"Good. Marta and Roberta, this is good time to stretch your legs or use the restroom before we make the final push to the Soo."

"I'm fine, Dad. That last rest stop wasn't that long ago," Roberta replied.

"Do your dear old dad a favor and humor me on this one. It's a long last leg of this drive."

With an eye roll and a huff, she complied. Marta was already out of the van and stretching.

"How about you, Tom? Do you need to use the restroom?" I asked.

"Naw, I'm okay. You go on ahead."

I took my wallet off the dashboard and my keys and grabbed my denim jacket off the back of the captain's chair. I noted that

Marta took her purse with her. Roberta was already out of the car and walking to the toilets. I sidled up next to Marta on the way to the rest area kiosk.

"We're not getting back in the car with our young friend. Take some time at the information booth. I'm calling a cop."

"You're sure?"

"Oh, yeah. I can hear the frigging hum like it's "The Battle Hymn of the Republic." This is either a bad guy or a badly confused guy. Either way, he's trouble and we're done with him."

There was a matronly volunteer at the information booth. She said "oooh" when I asked her for a telephone number for the state police. Another time, another place, I would have tried to handle this by myself. Calling for help was the smart call. No one—no one—messes with my family.

Chapter 28

September 1973

The power of positive thinking appeared to be working. The driver of the Riviera was a retired police chief from Columbus, Ohio. He was on his way to his winter home in Bonita Springs, south of Fort Myers on Florida's Gulf Coast, almost 250 miles away. His name was Chief Howard Kowalski, and his six-foot-four, two-hundred-pound, ramrod-straight frame filled the driver's seat. He had the largest head I had ever seen. It looked like it was chiseled out of marble. His all-white brush cut stood up on his head like wires. The chief informed me that he was making his annual trek south for the tenth straight year since his early retirement. He made the trip in two days, driving straight from Columbus to a motel south of Atlanta, where he slept for seven and a half hours and then drove straight through to Bonita Springs, an eleven-hour haul. He had been a widower for three years and missed the company of his wife of forty-two years. At sixty-five years old, he was a model of discipline, good dietary habits, and exercise. He looked like one tough bird. He occasionally picked up hitchhikers for the company during the past three years, "if they look okay. After more than thirty years as cop, I can usually spot a bad apple a mile away."

I told the chief to call me Mort, and that I was traveling from Michigan to meet my father, who owned a bar in Key West. My story: I was laid off from my job as a construction worker and was looking for work in South Florida's booming construction market. The chief and I talked easily about the tough economy in the Rust Belt, the fortunes of the Cleveland Browns and Detroit Lions, and laughed about our difference of opinion on the fierce football rivalry between Ohio State and the University of Michigan. Our relative, although unlikely, compatibility established, the chief suggested that I might want to accompany him all the way to Bonita Springs, even though it took me to the wrong side of the state for my Key West destination. We pulled out his map and quickly saw that, while I would still be over 150 miles from Miami, I would be in a comfortable car for most of the night. I also saw that Miami was a straight shot across Alligator Alley through the giant Everglades swamp, a road I had never traveled before. It was a bird-in-hand decision. I thanked the burly chief for the opportunity.

It was a dream ride. The tough chief was childless, and with the death of his beloved Hildegard and his career as crime fighter behind him, he was lonely and thick-skinned. Even though I was a wild, pot-smoking, beer-drinking youth who lived close to the fringe of illegal activity, I hit it off with him. I listened with fascination as the chief poured out his life as a rookie patrolman who worked his way up to the chief of police of Ohio's third-largest city. He was as tough as nails, a law-and-order kind of guy, but generally fair-minded, it seemed. The chief had a soft side that showed through when he tenderly described his wife and his work with troubled kids. He had established a police mentoring program in Columbus to work with kids who were in trouble for the first time. He talked about the thrill of the dozen or so kids he had caught in time, and how they had finished high school and found jobs and were now raising families. He was also vehement about the drug dealers he had put away and how drugs were the scourge of American society. I easily chameleoned myself away from the evildoers and positioned myself as a hardworking kid from Detroit who raised a little hell, drank some beer, but certainly didn't do drugs. The chief was fine with that, and as the miles and hours passed, we fell into a comfortable silence.

At the second gas station stop north of Tampa, the chief asked if I would like to drive for a spell. I agreed quickly. I had served as a substitute driver several times during my years on the road: I loved being behind the wheel of a car, especially a big old honkin' Riveria.

I didn't mention that I hadn't received my driver's license until I was eighteen. I had flunked out of driver's training at age fifteen.

The Royal Oak driver's ed teacher took a half-hour cigarette and bathroom break every day that took up the middle of the hour-long roadwork class located on the figure-eight track that simulated real traffic conditions with a traffic light and stop signs. No one ever flunked this part of driver's ed. You just had to stay on the road and pay attention to the twenty-five-mile-an-hour speed limit, the traffic light, and two stop signs. No radio playing or smoking was allowed in the cars, but smokers were allowed to puff their Kools and Winstons and Lucky Strikes at a picnic table immediately before and after class.

I saw the instructor's absence as an opportunity to break all the rules. I immediately rolled down his window, lit up a Winston, and proceeded to pass the other six cars on the course at speeds topping forty miles an hour. I would do rolling stops at the stop signs and my only conformance to the rules was to stop at the traffic signal in the middle of the figure-eight. On the second-to-last day of the class, I was testing out a transmission-busting maneuver known as a hole-shot. Mark McInerny, who had already finished driver's ed, had told me how cool it was to put a standing car in neutral, rev the engine up, and then drop it into drive. This would cause the car's back tires to screech and lay rubber as the car screamed from a dead stop into a barreling ton-and-a-half of race car. Mark noted that you didn't want to do this to a car you actually owned, because it "could really screw it up royal." On this day, with the teacher off to the bathroom, I pulled up to the red light, put the car in neutral, turned the radio up to listen to the Stones' "Satisfaction," cigarette dangling from my left hand out the window, and revved the 1970 Pinto up to six thousand rpm. With my right hand, I dropped the transmission into D, and Bam! The wheels spun as predicted, and the car shot like a bat out of hell, straight through the light, off the track, and into the infield of the course before I finally regained control and brought the car to a halt. I was laughing as I regained my composure, listening to "I can't get no dirty action, I can't get no satisfaction . . ."

What I hadn't counted on was the driver's ed teacher being confronted by the principal as he entered the bathroom, newspaper and Marlboro pack in hand. The principal told him bluntly that he was never to leave seven potentially unguided auto missiles on the course unattended again. The chagrined and bowel-constricted teacher made his way back to the track just in time to see me scream through the light, tires lit up. He ran fast and straight to my Pinto, angrier by each stride. He reached the car as I was still chortling and singing along with the Stones.

I didn't notice him until his face glared down at me through the Pinto's windshield.

"Oh, crap," I muttered.

"*Oh, crap* is right, mister. Get your smoking, radio-playing, hotshot butt out of this car. Now!"

I exited the car and stood in front of the irate Mr. Tasselbaum.

"You, you, you, are O-U-T, out! Out of this car, this class, this program. Don't you even think of reapplying. You are a driver's ed flunk-out, Mr. Whatever-Your-Name-Is!" he stammered and fumed.

That was it for my license. I had to wait until I was eighteen, when the law allowed me to take the written and driving test. In a way, it was a blessing. I would have surely crashed Ann's car if allowed to drive at sixteen, for any number of reasons. I did get some experience driving my friends' cars on back roads, but I was neither naturally talented as a driver nor reliably trained under a parent's watchful eye. The lack of skill and experience didn't dampen my enthusiasm for driving as I climbed behind the wheel of the chief's luxurious Buick Riviera and into the eight-way power seat.

I adjusted my seat to push myself much closer to the steering wheel. The chief advised me how to use the cruise control after we reentered the highway pointed south toward Fort Meyers.

"Okay, Mort, the driver gets to pick his radio station, but as navigator, I'd advise against a hard rock station. Capisce?"

I smiled and fiddled with the radio dials, finding a Miami Dolphins–San Francisco 49ers football game, to both of our satisfaction. The chief settled back and half-closed his eyes as I focused on the dark highway. As Larry Csonka dove for three yards and Griese passed for eighteen, I looked over and noticed that, while the chief was relaxed and near sleep, his sixth sense was still tuned into the game and any sudden movements of the car. *Just like me,* I thought as I cruised at seventy-two and a half miles an hour, just above the speed limit.

I liked night driving. Traffic was sparse and the miles clicked by as the football game progressed. The chief snoozed, his large body relaxed. My highway angst disappeared as I scanned the Riviera's roomy interior and smartly designed dashboard. *Here I am driving this beautiful vehicle, with the retired Columbus ex-chief of police snoring beside me.* The chief had bought us each a road-buddy coffee and candy bar at the gas station where we switched places. I pulled the Baby Ruth out of my shirt pocket and carefully unwrapped the top quarter and bit into the chocolate, nutty bar, careful not to let any of the crumbs hit the leather seats. This was living.

I drove for two hours, 145 miles, negotiating my way around Tampa and through Sarasota, before the chief rustled and woke fully. The first Fort Meyers exit appeared on cue, and the Chief sat up, rubbed his eyes, and said, "Good timing, Mort. Why don't you pull it off here and I'll take over?"

I eased the car off the exit and into the Mobil station, the only station at the exit with lights on. We both used the station's restroom, the attendant gassed up the Riviera, and the chief bought two fresh coffees and a package of doughnuts.

It was close to midnight, and the chief looked over at me and said, "Young man, how about you spend the night at my place? I'll get you a hot breakfast in the morning and then get you on your way."

"That would be greatly appreciated, sir."

I sat back in the reclined passenger seat and talked with the chief about every sport from football to golf and even curling, which we had both watched on the Canadian Broadcasting Station, and which the chief could tune into under certain weather conditions. We agreed it was the most boring sport we ever watched, but were still amused by the guys with brooms and funny accents chasing the "rocks" down the ice. We passed Fort Meyers toward Bonita Springs. It was after 2:00 a.m. when we reached Chief Howard Kowalski's townhouse, part of a nicely maintained complex that suited upper-middle-class snowbirds, located about three miles off the Gulf Coast.

I helped the chief bring his bags into the first-floor, two-bedroom condo. He showed me my bedroom for the night, with an attached bathroom. We were both tired from the drive, so the chief told me to sleep in and that he would wake me about ten. I took a long shower, arranged my meager toiletries on the bathroom sink counter, looked at myself in the steam-shrouded mirror, and smiled contentedly. The bedroom had been decorated with Hildegard's touch in Florida pink and aquamarine. I pulled back the quilt and fell into three pillows. The chief had turned the air conditioning on full blast, and as I settled into the bed, the room started to cool. I rubbed my feet against the stiff, fresh sheets. I was in a comfortable, clean bed. I hugged a pillow, curled up on my side, and slipped off into a deep and full sleep.

I awoke to the smell of coffee and bacon, noticing the alarm clock, sitting next to a ceramic figurine of a Scottie terrier, that displayed 9:45 a.m. I felt good. Clear-minded and well-rested, I left the bedroom and walked through the short hallway into the living room. The chief wore Bermuda shorts and a lime-green T-shirt in front of the stove, stirring a pound of bacon while keeping a watchful eye on a panful of scrambled eggs.

"Good morning, sir," I said approaching the kitchen.

The chief turned and smiled. "And good morning to you, young man. It is a beautiful, warm and sunny morning in Bonita Springs, Florida. You had quite a sleep. Now, sit down, and let's have breakfast."

We picked up our sports conversation over orange juice, scrambled eggs, bacon, wheat toast, raspberry jam, and coffee, before the chief started talking about his life in Bonita Springs with Hildegard—how they golfed together, shopped at the mall, took long walks on the beach. Chief Howard Kowalski was wistful and lonely, and I listened with sincere empathy and understanding, as I had so many times with the down-on-their-luckers, whether rich or poor. I knew my role was companionship, even though I was just a scruffy hitchhiker. I figured it was an even trade for the hospitality and the ride.

He snapped out of it after a few minutes and smiled. "Listen to me carrying on. You're a good kid, Mort. Although I'm guessing there's a lot more to you than you're letting on. But that's your business. You know, you're welcome to stay on a day, if you want to. I have some maintenance work I need some help on here, so you can earn your keep. Or if you want to get moving on, I'll give you a ride south to where I-75 ends and Alligator Alley starts up. Whaddya think, Mort?"

"I'd love to help you out today, to pay you back for the ride and meal. I'm thinking of getting started tomorrow morning, if that's all right with you,"

"Sounds good, Mort. Why don't you get your clothes together and run a load of wash, and then we'll get started?"

As it turned out, the maintenance chores were minor and con-trived. After a sandwich break, the chief suggested a round of golf. I had golfed only three times, and after confessing I was a hacker, we drove to the Bonita Glades Public Golf Course, which bordered the Everglades. We used a cart, a first for me, and spent the next three hours spraying golf balls through nine holes of saw grass and marsh-lined fairways and greens. I lied freely about my divorced parents, one in Michigan and one in the Keys, inventing family members and situations that seemed real and natural to both me and the chief. It was a grand afternoon for both of us. When we reentered the condo in early evening, the chief offered his under-age house guest a beer, a gesture of friendship belying our disparate ages and positions. He didn't offer a second one as he grilled ham-burgers for dinner. The night ended as I collected my laundry and turned in early, content again with life on the road.

I woke again to the smell of bacon and coffee and the figurine Scottie still poised next to the alarm clock: 8:00 a.m. I replayed my entry to the kitchen, offering another "good morning, Chief." He was still in the same Bermuda shorts, but with a fresh, gold T-shirt. We didn't talk much, rather shared the *Tampa Tribune*. I packed, and by 9:00 a.m., was out of the condo and in the front seat of the Riviera. The chief had prepared a bag lunch for me and, not known to me yet, included a ten-dollar bill in an envelope under the ham sandwich, apple, and two raisin oatmeal cookies. It was a twenty-minute drive to the drop-off point the chief had selected on I-75. The chief asked me what my opinion was of Bo Schembechler, the University of Michigan's successful coach, who had once coached for Woody Hayes at Ohio State. Now they were fierce rivals. The chief was a Woody man, but he liked Bo. We gently argued back and forth over our favorites' strengths and weaknesses.

I made the Chief chuckle by saying, "Well, Chief. The buckeye doesn't fall far from the tree. They're both three-yards-and-a-cloud-of-dust men."

As we drove the last miles toward the departure point, the chief surprised me. "Mort, do you believe in God and Jesus as your Savior?"

I thought about starting in on the usual: *Sure I do, God is my savior and inspiration* spiel, which is what most adults I knew on and off the road wanted to hear. I paused, sat up straight in the car seat, and told the truth instead of what I thought the chief wanted to hear.

"Well, Chief Kowalski, that's a tough question. Everything I've ever been taught tells me that there's a God who loves and cares for me. That Jesus and what he taught will lead me to a place that's better than what I—we—have on earth. It sounds good, and I believe Jesus was a remarkable human being who left a path full of true messages and examples for us to follow. But accepting Jesus as the one and only pathfinder is just too much of a stretch for me. Billions of other people have their own version of the one true path and God that pretty much offer the same bargain of a better life after we die. It's not hard for me to understand how billions of poor, hungry people trying to get through life one day at a time need to believe that there's some pot of gold at the end of the rainbow. That makes sense to me. I also understand that in a country like ours that is so wealthy, God and religion can give meaning and order to our lives beyond our jobs, homes, cars, and the ups and downs that life deals us. What I have a hard time getting my head around is the overwhelming number of human beings that believe their god is the only god. The exclusivity is frightening. I'd love to hear from a religion that says, 'hey, we've got this great god we believe in. But that god of yours sounds pretty cool, too. And it looks like both our gods are leading us to a better place.'

"What I'm saying is that whether it's Jesus or Mohammed or Buddha or Zeus or the Spirit Guide might not really matter. It's the acceptance of some divine being as God, for that individual, no matter how they get there. If that's the case, then it's hard to argue with the believers, which I'm thinking must number darn close to 99 percent of the people that have ever walked the earth. That leaves a pretty lonely group of 1 percent cutting against the grain. But, Chief, I gotta tell you, I waver back and forth on which group I think I belong to. You were right when you said I haven't told you my whole story. I'm only twenty years old, and there are times when I can tell you that no good god could possibly exist and allow evil to rule and destroy the lives of good people. That black shadow dims all the good I see on some days. I know my pain may seem inconsequential compared to some Ethiopian family watching their babies' bellies swell before they die, believing some god will give them a better place to be after they watch them wither away. Still, it's my own personal misery, and it's lodged deep in my gut. Maybe it all leads to some better place and the suffering of all of us will make us blessed in heaven. I'm just not so sure. In the end, it's what the philosophers tell us; a leap to faith, a belief that Jesus is truly the path, not just a ranting, genius madman. One thing I'm sure about, you can't find a middle ground on God. If you are a believer, God is divine. If you don't, the prophets are just wild-eyed, charismatic dreamers."

I finished my soliloquy, surprised that all of my reading and solitary thinking had erupted into a semi-coherent expression. The chief pulled off the last exit of I-75, the end of a road that started in Sault St. Marie, 1,700 miles north, and three cultures away from the world's largest swamp. He pulled the Riviera over to the sign that announced Alligator Alley. He looked at me with his brow furrowed. He reached over and set his massive hand gently on my shoulder.

"Mort, that was . . . that was . . . well, that was as descriptive a summary of what God is all about as I think I've ever heard. I've been struggling with my faith ever since I lost Hildegard. I've been thinking about all the bad, the evil things I saw as a cop, and wondering how it all fit in with my Presbyterian upbringing. Frankly, Mort, it's been a challenge to my beliefs. I don't know why I asked that question, but, son, you have a handle on the problem. In my case, I do believe in Jesus as my Savior. I've made that leap, but it's across a river of fire and doubt. You, young man, have a gift for putting it into words. You should figure out a way to use that talent. God bless you, son."

"Thanks, Chief. I do a lot of reading, and I sure as hell have a lot more reading and thinking to do before I can get that question answered, if there is an answer. It seems it's worth the effort, though," I replied.

"Amen to that. You know, Mort, I could give you a ride across this road to Fort Lauderdale. There's nothing between here and the coast but marsh, alligators, and mosquitoes. You know I don't have a lot to keep myself occupied, so it's no trouble," the chief said.

"Thanks for the offer, Chief, but I'll be fine. I'm sure I'll get a ride, and to be honest, the waiting for the next ride is part of the adventure."

"Okay, Mort, but if you're stuck for too long, you call me, and I'll get you to the other side," the chief said as he wrote his phone number on an old business card.

"Chief, the name is really Luke, Luke Moore. Sorry about misleading you," I said as I opened the car door and stepped outside.

"You son of a gun, I knew you weren't giving me the straight story. Cop's intuition, you know. Thanks for coming clean. I'd love to know the rest of your story. Maybe another time, young man. I'll tell you this, my old cop's instincts tell me you're a good soul, maybe a bit off the road, but a good man underneath what you're hiding. So God bless you, Luke Moore."

The chief smiled as he watched me collect my bag from the backseat and walk toward Alligator Alley. The Riviera made a U-turn back to the I-75 entrance. I smiled and gave the chief a salute as I stood in the morning sun waiting for a ride.

I looked eastward across Alligator Alley, two straight lanes without the slightest undulation as far as I could see. Heat waves rose from the asphalt, distorting the view of the highway. The morning sun was moving fast above the southeast horizon, where I supposed the bottom of Florida's tropical peninsula ended and the water separating the United States and Cuba began. Sweat formed in my armpits and on my brow. My clean T-shirt clung to my back. A trio of mosquitoes buzzed around my head. I flailed at them, killing two eventually, but two, three, and four appeared in their place. With the temperature rising and mosquitoes swarming, I thought about calling the chief and starting another day with a can of bug repellant.

Traffic was slow, a car passing every ten minutes or so. Finally, a green 1959 Bel Air pulled alongside me, blue smoke billowing out of the tailpipe. A bleached-blonde woman about thirty-five leaned toward the open passenger window and beckoned me with a look and the crook of her index finger.

"You look a little lonely out there, handsome. Where ya headed?" she asked in a Southern drawl.

I thought, *where else could I be heading but the other side of the swamp? There's nothing between here and Fort Lauderdale, is there?* But I answered politely, "Miami, ma'am. Where are you headed this fine Florida morning?"

"I'm going to Hollywood," she laughed. "Not Hollywood, California, of course, but Hollywood, Florida. I can get you pretty close to Miami. Now, before I let you in, take a step back and let me look at your aura. I don't wanna be picking up no low-life scum that might cause trouble for a single woman like me, you know!"

I took a step back from the car and smiled wanly. The blonde squinted through the open window and looked me up and down for a long minute.

"Hmmm, you have a lot going on in your aura, young man. It's just about leapin' off you into this car and beyond. Whooee, I don't think I've ever seen this combination of color and energy. Nothing bad, though, just a lot of mixed-up, high-po-ten-cy energy. All right, then, in you go. Let's get this show on the road."

I put my bag in the backseat, thinking, *She's out there, but harmless.* As I sat in the front seat and closed the car door, she extended her hand and said, "I'm Cecilia Barnes, pleased to meet you, Energy Man."

"I'm Luke Moore, and thank you very much for picking me up."

Cecilia decided to tag me as Big Aura. She was a wired woman filled with nervous energy. She was about five foot one, sitting on top of cushions that allowed her to see over the top of the steering wheel, which she clung tightly to as she spit out her story frantically.

"Here we are now, traveling together, Mr. Big Aura, headed across the mystical Everglades, where evil and good meet every day in the mist and muck. Reptiles and fish and birds living in a violent prehistoric environment oblivious to our human existence until some goddamn fan boat races across this godforsaken swamp interrupting all that is natural and real, ripping a seam into nature and disrupting all the natural balance that nature took a billion years to put in place! I mean, nature manifested here can be a bloody, horrible place with gators ripping an injured flamingo to shreds in a horrific show of the food chain manifesting its power. But, Luke, that is nature's way. You enter the way of man into this mix with machines and greed and lust and it screws up the whole balance of things. You certainly have to agree with that, don't you?" Cecilia finished, her eyes wide, her knuckles white on the steering wheel, looking at me for assent.

I thought, *Oh, no, a nut job, worse than I thought, but probably manageable if I go along with her.*

"Ma'am, I'm not from around here, but your way of thinking makes a lot of sense to me," I said.

Cecilia relaxed just a bit, settling back into her seat, and said, "I knew you would understand. I wouldn't open up this fast to just anyone. Let me tell you how I came to understand the universe and how it unfolds to anyone who has the fortitude to accept nature's manifest plan for all of us."

She took the next thirty minutes to explain how her hardscrabble past had led her to crossing the Everglades in a broken-down Chevy with me as her coincidental companion.

A product of a broken, incestuous home in Biloxi, Mississippi, Cecilia escaped to a foster home where discipline was administered with a paddle on a bare bottom. She didn't care about the paddle, or anything else for that matter. She started shoplifting, which led her to a girls' juvenile facility where punishment was atrocious, including solitary confinement with visits from women guards with broomsticks. Redemption was several years away after her release at age seventeen. Several years of prostitution followed in Birmingham, Mobile, and Atlanta, and incarceration in a women's prison.

Most of her life she could remember was in an institution, and she finally tried to rise above her seemingly inevitable fate. She ended up in an ashram just outside Gainesville, Florida. There she learned deviated versions of Eastern religions and the power of individual auras and nature. It was the first partially positive experience in her young life, even though the free-love aspects of the ashram didn't include payment for the use of her body in frequent sexual liaisons with every number of the hippie group, including what would have been called "gang bangs" in less polite company. She finally left and found work as a waitress, hotel maid, or any other position that would keep her afloat. Cecilia had limited formal education, but she had become a hungry reader in prison, discovering science, nature, and ecology as her favorite subjects. She was a bright woman dimmed by a hard life.

She told her life story with such intense sincerity that I didn't feel sorry for her. She had somehow managed to survive and kept a positive perspective. Cecilia was an itinerant worker and part-time hooker, keeping her head just above the water, mostly. She laconically told accounts of the men who had entered and exited her life. Once again, I heard a tale of life filled with pain that easily matched and exceeded my own. I respected this smallish, washed-out, part-time hooker who was racing to another dead-end waitress job in Hollywood, Florida, but with a sunny attitude and an eye for good aura.

Alligator Alley was eighty-five miles long, a straight shot from Naples into Fort Lauderdale. Cecilia's Chevy labored under the speed limit at only fifty miles an hour. I figured we would get to Hollywood, which was just south of Fort Lauderdale, around 7:00

p.m. I felt confident Cecilia would be easily convinced to take me to Miami and the Delgado family home in exchange for gas money.

My relationship with the Delgados was unusual. The family had moved from Miami to Michigan to continue a life that had restarted when the family fled Cuba in 1966. They were quiet about their emigration, which I learned about after splitting a six-pack of Stroh's on the railroad tracks with my classmate, Gus.

He and his brother Vincent were eleven and twelve years old when they left Havana. They had to start completely over in Detroit, spending six months in the tough Herman Gardens projects before their father saved enough to move them to a bungalow in the leafy suburb of Huntington Woods, adjacent to Royal Oak.

Gus was a freshman and Vince a sophomore when they enrolled at St. Mary's. Both were darkly handsome, good athletes, and better students. Vince, more than Gus, dabbled in the wildness of the Lost Souls, but their respect for their conservative and very strict Catholic parents kept them in check. A visit to the Delgados' home in Huntington Woods was like touring a foreign country, with Spanish spoken quickly and the distinct smell of Cuban dinners filling the home. Mrs. Delgado was wary of whom her sons befriended, but warmed up to me and John as the visits increased and the good manners taught at the Moore and Parcell homes won her. Gus's five younger brothers wrestled with us and tried to teach us soccer as our cultures meshed. After his junior year, Gus told me that the family was moving back to Miami. We were all crushed. Gus would have been a star in all the sports at St. Mary's his senior year. We vowed to stay in close contact. This was a personal strong point. My first hitchhiking trip was to Miami, a week after graduating from high school. I was greeted warmly in the crowded Delgado home, Mrs. Delgado appalled and amazed that I had hitchhiked all the way from Royal Oak.

"You are foolish, Luke. Why would you do such a thing?" she asked every day I visited in Miami. There wasn't an explanation she would accept. I just smiled and agreed, assuring Mrs. Delgado I would take a bus home.

I knew the Delgados would welcome me again. I thought Larry Lavalier might be a good contact to help me get my feet on the ground. This time I was looking to establish a beachhead; I was on more than just a lark. If I wanted Marta to follow, I would have to find work and a place for us to live. This was new territory for me. I had something to lose. And just under the surface of my own life, I knew this trip to Miami could lead to the completion of unfinished business: my promise to Annette.

The green Chevy backfired and shook me out of my reflection. Cecilia had been talking nonstop for half an hour, while I heard half of her evaluation of the great marsh that surrounded us on all sides. She began to repeat her rants.

"We're in the middle of hundreds of miles of nature, nature so powerful that if left alone it would devour anything in its path. It's nature, Luke! Look around, the energy is unbelievable. Right now, just off this road, the battle of good and evil is being fought by snakes, gators, lizards, fish, birds, and a billion insects. Something's getting eaten right now. And something's escaping its death. I can hear the battle, Luke, can you?"

The car backfired again, interrupting Cecilia's train of thought and the need for my obligation to answer her question.

"Oh, no, we're losing power," Cecilia cried. The Chevy shuddered, shut down, and coasted, Cecilia steering onto the shoulder next to the sign that announced, "You Are Entering the Missaukee Indian Reservation."

"Damn it! This isn't a good sign. There's bad energy going down here. We need to get this car moving, Luke, and get the hell out of here. I can feel it! Can't you?"

I did my best to calm Cecilia down, who was visibly agitated and trembling. "Hey, it's okay, we'll see if we can get the car started. But if we can't, and I'm not much of a mechanic, somebody will stop by to help us. I can feel it," I pronounced energetically, trying to offset Cecilia's fear.

"You feel it? The energy is bad here, Luke, real bad!"

I put my hand on Cecilia's forearm and said, "Don't worry, I'm here with you. This isn't so bad. Let's get the hood up and see what's up." But the fear in her eyes was real. I could almost feel it when I touched her. And for an instant, I heard my own foreboding rumble. I shook it off, getting out of the car and playing with the hood's latch until it opened and I propped it up. I knew next to nothing about cars, but I had seen Mark McInerny play around with the carburetor before, so I carefully unscrewed the hot wing nut on top of the air filter and lifted it off. As I did, a car passed us fast, then hit the brakes hard and skidded to the shoulder a hundred feet ahead of us. I watched the bed of the Dodge pickup truck reverse just as Cecilia appeared at the front of the Bel Air. The truck stopped abruptly ten feet in front of us, and two muscular men in matching, dirty white tank tops jumped out of either side of the truck's cab and moved toward us too quickly for comfort.

Then the sound of the hum, my hum, rumbled in full. It was resonant and haunting this time. It rose in volume. I felt it more than heard it. The sound crescendoed into a subsonic boom that jolted me. *It's a warning.* I looked over at a cowering Cecilia as the men reached us. I knew something bad was going to happen and felt nauseous, almost gagging. I caught myself and walked over to Cecelia.

Both men were over six feet tall and had a hungry muscularity. The driver had a bottle of Pabst Blue Ribbon in hand. He had a close-cropped haircut and a tattoo of a dragon covering his right shoulder and large bicep. The other man had a matching haircut and waved a half-bottle of Wild Turkey as he approached. They brought unfriendly smiles, and their bloodshot eyes told me they were at the end of a long night.

The tattooed man sidled up too close to Cecilia and said, "Well, lookee here, a pretty blonde bitch and her hippie boyfriend have broken down in the middle of nowhere."

"Ain't that a cryin' fuckin' shame, Harlan," the Wild Turkey man said.

"That's right, Harlan," the other man responded. "A cryin' fuckin' shame. We should help this little couple out, shouldn't we? Be real neighborly, right, Harlan?"

Harlan put his hand on Cecilia's head. She was hunched over, looking at the ground. "We should be real, real neighborly with this little piece of ass," Harlan said.

I quietly said, "Hey, you guys are both named Harlan? What a coincidence. We really appreciate your help, but we have a carful of friends just behind us who will be here any minute, so we really don't need your help. But thanks anyway for stopping and—"

Wild Turkey Harlan cut me off. "Shut the fuck up, hippie boy. You got it right, I'm Harlan-your-worst-fucking-nightmare, and this good ol' boy is Harlan-gonna-kick-your-fucking-ass."

From this point, everything unfolded badly and in fast forward. Wild Turkey Harlan moved in on me as Tattooed Harlan threw Cecilia onto the ground in front of him. I was hit with an overhand right, and as I fell, I threw myself at Tattooed Harlan and knocked him down to the ground, pummeling his head with my fists, two, three, four times before Wild Turkey Harlan was on top of me, trying to pull me off.

"Run, Cecilia, run," I yelled, amazed that she was able to scramble onto her feet and run off the side of the road into the deep saw grass.

I felt their fists first, then their boots as I curled up in a ball. The pain was excruciating at first. One boot was pointy, and the kicks stabbed. One Harlan swung a work boot, and the rounded toe met my body like a two-by-four.

I could hear them scream, "You stupid motherfucker. You faggot hippie fuck. We'll fuck you over, big time," until their voices faded to a muffle. I knew I was being beaten, but I couldn't feel their blows anymore. Before I slid into blackness, my last thoughts spun wildly.

Was I being beaten within an inch of my life? Or was it a few inches, maybe a foot? How could I tell?

Then the agonizingly familiar image of my dad jolted me. I couldn't conjure up an image to thwart him. My head felt like it was going to explode. I was dying, and he was going to be there when I slipped into the abyss. Was he the abyss? I panicked and Dad turned gray; everything went dark.

I gasped, the blackness sputtered, and faint pulses of light appeared, and the ghostly figures of the two state troopers outside Cincinnati, Glenn and Gilbert, and Sisters Jean Rosina and Rose Margaret appeared. One of the troopers was blowing into a long telescopic tube made of copper or brass with elaborate cloisonné decorations. It was nearly ten feet long and curved up slightly as it met the ground. It emitted a rumbling, otherworldly sound. The other cop was talking. I couldn't hear him at first.

"It's a *dung-chen,* Luke. Beautiful isn't it? It's used by the Tibetans to remind them that the music of nature can unite Heaven and Earth, and eternal truth can be found in both our world and yours. Of course, Officer Leo here—" the cop pointed to his partner "—likes to use it as a fog horn to wake people up when danger is afoot!"

Officer Leo smiled, and I laughed. He passed the horn carefully to Sister Jean, who made the Tibetan trumpet emit a lighter, melodious tone. Sister Rose smiled, watching her partner play.

"Ah," Sister Rose said. "Now that's how a dung-chen should be played. It's Buddhist, you know, Luke. They believe that these low sounds, when played off the mountain, create a marvelous echo and can influence a person's way of thinking. Cosmically speaking, of course. These cops wouldn't know a good dung-chen chop if it hit them in the face!" That made the cops, nuns, and nurses aides all laugh, and the hum echoed into a declining reverberation as they disappeared.

I heard voices talking over each other and had to concentrate to make out who they were and what they were saying. It was Marta, Mrs. Brady, and Kate at first, all repeating conversations from the past year.

I struggled to hear what Marta was saying, trying to separate her from the other voices. "I do believe I'm falling in love with you," she said, followed by her loud, earthy laughter. The women's voices came together again, and, while I couldn't make out the words, they were soft and comforting.

Light flashed and flickered. A deepening wave overtook me. As the voices faded, I saw Marta's face, her robust lips saying something I couldn't hear. Voices entered the dream again. I heard Annette and my mother. Then I saw them, sitting on an old sofa, relaxed, smiling and laughing, talking lightly to each other.

My mom said to Annette, "Oh, that Luke, you have to love him. Inside that head of his are ideas just waiting to explode. He is a handful, and I know I'll be worrying about him forever. But he has a world of joy bottled up in him that I can't wait to see unfold. He is my lovely, complicated little boy."

My mom looked at me and said, "Son, finding Annette in this other place was a gift from God. We have a lot in common, but most importantly, we have you. We thought you could use a little help, so we did what we could from our side. We sent some of our friends. They *are* characters, aren't they?"

Annette laughed, and then turned and looked directly at me. She was saying something to me. I strained to hear and then the words jumped out at me. "Gerard LaFleur. Talk to my dad. You'll know what to do then."

Annette smiled and put her hands on top of Roberta Moore's hand. They both looked straight ahead as the bright light enveloped them until only their piercing eyes were visible to me.

"I love you, son," Mom said as the light brightened intensely and the swirl of voices returned momentarily until only Marta remained. I curled up in her arms. She stroked my hair once and her hand rested on my forehead. The voices fell silent and the light disappeared.

Chapter 29

September 2003

The slightly startled information booth attendant had phone numbers for the Mackinac County Sheriff's Department and the state police stationed in St. Ignace. She wrote both numbers down on the back of a Tahquamenon Falls brochure. I walked around the main rest-area building down to the dog run, where tourists were airing out their golden retrievers, poodles, and mutts. I draped my jacket over one arm and punched the state police number into my cell phone. As I reached to hit the send button, I saw the blur of a foot, too late. A boot struck my forearm, and the cell phone skittered across the grass.

"You don't want to do that, Mr. Moore." A wild-eyed Tom Lutac was on me like a hungry cat, one hand on my neck, the other pressing the point of a knife between two ribs. He guided me away from the dogs and their owners to a small grove of trees and bushes. He moved us swiftly; I wasn't the first person he had strong-armed.

"Let's do this easy, Mr. Moore. That was a nice move to get your sweet daughter and wife out of the car. But it's not quite that easy. You and I are going to head back to your van, and we're going to have a little talk about how Mrs. Moore and Roberta are going to finish this trip. No one gets hurt if I get what I'm after."

Sociopath, psychopath—my professional diagnosis was needless. He wasn't capable of speaking the truth.

"You hear me, Mr. Moore? We're going to walk real slow back to the van and get this over with. I promise you, if you make a move, I'll find your daughter or your wife, and I will cut them up bad. And, Mr. Psychology, I think you know I mean exactly what I fucking say. Right?"

"Right, Tom." I put my head down compliantly.

"That's the spirit. Now, start walking."

He took his hand off my neck and put it on my elbow, guiding me from behind. I could feel the knife point jab me each step we took. I knew this was going to finish badly. The only guess was where. It damn well wasn't going to end anywhere near my family. It had to be here and now. Are we there yet? Yep. Was any of the old immortality left?

Ready to make my move, tendons and muscles tensed. Blood rushed past my eardrums, rumbling. One more step, and this ended. Then her voice shouted out with anger and fear.

"*Luke!*" I saw Marta running down the incline toward us, her eyes knowing that trouble was upon us.

Tom turned at Marta's scream. I turned quickly, my elbow and forearm catching his nose. It was enough to break free without getting stabbed. Now I had an angry, bloodied bull in front of me with his knife extended, and my wife running toward both of us. I put myself between them and yelled over my shoulder to Marta. "Turn around, Marta, and call the cops."

She stopped just behind me and said, "Roberta's getting help. Leave us alone now, Tom. You don't want to hurt anyone."

Tom wiped his nose with his shirtsleeves and smiled sardonically. "Your husband is dead, lady. And you're next."

He charged at me, but I was lit up with adrenalin and the powerful instinct to protect what meant most to me. I sidestepped past him and away from Marta. He charged again, and I used my denim jacket as a cape of sorts, to keep some distance from his blade.

I can't say that my thoughts were fully formed, but as I dodged, backing away from Marta, a visage of Cecilia pulsed past me, then the two Harlans' faces, like Halloween masks.

Run for your life, Cecilia. Run away, Marta, run.

I couldn't run. But I wasn't curled up in a ball this time. This maniac had to go through me. I waved my jacket in front of him. This washed-up matador wasn't dodging cars. I was trying to keep the mad bull off me and away from my wife.

Marta didn't run. I didn't see what she held in her hand as she ran down the hill toward us. She startled me by not backing away from our awkward parries and thrusts. I half-sensed, half-saw her following us, resolutely. Tom lunged again, grabbing my jacket, pulling me forward a step before I let go. His knife lashed out at me again and found my exposed arm. I stumbled backward, and his eyes lit up like a B-movie vampire as he moved in on me. Marta rushed him and swung the minivan's tire iron upside his head, twice. His body had a cartoonish quality as he staggered forward a step. His knees melted and he was on the ground. Marta stood over him, the crowbar above her head. Her expression bore an eerie similarity to Tom's when he was coming in for the kill.

Tom didn't move. Marta's face changed. She looked over at me, worried at the sight of blood covering my arm. Travelers came down the hill. I moved to Marta and took her elbow to lower the tire iron. Her eyes were glazy and her lower lip trembled, but she didn't cry.

A big man reached us and looked down at Tom. "Ma'am, you cleaned his clock good. I saw the whole thing. Cops are pulling up now. I'll stick around and make sure this guy don't cause any more trouble. How bad's that arm, fella?'

I looked down and saw about a six-inch gash. It wasn't deep, but it was seeping crimson, making it look worse than it was. "It's not bad."

Marta snapped to attention at my voice. "Let me look at that." Marta was a registered nurse, and I was the family wimp. "Lots of stitches and some good stories sure to follow. But you're white as a ghost. You're going to wake up from this bad dream and start shaking. Let's get you up to the parking lot and a first aid kit."

We turned to walk up the hill. Small groups of tourists gawked. Two cops appeared at the top of the hill with Roberta. They were both very tall and wore oversize sunglasses. I started to get woozy. The hum melted away as I fainted.

Chapter 30

T here were no voices or bright light. There were no thoughts. Like a distant drumbeat getting closer, I only knew a searing, unyielding pain. There was a suffocating pressure in the center of my mind. Time was irrelevant, jarring back and forth from infinity to instants. I sensed only the pressure, a throbbing metronome spreading like a rapidly blooming rose, working its way down my entire body into a deadening, agonizing ache into the center of my bones. My body knew I was alive, but that was it.

It had taken three days in a coma before my body acknowledged the first bite of pain, and another week to wind its way through my entire nervous system. I was in the intensive care ward of the hospital for a week before the first thought jumped into my brain. *I'm thirsty.* This led to a jumble of truncated and disassembled emotions, ideas and thoughts. I was fighting something, for something, but without understanding what. Images from movies, television shows, and rock songs began to creep into my mind. I saw John telling a story. I laughed in my mind's eye. The mélange of notions and visualizations began to link and take shape; ego meeting id through the Demerol drip and slow healing.

Days later, I knew who I was. Luke Moore. A vision of Marta crept into view, and I held the idea of her. Images of Ann, Donnie, Angela, April, my mom and dad appeared. The pain overcame thoughts again before finally, my eyes fluttered and opened. My pupils dilated wildly and then focused on Marta, her eyes closed, lines showing on her face. Her hand was on my forehead, matching my last full thought before death had arrived and departed. I fell back into a deep sleep, the first alive sleep I had felt since the pummeling.

When I woke, Marta was still there, hunched over my bed. She lifted her head, saw my open eyes, and lit up.

"Luke, Luke! I'm here, I love you, come back to me. Don't leave me." She covered me with kisses on my cheeks and forehead and lips, her hands surrounding my head.

From there, it was a slow, but steady recovery and recognition of how badly the two Harlans had beaten the living hell out of me. It took a week before I was able to converse and learn what had transpired since the last boot had landed on my back. The injury tally was long. They had broken my left arm and my head had swollen into a lumpy mess. Curling up into the fetal position had saved my face bones from being broken, but they didn't miss much else. My entire body was bruised deeply with serious injuries to my internal organs. The tissue surrounding my spine was so traumatized and inflamed the doctors initially couldn't tell how badly I was injured. When the swelling retreated, the damage was determined not to be permanent.

Waking was the first step of long regimen of therapy and healing. I had dodged death and survived, but I was tattered. My sense of time had been altered, and while minutes seemed like hours, I didn't care. As I healed, I was numb. This recovery was a snail's race. As I inched along, it was as if I was watching myself in a long, boring art film with subtitles.

When my mind felt less like Swiss cheese and my response to my visitors was more than a languorous stare, Marta told me how I had been saved.

It was Chief Kowalski who had arrived at the scene of the beating. Marta explained how the chief had stopped at a local Naples restaurant after dropping me off at Alligator Alley. As he stood in line to pay his bill after a slow cup of coffee, an elderly couple behind him struck up a conversation with him. The chief said that the couple was strangely consternated, asking him questions about his morning activities until he revealed to them that he had dropped off a hitchhiker a short while ago. He told Marta that the couple looked remarkably alike, like twin brother and sister. They both had thick white hair and were impeccably dressed in matching white Lacoste polo shirts with monogrammed alligators on the chest.

When he mentioned dropping off the hitchhiker, they became agitated, and the old woman told the chief, "How could you leave that poor lad out there to hitchhike across that swamp? He's in trouble, you know!"

The old man chimed in, saying, "You know that boy needs your help, don't you?"

The chief told Marta that the funny thing was that he knew what they were saying was true. He had a premonition, a cop's instinct, that something bad was going to happen.

He paid his bill quickly and decided to track me down. After an hour's drive, halfway across the Everglades, he saw the Chevrolet Bel Air on the side of the road, the Plymouth pickup parked in front of it. As he slowed his Riviera, he saw the two men, and as their eyes met, he saw my bloody body lying between the two vehicles. They sprinted for the truck, but Chief Kowalski was in his element. He pulled the Riviera abruptly in front of the truck, cutting off any escape route. He reached under the seat and pulled out a long-handled flashlight and a service revolver.

Adrenalin overcame age. The chief spun into action quickly and violently as he accosted my attackers, bringing down Tattooed Harlan with a flashlight to the back of his knees and then to the back of his neck, leaving him prone on the road. Wild Turkey tried to run ahead of the truck, but the chief caught him in ten yards, administering the flashlight again, knees and neck. He moved nimbly for a large, older man, grabbing Wild Turkey by the neck, marching him back to the Riveria, keeping an eye on Tattooed Harlan, still writhing on the road. He popped open the trunk, pulled out a suitcase, opened it with one hand, and grabbed two pairs of handcuffs. He cuffed Wild Turkey Harlan behind his back and threw him in the back of the Riviera. Springing to Tattooed Harlan, he did the same. The chief scooped me up and gently placed me in the front seat of his car.

He realized we were halfway between Fort Lauderdale and Naples, and chose east, where he figured the hospitals would be better equipped to handle my injuries. He drove over a hundred miles an hour, leaning over the front seat to the two Harlans with the Lugar pointed at them, telling them, "Okay, deadbeats, you have one minute to tell me what happened before I stop this car and feed you to the crocs, capisce?"

The thugs were quick to confess, which produced a dilemma. Should he go back and try to find the girl, or continue on? At his rate of speed, he knew he would find a phone in thirty minutes or less, and I looked bad, so he sped onward. He reached the town of Weston in thirty-three minutes and pulled over at a gas station with a pay phone.

"Move and you'll die," he told his prisoners before leaving the car and depositing his dime for the Florida State Police.

The state police advised him to drive to the Fort Lauderdale hospital, and they would expedite troopers to search for Cecilia. He roared the Riviera to the Fort Lauderdale Community Hospital, where an emergency room doctor told him that St. John's in Miami was better equipped to handle someone in my precarious condition. Chief Kowalski watched as an ambulance sped off with me inside. Fort Lauderdale police arrested the Harlans and led them, limping, to the county jail to be booked.

I remembered most of Marta's version of the chief's story. I knew he had saved my life. I knew the unusual duo in the coffee shop had saved my life. I knew that Marta had saved my life. I knew that Annette had saved my life. I knew my sister Ann, Donnie, April, Angela, and the Lost Souls had a hand in the rescue. And I knew my mom was still there to save me. I knew it was all connected.

Marta was my lifeline to recovery, coordinating everything after she drove nonstop from Cincinnati in a friend's car with her mother's blessing. The chief had pulled my address book from my bag and made the phone calls to family and friends. Ann had flown to Miami the day after the beating and spent three days hovering over me as I lay in a coma. Marta was already in my recovery room when Ann arrived. They watched me together. Ann understood it was okay to leave me under Marta's watchful eye when she had to return to keep her job and care of Donnie.

Ann had flown in with Kate Brady, both of their fares gifts from Helen Brady, who arrived soon after Marta, Ann, and Kate. Helen assumed the role of field marshal for my recuperation, renting a spacious three-bedroom apartment next to St. John's and insisting she cover all expenses.

Helen spent the next two weeks in Miami, waiting for improvements in my condition before finally returning to Knoxville. She also arranged for Marta to fly home and make arrangements for additional caregivers for her mother Lila at Helen's expense. Marta's mom was stable, and Helen's monetary contributions took the immediate anxiety of two dying loved ones off of Marta's shoulders.

I learned I was in St. John the Baptist's Hospital, run by the Dominican nuns, the same order that taught at St. Mary's.

"You just can't quite seem to escape the Catholics," Marta said. I laughed out loud for the first time.

The generosity of friends became apparent as I recovered. Helen sponsored airfare for a parade of people: April, Donnie, Kate, John Parcell, Mark McInerny, Elvis, and Lois. They joined Chief Kowalski and the Delgado family. It was a reunion, first at the Delgado family home, where they traded stories. Chief Kowalski found his role as a hero among my family and friends unsettling at first. But, amidst the constant hugs and tears, he found the solace and comfort he had missed since losing Hildegard.

I had mended enough to see the entire group—family, old friends and new. Ann, April, Angela, and Donnie doted while John, Mark, and Elvis made fun of my incapacitated condition. Kate and Helen reassured me about my rehabilitation. Vince and Gus Delgado told me that I was an honorary citizen of Miami, with Gus surprising all of us with his announcement that he had recently joined the Dade County Sheriff's Department. That allowed Chief Kowalski a point of reference and comfort in the midst of the eclectic group.

Marta sat by my side, holding my hand. I soaked up the love and attention, still immersed in pain and painkillers. Helen orchestrated a visiting schedule after the initial reunion that didn't overwhelm me and allowed for the long rehab that lay ahead. She rented an apartment for Marta in Miami after approval from Ann. Big Ann relinquished her primary claim to me after watching Marta at my bedside. When Marta needed to be back in Cincinnati with her mom for her cancer treatments, Helen flew in one of my sisters, along with Mark, John, and Elvis. As I recovered, I was overwhelmed by Helen's generosity, knowing that the cost of my medical bills and the rehab was already in the tens of thousands of dollars.

Helen was obdurate with me when she visited, when I tried to thank her. "Let me make this perfectly clear, Luke Moore. You have no choice when it comes to how I spend my money. I love you like my sons, and I will never forget what you mean to me and my family. I just want you to promise that you will never, ever hitchhike again!"

I laughed through the pain. "That's a pretty stiff price, don't you think?"

As time passed, I started to better understand how close to death I had come. Improvements in my condition came slowly, with good days and bad. A good day came when Cecilia came to visit.

She had survived, and that was as remarkable to me as the miracle of my rescue. I had thought it was her time to die, and so had she. It turned out differently. Cecilia came into my room with the chief. She wore a yellow sundress and had a little color in her cheeks. She nervously pulled a strand of hair into her mouth and waited at the hospital room door as the chief started toward the two visitor chairs next to my bed. The chief stopped and turned back toward her.

"C'mon, Cecilia, Luke is glad to see you. Right, Luke?'

I pushed myself up on my pillow. I could see she was taken aback by my lumpy and discolored head.

"Hey, Cecilia, I'm glad you came by. Sorry I look so bad. You are sight for sore eyes. You look terrific."

She smiled weakly, and with her chin hanging near her shoulder, she moved across the room and sat in the chair next to the chief.

"I'm glad we didn't die out there, Luke. I think you and the chief saved my life."

"Me too, Cecilia. The chief ended up saving both of us. I know how he found me, but I'm not sure on all the details on how he found you. You mind telling me the story, Chief?"

"You know, it's not my nature to tell war stories, but finding the two of you in the middle of the Everglades has softened me. I guess you two deserve all the details. Stop me if I start boring you."

The chief settled back in his chair and gave a cop's report.

"After watching you get carried off in the ambulance to the hospital, I rushed back to Alligator Alley to look for Cecilia. By the time I arrived, the state police had gone into the swamp in waders without finding a trace of her. I sat on the hood of my Riviera and watched Cecilia's car being hoisted by a tow truck.

"State Police Officer Wade approached me and said, 'Sir, we'll be sending some fan boats into the Glades to see if we can find her, but it doesn't look good. We're going to wrap up here and be on our way.'

"'I think I'll stick around for a while, Officer.'"

"'That's fine, sir. We will need you to help us with the paper-work on the two scumbags. Tomorrow will be fine,' Officer Wade replied to me. I told him I'd be there at 8:00 a.m. sharp. The officer nodded and walked toward his car. I asked him if he had a smoke. The officer smiled and said, 'Sure, Chief. Here. Take the pack.' He handed me a pack of Tareytons and a book of matches. 'Much obliged,' I said. Officer Wade tipped his hat and walked away.

"I tapped a cigarette out of the pack, put the charcoal filter to my lips, and took a long drag. It was the first cigarette I had touched since the day I retired. I always had a cop's coffee and cigarette addiction. They just fit so nice together. This was my first arrest in over ten years, and I was shook up. I needed an old cop's fix.

"Two hours later, I finished the pack. The sun had crossed over to the Gulf's side. It wasn't going to be long until sunset. Maybe two dozen cars had passed as I sat and waited. Two cars even pulled over to see if I needed help. I walked up and down the roadbed about a mile each way, looking hard into the side of the swamp the girl had run into. I saw nothing but clouds of bugs and heat rising off the marsh. There was nothing more I could do. I climbed back into my car and stared out over the steering wheel. I decided to drive to Miami and find out how Luke was doing. I knew it was going to be touch-and-go.

"I started the car up and pulled onto Alligator Alley slowly. I squinted into the fading sun, taking what I thought was one last, hopeless look. I drove at twenty miles an hour for a quarter-mile, and as I pushed the accelerator hard, I adjusted the rearview mirror. I saw Cecilia.

"I swung the car into a broad U-turn and saw her crawling, trying to stand. I was out of the car, and she collapsed in my arms.

I put her in the front seat and made another mad dash toward Fort Lauderdale. I remember I gave Cecilia a cup of lemonade from my thermos. I'll never forget what she told me. 'I have seen the face of evil and lived. God bless you.' Then she closed her eyes and slept with the cup in her lap sloshing lemonade back and forth."

Cecilia blushed at the quote. The chief had become her mentor. He had no illusions about Cecelia's capability of holding her own in life. He had found a rooming house for her, helped her find a job in a Fort Lauderdale restaurant, and loaned her money to fix the Bel Air. They talked on the phone every other day and went over a list of goals the chief had helped her develop. At the top of her list was: *don't be afraid* and *find love.* They talked on the phone on how she might put herself in position to find those things.

We chatted awhile about this and that until Cecilia stood up and said, "Well, I'd better be going."

She leaned over and kissed me on the forehead and said, "I'm glad we both survived."

I held her wrist and whispered, "You were right, Cecilia. About the evil. I could feel it, too and hear it—a rumble or a horn or something. I've heard it before."

As she turned to leave, she told me, "Luke, I heard the sound of a horn, too, you know. I heard it and I felt it. It was warning you, not me. I already knew we were going to die. You have something protecting you. We should have died out there. I knew you had a big aura."

Her eyes were frightened again, like out on Alligator Alley, and they gave me a chill.

She shook a little, and the smile returned to her eyes. She hugged the chief and waved good-bye to me, calling out as she left my room. "Get on with your life now, Luke."

The chief leaned forward in his chair toward me.

"You know, you probably saved her life, Luke. Who knows what those two would have done to her."

I shook my head and said, "I should have listened to her. She knew something bad was going to happen, and I just ignored her. I tried to help her, but to think she just disappeared into the Everglades after all she said . . . maybe I shouldn't have told her to run."

"There are a lot of maybes in life, Luke. Maybe I should have returned to find Cecilia instead of getting you to the hospital first. Maybe I should have never left you to hitchhike across the Everglades. But I didn't, and I did, and here we are, and Cecilia made it. Who knows why? I'll tell you, Luke, I'm glad I met you, Marta, Mrs. Brady, and the whole crew you have praying for your good health. You have been through a world of shit—excuse my French—but you are a survivor, son, with a whole bunch of people rooting you on. What I've learned is there is a time to mourn and then start living again. That's what I learned from this unholy episode. I was just rotting away since Hildegard passed away. While you've been lying in the hospital bed, I remembered I was pretty good at spotting the good kid getting ready to go bad. So I volunteered down at the Naples probation office, and I'm working with three kids. And Cecilia. I might add, Mr. Mortimer Molesky, that after hearing the stories about the real Luke Moore, you're on probation with me, too!"

Three months after my arrival with a wrecked body and barely alive, I was released from St. John's. I moved to the apartment Mrs. Brady had leased, with a part-time nurse, whom I had unsuccessfully lobbied against. Friends and family rotated through in weekly stints to help me through rehab sessions at St. John's. Marta's mother, Lila, was in remission, but she needed Marta's nursing and income. Marta had taken her mother's place at Karen's Kafe, so she could only visit for two days at a time. My family and friends were all employed, and although Mrs. Brady insisted in ferrying them back and forth to Miami, I informed Helen that I was well enough to continue therapy alone. There was a fight, but I was adamant and finally won an argument: a sure sign I was recovering. After confirming the chief's support that he would check in on me once a week, the arrangement was agreed upon. My injuries were healing rapidly, and there was no permanent damage to my guts. I had bouts with dizziness and occasional vertigo, but the doctors were carefully optimistic I would recover fully with time. A couple more months of rehab and I would be a free man. I started to plan. I was certain Marta and I would live together. I also knew it was time to stay in one place and get a job and start college. The rest was in flux. I had exchanged long letters with Marta, discussing the necessity of settling in Cincinnati near Lila.

The beating had one other effect: I was no longer immortal. It wasn't a mighty revelation, just the acknowledgment of the inevitable after coming within an inch of losing my sorry-ass life. Living on the road, on the knife's edge, had a powerful pull, but it wasn't sustainable. While it provided moments of startling clarity and thrill, I saw that it was also an addiction.

I realized and accepted that a life filled with periods of tedium was compensated by the unrolling comforts of love with a woman and the surrounding relationships, as satisfying over the long run as the rush of the road and living alone by one's wits. It was a reconciliation I could live with. I also knew it was an acknowledgement of beginning to run toward life instead of away. No matter where I landed up, it would be with Marta, building a life.

I ventured out beyond the hospital and my apartment as I gained strength and spent time at the Delgado family home. One night, I rode with police cadet Gus Delgado in his car, and, without much of a segue, asked him if he knew anything about a nightclub called La Bohème in Miami Beach.

"You mean the Queer Lounge? What do you want to know about that for?"

I framed the Brady story carefully, telling about Kate's dad and how this all fit into my unusual relationship with the Brady family. I did not reveal my hidden purpose. I asked Gus if he would mind giving me a ride to Mr. Brady's nightclub. Gus shrugged and pointed his car toward the bridge leading to Miami Beach. Gus had a cop's disdain for homosexuals, but he told me the police accommodated the club because it didn't cause the daily problems they found with more dangerous behaviors, like the emerging problems with the Colombian drug traffickers. I asked Gus to pull over just past the club and told him I was going in to try my luck with meeting Mr. Brady. I didn't ask him to come in with me, and he didn't volunteer.

"It's your call, Luke. I'm sure it's harmless enough if you don't mind fending off the dirty old men. You need a ride back, you call me."

"I'll be fine. I'll take a bus back, but thanks for the offer."

Gus pulled a U-turn toward his home in southwest Miami. It was a steamy night in Miami Beach. I looked down the street at the neon sign in turquoise and pink, and felt my chest tighten and began to perspire. This was the beginning of the end of this story.

Chapter 31

September 2003

My bullfight, ended by my angry and lethal wife, was followed by a visit to the hospital for twenty-two stitches. I traveled in the back of a police car, lights flashing and sirens wailing. Marta and Roberta followed in the van. Another police car brought Tom Lutac to the same emergency room. He was incoherent, but dangerous enough to make the hospital trip in handcuffs. We were discharged in tandem and then found ourselves in the St. Ignace Police Station at the same time. I filed an official complaint. Tom was booked for assault with a deadly weapon. He had the opportunity to acknowledge me, but was desultory, head hung almost to his knees. He turned in my direction once, and all I saw was a vacant stare. Leading up to and during the assault, he was alive as a nut job. After losing the match, he was meat for the slaughterhouse.

The police were indeed tall in the Upper Peninsula, but not mythical or mystical. They were big guys doing their job. They took all three of our statements, which, when added to the accounts of the rest area witnesses, created a damaging picture for Tom Lutac. He was being held over in the county jail for a pre-trial hearing. Every cop in the station was empathetic to our situation when they learned we were dropping Roberta off at Lake Superior State College. They rushed us through the paperwork and told us we might or might not have to come back to testify. Their instincts told them Tom was likely to fold his hand and plead guilty. Not surprisingly, his real name was not Tom Lutac. Tom Mikowski had a rap sheet that began when he was twelve. He was going to prison for a while, the cops assured us.

Marta, Roberta, and I sat on a sturdy slat-backed bench, a twisted pretzel of a family. Marta's and my sides were glued together, while my gauzed arm lay lightly on her lap. Roberta's head was on my shoulder, her arm locked with mine. I wouldn't recommend getting stabbed by a crazy dude as a technique to encourage family intimacy, but it was a memorable vignette for the Moore family.

Given our walking papers, we thanked all the officers for their help. The precinct doors opened for us, and we walked down the steps toward our van, arm in arm.

"Dad, would it be safe to say that this ends your self-described perfect record of being able to spot a bad-apple hitchhiker a mile away?" Roberta asked.

"I think that record just ended with a resounding thud." My father-daughter credibility fell just as fast.

"It's okay, Dad. I'm part of your stories now. Not as big a part as Crowbar Momma Moore, but I'm in the picture. I like that."

"You'll always be part of the story, Roberta. We don't need a ruckus like this to make our stories."

"Amen to that," Marta said.

Marta had been unusually quiet during the entire ordeal. She kept close to me: holding my hand, pushing a loose strand of hair back over my ear, hand on my shoulder, arm slipped through the crook of my elbow.

"I almost lost you thirty years ago. I don't like the damn drama. I want to grow wrinkled and gray with you, Luke. It's been a long time since that special blend of Luke Moore excitement paid us a visit. I can do without it."

Her eyes fiery and defiant, her complexion pinked up. She didn't have to say a word. She was telling me that picking up Tom Whatever-His-Name was reckless and arrogant—a know-it-all move that put my family in mischief's path. I was a nimrod of the first order.

"I understand, dear." I capitulated.

"I know you do, Luke." Her face softened. "And I do believe Crowbar Momma could grow on me."

We all laughed. We decided to complete the drive to Sault Sainte Marie, two hours away. The last leg of I-75. The final installment of a road trip started thirty years before.

Chapter 32

September 1973

I strode toward La Bohème. It was autumn in Michigan, but in Miami, the September air dripped humidity. My high-performance sweat glands were open for business. Collins Street was a parade of bars with brightly attired crowds gyrating inside and outside the bars to the local salsa and Latin bands. I remembered the details Mrs. Brady and Kate had given me about Curtis Brady. La Bohème was a corner cabaret until Curtis Brady and Martin Lane bought it in 1963. They had transformed it into a chic, see-and-be-seen club, while still remaining friendly to the large crowd of regulars who loved the music.

I presented my ID to the tightly dressed, muscled bouncer just inside the door. I peered over the bouncer's shoulder and saw a long bar that stretched almost to the tiny stage. The padded bar stools with backs were nearly all occupied. There were numerous four-top tables that filled the room, and ten booths on the opposite wall from the bar. If the club held 150 people, it was past capacity. The cigarette smoke was thick, curling up to the overburdened ceiling vents and bouncing back in cirrus cloud formations just above the heads of the animated patrons. Conversation near the front door was loud, competing with a soaring trumpet solo. A small sign on an easel identified the avant-garde jazz group that was finishing their set. The jazz lovers near the stage were enthusiastic in their support of the young trumpet player. I put my ID back in my wallet and started to wade into the crowded bar.

The bouncer put his thick forearm in front of me, "Ten bucks, fella."

I had twenty-two dollars in my wallet and handed over two fives reluctantly. I found a seat in the middle of the bar and slid between a man smoking through a cigarette holder and an overly thin woman whose makeup failed to hide her real age. The bartender approached the woman, who ordered a refill on her martini—dry, two olives.

"Oh, I just love martinis," she turned and said to me. "Don't you?"

"I'm more of a beer guy."

"Well, then, bartender, get this young man a beer. I'm buying."

"Thank you, ma'am. I'm Luke Moore." I extended my hand, which was readily accepted by the tall, elegant lady sitting ramrod-straight at the bar.

"And I'm Mrs. DeWitt, Ruth DeWitt," she replied.

We chatted for a while as the band took a break. I finally asked Mrs. DeWitt, "Do you know if the owner, Mr. Brady, is in the bar tonight?"

"Well, yes, sweetie. That's Mr. Brady sitting right next to you." Mrs. DeWitt reached her long left arm past me and touched the man on his left shoulder and exclaimed, "Yoo-hoo, Curtis, this young man wants to meet you."

Curtis Brady turned away from the man he was talking to and looked at me, sizing me up.

"Curtis, this is Luke Moore. Isn't he lovely?" Mrs. DeWitt burbled. Curtis Brady put his hand lightly on his forehead, pushed back his longish, graying hair over his ear, and smiled sadly.

"Luke Moore," he stood up and extended his arms and clasped my shoulders. I watched his eyes water up, and through a quivering, clenched jaw, he said, "I'm so very glad you found me, and that you are getting better!"

He stepped forward and embraced me, holding my head with one hand. The hug lasted for a long moment. I was slightly embarrassed with the emotion, but understood that Mr. Brady had learned all about me from Kate.

Curtis announced to all around him that a great friend was visiting with him tonight. "A round of drinks, on the house, to celebrate the arrival of Luke Moore to La Bohème. A friend forever to the Brady family!" he announced to the crowd.

The man sitting next to Curtis Brady stood up and extended his hand to me. "I'm so pleased to meet you. I'm Martin Lane, Curtis's partner in this club."

"My pleasure, Mr. Lane. Kate Brady told me about you."

"Yes, I guess that would be so," Martin replied. "Curtis, why don't we take Mr. Moore back to our office where we can talk privately?"

"Excellent idea, Martin. Luke, do you mind?"

"I would enjoy that, Mr. Brady."

Curtis Brady put his arm around my shoulder, and we walked with Martin past the stage, through a corridor leading to a small and elegantly furnished office. There was a partner's desk that sat between a large bookcase and a sitting area, with a loveseat facing two overstuffed leather chairs.

We sat and talked for hours, only interrupted by the timely visits of a waiter named Richie, who kept me refreshed with a stream of Heinekens, and Curtis and Martin with club sodas with a twist of lime. I told my stories chronologically. The account of my years and subsequent months, finally woven together with my listeners' lives, was a spider's web. I finished, exhausted, and became more of listener than a talker as both Curtis and Martin talked about their year with Annette. As I listened, I balanced two trains of thought. I could see the affection that existed between the two middle-aged men. I knew enough of their history and was moved. Conversely, it was my first experience observing love between two men, and I attempted to overcome my mental image of homosexuals exchanging hand jobs in public restrooms.

At 2:30 a.m., my face was flushed from beer, and I was almost chain-smoking cigarettes, a sure sign I was getting bombed. Martin asked me to tell them more about myself. I needed to steer the conversation to my primary reason for finding Mr. Brady. We were all puffy-eyed and spent from telling stories that made us cry and laugh. There wasn't going to be a painless transition, so I let it fly. I pulled myself up in the chair and exhaled.

"Mr. Brady, Mr. Lane, I would like to talk to you about Gerard LaFleur."

They both froze, their relaxed countenance on the loveseat broken. Half a moment passed, and Curtis Brady put his hands over his face. Releasing his hands, he sat up straight and looked at me. "Only Annette knows. Only Annette knew," he corrected himself, "about Gerard. And she made a promise to him that I know she would keep. So how is it that you know anything about Gerard?"

I was taken aback by Mr. Brady's graveness. "I also made a promise, and I am asking both of you to help me honor the promise. I need to meet with Mr. LaFleur, and you know that I need your help. I need it with no questions asked."

Curtis and Martin stared at each other before Martin broke the silence. "Luke, you may not believe it, but we are men of honor. Actually, we have learned to honor promises made by ourselves, and in this case, dear Annette. Your request poses a conundrum for two old queers who have pasts filled with lies and the pain caused by years of deceit and deceptions. But we've reclaimed ourselves, and that's in no small part because of Annette. Can you at least tell us if your promise was made to Annette?"

I tossed over the promise in my mind. "Yes," I finally answered. "I made the promise to Annette just before she died in my arms. I'm not completely sure where it all leads, but I do know that Gerard LaFleur is a part of it."

Curtis and Martin looked seriously at each other again, and Curtis spoke, his eyes brimming over. "This has been an important night for us, Luke. You have helped us share our grief over Annette who we both miss beyond words. You've interrupted our safe, yet fragile world. But, Luke," he paused and looked over at Martin. "I trust you. For Christ's sake, my daughter died in your arms. We are going to help you, no more questions asked. I'm afraid, and not afraid, of what happens next, if you know what I mean."

"I think I do, Mr. Brady," I replied.

"All right, then. Let me tell you what you need to know about Gerard LaFleur."

As I listened, I was astonished once again by how remarkably complex and interconnected life could be.

The following afternoon, I drove south from Miami in Curtis Brady's Lincoln Continental with directions to Gerard LaFleur's restaurant in Key West.

I started out in clean clothes Martin had laundered for me and with five twenty-dollar bills Curtis insisted I take with me. My goal was to meet Gerard, finish my business, and head back to Miami Beach the next morning. Curtis and Martin insisted that I should spend at least one night in glorious Key West.

They accompanied me down to the underground parking garage, looking wistful and worried as I pulled away in Curtis's Lincoln Continental. I steered onto Highway 1 leading to Key Largo and pushed a Miles Davis tape into the Continental's eight-track player. I had never visited the Keys, and, while my mission was paramount in my thoughts, I marveled that I was traveling in this boat of a car through the exotic Keys, erstwhile home to good ol' Ernie Hemingway, one of my favorite authors.

It was about a three-hour drive to Key West from Miami Beach. As I passed through Key Largo and onto Plantation Key and Lower Matecumbe Key, I was tempted by the beaches and the ocean that lay both east and west of me. I succumbed in Marathon Key. I bought an unfashionable swimsuit emblazoned with seashells and sea horses for $1.99 and a beach towel decorated with the Florida Keys at a souvenir shop. I pulled over at a pristine beach on Big Pine Key and found a spot well away from the crowd. I removed my shirt, sprinted fast enough to avoid stares, and plunged into the tepid, sparkling Gulf of Mexico. The saltwater stung my eyes. It wasn't the cold, freshwater swimming experience of Michigan's inland and Great Lakes. The waves were gentle, and I bobbed easily on my back.

It was six months since I had made the promise to Annette. I knew I had to meet Gerard, but what the hell happened after that was eluding me. I knew from Curtis and Martin's reaction that I wasn't likely to receive a warm welcome. I was going to have to wing it. I was resolute, but with more than a whiff of worry.

After my swim, I sat on the beach and air-dried in the hot afternoon sun. I was far enough away from the other beachgoers that I could sit with my shirt off. Half an hour later, I brushed the sand off my feet, laced up my All Stars and pointed the car toward Key West.

The town of Key West, at the farthest tip of the Keys, perched between the Gulf of Mexico and the Atlantic Ocean, looks out toward the Caribbean, facing Cuba. Rich in pirate history, it had become a counterculture haven in the late sixties, where hippies often clashed with the retired senior citizen establishment. As I drove onto Duval Street, the town's main drag, at 6:00 p.m., the street was alive with young and old making their way to dinner and drinks at the numerous taverns and restaurants that coexisted with the tourist stores and fishing shops. I spotted my destination at the very end of the street, just before the public beach. I parked the Lincoln in an opportune spot right in front of Limbo, the quaint restaurant and bar Gerard LaFleur managed.

The sun was directly above the white clapboard structure, ready to set over the Gulf, reflecting an orange glow over the restaurant.

The restaurant's name made me smile. While I guessed the name was connected to the dance, I thought of limbo as that singularly Catholic place where unbaptized souls stayed until Judgment Day. I remembered when I first learned about limbo in second grade, from Sister Dennis Margaret, one of my favorite teachers. In a classroom packed with fifty-one students who ranged from brilliant to dumb and from somnambulant to agitated, she ruled with the necessary doses of sternness and kindness. She was launching the annual school drive to "adopt" pagan babies. Sister explained to my astonished class that, for five dollars, our class could sponsor a pagan baby stuck in some woebegone village in Africa, South American, or Asia. The five dollars would pay for inoculation against horrible diseases and for a baptism, so that the pagan baby would no longer be pagan, but Christian! Then they would escape the fate of dying and going to limbo.

John Parcell had raised his hand and asked Sister, "What's limbo?"

"Limbo is the place where all unbaptized souls must go until the end of time, and God delivers us on Judgment Day. It's not a bad place, John; it's located between purgatory and heaven and is like a waiting room in a train station. It's comfortable enough, but frustrating, because you can't board the train for heaven. Now, these unbaptized souls aren't bad people. If they were bad and un-baptized, they would be going to purgatory, which, if you remember last week's lesson, is the painful place sinners must wait until they are ready for heaven's grace. Of course, if you are a mortal sinner when you die, hell awaits your damned soul."

The class tittered at the word *damned.*

"Most of the souls in limbo are babies and young children who haven't yet sinned, and yet can't enter God's kingdom because they aren't in God's Catholic Church. They are Lost Souls," Sister intoned.

John raised his hand again. "That doesn't seem very fair, Sister. Those pagan babies didn't do anything wrong. Why should they have to stay in limbo? God isn't unfair, is he? Why would the Catholic Church have a place like limbo? The pagan babies should get to go to a place like Disneyland to wait."

Sister Dennis Margaret just shook her head and said, "They're just Lost Souls, John. Just little Lost Souls."

I entered Limbo and greeted the hostess at the reservation podium. "Hi, I'm wondering if Gerard LaFleur is working tonight."

"Yes, but we don't expect him for another hour. Can I help you?" the perky blonde hostess said.

"My name is Luke Moore, and I'm here to see Mr. LaFleur. I'd like to wait if that's all right."

"Of course. I think you'd like the veranda out back. The sun will be setting in about an hour. It's quite beautiful. Follow me."

The hostess led me past a circular bar that separated the restaurant's tables from the wide veranda, half-covered by a porch. The full sun was blinding as it bounced off the Gulf water. I covered my eyes as I was led to a waterside table next to a railing, settled myself, and scanned the veranda. Looking out over the Gulf, I took a deep breath. It was warm, and sweat started to form in all the familiar places.

This was the very end of the road, I thought. What a fitting place to try to fulfill my promise to Annette. I turned and surveyed the other diners. The sunlight made me squint and blink, but I thought that the group at the large, round table in the center of the porch looked familiar. There were two giant brush-cut men, two matronly gray-haired ladies, an elderly couple dressed in white polo shirts, and, finally, two men in Hawaiian shirts who were look-alikes for Gilbert and Glenn from Cincinnati.

They laughed easily among themselves, sipping champagne from long-stemmed flutes. I took a harder look, but I felt woozy. My head started to swirl as I became certain I recognized the two cops who chased Kate and me off the highway in Cincinnati, then Sister Jean Rosina and Rose Margaret, and Gilbert and Glenn Standish. The remaining couple matched the description of Chief Kowalski's coffee shop interlopers. Uncomprehending, I stared at them. The group suddenly paused and raised their champagne flutes toward me, simultaneously.

"To Luke Moore, a job well done!" they toasted.

Behind the assembly, the air moved like heat waves rising off summer asphalt. Two women emerged, hazy at first, and then sharply distinct.

I lost my breath when I recognized Annette and my mother standing behind the group. They were ethereal in their flowered sundresses, almost floating behind the assembly of duos.

Mom looked at me and all the love I had missed was shining through her pale, blue eyes. She blew me a kiss as she had every day of our life. I trembled as the sobs overtook me. All my anguish and loss collected in my chest and washed through me. I could see what I had lost. It was too much. I would never recover. Why try?

Mom called out to me, "Luke, I know. I know. It's too much to bear, isn't it? It is a marvel isn't it, that I'm here and still part of you. I can't erase the past or your pain. It will always be there. But, son, you can't leave me behind, either. And every step you take away from that black day is a leap toward the best part of the story. I'm part of it, Luke. Let me in. Let your life in. I'll be there for you. You just have to look. You're almost there, Son, almost there."

I heard her laugh, deep and loud, and watched as her head lifted back, opening her mouth, revealing the flash of her teeth. She gestured to the odd collection of twins in front of her. They were waving and laughing and generally behaving like goofballs.

"They were guides for the journey, son. You can make it on your own now. God bless you. Go live your life."

Annette Brady smiled and mouthed, "Thank you, Luke. You made it."

My body went cold. I felt myself swooning as the sunlight danced off the group's champagne flutes.

I awoke on a chaise lounge on the beach just a few feet from the restaurant table. I felt a cool towel on my forehead. Seated next to me was a handsome, dark-complexioned man in his midtwenties.

"Feeling a bit better now, aren't you?" he asked. I tried to sit up, but the man gently restrained me.

"Just relax, Luke. Here, have a drink of water."

I sipped the water and handed the glass back to the man. "Well, Luke, I'm Gerard LaFleur. Curtis Brady called and told me we have some talking to do. I didn't expect to find you passed out in my restaurant, but given the reason you came to find me, I suppose nothing is too surprising, is it?"

"That's a good way to put it. I am here for a reason, but I don't really know where to begin."

"Let's get to know each other and then we'll get to your mysterious mission. How does that sound?"

I knew Gerard was not that much older than me, but he had a maturity that seemed a generation older.

"That would be great." My head was clearing, so I sat up and pulled off the blanket that had been wrapped around me.

We sat and talked. I learned how Gerard, Walter William Prescott's bastard son, made his way to Key West and became manager of Limbo. Gerard LaFleur was Helen Brady's nephew, cousin to Kate and Annette. It didn't seem unusual, when held up against the last six months of my life, that Gerard LaFleur, Curtis Brady, and Annette Brady had been thrown together in a jumbled stew of destiny.

Gerard's mother, Marion White, was sentenced to twenty years for manslaughter in the shooting of W. W. Prescott III. When Marion delivered a baby boy in prison, the Prescotts whisked him away to an orphanage in Baton Rouge, Louisiana. His first good fortune was to be adopted by a Cajun couple from New Orleans, René and Michelle LaFleur. They named him Gerard after Michelle's father. The LaFleurs were the owners of an antiques store in the French Quarter, where Gerard grew up with stern and loving parents who emphasized education and hard work. When he was fifteen, they sat him down and explained his past, coinciding with his mother's early release and parole from prison. René and Michelle had arranged for his mother to move to Miami, where René's brother owned an import business. Marion White took a job as bookkeeper, a skill she learned in prison, and René and Michelle traveled with Gerard to meet her. He was torn between his loyalty and gratitude to his adopted parents and his natural ties to his birth mother, who had lost everything. He loved all of them and made the wrenching choice to live in Miami with Marion White. He vowed never to lose his connection to his parents.

"I was a normal fifteen-year-old kid with good parents and a good life, and then my world was turned upside-down. I hated leaving my parents, but how could I leave my mother, my birth mother, after all she had been through? I cursed the Prescotts for what they had done to my mom and me. I learned how to hate."

I knew exactly what he felt. His faced was lined with years of bitterness. I wondered if my face was beginning to weather like Gerard's. He continued with his story.

While finishing high school in Miami, Gerard applied for a part-time job as a waiter at La Bohème and met Curtis Brady. After six months' employment with La Bohème, Gerard overheard Curtis and Martin talking about the Prescott family. He dropped his tray of wine spritzers and martinis. The ensuing cleanup led to the realization that Curtis was the ex-husband of his aunt, Helen Prescott Brady. Their mutual hate of all things Prescott fed their relationship, and Gerard became Curtis's protégé. Gerard had inherited the Prescott musical gene and played piano beautifully. The terribly coincidental, ironic past was a strong bond between the young, talented mulatto and the tormented homosexual nightclub owner. While their Prescott history was the instigator of their relationship, they found an unusual, almost father-and-son connection developing. Gerard learned the club business from Curtis and the financial business side from Martin. He played background piano for the lunch crowd.

Everything changed when Annette arrived. He tried to hate his Prescott cousin, but it was impossible. He began to accompany her on piano for her sets at the club. They connected, first musically and then as friends and confidants. Annette persuaded Gerard that her mother was not cut from the same cloth as her brother and father. She explained what had transpired after her grandfather's death and how her mother was dedicated to righting wrongs left by Walter Prescott's legacy. But when Annette suggested making amends between the Bradys and Marion White and Gerard, he was adamant that reconciliation was impossible. He had never told his mother that he worked with Curtis Brady, or of his connection to the Prescotts, and he never would. He asked Annette, Curtis, and Martin to solemnly vow they would never mention his existence to the Bradys. His mother had put the past behind her and was struggling to make her freedom work after spending half her life behind bars.

Gerard worked at La Bohème and kept his secret for ten years while learning the club and restaurant business throughout Curtis

Brady's travails, troubles, and recovery. A year ago, Gerard had accepted a job at this large, successful restaurant in the Florida Keys. Curtis Brady knew the owner and suggested Gerard was ready for a bigger challenge than La Bohème. It was a great opportunity for a young man.

He anonymously attended Annette's funeral in Knoxville. He had learned from Curtis Brady of the circumstances of Annette's death and of my role in the tragedy. The funeral was wildly emotional for Gerard, grieving for Annette with his blood family, yet unknown and separated in the shadows of the church with his secret. The terrible harm the Prescotts had inflicted upon him and his mother was unforgivable and irreconcilable.

"So, you have had your share of bad times, too, haven't you, Luke?"

"That's for sure, Gerard. But I'm learning something. No matter how screwed up my past was—and my present isn't that much better—there is plenty of pain to go around in life. I'm not sure who would win the hard luck award, you or me. One thing's for sure, I'm seeing things in a goddamn different way. You wouldn't believe—hell I'm not sure I believe—no, I am sure I believe what happened to me before I passed out. Gerard, I saw my mom, I saw Annette, I saw a whole bunch of people who had been warning me, or helping me or telling me—hell, I'm not sure what they were doing, except they were all real, and it all started that night I found Annette. Or she found me. Everything since then has been—it's been a wild ride of events that has led me here. This is not coincidence, Gerard. Not at all. I mean, for Christ's sake, even the name of this restaurant is "Limbo"! We're all somewhere between heaven and hell. And then there's the frigging horn that sounds every time something bad is about to happen. I'm telling you, Gerard, I'm the last person who should be a messenger for you. I know that I'm here for a reason. You and I have unfinished business with our past, and it's eating us from the inside out. Annette sent me here to end the pain, to help you face your devils and embrace your angels. And on the way here, I can see I had to be smacked upside the head to see the same thing. We're here for us and for Annette and my mom and for all of the crap that has landed on the Bradys, caused by those son-of-a-bitch Prescotts and my dad."

"You heard the horn? I've heard it, too." I watched Gerard's face turn animated at the mention of the horn.

"Ever since Annette died, I hear this rumbling, and then this deep contralto, just when I'm ready to do something stupid. You're telling me that it's Annette? That's crazy. But maybe not. I've been having the strangest dreams. Annette has been in them, and some other woman, older, beautiful—don't tell me that's your mother. This is the craziest thing I've ever heard, Luke. You are one loony tune if you believe all this stuff you're telling me."

"C'mon, Gerard, you and I both know this isn't any accident I'm sitting here having this conversation. The whole thing is impossible. But here we are, sharing our whacked-out past, and, of course, there's more."

"And what the hell would that be?"

"Gerard, do you know why I'm here?"

He stared past me and said, "Annette died with you by her side, right? She was an incredible, generous person, with a pure heart, and she was very determined, wasn't she? I believe she sent you to me. She kept her promise to never tell her family about me. But then she made you promise to find me and how did you put it, 'face my devils and embrace my angels'? God, she found a way, didn't she?"

"Yep, she did. Annette didn't die thinking about herself, she was thinking about you and your mother. She was thinking about her mother and her family and that the final part of . . . of redemption for her family. The final part of completing a family busted wide apart. And the way it worked out was that I'm the messenger, from another family that's broken all to hell. Sitting here talking to you, it sounds like the pieces of the puzzle fit pretty neatly together. But, man, Gerard, it's been a tough goddamn year. And the year before that was bad. And the year before that—a disaster. I just couldn't keep my head on straight. I couldn't even help my own brother and sisters, who really needed me. I was just filled up with hate. Pure, true hate of my goddamn father, who was so completely screwed up he made his lousy deal with the devil and burned my mother to death. God, I hate the man every day until it hurts. But now I understand it's killing me. I run. I take off and get away from the scene of the crime. Only it doesn't help. I'm slowly sinking under the waves. My family and friends keep grabbing me by the arms to keep my head above water, but I'm a pretty determined guy, so I keep going back under. Then almost out of the sky, Annette falls into my life, shows me where God lives, makes me promise to put her family back together without explaining exactly how, and dies. With her blood on my hands and a promise to keep, I start to dog-paddle and good things, weird things, start to happen to me. It wasn't a straight line, but I found some good people along the way, and a woman I love and who loves me. I was kicked half to death and now here I am, sitting with you, living under a black family cloud, like me. And, oh yeah, every so often the earth shifts a few degrees, a vent opens, and some wild, Tibetan-horn-playing webe-los spirit guide shows up—sent by my dead mother, who's rooming in the netherworld with Annette—and warns me I'm headed for some big trouble. But I'm so thickheaded, I don't have a clue they're trying to help me. Yeah, Gerard, it's been a tough year, but a year that saved my life. Now I can start living. I'm forgiving myself for forgetting about my family and friends, even though they kept me alive. I can love again. And what took me here was you. We have to finish this, Gerard."

Gerard lifted his head from his hands.

"I can see it now. Annette always told me she was more stubborn than me. She wins. I'm not sure how to start this, but it's time for reconciliation. I'm not going to fight her. Especially since you're telling me she's looking over my shoulder."

"I think we all win, Gerard. That's why it's going to work, somehow, someway."

"We'll see. Are you feeling well enough for a beer?"

"That sounds perfect."

We sat on the veranda, the restaurant bubbling with activity around us. The sunset was glorious. Two Lost Souls, drinking a cold one on a tropical finger of sand, healing together.

"Marion White, this is Helen Brady," I said. "Helen, this is Gerard LaFleur," I said to Helen, with Kate Brady and her brothers and father and Martin Lane standing by. Marta held my arm as I made the introductions in my Miami apartment. I didn't know which way the reunion was going to turn. Tears and hugs relieved and vanquished initial awkwardness. Marta served a pan of lasagna over a makeshift table, the Chianti and conversation flowing. Annette and music created a common bond. The singing started as the dinner was cleared.

The doorbell buzzed. Matthew (a.k.a. Elvis), Mark, and John arrived after announcing they were driving down in force to load my acquired possessions from the Miami apartment into a U-Haul. We were scheduled to pick up Marta's mother in Cincinnati and then drive north to start a new life in Royal Oak.

Helen Brady had provided the impetus by offering me a grant, which I insisted would be a loan, to start college. She had offered Marta the same opportunity. And so it happened I was shifting gears from shiftless scalawag to a man with a live-in girlfriend and a prospective mother-in-law. At least my reputation for leaping first and looking later was intact. I had already been accepted at Wayne State University and had a line on a decent-paying work-study job in the library. And I was looking forward to it. My life was moving very fast, exhilarating and frightening, just like the road.

My friends, the not-quite-Lost Souls, mixed easily with the family in the cramped living room of the apartment. After a while, I retreated to the kitchen with Marta.

"You're feeling pretty good about yourself, aren't you, Mr. Moore?" Marta said.

"It's a good day, Marta. I did my job."

"Yes, you did." She put her arm around my waist and cradled her head on my shoulder.

Helen Brady's voice singing "Summertime" soared in from the living room. The Brady family, Gerard, Marion White, and the Lost Souls joined the sing-along. Marta and I listened from the kitchen and gently swayed into a dance as the harmony filled the room. I held Marta tight and loved her. I finally understood where God lives.

Chapter 33

September 2003

After the rest area pandemonium, we drove the sixty miles to the Soo, stopping near Kinross for a dinner of Upper Peninsula pasties, a specialty meat pie. We kept our reservation at the Hiawatha Motel, a mile away from the college. We woke the next morning, and with stunning speed, our daughter left us physically, emotionally, spiritually—Christ, she even left us intellectually—behind.

Marta and I watched the separation happen with our jaws hung open, as the process of becoming empty-nesters blazed past us like time-lapse photography. Roberta was polite, but after a Kmart stop and helping her settle into her room, it was painfully clear our usefulness had terminated. It was simply and shatteringly obvious: in with the new and out with the old. My silver-dollar bald spot bloomed into full-monk circumference over the course of the day. The Freshman Parents' Orientation Continental Breakfast warned of the angst of separation. Separation my rear end. It was a good, old-fashioned heave-ho, with a forced smile. I even unraveled the dressing on my wounded arm, hoping to attract Roberta's attention and sympathy. But she was off to the Freshman Dorm-Living Brunch, followed by Freshman Dorm-Meeting Pizza.

"Aren't our tuition dollars paying for all these meeting meals? I'm surprised they don't have Freshman Sexology Beer-Fest Seminar," I told Marta.

I don't think she heard a word I said. She probably realized she was not only losing her baby, but was going to be stuck alone with me and my stories, without the diversion of her daughter's female companionship.

Our good-byes with Roberta were heartrending and heartbreaking. She gave us letters to take home with us that were filled with our golden rules, to reassure us she had listened. It was very sweet. Although I imagined a different scene: R&B music kicked up high on her dorm room stereo, Jell-O shots readied, and lust-filled young men flooding the dorm with male hormones. I quickly jettisoned that image.

We both sobbed as we departed Sault Sainte. Marie. I pulled over at a gas station to buy a box of Kleenex. The mustached counter girl asked me if I was okay, as I blubbered trying to find the right dollar denomination to pay her.

"I'm okay. It's my daughter. We just dropped her off at college."

"Dropped her off at Lake Superior, eh? Yep, we get two or three parents crying in here every fall. I'm sure she'll be okay."

I thought about giving a smart-ass response, but I really wanted to be back in the van to continue wallowing with Marta about our new, daughterless cocoon of a life.

We told each other favorite recollections of our daughter on the way back to St. Ignace, and by the time we arrived, we were all cried out. I parked in Arnold's Ferry parking lot, and reached over to hold my Marta's hand tight.

"Please don't leave me for Raul, the pool boy," I pleaded.

"We don't have a pool, Luke."

"That doesn't mean there isn't a pool boy named Raul to run off with. Or maybe a doctor—yeah, that's it. Please don't run off with a rich doctor."

"Luke, you're still the one. Often trying, but always the one. We'll be okay."

I sighed deeply and kissed her hand before letting go. We walked aboard the last ferry to Mackinac Island for the day. Marta and I had returned to the island twice since our thirty-year relationship began there, once on vacation with Roberta, who wearied quickly of the island's eighteenth-century history and the retelling of the beginning of her parents' unlikely love affair. Our second visit was for a nursing convention in 1985. That visit was a lot more fun.

Marta and I attempted to recreate the Night of Impossible Positions, and nearly succeeded. We would have made it if I hadn't pulled a hammy on the Inverted Reverse Lotus Curl position. We reserved the same room at the Chippewa on both occasions and sat on the same bar stools in the Pink Pony, toasting each other on our impossible good fortune.

The ferry pushed the dark blue water of Lake Huron forward into a churning froth. The oncoming night temperature was dropping in synchronization with the northern sun. We stood starboard with sensible layers of fleece and windbreakers, watching the peach sun begin its descent toward the main arches of the Mackinac Bridge. I held Marta from behind, nuzzling my chin into the crevasse of her neck and shoulder.

"Breathtaking," I said.

"It is a magnificent view, Luke."

"Not the view, Marta. You."

Her mouth opened into her toothy smile. "I'm glad you're happy, Luke."

"I am. I could die tonight and I would die a happy man. How about you?"

"Yes, Luke, I'm happy. I like to think back to where we came from and pause at the intervals. We've had our share of bitter pills, but it's been a good life. A very good life. Think about us when we met, Luke. God, we were so young and dumb. We've come a long way together.

"But you should know that after thirty years, you still scare me. Even though we've become a predictable, boring, and middle-aged couple, you still have the seeds of danger buried deep inside you. I worry about you. And I don't want you dying, happy or otherwise, tonight."

"No, not tonight or any night in the near future. We don't want to miss our big night in the Grand Hotel."

Tight against each other, we watched our twilight approach the island harbor.

The horse and carriage met us at the dock, courtesy of Mrs. Brady. Our reunion had been orchestrated by her and Kate: a celebration to honor the significance of the momentous year that had introduced or renewed us back into each other's lives. The relation-ships were tumultuously born, but flourished in unforeseen ways, and the years tumbled by. It was also the thirty-year anniversary of the beating that began the redefinition of my life. My journey in 1973 up and down I-75 resulted in death, new friendships, requited lust, love, arrests, celestial twins, mayhem, family unity, and a trove of road stories for the ages. It nearly killed me, but in the end, I survived to tell the story.

The invitation read, "Family of Families Reunion, Mackinac Island, the Grand Hotel." The invitation list was my life in living color. It was going to be quite a soiree.

We walked up the stairs of the Grand Hotel, the bellman car-rying our bags behind us. We looked like we belonged this time. At the top of the stairs, the Great Porch greeted us. Halfway down the Porch's west wing, our friends were all gathered to watch the bril-liant fall sunset. Marta and I walked toward them, hand in hand, unnoticed. Mrs. Brady's hair was fully silver, her face aglow from the sun's reflection. She sang with her grandchild, named Annette, who was celebrating her twenty-ninth birthday. She was Elvis and Kate's daughter. Kate smiled with the same glow on her face as her mother's.

Kate married Elvis in January 1974 after a case of "conception, reception, what happened to the contraception?" Helen Brady was furious like a Prescott, for about fifteen minutes, and then remem-bered her estrangement from her parents. Elvis insisted they live on the money he earned, so they struggled happily until he wrote a song that was covered by Bob Seger. The royalties dribbled in, and he took his first strides as a songwriter. Heartbreaking news fol-lowed a year later. Elvis called us and asked us to meet him for what was becoming an uncommon after-work beer at Lum's.

"Guys, you're not going to believe this. I have cancer of the nuts. Can you believe that? Me? I have cancer of the fucking nuts!"

We thought he was kidding, and laughed. He wasn't. Eighteen months later, testicular cancer killed him.

Kate Brady Muldoon was devastated, again. This time, my own ship righted, Marta and I helped her through it. We became Annette's surrogate godparents. A bond tightened between us when Kate was there for us through Marta's two miscarriages. After nearly a decade of every pregnancy test imaginable, our Roberta was born. Kate's daughter became our babysitter. Helen Brady was a constant visitor and became a friend to Marta's mother, who moved with us to Royal Oak, but soon insisted on her own apartment, after she found a job waitressing at the Delmar restaurant.

Lila's cancer remained in remission until her granddaughter was born. She held one-year-old Roberta in her arms the day she died at our home. Our lives did indeed braid together through joy and sadness.

John and Sydney lasted five years before John left Indian River to chase the entertainers' dream to Los Angeles, New York, and finally Chicago. There he found his place in the Second City comedy troupe. Sydney left him as his cocaine use soared out of control. He returned to Royal Oak to visit his family and friends, and he never stopped making us laugh. In our twenties, we shrugged off his drug and booze problem. He was succeeding as a comedy writer, and we viewed his career as a balance to his cockeyed private life. In his thirties and then forties, we knew he was an addict to bad behavior fueled by a potpourri of substances. Five years ago, he drove his Porsche off the Pacific Coast Highway and nearly lost an arm. Three months in the hospital, six months in rehab, and one year of community service later, he was clean. John wore the hollow look of a surviving addict, his soul straggling alongside him. He could still make us snort and chortle on visits, but it was pain mixed with mirth.

Mark and Lois became the models of their parents' youth; practicing Catholics with five children, an ice rink in the backyard, and still playfully in love. Our Roberta and their youngest daughter were best friends. Mark and I looked anxiously for signs of the genetic code that might lead our daughters down our path of teenage lunacy by the time they were preteens. We never stopped worrying, even when it was clear they were much wiser kids than we were. Mark concluded that the lunacy gene skipped a generation. We immediately began worrying about our unborn grandchildren.

Ann, April, Angela, and Donnie were also with us. All married, ten kids between them. Ann still lived in the house on Hoffman with a professor husband and two daughters. April and Angela both lived in Ann Arbor, their lives reverting to twin symmetry after college. They lived on the same block, had three children each, and both taught at the University of Michigan. Donnie worked as a graphic artist for an advertising firm and painted contemporary action portraits of professional athletes. His work was in high demand for posters that graced the bedrooms of young dreamers like himself so many years ago. He married late, at forty, and his wife had three-year-old twin boys. We all lived close enough to celebrate the major holidays together at my drafty, old, and big house in Indian Village, a well-preserved neighborhood on the east side of Detroit. We visited Mom's grave together once a year, at Thanksgiving. We told Roberta Moore stories over turkey dinner to keep her with us. Every year, as the pumpkin pie à la Roberta Moore was served, I told the next generation about how my mom, their grandmother, along with Annette Brady and a fabulous cast of etherealites, had saved me from myself and the bad guys. They loved it as children, questioned it when they grew older, and as I concluded the story, there was discussion and debate on whether the story was real or was it a figment of wacky Uncle Luke's imagination. They debated whether God was involved, what was real, what wasn't, what caused the sound of the dung-chen and the cosmic hum. Was it a signal or warning? If not, what was it?

I didn't participate in the animated discussions. I would occasionally answer a question or add a detail, but the story had become our family fable. I knew, somehow, this provided great joy to my mother. Her family together, discussing with love and fervor whether she was an angel or the product of her son's imagination, and what God's role was in her appearance. It kept my mom's life vibrant and real for me, my siblings, and our children. Her life had become a triumph of her love, trumping the smoke and ashes that nearly ruined us all.

This brought me to Mom's only golden rule I could not abide by: forgiveness. I remembered the kitchen table talk about not allowing hate to consume a person's life. And that the only path to living a life free of hate was forgiveness. And that forgiveness was a one-way street.

Which brought me to Dad. The opposite of Mom. I spent five years in therapy working through the obvious. I loathed my dad, and the abhorrence was an encapsulated cancer inside my soul. He couldn't hurt me anymore; I wouldn't let him inside long enough to do any damage. But there he was. There he dwelled, and he wasn't going away. I quit the therapy and accepted my condition and the periodic headaches as payment for my incapacity to forgive the monster. That was the state of my soul for decades.

Until a month ago. Ann brought the letter to my house and watched me read at my kitchen table. It was another parole hearing, with a twist. The parole board had been asked by my dad's court-appointed lawyer to consider a humanitarian release. Emphysema had riddled my father's health, and after thirty-five years in prison, he was no longer considered a threat to anyone.

I was the last holdout to tread down the trail of forgiveness. My sisters and even Donnie had honored Mom's golden rules and made their peace with Trygvi Moore. It had taken decades, a zigzag to absolution.

"It's up to you if we stand in the way of a parole, Luke. None of us will agree to support this unless you agree," Ann said.

I clenched my fists and ground my teeth.

"Luke, there's a way to find out. Go see him. That's my advice."

I hung my head. "Let me think about it, Big Sister. Let me think about it."

Helen Brady and Annette finished their song as we approached the party. The better part of my life spread before me in embraces, handshakes, and kisses. Helen Brady ordered champagne for a twilight toast. As the ginger sunset met the straits, John raised his flute of orange juice to Mark, me, Kate, and the group.

"Lost Souls, my friends," John toasted.

"Lost and found. Lost Souls and friends found." Kate lifted her glass to us.

As I raised my glass to those I cared about the most, I understood it wasn't the end of the story. It was a very satisfying interlude.

Acknowledgments
How I Got There

The parade leading me from storyteller to writer-in-progress has been a most humbling journey. I've been telling stories since I was a boy, always in an attempt to keep the fickle spotlight of attention pointed straight at me. In the fifth grade, Mrs. Smiley offered my fellow students the opportunity to make a speech on any topic; I jumped up and presented my tale of the Yowser, the yellow bellied sapsucker in a seersucker suit, a bird whose sartorial gifts weren't appreciated by his sapsucker clan. The class started to laugh as I extemporized about that crazy bird's exploits, and when I noticed that those cute girls in the front row were laughing too, an addiction was born.

It never stopped, and even when the attention-seeking reached epically ridiculous heights, at least the high jinks provided continuing fodder for a laundry list of stories.

I learned that good manners and a good story could make up for all sorts of bad behavior, and both played a role in keeping me safe when I took to the road. As the years rolled by, the stories became sales tools in a business career, and, more importantly, they served me well as I became a yarn-spinner to my four children.

Several years ago, when I finally decided I was going to try to realize my next dream of being a reasonably accomplished writer, I thought that the storyteller talent would surely prevail over any obstacles I might bump up against. So, I pulled out my yellow legal pads and wrote, in longhand. Then I asked a range of assistants, at the business I co-owned, to type up my chicken scratch. Really, I was that big of a dope. I wrote on until my middle-aged right hand started to protest by cramping up at the mere sight of another legal pad. Then I retaught myself to type, and the process moved much faster. Faster was not necessarily better.

Finally, my tome was complete. I couldn't wait to show some-body, anybody, what a good story I had written. In a moment of clarity, I decided that maybe I needed an editor to give the book a once-over. I called my neighbor Cindy LaFerle, an author and lovely human being. She referred me to two pros who were willing to edit a rookie's manuscript. I passed my baby on to Iris Under-wood and Virginia Bailey Parker and waited to hear back. When I daydreamed about what I would hear back from these two ladies, the scenarios ranged from "You're brilliant! What a talent!" to "I can't believe I actually read this trash!"

What I received back were two identical editorial reviews. It was just short of brutal and descriptively direct, very direct. It was also enormously helpful in two ways: First, I was told that a good story wasn't necessarily a good novel. Secondly, I might possess some raw talent, but at this point it was more "raw" than "talent." I learned that if I was going to get any further, I was going to have to get serious about the craft of writing, and while I was late to that party, it's never too late to begin.

After a lot of discussion with both ladies, I asked Iris and Vir-ginia individually if, in spite of the shortcomings of the first draft, they thought the novel was worth pursuing. They both protested that they couldn't answer that question; only the author could make that decision.

These are two tough ladies, but they finally relented when I threatened to inconsolably weep, and the answers they gave me were again identical: yes, the novel was salvageable, but it would need a significant rewrite, which would lead to more than a couple drafts. The final advice was a killer. I had written the novel in third person. It needed to be personalized and rewritten in first person. After that little morsel of advice finally sank in, I realized what they were saying. "How serious are you about this novel, and what are you willing to sacrifice to make it a worthwhile book that people will enjoy reading?"

The rewriting process was the toughest work I have ever done, completed over a long period of time and with one very patient editor, who stayed with me through the entire process. Yes, it was a job, Iris, and you performed it with professionalism, toughness, and skill. I became a writer along the way, with plenty of road in front of me to improve. You also gave me *On Writing*, by Stephen King, which is a must-read for every aspiring writer. Thank you, Iris; you were the first "I couldn't have done it without you" friend along the way.

When the story was finally in readable shape, I called on the best readers I knew. All of them took the time to read the story and truly help improve the novel with their comments and help. Thank you, Jackie and Karolyn; you were generous readers and better friends for a lifetime. Helen, you gave me stopovers in Knoxville in both 1973 and 2003 that provided the southern core of the story. Carleen, you did the same, inspiring the Indian River setting. Plenty of beautiful women helping me, and a wife who only rolls her eyes at the friendships.

My other readers were Del and Scott, who were college roommates many years ago when I crashed on their dorm room floor for months. Del lent me his time, his inimitable intensity, enthusiasm, and passion for my project, and helped me get there.

Scott was there for the real-life story of *Getting There*, along with Jerry, John, Mike, Joe, Cal, and a host of very real people who remain my friends today. Early on, we adopted a broad title for an extended group of pals, calling ourselves the JOs. (How that name came to be is another good story, but don't let anyone convince you that it stands for Jolly Olly.) This was not an exclusive club, just a group that gathered through our love of sports, music, and thrills in every size, shape, and color. We came from the suburbs Royal Oak, Huntington Woods, and Berkley, Michigan.

Friendships that last past forty years and start reaching toward the half-century mark are extraordinary. They are filled with the pain of watching pals die too young or wound themselves with self-inflicted arrows. But they are also filled with the quiet pleasure of seeing some of us who stumbled, found our feet, and move through life almost normally. With my friends, I have been frightened to the marrow, foolishly tested immortality, and raised bail.

Beyond all the serious stuff that bonds us together, we have sung and laughed. Oh, how we have laughed—at each other, with each other, and at the rest of the world. Because we have seen each other angry, sick, ecstatic, pie-eyed, churlish, generous, caring, and selfish, not to mention having seen each other in our underwear at every phase of our life; there are very few unknowns or secrets about or between us. For example, my friends have seen me successfully explain to a cop, at two a.m., why I was certain there was no need to bust this seemingly out-of-control party…while wearing women's underwear on my head!

All this created bonds that, while tested, have stood the test of time. My testament to the friendships is this novel. Thank you, one and all.

I'd also like to thank the team at Synergy Books for literally "getting me there." The process, beginning with editing and proceeding through cover design and to finally seeing my book in print, has exceeded my expectations. What more could an author ask!